From Tormented Tides

Tides

Val E. Lane

wave song publishing

"The heart of man is very much like the sea. It has its storms, it has its tides, and in its depths it has its pearls, too."

Vincent van Gogh, The Letters of Vincent van Gogh

PLAYLIST

Scan the code or click to listen. Each song corresponds to the chapters in order, plus additional songs at the end. You can also search for the playlist on Spotify by book title.

CONTENTS

PROLOGUE

I had expected danger when I met him. After all, he was supposed to have died centuries ago. But even in the nightmares that plagued me, I'd never dreamed he could resort to this.

He pressed the cold cutlass blade to my throat as the captain looked on from the deck. My silent salt tears trickled down, mixing with the raging seawater below.

"Don't do this," I whispered, quietly enough that the rest of the crew couldn't hear me.

"I have to." He spat out his words through gritted teeth. I could feel the steel blade shaking against my skin as his hand trembled.

Was he truly capable of doing this? Could he really bring himself to kill me after everything else he'd lost? I knew that he was driven by his pain, but I still trusted him. We were two broken hearts, both fated to a dismal end, and I had accepted mine by now. This semester would be my end. I was ready. But even 300 years wasn't enough for him. He wasn't going to let me save him.

He loosened his hold around me just enough to allow me the freedom to turn my head. Turning my face toward his, I looked up into his eyes one last time. I prayed that somehow my desperate gaze would be enough to turn the tides of his will. He blinked through his own tears and swallowed, and I thought, for just a second, he was going to change his mind. And he did. He tightened his grip and lowered the edge of the sword to my chest, right over my pounding heart.

The dreams were right. I'd always known the sea would bring my downfall. But I thought it'd be different. I thought I'd drown beneath the waves, not be brutally murdered by pirates. But here I stood, betrayed with a blade at my chest as the waves battered the ship's hull, heralding the coming maelstrom. One haunting phrase echoed over and over in my head, louder than the sound of the storm. It was a familiar warning I knew I should've heeded from the beginning: *Never trust a pirate.*

1

TRIM THE SAILS

"Mommy, did you have another bad dream?"

It was impossible for me to glimpse that painting without hearing that echo of my childhood voice. And here, now, as I walked into the room, I couldn't keep my eyes from jumping to the wall where it hung. I remembered all too well the dim room, colored with hues of gray and midnight, and the door cracked open just enough to let in a sliver of golden light from the hallway. The dark-haired woman sat up in her bed, framed in dark purples and blues, her shadow cast against the wall. The focal point stood in the doorway—a small girl in PJs, clutching her plush bear.

It was easy enough to assume that painted scene portrayed a child coming to her mother's room to be comforted from a nightmare. But very few would have guessed it was, in fact, the other way around. Eventually, I understood why my mom had to drink herself to sleep. But understanding didn't necessarily come with forgiveness.

My gaze lingered over this long-past moment that I had captured with my paintbrush so many months ago. 'Bad Dreams,' I called it. From its place on the wall of my dorm, the watercolor piece offered a haven of pastels in the otherwise dull, gray room here at Isabel School of Arts in Constantine, Florida, miles from home. Despite the unfortunate circumstances that inspired its creation, I was proud of that stupid painting on the wall. I replayed each painstaking hour spent layering the watercolors on the page and the pride of finally signing my name in the corner of the finished piece—*Katrina Delmar*.

Still, on those days that reminded me Mom wasn't home–like my 19th birthday just three days ago–I wanted to rip it off the wall and hide it away. So I stood there, remembering a past I was trying to bury, until I decided I didn't want to remember anymore. With one last look at the canvas, I pulled it off the wall and slid it underneath the bed frame with bitter mixed emotions.

Happy Halloween to me.

With the painting out of sight, I snapped myself out of the moment and returned my attention to the object I had come for. I strode to my small dresser where it lay, still nestled in the same box it was in when it arrived in the mail three days ago. A necklace. With slow movements, I picked it up by its delicate chain and then made my way back toward McKenzie's side of the dorm where we were getting ready for tonight's party.

We had attempted to style my hair, but I knew that my out-of-control waves would make their appearance no matter what I did. That was the Cuban side of me showing, in its natural state of loose curls and wild ringlets of dark brunette, nearly black, framing my heart-shaped face. My expressive brows were just as dark, but balanced out by my full lips. My olive skin was slightly darker than when I had arrived. Somehow, I managed to avoid sunburn here despite the intense sunshine. Overall, I looked a lot like my mother, much to my disdain. I always thought she was beautiful, but everything else about her blinded me to that.

McKenzie's costume of choice was a "sexy cheerleader," and to be honest it suited her well, her ginger hair tied in a half-up half-down style tied with a big navy bow, garnet red lips, and mini-skirt complementing her slender figure. I, on the other hand, felt like my dark eyes and hair clashed with the feather-white dress and wings strapped across my petite frame. McKenzie had loaned me her angel costume from last year. I hoped I wouldn't look too ridiculous.

"Don't forget your halo." McKenzie handed me the fluffy halo-on-a-spring headband, and I begrudgingly placed it on my head.

I felt slightly exposed in the tight satin dress that just barely reached the middle of my thighs. It wasn't exactly what I would have chosen for a Halloween costume, but I was in no position to be choosy. Until more of my paintings sold at the antique store downtown, I was at the mercy of luck, McKenzie's generosity, and my quickly dwindling savings account. But there was at least one way I thought I could make the costume my own.

"Oh, great idea! That looks so cute with your costume!" McKenzie's bright eyes lit up as I returned with the necklace. I secured the clasp into place around my neck with a weak nod.

"Well, you're not wrong." I agreed, glancing into the mirror.

But that wasn't why I had put it on. Aside from being the only thing I could add that was truly mine, I hoped it would serve as a reminder to keep my head. My own good luck charm from Dad.

My stomach knotted with a pang of guilt as I thought of him. I'd promised him I'd stay away from booze here. But just two weeks ago I'd been drunk. Very drunk. Maybe he'd get it. Or maybe he'd just think I was doomed to follow in Mom's footsteps. And now I was headed to *another* party.

"I still can't figure out how my dad managed to send me something like this for my birthday." I breathed out, studying the peculiar pendant hanging perfectly past the groove of my collarbone. "He usually just gets me something like painting supplies or some weird car accessory. You know, lame Dad gifts."

The pendant caught the light as I shifted, dazzling like the blue and white sunlight on the bay from its thin silver chain. Secured within a subtle setting of silver twisted prongs curling around it, it was almost oval-shaped, but not quite that symmetrical, and nearly flat, almost reminiscent of a seashell. But somehow it wasn't a shell, or a jewel, or a stone. It was something unlike anything I had ever seen before, and looked somehow natural, despite its ethereal beauty. It shone like glass, through a thin pearly glaze, shimmering with an array of colors anywhere from an icy blue to hints of green to white silver. I couldn't shake the strange sense of Deja Vu I felt while looking at my reflection wearing it, as if I'd somehow seen it before.

McKenzie nudged me with her elbow. "Well next time just let him know when it's *my* birthday. It's so pretty!" McKenzie's energy could sometimes be enough to power a rocket launch, which made me thankful for the large dorms on the East Wing of ISA, with small separate bedrooms on either side and a tiny, shared kitchenette in the middle.

"Where did he even find this?" I had to dig the words out of my throat as I was still held captive by the necklace.

"I dunno, but who cares! It's gorgeous." McKenzie flashed me a toothy grin. "But let's get a pic while our hair and makeup still look good. Once we're out on the yacht, all that sea wind will probably ruin it."

"Yacht?" I repeated with surprise, my voice rising. "You said the party was on the beach."

Without offering a response, my redheaded roommate sprang to her feet and disappeared for only a moment before returning with her treasured vintage Polaroid camera. She carried the obnoxious thing around everywhere and took every opportunity she could to snap an instant-print photo to add to the collection held by clothespins on string lights hanging over her headboard.

"Well, it *is* on the beach," she said finally, acknowledging my tightened expression. "Just further out."

"What is that supposed to mean?" I folded my arms. I was agitated that I had even let her talk me into another party.

"Listen, Ty's parents are letting him use their yacht for the Halloween party. I know you don't like going in the water, but we won't technically even be touching the water. It's much too cold for that." McKenzie's expression immediately returned to its natural perky state as she referred to the 80-degree days of October in Florida.

"Right, even worse," I huffed, trying to mix a laugh in with my groan to soften my sarcasm as I thought back to my own nightmare the night before. "I'll just be *on* it, surrounded by it."

"Please don't bail. Pleeeeease. This will be the last party I ever drag you to. I promise."

I knew that was not true. And surely, she had to know it, too. McKenzie had a heart of gold, but it definitely ran mostly off emotions.

"You said that last time." I reminded her, tucking in my chin. I fought the urge to roll my eyes and a shudder tickled my shoulders. Sometimes my roommate's enthusiasm for trying to help me make the most of my time at ISA backfired. Like when I stumbled out the doorway of the last party after one too many drinks.

"I know. I know. I know." The words rushed from her ruby lips. "But tonight will be different. It's a costume party, not just some random Friday night dorm party. It'll be legit."

I stared at McKenzie in silence, mulling it over in my mind. Finally, I looked down before speaking.

"It's not that I don't like parties. But..." I closed my eyes and took a deep breath. "I don't want to end up like my mom. She started drinking and never stopped. So I don't even want to start. But at these parties sometimes I just feel like such a fish out of water."

"Oh." McKenzie set down her tube of lipstick. "Okay, okay. If you really don't think you should go, you don't have to."

Something about her words activated a defensiveness within me. Could I really not control myself? Was I already just as bad off as Mom? If I failed, it wouldn't be the first time. But if I didn't, it could be my chance to prove to myself that I really could change everything. I could be stronger than Mom. For some reason, I clutched the necklace at my neck, as though it represented some sort of internal encouragement from my dad.

"It's fine," I said, more to myself than to her. "I'll go."

"Yay!" McKenzie clapped her manicured hands together as fast as a hummingbird flapping its wings. "I owe you a cinnamon chai latte from Sea Dogs for this! You won't regret it, you'll see."

We'll see.

I shook my head, still not sure of my feelings about attending this party. I hoped if anything, it could give me some spark of inspiration for the student art showcase next month. But the blank rag paper canvas still taped to the desk in my room was a reminder that I had stalled out. Inspiration eluded me lately. I couldn't seem to get my head into my work since my nightmares had returned. I was struggling to make it mean something. And I didn't know if I could paint something again that had quite the same impact as the painting that brought me here to begin with.

"All right then. Let's go." I gritted my teeth, determined not to repeat the mistakes of the last party. I knew that night I never wanted to be drunk again. It was the worst feeling I'd ever experienced. But the one good thing about that night—and the one thing that scared me the most—was that for the first time in weeks since moving to this beachside town, I slept through till morning without a single nightmare of drowning.

2

LIKE SHIPS IN THE NIGHT

I t was time to get going. I'd committed to my decision. We slid into McKenzie's yellow Miata as she lowered the top, and headed straight for the harbor, only a few blocks from campus. We passed the far side of the campus, where most of my art classes were held, opposite the dorms beside Matanzas Bay. Crossing the campus meant a breathtaking tour past towering Spanish rooftops and the elegant colonial statues nestled throughout the cobblestone pathways. Manicured palms lined the walkways that twisted through the grounds, swaying with the breeze from the bay. The older authentic buildings echoed their history of a golden age of exploration, and the newer structures were built to match.

It was hard to deny the romantic feel of the old castle-like buildings, especially when the sun lit their golden color on fire in the twilight.

As we drove, I admired the bay, which flowed along the border of Constantine, and its neighboring, more well-known city of St. Augustine, separating both towns from the Atlantic beaches. My watercolor eyes couldn't help but drink in the magnificence of the deep indigo water and white crystal sunlight dancing across its surface as the anchored boats bobbed up and down. The gulls perched along the stone wall that lined the bay at my side, mocking me with their calls before taking flight just to soar back to the top of the bridge. Just beyond that bridge was the vast ocean that I'd spent every moment avoiding since I arrived here. How could I not? After a dream like last night's, it was hard not to fear the ocean, which was disheartening, since I was otherwise drawn to its beauty.

I gazed up at the arched sign above us as we walked onto the docks. *Gull Marina*, it read in pink faded letters, once red before the Florida sun had sapped them of their vibrance. Here we met McKenzie's "friend" Ty, welcoming his friends onto his family's luxury cruiser. As we neared the water, my pulse sped up in my tightened chest. It was almost as if I was actually underwater, struggling to breathe as I forced myself to take hesitant steps towards the boat. When I made the mistake of glancing down at the roiling water below, a knot formed in my stomach, a sickness creeping upward, and I did my best to swallow it down. I took a deep breath as we boarded, but it felt like breathing through a snorkel. With trembling steps, I was careful not to fall as I climbed onto the gangplank leading to the open platform at the back edge of the boat.

I was glad that I chose to wear my sneakers, instead of the white pumps McKenzie had insisted on. All the while, I still couldn't wrap my head around the fact that it was 83 degrees on October 31st. Back in Arkansas it would have at least been chilly enough to need a sweater by this time of year.

Ty's yacht was impressive, even being one of the more compact vessels, the open deck on the back of the boat could easily hold two large tables. A straight stairway along the side of the ship led from just behind the bow of the boat to a higher deck up top. The inside cabin boasted a lounge area, where a dozen or so unfamiliar faces sat, drinks in hand, laughing and commenting on each other's costumes. Music boomed with Michael Jackson's *Thriller* first up on the playlist, a given for any Halloween party.

McKenzie somehow managed to get invited to all sorts of get-togethers like this. She knew everyone and everyone knew her, but I, on the other hand, felt like a square peg in a round hole in these places. Most of the partygoers looked like other college students, though there couldn't have been more than 25 or 30 others. I had made a few acquaintances at Isabel, but so far, we had toured the entire length of the boat without seeing another face I recognized.

At seven-thirty on the dot, the boat left its port, the faintest remnant of orange glow fading behind the blue horizon. When the salty air intensified as we began moving out to sea, a sensation of nervousness began welling up in my chest. I felt my heart flutter as the small ship bobbed up and down in the wake, picking up speed. I tried not to think about the fact that there was nothing but vast ocean surrounding us with nowhere to go but down.

What did you expect, Katrina? It was just a dream. Suck it up.

However, no amount of self-encouragement could banish the clarity of the nightmare from last night that held my thoughts captive. As I stared down at the black water it all came back to life in my head.

A mammoth wave curled over me, sucking me under as if I was no more than a lifeless piece of seaweed. The water collapsed down on my chest like a crushing boulder. It was all a blur of blue, crystals of foaming bubbles swirling in a frenzy around me. I attempted to swim back up, kicking furiously, but I was no match for the current. The surface glimmering tauntingly right above me remained out of reach. The sound of my own racing heartbeat thundered in my head. My searing lungs felt like they would explode, but I knew if I attempted to draw a breath it would be my last. Yet it was no use. I could no longer resist the burning need in my body to breathe. The urge to inhale was a raging fire consuming me from the inside, and at last, it had won. Opening my mouth to gasp for air that wasn't there, I braced for the sting of salt water that would rush to fill my lungs...

"Don't worry. It's okay." McKenzie must have noticed my white-knuckle grip on the railing of the hull where we sat looking at the water trailing along the side of the boat.

"I know. I'm fine." I nodded, but my shaky voice betrayed me. I didn't expect to react this way, but my nightmare had resurrected old fears that I had forgotten were so strong. I hated that dream. I'd had it a few times since moving to Florida, but it had become a near-nightly occurrence these past few weeks.

"Ty's been boating since he was like five." She tried to reassure me. "He's got this! No need to worry." She patted my hand playfully, batting her eyelashes.

I nodded unconvincingly. I tried to enjoy myself, but none of this felt like me—the skimpy costume, the booze, the crowd. I was just a small-town Arkansas girl suddenly trying to blend in with elite art students whose allowances probably rivaled my dad's yearly income. I tried keeping my focus on the reason I was here—my full-ride scholarship and a chance to focus on my art and leave the baggage behind. Yet somehow, I kept ending up at these pointless parties.

Just a moment later, McKenzie saw someone else she knew and waved her pom-poms at them from across the boat, springing up to head over in their direction.

I tried to focus on the beauty of the water instead of my fear of it. As I watched the black water rolling underneath the boat, its unstoppable nature captivated me. Golden and neon blue lights from the ship danced in the ripples as the boat moved forward smoothly. For whatever inexplicable reason, I started to feel less afraid.

"Who's ready for Boozing for Apples?!" Ty stood up from the helm, dressed like a gladiator, throwing up his hands like some kind of Roman Caesar demanding cheers from his subjects. I couldn't help but roll my eyes. That seemed like a horrible game to play on a moving vessel at sea.

Everyone whooped and cheered. McKenzie came back and sat down beside me just in time as everyone began playing. I could tell McKenzie wanted to get in on the action, but she was staying with me instead. Guilt washed over me like the sea spray misting up from the side of the boat.

Though Ozark, Arkansas held nothing for me and reeked of stale friendships, small-town gossip, and painful memories, in that strange moment I missed it. I missed the cool Octobers, I missed the orange and red leaves peppering the mountains as the grip of autumn strengthened, and I missed Dad's store-bought chocolate cake every year on my birthday.

While the party-goers carried on, pressing their faces into a full tub of water that was sloshing over the sides with the boat's movement, Ty suddenly stood up to make another announcement. "Okay people, the island is just a few minutes out! We should be there soon!"

I shot a panicked look at McKenzie. "What is he talking about? What island?"

McKenzie pulled her bottom lip between her teeth and squinted as if to look like she was aware that she'd made a mistake.

"McKenzie! What is going on?" My voice cracked.

"I may have forgotten to mention that part of the Halloween party is sailing out to the island and making a bonfire for a few hours to hunt for ghosts."

I sucked down a breath deep into my chest to keep calm.

"Excuse me, what?"

McKenzie's face became a little more serious, but I could tell she still didn't understand the severity of the fear she'd just stirred up within me. "Okay, so here in Constantine, there's a little island way off the coast that's got like a bunch of creepy ghost stories and stuff about it. Did you know about that?"

"Not at all." I shook my head, urging her to go on as I chewed my lip in distress.

"Ty thought it would be cool to go check it out and spend part of the night there. Ya know, make a bonfire and stuff. And like, maybe we'll see a ghost or something. I mean, it's Halloween, come on!"

"McKenzie." I groaned in angst, but didn't even know how to finish the sentence beyond saying her name.

"Don't worry!" Her eyes lit up, as if she'd just discovered the solution to a puzzle. "I'm pretty sure no one has actually seen a ghost there or anything. It's all just stories. Like there's this one story about a girl who mysteriously died out here back in the eighties or something like that. It'll be fine, I promise!"

"And that's supposed to make me feel better?" I muttered. She looked down and her lips parted as she expressed eyes full of genuine pity.

"Well, I'm sure you can stay on the boat if you'd rather not go with us." She was serious, but the way she said it irked something under my skin. I could tell by the nearly empty cup in her hand that she was already a little tipsy. Regretting my choice to come, I took a breath, accepting that the only way to get through the night was to just manage as best I could.

With another wave from some obscure figure on the other side of the yacht, McKenzie's attention drifted away. She told me she'd be back again in a minute and stood up to scurry over to another small group of people.

I remained in my spot on the edge of the yacht and glanced back around to stare out at the dark horizon, thinking about what would await us on the island. It seemed like a terrible idea, but what did I know? I had never been on a boat before. I didn't grow up around the ocean and all its mysteries. Maybe it was perfectly safe, I had to tell myself to keep the fear at bay.

As I watched the outer waters, I blinked to steady my vision as I noticed a shadow looming on the surface of the ocean in the distance. The more I strained to see it, the more I could make out the large silhouette of another boat, drifting in the shadows of the horizon. Turning around to scan the deck of the yacht, I wondered if anyone else had seen the same thing, but everyone seemed a bit too buzzed or immersed in their conversations to notice. When I looked back, the shadow ship was gone, so I supposed it must have been my imagination, or maybe a trick of the light. There was only a sliver of the moon out tonight, making it darker than usual. So, I convinced myself that the obsidian sky and black water were just making it all too easy to see things that weren't there.

3

LAND HO

"Land ho!" Ty shouted with mischief in his voice.

I watched him from my seat as he maneuvered the wheel at the helm. He had seemed like a decent enough skipper for the most part, but as he inched the boat closer to the island, I started to feel uneasy. I was a little worried his judgment was getting impaired from the alcohol I had watched him guzzle down since before we had left the marina.

The crowd on deck became livelier, voices and spirits lifting as they turned their attention to the dark little mass ahead. Illuminated only by the boat's single headlight, the little island stood as creepy as ever, as if levitating on the ocean's surface. As everyone excitedly rushed to the edge of the boat to see their destination, the boat rocked as it struck something solid underneath. I grabbed the railing to keep my balance, looking around for McKenzie. I didn't see her.

I felt the yacht's vibrations through my bones as the underside slid against the sand. I gripped tighter, trying not to panic as everyone grew silent. Ty let out a slew of curse words as he realized he had sailed a bit too close to the island. From it extended a hidden sandbar that apparently reached out much farther than he realized.

Oh, no.

Close to the same area where I thought I had seen the shadow ship, the visible edge of the island skirted just a few meters away. Thankfully, the lights from the mainland back in Constantine were still visible behind us, reminding me that we hadn't entirely disappeared into a shadowy void. But still, the lights were tiny dots barely shining in the distance, and they didn't change the reality that we were much farther out than I thought we would go.

Once the boat had settled, the chatter returned, but this time there was a sense of panic present in the voices. People spoke faster. Some were tapping their fingers impatiently. A few other guys in the crowd rushed to Ty and tried to figure out what to do next. I stood up to get a better view. McKenzie came bounding down the steps from the top of the boat and hurried over to me. How she managed to keep her balance while running in her high heels, I'll never figure out.

"Are you okay?" She exclaimed.

"Yes," I said, still holding the railing. "But just so you know this is not helping." I tried to sound playful, but I certainly wasn't kidding.

"I'm sure it'll be fine! Ty can get us out. I'll go ask him and see what's going on." McKenzie scurried away before I could even begin to think of a response.

I stood, braced against the railing, watching the water rippling below against the now stationary boat. A couple of frat boys appeared at my side, pushing each other with incredible energy, as though they were trying to urge each other toward me.

"Hey, gorgeous." One of them cleared his throat as though holding back a laugh, leaning onto the railing next to me. "Some captain we got, huh?" He snickered as the golden lights off of the boat caught the sheen of his slicked-back copper hair. He wore a Wonder Bread race car driver suit, clearly paying homage to the movie Talladega Nights. His friend's face was obscured by smudged makeup drawn to look like a skull, but it wasn't enough to hide his smug expression.

When I simply nodded and half smiled in reply, the Ricky Bobby wannabe inched himself closer. With my guard up, I closed my arms around myself tightly, letting go of the railing to do so.

"Hey, I remember you from that party back in Caylin's dorm. We practically carried you to the door that night you were so trashed!"

I didn't exactly remember the referenced incident at all, but I couldn't deny it. That night I *had* gotten too drunk to walk straight. McKenzie told me I had to have help making it to the door and up the stairwell back to our dorm. Was it really these two goons who did the honors? I recoiled, embarrassed to talk to these guys if they had truly seen me like that. And I couldn't figure out why it mattered because I found their presence quite unappealing.

"Well, don't worry, I won't be needing any help getting off this boat tonight. I can't believe I even got on in the first place." I tried to sound light-hearted, but my nerves were fighting to be front and center. The worst part was that I couldn't tell if the twisting in my gut was from watching the water too long or the two obnoxious prep boys flanking my sides.

Skeleton boy now stood on my left side and placed a beer in my hand. I ran my thumb along the glass bottle's cold surface before setting it down at my feet. "Not tonight," I uttered, not unkindly. "I'd like to walk myself out this time."

"Aw come on now, don't be so salty." Ricky Bobby stuck out his bottom lip in a mocking pout. "How do you expect to build your tolerance if you're gonna give up that easily?"

"I appreciate your concern, but really, I'm good," I said, trying to sound more insistent. I looked back out into the water, somewhat hoping to catch another glimpse of what I thought I saw before.

"Whatever's out there, babe, I promise it's not as interesting as what's on this boat." Skeleton boy grinned in an annoyingly confident way that mismatched his teeth's alignment to the white skull lines around his jaw.

I tried to turn away slowly, hoping they would get the hint that I wasn't interested in continuing the conversation, but they persisted.

"If you don't like to party, what do you like to do?" Skull Face laughed as he lightened his voice as though speaking to a child.

"I—Usually painting. It's why I'm here."

"Painting," he repeated, looking down at his feet as he kicked at something invisible. "That's cool, I guess."

"Well, we are at an art school," I added, swallowing down a lump of self-doubt. I was holding onto the railing again, twisting the skin of my palm against it nervously like throttling a motorcycle. I didn't know what else to talk about. I didn't *want* to talk. But that was precisely why I was forcing myself to do it anyway.

"Yeah, but who's thinking about that at a time like this? It's like bringing homework on a vacation." Ricky Bobby laughed again, the tone in his voice rising and falling. Some frustrated cursing came from the direction of the hull, catching Ricky Bobby's attention.

"Well, it was nice talking to you, but seems like Ty still doesn't have a freaking clue. Maybe we should go offer our expertise."

"Yeah." Skull Face nodded. "My parents would kill me if I got their yacht stuck like this."

They walked away without another word to me, but even as the distance between us grew, I could still hear them snickering again as Skull Face jabbed his friend's side. "Okay, hand over the twenty bucks since I made the first move on watercolor girl."

I shook my head. Stepping back a bit from the edge of the boat, I glanced at the hull to see if we were any closer to getting the vessel freed from its gridlocked position.

From what I could tell, we were not getting out of this situation any time soon. After plenty of wasted time trying to no avail, as the yacht engine sputtered uselessly, Ty reassured us all that when the tide rose a bit more, it would free up the boat. So, it was just a matter of waiting it out. He announced to everyone that the party was still moving to the island as planned and that we wouldn't be passing up the opportunity for a beach bonfire and some ghost hunting.

Interestingly, the notion of a yacht running aground on a supposedly haunted island in the middle of the ocean seemed to stir up more excitement as the others leaped and crawled over the side of the yacht into the shin-deep water below.

I, however, was not looking forward to the idea of blindly wading into dark water to get to the island's edge. The whole situation seemed incredibly unsafe, and my heart filled with dread just from thinking about it. Looking down over the boat's edge, my mind whipped up memories of the nightmare, and there was nothing I couldn't do to convince myself to follow everyone overboard.

"McKenzie, I think I'm just going to stay here."

"Are you sure? You're gonna be all alone."

"Yeah, I'll just catch up a little bit later," I explained. "I can see you guys from here." I could see the first orange flames catching as they were already getting the bonfire started on the shore. More cheers and laughs arose. Someone turned on a radio.

McKenzie waved me goodbye and followed the crowd off the boat and onto the island. I felt bad for being such a drag, but it didn't seem to dampen her bubbly spirit in the slightest.

As I sat there on the empty yacht, I ran through ideas for my showcase piece. Should I use regular watercolor paper? Or maybe go a little less traditional and prime a canvas for watercolor? It all depended on what I would create. I checked around me for inspiration. I looked at the glowing cinders rising into the night sky from the fire, the glitter, and colors of the costumes, the midnight canvas of the sea and sky that blended into one dark endless void. But nothing felt right.

Suddenly my phone chimed. It was a text from Scott, my Dad.

Happy Halloween, Trina. Te amo.

He almost always told me he loved me in Spanish. Even after living in Arkansas for over twenty years, a slight remnant of his Cuban accent still decorated his words when he spoke. Halloween was his favorite holiday, and I knew he was alone. Mom had been gone for over a year now. I felt horrible at the realization that I hadn't spoken to him since my birthday, I texted him with a grinning emoji and something I hoped would make him smile.

Happy Halloween Dad. And btw no promises, but I'm going to try the showcase. For you. Now if I could just find a way around the whole black tie dress code and gala part lol.

He replied almost instantly.

Bueno, hija. I knew you wouldn't pass up a chance to knock their socks off again.

The corner of my mouth lifted into a little smile at his corny expression. But it disappeared when I thought about the showcase and the fact that I hadn't even started. I prayed that something would come along and inspire me as I waited in the empty boat.

I'll do my best, Dad. And before long it'll be Thanksgiving break and I'll be home for a while. I miss you.

I sent a heart emoji to follow.

I miss you, too, Trina. But as much as I worry about you being so far away, I know you deserve to be there.

A tender smile formed on my lips at my Dad's encouragement. He was always ready with something reassuring to say. I wondered if he was in the house or still in the shop covered in grease working on a car he just couldn't leave alone.

I laid my head back on the railing, pulling the halo headband off my head. As the stars twinkled overhead, the sound of the waves lapping at the bottom of the boat was drowned out by the noise from the island beach, which reverberated with loud music, talking, and laughter. By now it was half-past eight. The tide had crept up a bit and some of the partygoers were having quite the time wading around in the water and dancing around on the shore. I started to wonder if McKenzie was as concerned with getting stuck out here all night as I was. I took a moment to search the tide times on my phone just to get an idea. High tide was supposed to peak in just under an hour. I hoped it would be enough to get us out of this mess.

I mustered the courage to look back over the edge of the boat at the water. It was higher now, and I hoped Ty had the sense to remember to put the anchor down. I had texted McKenzie, with no response. Eventually, I realized I would need to find her face-to-face if I wanted to talk to her.

I hoisted myself up along the edge of the boat, and made my way down the ladder, grimacing as I forced myself to dip my toes into the water.

Come on, Katrina. You can do this.

My self-pep talk was only so helpful. But I knew if I didn't remind McKenzie and Ty about the tide, they all might just be swimming back. I was still in disbelief at how no one seemed to realize how dangerous this whole situation was. But I wasn't a Floridian. I didn't grow up near the beach like they had. The ocean scared me; it held power and strength greater than anything. There was no telling what secrets lie within its trenches. And I didn't like that. Maybe I was being paranoid about what I knew little about, but I didn't care. I wasn't about to get stuck on some island miles from shore all night because these party animals lost track of time.

Considering that possibility was just the boost of courage I needed to take one step further down and let myself slide feet first into the water. It was a little higher than it had been an hour earlier, but not so much that I still couldn't wade through it without much difficulty. In that moment I was thankful for my super short angel dress, as its hem was well above the water line. A knot formed in my chest as I entered the water with trembling hands, but as I stepped forward, the fear eased a bit. Something about the water against my skin, as foreign and unnerving as it was, stilled my breathing as I realized it wasn't pulling me under. It was nothing like the sea in my dreams. That one was brutal and relentless, using all its force against me. But this placid glass water was gentle, encasing my frame delicately as it lapped up lazily along my legs. For a moment, it wasn't so bad. But then I started moving forward into a black abyss into which I could not see below.

After trudging through the water, trying not to think about what I might step on, I finally made it to the island's edge. With a long sigh of relief, I marched forward towards the crowd on the beach, the bonfire's glow flickering off their dancing bodies. I could see McKenzie's bright cheerleading dress even from there, and I made my way to her, passing up multiple offers for a drink or a joint. I didn't see anyone ghost hunting. I figured they had either forgotten about it or chickened out, as the rest of the tiny island was quite dark and foreboding.

"Aww yay! You made it! Couldn't stay away from where the fun is, could ya?" Her words came out a bit slurred.

"No, I came to check on you." I responded a touch more sharply than I had intended. "Does Ty have a time in mind for going back to the boat? The tide will probably be high enough in an hour or so."

"Oh, well yeah, we'll be fine. I'm sure he knows. Stop worrying, Katrina. Just have fun!" She spoke, trying to dance, stumbling in the sand, while not even looking my way. I realized she was a little too wasted to have this conversation.

Right then and there it occurred to me that I would be stuck here, completely at their mercy for returning. This was without a doubt the last party I was going to let McKenzie talk me into.

I turned away, determined to get back to the boat before the rising water made it impossible. As I stepped back into the water, it felt much deeper than it had been just a short moment ago. The high water sloshing around my hips was a warning signal that our time was running short. As I closed my eyes again, trying not to look at the dark water below, a jolt of fear shot across my body as my toes didn't reach the bottom with my next step forward.

The sudden drop off the sandbar sent me tumbling forward, and the stupid wings on my costume acted as sails in the current that sucked me out further into the water. With the lower half of my body now immersed, I began to fight the current, but quickly found it was no use. I tumbled amongst the torrent, salt water splashing around me. Panic welled up in me as I remembered the dream from the night before. Was this what it was trying to warn me about? I opened my mouth to cry for help, but no sooner had my lips separated than the seawater rushed in with a quick lap of a wave, burning my eyes and forcing my scream back down.

For a brief moment, my head went under, my soaked wings now heavy and weighing me down. I wasn't the best swimmer, as I'd never had many opportunities to practice, so the drenched feathers at my back only added to the difficulty of trying to fight against the rip current. My arms grew tired as I fought to swim back to the boat, but I could tell I wasn't getting any closer. If anything, the hidden torrent was washing me farther and farther out. My heart beat so fast it felt as though it could've been heard all the way to the ocean floor.

Terror pulled me under as fast as the current. Just as I thought I'd never make it back up above the water, I felt something lift me from the bottom. Arms, strong and sturdy, raised me up back to the surface, and somehow we were right at the island's edge. In the dark I couldn't see my rescuer, but they lifted me gently to the sandy shore of the island, on a side far enough away from the party that I could catch my breath in peace. After I coughed up the seawater caught in my throat and rubbed my eyes to soothe the salty sting, I glanced around, looking towards the partygoers, to find whoever it was who had brought me here, but I didn't see a soul who seemed close enough to have managed such a feat. But I knew someone helped me. Whoever it was, they had vanished. I checked my phone, grateful it was still secure in its waterproof case, a wise investment I was glad I made since moving here.

Once I caught my breath, I stood, tearing the heavy, dripping angel wings from my back and tucking them under my arm. They had almost been the death of me, and I certainly didn't plan on wearing them on the way back. I began to make my way toward the party in the distance, but then I decided I'd rather not get caught up in all that again. I needed a moment alone, and going back to the yacht alone was not an option after what had just happened. In search of a moment away from the chaos, I wandered away from the bonfire and walked along the edge of the shore. The island wasn't very big at all, likely too small to appear on any maps. It could probably be crossed on foot in no more than five minutes if you could manage to get through the thicket of trees condensed in the center.

I was thankful for those trees as I walked around the corner, hidden by wild unkempt palms and wide-leafed brush that acted as a barrier to the chaos behind me. I plopped down into the sand, exhaustion settling into my bones. With the light of the fire blocked by the trees and the moon hidden in the sky, it was quite dark there in my little corner of the island. But I didn't care. Setting my phone out beside me in case McKenzie texted, I leaned my head back. I looked up and noticed the stars, nestled in their places against the black heavens. Out here they looked brighter than I'd ever seen, and they appeared clustered together, feathered by wisps of starlight. For nearly the first time since I'd come to Isabel, I felt like myself as I sat there alone beneath the night sky.

Suddenly, an unfamiliar voice made me jump.

4

Fair Winds

"Are you looking for constellations?"

I whipped my head around to see a guy, close to my age, maybe a junior or senior, sitting in the sand about 15 feet from me. How had I not seen him there when I first sat down?

"No, just catching my breath," I replied, squinting to see him in the shadows, then looking back up. It was difficult to make out his features, but I could at least see his light brown hair that was just sun-kissed enough to appear golden. "But I've never seen stars this clearly before."

"Then you need to get out on the sea more. No better way to stargaze." He chuckled. I couldn't help but notice his accent, which held a timelessness about it, not quite American, but not quite English, and felt like soft satin against my ears.

"No thanks." I shook my head and tilted my chin back toward the crowd. "I can't even believe they talked me into this."

He didn't respond. The night sea breeze sent a small chill over my bare arms and legs, and my mini dress did little to offer much warmth. I brought my knees up to my chest. For a while, we just sat there in silence.

"Nice costume, by the way," I said, noting his pirate attire. "Though I'd expect a peg leg or an eye patch."

"Well fortunately I've never had need of either," he joked. "And what are you?"

"I'm supposed to be an angel."

He nodded. He must've noticed my shivering because he stood to walk over and offered me a blanket that he produced from seemingly nowhere.

"Where did you get that?" I took the blanket from him and quickly wrapped it around my bare shoulders.

"I brought it with me from the ship. It can get cold out here on the water. I just needed to get away for a bit, find some peace."

"Me too. Thanks."

"Of course."

There was another minute of silence between us. I felt a strange comfort with him, and I didn't even know him.

"What's your name?" I blurted out.

"Milo." His voice sent a wave of warmth through me, more so than the blanket.

"I'm Katrina."

"Lovely to meet a fair lass like you, Katrina."

"Okay, you are *way* too into your character," I laughed.

"What?"

"*Fair lass?*" I repeated.

"Well excuse my manners," he chuckled. "You did say you were an angel after all."

I rolled my eyes, but in a playful way. A few more notes of laughter escaped the both of us until we both settled into silence again for a moment. I was the first to break it.

"In Arkansas, I used to sit outside on summer nights to watch the fireflies near the woods behind our house." Here I leaned back onto my hands, moving the blanket to my legs, and kept my gaze fixed on the sky. "That's what the stars remind me of."

Even with the echoes of the party music behind us, the only sound that caught my attention was the gentle gurgle of waves rolling at my feet.

"Can you locate the North Star?"

Locate.

Something about that sentence, the way he spoke, sounded so poetic and formal, as if he carefully preselected each word before speaking.

"I honestly have no idea," I laughed. "Sorry."

"Don't apologize." He moved a bit closer to me, pointing into the sky. "Right there to the left a bit. That's it."

I nodded as my eyes locked onto the bright dot in the sky.

"Impressive," I said. "How does it work?"

"Any good sailor can find it. You use the angle between the skyline to the north and the star, and that will tell you the ship's position."

"You must spend a lot of time out on the water," I acknowledged.

"You could say that."

Suddenly we were interrupted by the sound of McKenzie calling my name and the thud of footsteps in the wet sand. Glancing up, I saw her bouncing towards me. Without a word, she grabbed my hand and pulled me up.

"C'mon, we gotta get back to the boat before the tide gets too high," she said.

"That's what I've been trying to tell you!" I snapped.

Ignoring my response, she pulled me back in the direction of the party. I turned around to make sure Milo was coming, too, but when I looked over my shoulder, he was gone. I clutched the blanket he had given me and inwardly hoped I would see him again back on the yacht.

The rising waves were lurching closer to the shore, snuffing out the last bit of dying embers from the bonfire. It was time to move, or we would be navigating some dangerously deep water back to the boat.

The water was nearly to my thighs now, and I held onto McKenzie's hand tightly from behind as she led the way forward, but her stumbling made me anxious. As I stared down into the water, I was grateful for the big light on the front of the yacht that illuminated the now fully submerged sandbar. I tried to suppress my nightmares as the chilled water tickled my skin.

Everyone cheered as the last person climbed up the ladder back onto the boat. We waited on the boat for another little while to allow the tide to peak. Without warning, McKenzie proudly took out her Polaroid from the backpack she carried.

"I think this calls for a picture," she laughed loudly. "Here, let me test the lighting. Smile for me!"

I flashed her a forced grin, and she snapped a headshot with a bright light snapping in my face. The camera spat out the image with its iconic printing sound. The small film slowly developed to reveal my brightly illuminated face and neck, contrasted heavily against the nighttime backdrop. McKenzie carelessly dropped the picture down on the edge of the boat as she pulled herself close into the frame with me for a selfie of the two of us. I fake-smiled for the split second it took to snap the photo. As the camera began to print again, a powerful burst of wind came from nowhere and whipped up the picture of me McKenzie had placed on the hull. My gaze followed the little white rectangle as it was carried by the gust back in the direction of the island. I tingled with an otherworldly sensation knowing a photo of me was now fated to float about wherever at the ocean's mercy, but I didn't dwell on it too long before the boat engine fired back up. I remembered Milo and looked around, hoping to catch a glimpse of him.

"Hey, McKenzie." I touched her shoulder to get her attention as she stared with a tipsy smile at her newly printed selfie. She glanced up at me, mascara smudged underneath her eyes from a mixture of sweat and sea, but her aquamarine eyes still sparkled with vibrance. "Do you know anyone here named Milo? He was dressed like a pirate."

She bit her lip, thinking for a second. "Hmm, I don't think so. At least not that I know of. I've never met anyone at Isabel named Milo."

5

ANCHORS AWEIGH

As we settled, and the cruiser prepared to take leave, I shuffled my things around on the boat looking for my phone, but it was nowhere in sight. I gasped, realizing I had left it back on the island. In my mind's eye, I remembered placing it down beside me in the sand before I started talking to Milo, and I never picked it back up. A dark cloud of dread engulfed me. How was I going to get it back? If the tide didn't get to it first. I told McKenzie and she immediately yelled for Ty to stop the boat.

"Hold up! Katrina needs to go back to get her phone."

With obvious aggravation, Ty snapped on a life vest.

"Well, we better freaking hurry. I'll try moving a little closer." He tossed me a life vest and I fastened it around myself as he nudged the boat just a couple of yards closer to the shore.

"Let's go." He jumped down from the cockpit, flashlight in hand.

I followed him to the boat's ladder, and we quickly climbed down.

"I'm so sorry," I muttered meekly.

"Whatever," he groaned, "just make sure you remember where you left it."

I hustled towards the spot where Milo and I had been sitting, passing the eerie sight of empty glass bottles and the dying embers of the bonfire. Ty followed me with his flashlight illuminating our path.

"It's over here!" I called. He thrust the flashlight into my hands.

"Go get it. Quick." He seethed.

Near trembling, I rounded the corner, leaving Ty behind where he seemed content to wait. My phone remained nestled in its spot in the sand, and I stepped forward to pick it up.

Just as I started to turn around and head back, the sand beneath my feet shifted seemingly on its own and stopped me in my tracks. A strange, unsettling breeze blew in from the ocean, a frigid air lingering.

I heard a faint whistle in the breeze that quickly grew louder into a wailing groan of creaking wood and wind. The gentle waves along the island's edge began to grow taller and aggressive, rolling and churning until they peeled back like petals to reveal an opening in the water's surface only about 100 feet from shore.

By this point, terror had gripped me and left me frozen in place. The water spiraled and sprayed sea mist into the air, catching in the ray of light from my flashlight like fog. Something menacing burst out of the water, along with the sound of old wood bending and aching under pressure. The wind grew stronger and whipped my hair back behind me, ripping feathers from what was left of the dainty angel wing remnants along the back of my shoulders. Hefty gusts bent the trees around me so strongly I thought they would snap in half. I felt weak, almost paralyzed from the scene unfolding just meters away. A ship. A rotting, algae-coated galleon was emerging from the ocean right before my eyes, like a whale springing up to the surface.

The faint moonlight gave me just enough clarity to make out the endless layers of barnacles climbing up the hull, coating the long-corroded mermaid carved into the bow. Saltwater gushed down in waterfalls off the edges as the ship righted itself onto the water. The waves began to die down and the wind became steadier.

Worn sails unfurled from the masts, mottled with tears and holes, yet somehow the strong wind still caught them. A harsh, gruff voice yelled out from within the ship.

"Hoist the colors and man the sails!"

A worn flag slowly began rising along the mast, equally ravaged by time as the battered sails. As the flag peaked at the top of the mast, the wind peeled it back to reveal an iconic black flag with a skull and crossbones.

More voices began coming from the ship. They were those of yelling men, but I couldn't make out what they were saying. Willing my legs to move with everything in me, I finally found the strength to turn and hide in the foliage. From there, I peeked out from behind a palm tree. There appeared a shadowy figure standing proudly just at the base of the bow, overlooking it all.

He was brooding and overpowered every other human on the deck, and his stature alone would be enough to send someone running in the other direction. His deep red captain's coat, the color of blood, caught in the wind and opened back, revealing the pistol strapped to his chest. He could've been my dad's age, and the harsh brow over his steely eyes made him look as though he was enraged with the world and ready to take it out on whoever had the misfortune of speaking to him next. Clamping his black captain's hat down on his head to keep it from blowing away, he looked in my direction. I felt my blood run cold when the moonlight hit his face. With the empty eyes of a broken man looking like he'd lost it all—and was furious about it—-he stared in my direction. Terror rippled through me as his unnerving expression remained unchanged, and I prayed he couldn't see me.

I could feel his stare piercing through the trees as my heart pounded in my chest. Soon the voices on the ship became louder and his deathly gaze broke. He turned away when a voice below called him to attention.

"Starboard side is clear, Cap'n, and anchors aweigh! Where'll we be sailing tonight?" Through the clink of swords, metal, and chains, I could just barely make out the words. "Drop that anchor back down," the captain ordered, his words pouring out like dark smoke as he looked back at the thin bit of shore separating us. "I have no plans to leave the island tonight." And finally, I found the strength in my legs to turn around and run.

I was frantic and out of breath when I made it back to Ty. Running past him, I sprinted back through the water without a second thought, eager to get off the island.

"What the hell? Chill out!" Ty shouted behind me as he worked to catch up. Too shocked to form a coherent response, I just clambered back up the ladder into the boat, catching my breath, soaked from the seawater.

"Did you get the phone?" McKenzie asked. A shivering nod was all I could manage. I contemplated telling her what I had just seen, but I didn't know how to put it into words. Ty chucked his life jacket onto the floor and hopped back into the cockpit, unfazed. Had he not at least felt the strange wind or saw the waves foaming?

I looked back to see if I could still catch a glimpse of the ship I knew I had seen. The island had acted as a shield to those on the yacht, obscuring whatever supernatural event was occurring behind it in the seas. There was nothing. Not a shred of evidence of the pirate ship. The water around the island didn't even look like it had been disturbed. I, however, was still trembling. Now I understood why the island was rumored to be haunted.

"Are you okay?" McKenzie asked. "You look like you saw a ghost."

"What would you say if I said I did?" I managed to squeeze out between breaths.

Ty yelled from the top of the deck, "I'd say Happy Halloween, losers! That's what we came for!" A roar of laughter erupted across the boat. It was clear they wouldn't believe me if I told them, so to avoid further making a fool of myself I kept my mouth shut the rest of the night, aching to get back to land.

I t was sometime after midnight.

My skin felt sticky from the night on the sea. My wild hair stuck to my arms and neck from the humidity. I was itching from the sand in my dress scraping against my skin. I longed to get back to our dorm, take a shower, and fall asleep in my bed.

I knew McKenzie was in no shape to drive, so I took the keys from her backpack and placed myself in the driver's seat. She plopped down in the passenger's seat like a wet noodle and without objection.

The drive back to Isabel wasn't far from the marina. It was only a couple of blocks, but we couldn't get there fast enough. I practically jumped out of the car once we parked and speed-walked to our building.

We were one of the few inhabitants on the top floor. The privacy couldn't be better, but it also felt a little eerie sometimes, like tonight, when not a single other soul wandered the hallway overlooking the bay across the street. As I unlocked the front door, McKenzie put a hand on my shoulder in an uncoordinated way.

"Are you mad at me? You seem a little...bothered." I could tell she was practically pouting just from the dramatic melody of her voice.

"No," I sighed, not turning around. "I'm honestly just glad we made it back in one piece and that I came back sober this time."

Sorry if I'm distant. I just saw the Flying Dutchman rising out of the sea.

McKenzie didn't even make it to the shower, but instead toppled onto her bed, still dressed as a cheerleader, and within a minute, I heard gentle snoring. I slunk wearily into the hot shower and felt sweet relief as the warm water rinsed away the salt on my skin. I felt like throwing up, but this time at least I knew it wasn't from drinking. Slipping into an oversized T-shirt, I rolled myself up in my sage blanket and closed my eyes,

But I couldn't sleep. There was a churning in my stomach and a whirlwind in my head. I couldn't stop thinking about the pirate ship. Part of me wondered if

I had dreamed it. Did I make the whole thing up? Was I tripping on something I didn't remember taking? My sanity seemed a lost cause.

I suddenly sat up in my bed and slipped on a pair of socks. Without turning on the light, I got up and tiptoed out to the front hallway balcony. I stepped out into the second-floor hall. The cold stone against my bare feet contrasted with the heavy, wet heat that engulfed me as I walked out. Underneath the archway wrapped in my blanket, I leaned on the twisted iron railing and stared out into the blackness of the bay. Our dorm building in the East Wing of the campus was so isolated from everything else that it made the sky and sea appear that much darker. A faint rose glow from the city lights of downtown hung in the air like a ghost. I slid down along the stucco walls and sat with my back propped up against it. My mind couldn't stop reliving each detail of the wooden ship resurrecting itself from the depths of the water, half expecting it would reemerge in front of me again here on the bay. After a long while, the distant sound of the water crashing lulled me to sleep.

The next morning McKenzie found me lying outside our dorm.

"Why are you out here?" Her voice made me jump. "You have *got* to tell me what's going on. I have known something was up since last night," she said.

I sighed, sitting up and holding my head.

"I swear you're acting weirder than that night you got wasted."

I knew with McKenzie there was no way I could escape telling her the truth. I was a terrible liar, and she was too good at being relentless. The question was, would she believe me?

I reached up and grabbed her arm, motioning for her to sit down. She took a seat next to me on the porch.

"I'll tell you, but it's going to sound absolutely insane." I began.

She gave me a smirk and squinted at me through the thick frames of her glasses. She only wore them in the dorm.

"Well good thing I like insane," she replied.

I took a deep breath and then tried to think of a way to begin relaying to her what had happened on the island the night before.

"When I went back with Ty...He stayed behind. I...I saw something in the water. When I went back to get my phone —I swear I saw a ship—a pirate ship—come up out of the ocean, right off the coast behind the island."

McKenzie's eyes grew wide. "No way, no way! Are you sure?"

"Honestly, no, I'm not sure. I'm still questioning it myself," I said, looking down at my hands, "but it definitely screwed with me."

McKenzie started to laugh. "That is so wild! I guess those stories don't come from nowhere...."

"Stories? What stories?" My words came out with a hint of urgency.

"You know." She rolled her eyes. "Constantine is like Ghost Story Central. There's a ghost story for everything around here."

"So, you believe it?" I asked.

She looked shocked that I would ask.

"Well yeah!" She screamed. "I think a bit of pirate ghost drama is definitely possible, especially in this pirate-history city. After all, consider yourself lucky. You're the only one of us who got to see anything cool last night."

I was relieved that she didn't think I was crazy, but also a bit concerned at her lackadaisical attitude about it all. Could she seriously believe me but also be this nonchalant about it?

"McKenzie, just don't tell anyone," I pleaded. "I already feel like enough of a freak around here."

"Yeah, you got it!" I couldn't tell if she was playing or being serious anymore. "I'm sorry Ty was kind of a jerk to you last night."

"It's okay," I sighed.

That's the least of my problems right now.

That evening, I called Dad, hoping it would get my mind off things, even for just a few minutes. We talked about the usual things. His garage. A new car he got in to work on. My classes. But the moment the call ended, my head was back to spinning with thoughts of last night's incident.

At some point, I had to convince myself I had imagined the whole thing. It was the only logical possibility. Maybe I *had* been drunk and just didn't remember. Maybe I hallucinated every bit of it.

Turning the thoughts over in my head until I just couldn't accept them anymore, a yawn crept up on me. I could hear McKenzie's muffled voice through the thin wall separating our small bedrooms practicing a presentation for her communications class tomorrow. I decided to get in bed. I'd had more than enough action over the past few days.

6

ALL AT SEA

T he following Monday was rough. Of course, the pirate ship took its turn plaguing my dreams throughout the night, so my sleep wasn't very restful. It took a great amount of effort to focus throughout the lecture on the History of Illustration, seeing that my mind couldn't keep from wandering.

The moment my last class ended at 3:30, I immediately headed for my parking spot, but then stopped and thought it better to stay in the campus courtyard. I had a paper due the next day that I had completely forgotten about due to all the events over the weekend. Though I was glad the teacher reminded us in class, I knew that meant I was about to spend hours trying to finish it in time. Staying focused back at the dorm had become increasingly difficult, so I decided just to stay on campus and work on it there.

I carried my laptop and backpack out to the South Lawn, where it wasn't uncommon for students to set themselves up at a picnic table or hammock and hang out or study, even well into the evening hours. Picking a spot under a tree, I opened the document, staring blankly at the screen. I had started on it last week, but so far had only managed to get down a paragraph. Five more pages to go. Battling my thoughts, I had to push my desire to daydream about the ghost ship out of my head for long enough to get something down. By the time I looked at the clock, it was past 8:00 and dusk had turned to night. I was finishing up the last paragraph. My mind was spent, and I hadn't even stopped to realize how incredibly hungry I was. Closing my laptop and standing up, I made my way toward the campus library to print off the finished product.

My steps were brisk and quick-paced. I was eager to finish this and get home. Fortunately, Queens Library was right across the street from the South Lawn, so it wasn't a long walk, and as far as I knew, the library was open late most nights.

The layout of ISA was quite simple. It was essentially a big square, a cobblestone courtyard at the center, with most academic activities and classes taking place in the North Village, a collection of antique stucco buildings inspired by Spanish architecture, including Queens Library. As I strolled past the towering palms around the front of the building and entered the arched doors, the last bit of daylight dipped behind the building.

I printed the paper off quickly, and then I began to head back towards the door, but something caught my eye. In the corner of the library, I noticed a section of books titled "Constantine History." I briefly wondered if they might have something about the myths and ghost legends surrounding the city and thought maybe it was worth a shot to find something about the ghost ship. Even my rumbling stomach couldn't dampen my curiosity.

I headed over to the shelves, nestled away from the main lobby of the library. As I perused the titles, I couldn't quite find anything that seemed to contain the type of information I was looking for. My brown eyes quickly scanned the titles, but none of them seemed like they would tell me what I wanted.

Glimpses of St. Constantine

Constantine Under Three Flags
Stories of Old Constantine
Castillo de San Romero
The Hidden History of Constantine
St. Constantine Legends

The last one caught my attention. I picked it up and quickly scanned through the pages in my hands. I saw accounts of the Old Constantine Jail, the Castillo de San Romero, and others, but there was nothing about the island off the coast. I flipped to the back of the book where the last page closed with a note:

Constantine is one of the US's oldest cities, and as such there have been various reports of people seeing figures, ghosts of soldiers, pirates, and others. This nearly 500-year-old city has a history of haunting!

Upon reading this, I realized I was likely just one of the many people who thought I saw "something" lurking in the shadows. I had never been a believer in ghosts or haunted places, so I felt ridiculous to think how much the pirate ship had tormented my mind. But there had to be some explanation for what I saw. I began trying to downplay it, thinking it was nothing more than some exaggerated part of my imagination. But I still couldn't shake the doubt. As I closed the book in my hands, I was startled by a soft voice from behind me.

"Interesting book?"

I turned around to see a tall, attractive guy with raven black hair and piercing ice-blue eyes looming in front of me. He was smirking slightly, and his thick brows were lifted in a coaxing manner, like he was eagerly awaiting my response. It was hard not to notice that he was quite beautiful in a striking kind of way. The blueness of his eyes complemented his sharp, freshly shaven jawline. I hoped he didn't notice how I looked him up and down for a split second, noticing his unique choice of black pants messily tucked into dark leather boots, gray shirt, black jacket, and vest underneath. It seemed like a lot of clothes for a place with a climate as warm as Florida's. It had an edgy but classic appeal, certainly all his own.

"Not interesting enough," I replied, sliding the book back into its place on the shelf.

"Oh? What were you looking for?" He asked, his elegant accent caught me off guard.

"Just browsing," I said, not sure how else to answer his question.

"My apologies," he said, "I just thought maybe I could help. I'm in my last year here so I've spent a lot of time in this library."

"Oh. Nice." I grinned. "I just started here this semester."

"I can tell," he chuckled.

"What's that supposed to mean?" I asked, a bit annoyed.

"I'm sorry. Where are my manners? I'm Bellamy."

"Katrina."

"Lovely to meet you, Katrina." He said in that charming voice of his. "If you need anything, I'd be happy to help. I know it can be rough your first semester."

I began to slowly walk out of the book aisle and Bellamy took up stride beside me.

"Okay, um, thanks," I said, not sure what he was getting at. "So, are you, like, a foreign exchange student?" I asked, wondering about his accent.

"Oh. Well, no, not exactly. My parents are from Europe, and we moved here a few years ago. They wanted some sun and sand I guess," he joked.

"Must've been quite the move," I said quietly, still looking ahead.

"It certainly was. But I like it here." He paused, brushing his bottom lip with his thumb. "Will I be seeing you again?"

His forward question and brazen attitude took me by surprise. However, I had to admit, I wouldn't have minded seeing him again. His mysterious character drew me in.

"You might," I responded, curling the corner of my lips into a small smirk.

"When and where are my best chances?" He asked.

"Well, of course, I have classes tomorrow," I explained, "but after that I'm free."

"Any chance we could meet again on the South Lawn tomorrow evening, say 8?"

"Yeah, um, that's good for me," I said, brushing my hair behind my ear nervously.

"Perfect. I'll see you then, Katrina."

He turned to leave.

"Wait," I stopped him with my voice. "Don't you need my number or something?"

"Don't worry, I'll find you."

His reply shocked me, despite his friendly tone. Feeling unsettled, I didn't know what to say in response as I watched him turn to walk away. From around the corner, an elderly librarian stepped around to restock some books next to me.

"Excuse me," she interrupted gently. "Miss, who are you talking to?"

I glanced at Bellamy, who was now steps away, heading to the door.

I looked back at her, realizing she seemed confused as to what—or who—I was looking at.

Could she not see him?

My stomach growled. I thought maybe my hunger was distorting my experiences. I needed to get back and eat something.

Walking back to our dorm, my thoughts wandered to Dad. I was just about to give him a call as I navigated through the torch-lit campus, but before I could even pick up the phone, it started ringing with his picture on the screen.

Strange coincidence.

"Hey, Dad." I picked up, thinking it was strange for him to be the one to initiate a call this late.

"Katrina, I have to tell you something." His voice sounded stressed on the other end.

"What? Is everything okay?" I asked, suddenly worried.

"I found your mom."

7

A Shot Across the Bows

H is words came through the phone like knives into my chest. I felt a twisting in my stomach.

"I didn't know you were looking for her," I said.

"I know, *hija*. I wasn't exactly looking," he said, a sadness in his voice. "I did try to call her a few more times, *pero*...but she came back on her own. Said she's been in Missouri trying to let things settle." I was silent, not sure what to think. "I just wanted you to know that she's safe and she...she says she's doing better."

I finally spoke.

"That's...good, I guess."

This was difficult for me to take in. I was glad to know she was safe, but the resentment was still so strong. I also didn't believe her. It wouldn't be the first time.

"She's actually here and would like to say something to you." He started.

"Okay?"

"Katrina..." hearing her voice on the other end was unreal, nearly giving me a chill. Especially since it actually sounded clear and coherent, to my surprise. I couldn't remember the last time I'd heard her like that.

"What, Mom?" I said coldly.

"I just want you to know that I'm sorry for everything. I never meant for things to go this way."

I didn't respond.

"I had to go away for a while. I was trying to keep you and Scott out of it. I know you're tired of it. I know you don't believe me," she pleaded, "but you have to try to understand that there are things I can't control."

"Yeah, I know that," I said, "the biggest one being yourself." I didn't mean for my words to come out so harshly, but I had nowhere else to direct the anger inside me. She didn't respond. I let out a huge sigh and shut my eyes, trying to calm myself before saying anything else I'd regret.

"Where were you?'

"I promise, I was trying to get sober. I didn't want to come back until I could..."

"Well, we were really worried. But I'm glad you are okay." I told her, trying my hardest to soften my tone. "Can I talk to Dad?"

"Of course, sweetie," she said, sounding defeated and tired.

I heard some noise on the other end of the phone and then it turned into my dad's voice.

"I just thought you should know, Trina."

"Thanks." I paused. "So, is she staying at home?"

"For now, yes."

"Okay, well we can talk more later. Goodnight," I said.

"I know, Trina. It'll just take some time. Night. Mom says goodnight, too."

I hung up. How was I supposed to handle that? All that time without her presence and she just thought she could walk back in like nothing ever happened? Every milestone, every important moment, she wasn't there to see any of it. And for the past year, she was off on her own while we tried to make do without her. I had tried to help her time and time again, all too often throwing myself out to her only to face disappointment when I would walk in after school and find her passed out on the couch, glass bottles lining the floor around her. How many times I had waited anxiously for her to show up to my art shows that she promised to attend only to be left standing there alone with Dad feeling like a fool. I couldn't remember the last time I had spoken to her on the phone before then.

I trudged through the door to find McKenzie updating her social media feed while lying across the couch.

"Well, well, another late night?" She teased. "See any more pirate ghosts?"

I shot her a narrowing glance, wishing she would give it a rest. I also knew I was already in a foul mood from the news about my mom, but I directed my thoughts back to Bellamy.

"Actually," I said, "I met someone at the library."

A massive grin lit up McKenzie's face, and she shot up from the couch like a bullet.

"You met someone? I swear, Katrina, you don't tell me anything! Who is it?"

"Some guy named Bellamy. A senior. Do you know him?"

McKenzie tapped her chin and pouted her lips dramatically as she thought.

"Hmm, nope, I don't think so. Did you get his last name? Let's Facebook stalk him."

"I didn't."

"Ugh! Well, there can't be too many guys with a name like Bellamy here. I'll find him."

Right away, McKenzie got to sleuthing on her social media.

"Well, you let me know when you find him," I joked. "I'm going to chill for a bit," I said, already pulling my shirt off to get ready for a nice shower.

I let the warm water rush over me, and it felt like it was taking the day's troubles with it down the drain. My mom, the ghost ship, not to mention I had my first exam coming up in a few days and I realized I hadn't studied.

Maybe I really should take up drinking.

I chided myself for the thought. Once I was in an oversized T-shirt, some cotton shorts, and my freshly-washed hair wrapped tightly in a towel, I emerged from my bedroom to find McKenzie lying in her bed, still trying to dig up something on her phone.

"Find him?" I asked.

"Come here and look. Are any of these him?"

I walked over and quickly scanned her search results. "Nope, none of those."

"I give up!" McKenzie exclaimed. "Just get a pic of him soon!"

"It's nothing serious. I don't even know what I think about him."

"Is he cute?"

"Well yeah, he is actually, but I don't know, he's a little mysterious."

McKenzie made a little face, scrunching up her nose with a grin full of mischief. "Well, if you want to dig up any real dirt on him, just get me his full name. My cousin is a detective for the police department and he's just a text away."

"Don't worry, I don't think he's a serial killer or anything. Just a little...different."

"Sounds sexy!" McKenzie exclaimed. "If you don't take him, I will."

I laughed and told her goodnight. I walked back into my bedroom and took the towel off my head, drying my waist-length hair with one last squeeze. I rubbed some product through it quickly because if I didn't, my unruly waves would become frizz from the Florida humidity.

I lay down and closed my eyes, thinking of what more tomorrow could hold, because today had been full of unexpected surprises.

T he next morning, I welcomed sleeping in. My first class wasn't until 10 AM. I took advantage of the extra time to lie there beneath my covers, fidgeting with the pendant on the chain around my neck. I hadn't taken the necklace off since the night of the party. It was strangely comforting to me.

As I stared up at the ceiling, I thought about last night's conversation with my mom and wondered if maybe this really would be the time she turned things around. For just a moment, I was hopeful. I squeezed my necklace as I thought of her, as if to capture the glimmer of hope while it was there before me. I held on to it, but then as I relived every broken promise from years past, it fizzled out, and I let go of it.

As I scampered back to the dorm after my last afternoon class, a voice snagged my attention.

"No wild parties tonight, I hope." The groundskeeper, Russell, called as I passed him upon entering the wrought iron gates to the East Wing. I vaguely smiled at him with a look of guilt as he continued to sweep the corridor of the first floor. He seemed to always keep a watchful eye out for the students. Something about his humble demeanor in this extravagant place made me feel more connected to him than most. I had no real complaints about any of my professors, but sometimes the people here could seem just a bit out of touch with reality.

Scurrying up the steps, I opened the door to our dorm to find it empty. McKenzie's keys were absent from their usual spot on the square table by the doorway. I figured she must be out on one of her own adventures, so I took advantage of the emptiness to sit and stare at my blank canvas some more, hoping some source of inspiration would strike.

I happened to notice the blanket Milo had given me, still lying at the foot of my bed where I had dropped it that night upon coming home. His gentle voice echoed in my head. It had been too dark to see his face clearly, but that velvet voice I could never forget. For a moment, I relived our conversation on the island. That was it! His words about the North Star rung clear in my thoughts. That was my starting point.

Dipping my wet brush into a buttery smooth block of blue, I began to paint the background. Streaking the brush across the canvas, I felt the idea come together as I laid the foundation for a night sky reflected in the sea below. The reflection would be the focus, mirroring the light of the North Star. I'd figure out what else to add later, but at least I had something.

As I mixed some blue and white pigments, creating lines and creases on top of the thin layer I had already applied, I vividly recalled the North Star as Milo had pointed out, twinkling unwaveringly over the horizon. I wanted to amplify the vision in my head with my colors, to make the ocean waves reflect the starlight in waves melting into silver.

Glancing over at the clock on the wall, I realized the time was already ten minutes past seven. Forcing myself to set down my brushes in a hurried frenzy, I stood and began to undress, trying to decide what to wear for my meeting with Bellamy while also trying not to waste any more time. It was hotter than it should be in November, so I opted for a sleeveless plum-colored top with some light jeans and some leather flip-flops.

I reached for my mascara and a neutral shade of lip color, knocking over the small, packaged box that had enclosed my necklace days earlier when I'd received it in the mail on my birthday. Taking note, I reminded myself to do a bit of cleaning up later, knowing the chances of that actually happening were unlikely. The tissue paper fell out as I reached down to pick up the face-down box. That's when I saw the writing on a paper no bigger than a notecard tucked between the gift paper.

> *It's your turn to have this. Always keep it with you. It's been said that it can help with the nightmares. Maybe it can even stop them, just as long as you can figure out how. You'd be the first in our family. They've been trying for a long time. Whatever you do, don't lose it. It's the only chance we've got.*

I didn't know what to make of the message. The handwriting didn't look like my dad's, but who else could have sent it? He knew I had nightmares as a child. But how would he know they had come back now? Could it have been from

Mom? I refused to think she'd write something so cryptic when she could barely string together a sensible thought.

I shook it off for the time being. As odd as the message seemed, I knew I didn't have time to give it more thought. I'd call Dad about it later, but for now, I was running very late to my meeting with Bellamy.

It was a short enough walk from the dorms, so I left my old Cherokee parked in our lot. Stepping onto the South Lawn, I began to question if I should do this.

*What if he *is* a serial killer?*

Bellamy certainly had a dark enough lure about him. And he said he would find me. I didn't know exactly what he meant by that. My uncertainty began to strengthen, and soon it was talking me into leaving. I turned to go, deciding that perhaps it was for the best to put this idea to rest. It wasn't like me to get involved with a "bad boy."

I had only gone a few paces back towards the dorms when I noticed Russell struggling with some boxes he was loading into a school van parked by the lawn.

"Do you need some help?" I asked shyly, hoping not to offend him.

"I'm fine, missy, you just worry about staying out of trouble now." He uttered in his raspy voice. I liked to think his voice was weathered by the sea air from some past life in his younger years as a fisherman.

"Katrina!"

I looked over my shoulder in the direction of the voice that called my name. Bellamy approached from the right, dressed in dark attire, similar to the day before, but this time he made less of a statement in his black pants and button-down gray jacket that just reached his hips. It was still quite a vintage look, and it flattered him.

He walked up, nearly blocking Russell, who was still wrestling with the boxes.

"Let me lend a hand with that," Bellamy offered, taking one of the containers from Russell's hands before he could answer.

I couldn't help but notice a very peculiar moment between them, as Russell glared up at Bellamy coldly, and Bellamy shot him back a serious look, almost warning-like. I sensed some type of unexplained rivalry that neither was willing to acknowledge in front of me.

"What are you doing?" Russell asked under his breath.

"I'm just helping you, sir," Bellamy responded politely, but something about the way he said it sounded off.

The tension was overbearing, like a crushing weight that I couldn't ignore. Russell shot Bellamy one last glance through narrowed eyes before turning around to climb up into the driver's seat of the van.

"That was nice of you," I said. "Do you two know each other?"

Bellamy shrugged. "He's a...friend of my dad's. They aren't on the best terms at the moment." He paused after that sentence, then changed the subject. "Hope you're hungry."

"I'd be lying if I said I wasn't," I smiled at him. His concerned expression changed to a grin. I still wasn't convinced. But at least I knew now that contrary to my outlandish experience at the library, Bellamy *was* visible to other people. I wasn't going entirely crazy, at least.

"Come on then. Where do you like to eat around here?"

"You're the expert, remember?" I said. "You've been here a lot longer than me. You pick."

"Ah, yes." He nodded, turning his face away from me. It was then that I noticed the piercing in his ear, a small silver ring curled around his lobe. "Let's go into town and decide there."

The campus was a mere few steps away from the hustle of Constantine's central historical hub. A couple of blocks and we were there, surrounded by the tender glow of streetlamps and chatter of bustling tourists, with a lovely evening view of the bay at our side as we walked. We small-talked along the way, and I felt myself letting down my guard a bit more with Bellamy. I started to feel bad for judging him so harshly.

As we walked through the old city, palm trees planted along the sidewalk swayed in the evening breeze, carrying the scent of salt and fish to our nostrils. Tourists typically flocked the streets here, but now that it was autumn, vacationing season was dying down, leaving a more intimate feel.

A quaint little cafe right on the water over the bay with picnic tables outside along the deck caught my attention.

"This looks like a cool place," I suggested.

We seated ourselves at the little wooden tables lit only by the string lights hanging above them.

"Ever been here before?"

"No, actually, I haven't," he replied, running his hand through his soft trimmed coils of messy waves turning in every which way across the top of his forehead in an untamed sort of way. Just the faintest shadow of equally dark facial hair bordered his lips and jaws enhancing his sculpted cheekbones. His features seemed unreal, with seductive brazen eyes that delved deep, tugging at the devil in me.

"So, tell me this story of yours," Bellamy began, placing both elbows on the table. "What made you choose this school?"

A slight flush of embarrassment rippled across me, though I wasn't sure why.

"Well, I grew up in Arkansas, so this wasn't exactly where I thought I'd end up, but I wanted to get far away." I glanced down. "I'd been applying for art scholarships since junior year of high school. I didn't think I was good enough, but I guess Isabel did. Full ride."

"What kind of art is your specialty? Music?" Bellamy's eyes shimmered with interest.

I laughed at the thought. "No, never. I paint." My confidence rose greatly as I proudly spoke of my passion. "Mostly watercolors."

"That's fascinating. I hope that sometime, you can show me some of your paintings."

"I just started on one today, actually."

"Really?" Bellamy leaned forward, flashing his pristine teeth.

The server appeared in her ketchup-stained apron to take our orders, yanking us both out of the moment with her sandpaper voice. "What'll it be, folks?"

"I'll just have a burger and onion rings please," I requested.

When the waitress looked at Bellamy, he seemed almost surprised.

"I'll have the same."

"Keeping it simple. Love it." She snapped her notepad shut and sauntered off.

"So, what are your plans after graduation?" I prodded, putting my focus back on Bellamy.

"I, um..." He paused and looked down, tracing the cracks in the table with his finger. "I haven't really thought about it, to be honest. I'm just taking one day at a time. Who knows what the future holds?"

He suddenly stopped to stretch and took off the jacket, revealing a shirt with sleeves that just touched his elbows. I couldn't help but notice the inked images across his forearm, including an intricately drawn sparrow to an anatomically correct heart pierced by two arrows. "Hope you don't mind a little ink," he snickered. I continued admiring the patterns and finally my eyes began tracing the tattoo of a star on his skin.

An excited gasp escaped my lips.

"Is that the North Star?"

"Yes," he said, patting it proudly. "How did you know that?"

"Well, it's actually part of what I'm painting right now, believe it or not."

"You're kidding." He chuckled. "And what gave you that idea?"

My thoughts flashed back to Milo.

"This might sound crazy, but I was at a party a few nights ago on a boat. And we got stuck right on the shore of this little island a couple miles from the mainland. I met someone there who showed me the North Star in the sky, and I've been thinking about it ever since."

Bellamy's pleasant demeanor suddenly shifted to a look of eager curiosity.

"Island?" His question caught me off guard.

"Yeah, just off Constantine Beach. Do you know it?"

He nodded, but his face looked pinched like he was calculating some difficult math equation in his head.

"I know it." He let his words dangle in the air for a moment before continuing. "It's dangerous there. Sometimes the tides get out of control around that area. You shouldn't have been out there."

"Trust me, I found that out the hard way. But don't worry," I said, playfully putting my hands up in surrender. "I was just a passenger, but if I have my way, I don't plan on going back to that creepy island."

"That's for the best," he said solemnly.

I couldn't help but feel that he was acting a bit weird all of a sudden. There was a Tug-of-War raging in my mind on whether I should tell him about the phantom ship. Would he think I was psychotic?

"Sooo...Has anything strange ever happened there? Like a sunken ship, maybe?"

"There are rumors." I was not expecting his calm response. I anticipated he would find the question out of the ordinary, but he didn't seem at all taken aback by it. He looked away, not offering to say more, but now I wanted to press him. I still wanted answers for what I witnessed, and the way he tiptoed around my questions only made me suspect he knew something.

"Tell me," I demanded, but in a lighthearted tone. "You've made me too curious now."

Sighing, he rolled his eyes playfully "All right, fine. You win." He leaned toward me, and his gaze became more serious. I leaned forward, my ears itching.

"Some say that back in the time of pirates there was a cruel captain who captured the last mermaid in existence near the island. Supposedly a mermaid's tail could be used for magic." He almost whispered the last sentence, eyes drilling into mine like he was telling a scary campfire story. "But before his crew could kill her, she cut off her own tail and used the magic to send a storm. It was a maelstrom meant to kill the captain and his crew, but also cursed them to relive the same fate over and over forever. Legend says they're trapped with their ship at the bottom of the ocean, but they resurface with the tides from sundown to sunrise."

A morbid chill coursed through my veins as I remembered the pirate ship, and all at once, I believed in ghosts again. Once more I was certain of what I had seen. My stomach growled, but I was no longer looking forward to eating.

I realized how fervently I was staring into his eyes, and then silently told myself to ease up a bit. What he described sounded ludicrous, but there was no denying it correlated with what I had seen. I caught myself holding my breath and had to remind myself to exhale. Then, to my surprise, Bellamy began to laugh.

"That's the legend anyway. Something like that." He said, leaning back in his chair and breaking his air of seriousness.

"So.... Mermaids?" I asked.

"Mermaids. Sirens. So the legend goes."

"How do you know so much about this?"

Bellamy hesitated a moment, but just as he opened his mouth to answer, the server came by with our plates of food.

"Thank God, I'm starving," Bellamy expressed.

It felt like an awkward time to press him further, so I just picked around at my own plate of onion rings, trying to disregard my loss of appetite.

The rest of the night Bellamy asked me more about myself. I told him more about home and my dad back in Arkansas. The conversation took a much more light-hearted turn, and for a while I forgot about trying to find ways to prod him more about the ghost story.

"If you can believe it, I've never seen the ocean before this year. I can't believe I'd never gone sooner. I used to ask my mom if we could take a beach vacation, but she never liked the idea. I always thought maybe she was scared of the water or something. She was more of a cabin-in-the-woods type."

"Was?" Bellamy asked boldly.

"Well, it still feels like she's gone. She just came back after a year of doing who knows what. She's had some...issues...to work through." The conversation suddenly took a dismal turn. A second of silence hung in the air. Without thinking about it, I moved from fidgeting with my hair to subconsciously pulling up the little chain around my neck, revealing the pendant as I twisted the necklace between my fingers.

Bellamy's gaze suddenly fixated on my necklace, and he became strangely quiet. He appeared distracted, almost afraid, for a split second, and then he snapped back out of it. But I couldn't help but feel that something had shifted from that moment.

"Do you miss Europe?" I asked, hoping to break the tension.

"Well...I miss my old life, yes." He looked out across the bay. "But some things were simply not meant to last."

The way he voiced that last sentence caught my attention. Like he was alluding to something, a painful memory or sorrow that he was harboring. It had a way of bringing my own heartbreak to the surface.

"I know what you mean," I said, staring into a paint chip in the table. "It's like that with my mom. I still remember when it felt like we were a family, before she totally went off the deep end. But like you said, it didn't last."

He glanced up, looking defeated as he raised his brow. He began to speak, then stopped himself. Withdrawing his words, he seemed to search for the next thing to say.

"I feel like you're trying to tell me something," I urged him on.

"I have a lot to tell you, Katrina," his voice lowered, sounding more elegant than ever. "I'm just trying to figure out how."

"Well, to be honest, you are sort of confusing me. Just go ahead and say whatever it is."

He locked eyes with me intently from across the table. The dim light of the atmosphere framed his face with a golden glow. He was so somber. I couldn't decide whether I was uncomfortable or flattered by his deep gaze.

He put his hand in the pocket of his vest and pulled out something. He gently slid it across the table to me. There under his finger was the picture of me that McKenzie had taken with her Polaroid the night of the party, the one that had been whisked away in the wind. My heart nearly stopped.

Stalker. Serial killer. Both.

"How—how did you find this?" I asked, still shocked.

"Well let's just say it sort of found *me*," he paused "on the beach."

"Which beach?" I leaned forward.

"The island you're so curious about." His words slithered out effortlessly, startling me.

Inwardly my thoughts were spinning. I couldn't piece together how any of this was possible. Had the wind really blown the picture to him? How else would he have gotten his hands on it? Was he lying? Where was he that night? I couldn't recall seeing him on the boat at the party. I was sure he hadn't been there. The questions rolled over in my mind like tidal waves. I felt as if I was going completely insane.

"You were there on the island? How?" I asked him, leaning forward.

"Who do you think pulled you out of that rip current?" His demeanor became more serious as my breath caught in my chest at the revelation. "When I saw this picture, I realized that you might be in possession of something that is putting you in serious danger. Now I know my suspicions are true."

"What the hell are you talking about?" I stood up, ready to leave, if necessary, pushing the metal chair out from behind me. "That still doesn't explain how you got that picture."

"Katrina, I swear, the picture blew in on the sea breeze...to the island after you left. Something carried it there. I was there that night. We all were. When I saw this picture—saw what you have around your neck—I knew I had to find you before they did."

"We? They?" I said fiercely, raising my eyebrows "Who's they? And how were you on the island after we left? No one else was there except us."

"I can explain." Bellamy held up his hand and appeared concerned. "But you must calm down."

I pushed my fingers to my temples, rubbing them while closing my eyes. Convincing myself to stay to hear him out, I sat down with a grunt.

"You need to explain this all in five minutes or less because right now I feel like I'm losing my mind."

"I'll try." Bellamy nodded, then pointed at my throat. "The necklace you wear, it's something special, you're aware?"

"Well yeah, I guess so, it was a birthday gift."

"Sure, but do you know *what* it is?"

I was silent. Bellamy's voice dropped to a whisper.

"It's a scale. A mermaid scale."

"I'm sorry, what?" I had to bite back a laugh from the thought that my date might be delusional.

"I could be mistaken, but I've seen my fair share of mermaid scales, and that certainly appears to be one at the end of your chain."

"Mermaids," I repeated for confirmation. "You're serious? Geez, this city just keeps getting weirder." Of course, I didn't think mermaids were real, but a hint of curiosity still welled up within me, tugging at my doubts. Just a few days back, I didn't believe in ghosts either, but then I saw the phantom ship. I was no longer certain what was real.

"I half expected you to say that." Bellamy stood to his feet and held out his hand. "But can I show you something that might help you understand?" Reluctantly, I stood to join Bellamy and reached out with uncertainty to take his hand.

8

UNDEAD MEN TELL NO TALES

H e gently pulled me forward as he walked away from the table and took me with him. His grip was tight, but not forceful.

"We can't just leave without paying," I reminded him.

I caught a glimmer of mischief in his eye as he looked back at me over his shoulder. "Right. Wait here a moment." His sultry accent was reassurance enough. I watched him spin around and quickly leave what I presumed was the payment on the table.

He led me a little way down a section of the big stone wall that separated the sidewalks and streets from the waters of Matanzas Bay.

"Hmmm, no, not here. This won't work." He looked around, as if he had lost something. "We need to go to the ocean."

"Why?"

"You want to believe in mermaids, don't you?"

"No, I think *you* want me to believe in mermaids."

"I just want you to see things for what they really are." A lock of his midnight hair caught in the wind and ruffled. "Are you up for a walk?"

I hooked my thumbs in my pockets and tilted my chin.

"Only if it's supposed to somehow make all this make sense." Was I crazy for being curious enough to agree to it?

"It will," he uttered.

Together we began our mile-long trek across the bridge to the beach entrances on the other side, with Bellamy leading the way with sure steps. The words exchanged between us were few and far between. I supposed because Bellamy sensed that anything else he said was only going to confuse me further, and quite frankly I was too afraid to ask any more questions. I couldn't help but wish I had suggested that we drive there, to shorten what felt like the longest suspense of my life.

As we approached the beach ramp and trudged past the dunes, the shore appeared empty, as I expected this time of year on a Tuesday night.

"Just checking. You're not gonna kill me, right?" I asked, only half-joking.

"Such little faith in me. I'm more of a gentleman than you think." He smirked.

Within minutes, we stood along the coastline, the waves crashing feet from us, creeping up the sandbanks. A weak orange glow of city lights created an aura far in the distance. Miles of sand stretched ahead, following the edge of an ocean of trees inland. It was the border of Constantine against the edge of St. Augustine's forested state park, giving way to the sandy coast. Moonlight danced on the black mirror surface of the sea's horizon.

"If you didn't think I was crazy, and I wasn't trying to prove you wrong, this might almost feel romantic," Bellamy uttered, staring ahead as we walked. I rolled my eyes with a scoff. I waited for his next move, intrigued as ever, but also afraid of not knowing what to expect.

"Here." He took my hand in his and stopped abruptly. He pulled me toward him facing the ocean, in a mere gesture of repositioning, nothing more. Letting go, he stepped back towards the water behind him. With another step back, dark water enveloped the sole of his boot, then vanished as the tide sucked it back. I leaned forward, keeping my gaze on his footsteps. I was half expecting to see a mystical whirlpool appear for all I knew.

Then, his boot began to fade with a white illumination that rapidly worked its way up his leg. His edges became like mist. He reached out to touch my face, and I was too baffled to resist it. When his fingers touched my cheek, it sent a winter blizzard swirling in my veins. The rest of him glowed translucent white. As he faded inches from my face, I could suddenly see right through him. The color in him drained until he was nothing but a white shadow with a wispy outline of Bellamy's features.

In a twisting mix of terror and fascination, I reached up to touch the hand cradling my face. I realized I couldn't touch it, and my hand went right through his. Questions and chaos came rushing into my mind like a flash flood. Forcing myself to snap out of my stupor, I stumbled backward to pull away from his ghostly touch.

"What—what just happened?" I asked, my jittery voice trembling with urgency. "What is happening to you?" I corrected myself, swallowing the dry lump in my throat, my voice now a weak whisper.

Bellamy didn't respond. Instead, a low rumble of laughter came from him, which raised goosebumps along my arms. He stepped forward, out of the water, and like the first brushstroke of watercolor on paper, the hues of flesh rushed back into his pale being. His skin reabsorbed his natural color of slightly pale skin, as if kissed by moonlight. Here, even in the darkness, his topaz eyes glittered like the Caribbean Sea.

"Katrina, there's far more in this world than you realize. And not everything is as it seems." He was grinning audaciously, as if he found my confusion funny. "Still not certain about the mermaids?" I didn't respond partially because I was riled by his inappropriate laughter, but more because I was still replaying what had happened over in my head.

"Forgive me for laughing. I forget how terrifying that must be. But seeing you come to the realization that I'm telling the truth was very entertaining."

"Okay, but what does any of this have to do with mermaids? You just turned into a ghost. How is that possible?" The hysteric sound of my own voice was alarming. Sucking in my breath, I tried to settle myself.

He looked up at me, his brow lifted, and he placed his hands in the pockets of his jacket.

"Remember the mermaid story? And the curse?" He paused and took a step toward me. He leaned in, his lips mere centimeters from my ear. He tickled my earlobes with his whispers. "What if I told you, it was all true? What if I told you that I'm one of those cursed to die at sea every day for eternity?"

He pulled away. As if to drive his point home, he held up his hand in front of his face, and without even blinking, as if on command, his forearm became entirely transparent.

"So, you—" I took a step back from him, my every muscle tensing.

"I've been dead for 300 years, Katrina."

We stared at each other, as if there was an invisible taut string between us, neither of us willing to be the first to snap it by pulling away.

After a moment, his arm returned to its normal appearance.

"In all seriousness," he started, "when I saw the picture of you, I knew I had to be the one to find you." He took a step forward in my direction. I flinched.

Another step to me, and he was right in front of me again. He lifted my hand, coiling his fingers around mine softly.

I looked up at him, lifting my chin to meet his gaze towering over me. My mind seemed to have lost communication with my body, so I just stayed there, fixated on his starkly handsome face. His gaze slowly left mine and I felt his eyes snaking down my neck. He suddenly let go of my hand and then took a lock of my hair between his fingers gently. A shiver tickled the base of my neck.

"Don't fear me, Katrina." I felt him staring just above my chest, or perhaps a bit lower. Heat pooled in my body as he released my hair and traced my jaw, his touch gentle, but firm. A flight instinct rose within me, but some other part of me wanted to give into him. His fingers brushed my ear and then trailed down to my necklace, dancing across my collarbone. I started to pull away, breaking the trance he held over me.

"Don't," he muttered softly, using his other hand to take mine again. As he traced my fingers, I felt another rush of heat accompanied by panic. My breathing became deeper as his grip on me tightened. His scent of earthy spices, woodsmoke, and a hint of rum filled my nostrils. I didn't like that some part of me found it intoxicating. "But now that you know, I need to ask something of you." He reached up and took the pendant between his fingers. "I need you…" he breathed, "…to give this to me."

I felt a gentle tug that grew stronger, and I thought he was going to rip it from my neck. I reached up to stop him. But I didn't have to, because something else stopped him instead.

A strong, yet youthful voice shouted from behind Bellamy.

"No!" A shadowy figure wrenched Bellamy from our strange embrace. The impact of the tackle left me falling to the ground. I felt the thin chain snap against the back of my neck as Bellamy clutched it, taking it with him.

"You've been following me!" He seethed as he shoved the attacker's arms away from him. They both towered over me, just a few feet away, the ocean at my back. I glimpsed my necklace in the sand at Bellamy's feet. He must have dropped it.

"I'm no fool. Unlike Valdez, I'm not going to trust *you* to actually bring the scale back." The opponent growled in a voice that called to some hidden memory of mine.

"You have no right!" Bellamy flared up like an uncontrolled blaze. I witnessed desperation in him I couldn't have otherwise imagined.

Startled, I lurched forward and snatched up the necklace, ready to make my escape. When I tried to stand, a blunt pain in my foot hit me like a sledgehammer. I had come down on my ankle, twisting it in the sand when I fell. Forcing myself through the pain, I clumsily clambered up. I thought I could slip past the two by dodging to the left, where there was an opening between them and the sea, but I was wrong. Bellamy reached out to grab me as I ran past, stopping me with his arm and wrapping the other around my back in a bear hug.

"Let go!" I shrieked, holding onto the necklace with all my strength.

The attacker overpowered Bellamy, pulling him off me.

"Where is it?" The other voice demanded, ringing with an even stronger hint of familiarity. Bellamy swung into him, but the man grappled him and hurled him to the side, knocking him off balance. As Bellamy staggered, the man threw a punch that made contact with Bellamy's jaw. Bellamy was still recovering from the hit while his attacker changed course and rushed forward to me. Grabbing my upper arms, he pulled me to him. I looked into his face fearfully, with only the light of the full moon to illuminate his features. To my disbelief, I recognized him.

"Milo?" I gasped, terrified.

He peered at me with hazel eyes through a shaggy curtain of hair. The gentle nature he showed on the island was gone, replaced by a fierce, uncaged intensity. He looked just as surprised to see me as I did him.

"You?" He appeared conflicted, softening his expression, and blinking in confusion. "I...I won't hurt you," he uttered under his breath and nodded at the necklace in my tightly closed fist. "But you *can't* let that fall into Bellamy's hands. Run. Now."

"No, Katrina, don't listen to him!" Bellamy shouted desperately, back on his feet. Milo gave me a gentle nudge backward, my feet swallowed by the rising tide washing ashore. He used his arm as a guard to push me back as he stepped toward Bellamy.

"So, we just suffer for eternity, then?" Milo growled at Bellamy, a tinge of pain in his voice. "This may be the only chance. The crew shouldn't have to pay for Valdez's sins. All for *your* selfishness."

As Milo walked threateningly towards Bellamy, he drew out two swords from his sides and tossed one of them at Bellamy's feet. The blade was white and ghostly, as if from another realm. As he raised the other sword in his hand, it caught the moonlight, revealing the curved shape of a cutlass.

"Pick it up and let's settle this now."

Now both armed, they charged at each other with fury. Bellamy swung first, only for Milo to deflect it with a flick of his blade. Their swords sparked in the darkness, sending embers and shards of metal flying like fireworks. Trembling with fear, my mind racing, I ran toward the forest tree line behind the shore. My flip-flops had become separated from me long ago. I tripped as my bare feet stumbled over the uneven ground and sand went flying. I toppled down clumsily, wincing at my injured ankle. As I peeked over the edge of the dune, I strained to see in the shadows.

Wielding their cutlass blades, they ducked and dodged one another's blows, but Milo proved unrelenting. He was just a bit shorter than Bellamy but seemed faster. His weapon swung like lightning across the black horizon. He parried every blow with ease.

Bellamy fought well. At times, I thought he would best Milo, particularly when he swung towards Milo's neck, but he was always blocked at the last second. Metal clanged in the night as Milo whipped his sword across the air, towards Bellamy's shoulder, but Bellamy also deflected it with ease.

A strange sight it was, these two men dueling in the night along the coast, echoing a vision of fearsome buccaneers long past. Suddenly Bellamy's unique style made sense to me. The excessive layers, the boots. All pirate–but with a modern twist. And now here they were, wielding swords along the shore like it was still the 18th century. There was something strangely beautiful about the way they handled their blades, dancing along the sand in a very dangerous game of tag. I was mesmerized.

Mesmerized and confused. I still didn't understand what they wanted from me, nor could I choose who to believe. Bellamy was a ghost. Milo was a pirate. My necklace was a mermaid scale, supposedly. It was too much. I managed to convince myself that maybe it was just another, different bad dream. As I watched them with these thoughts bombarding me, Bellamy attempted one more swift swing, aiming for a head blow, but Milo ducked with unbelievable speed, managing to plunge his sword directly through Bellamy's abdomen.

A chilling wail escaped my lips when I saw Bellamy reach down and rip the sword out of himself, unwavering. Blood rushed to stain his shirt, but he barely grimaced from the pain. He tossed the sword down to the ground, uttered something I couldn't make out to Milo, then took his form of a white ghostly wisp while pressing his hand across his wound. He stepped back into the water, holding his free hand out at his side in a mocking gesture of surrender. I could suddenly feel his eyes on me.

"Whatever he tells you, Katrina, don't listen." He called out. Then, he vanished in a swirling mist under the water, like the smoke that shrouds a freshly put-out candle.

Milo then turned to look in my direction. He began walking towards me, and my heart, already racing, began to pound so hard I thought it would explode. I wanted to run, but I knew I couldn't escape quickly enough. I hurriedly opened my hand, glancing down at the coiled-up necklace buried in my sweaty palm. In a last-ditch effort to keep it safe, I quickly tucked it away in my bralette just before he reached me.

"Are you alright?" His voice was smooth and lacked an edge that had been present in Bellamy's voice. It was softer, a bit deeper, and made me feel sudden warmth. But I couldn't forget what I'd just seen.

"You—you just stabbed him!" I managed to exclaim shakily between my panicked breathing, very near tears.

I looked up, sand falling from my tangled hair and my face smudged with dirt. He glanced down at me, clad in his dark jeans tucked into black boots, and a long loose-fitting brown shirt, unbuttoned all the way to reveal a white undershirt. His sword hung from a brown leather sling across his torso. He ran his hand through his dark golden hair, brushing it over his head out of his face. I could see the moonlight reflected in the small sweat beads across his forehead. He was still breathing hard, his full, pink lips parted just enough to reveal a row of gleaming teeth. His angular features were softened by his thick tousled hair just reaching mid-neck. A light scruff of the same golden-brown hair lined his jawline and cheeks.

He didn't respond, only turned to look back at the spot in the waves where he had ended the duel with Bellamy. Then, back down at me.

My head was spinning, and I thought I was going to faint. Milo reached down and began to gently lift me from the sandy dunes and brush. I felt my consciousness slipping.

This has to be a bad dream.

9

CALM BEFORE THE STORM

The darkness that had overtaken me slowly released its grip. My eyes fluttered open to the night sky. For a moment, I saw only the stars, clustered overhead in a cloudless backdrop. I turned my head weakly to see Milo.

All at once, the memory of the previous events came flooding back. I remembered the fight between Bellamy and Milo ashore before Bellamy vanished into the ocean. Right after Milo stabbed him.

I instantly shot up and scrambled to my feet, ready to make my escape from this psychopath.

"Wait," he said.

I offered him no response as I found my balance and turned away. He slowly stood up.

"Are you sure you're alright?" he called.

"No, of course I'm not alright." My face felt hot and every muscle in me tensed like a tightwire. "This week I've seen a pirate ship rise up out of the ocean, I went on a date with a guy who turned out to be dead, and to top it all off, I just watched you try to kill him." My words streamed out all in one breath.

I yanked my phone from my jean pocket, grateful it had managed to stay put in all the chaos. I was going to call someone to come and get me, maybe McKenzie or the police—I honestly hadn't thought that far ahead yet—but it was no use either way, as I quickly realized I had no service.

"Well, if you don't give up the scale, that won't be the last of it. They—we—won't stop coming for it."

I stopped. I didn't know what to say. The words on the note from the necklace box flashed in my mind's eye.

Always keep it with you.

Had Dad known it was allegedly a mermaid scale? I couldn't bring myself to believe that my corny, overly logical dad could have any part of something this fantastical. But why did whoever wrote the note tell me to keep it safe?

And the nightmares. What if this freaky necklace was my only hope for stopping them? It could help with those, the note said. Maybe it could help Mom, too...

Rhythmic footsteps padded in the sand from behind, pulling my attention away from my thoughts. It was Milo catching up to me.

"I didn't kill Bellamy." he panted.

"Obviously. But you tried," I muttered as I tucked the phone away. My ankle throbbed with each step. I must have twisted it further when I stumbled over the sand dunes. But I kept pressing forward back towards the shore.

"I *can't* kill him. He can't —*we* can't die because we're sort of already dead." He spoke in a strangely casual, calm way, as if it was a perfectly normal thing to say.

My steps slowed, and my eyes narrowed at him. "So then what happened to him?"

"He returned to the ocean. He'll probably go back to the ship. He'll deal with his injury for tonight, and he'll be good as new with the next tide. We die every night. He's used to it."

"So...are you a ghost, too?"

Milo pretended to study his knuckles, smiling a sultry crooked smile that made me want to look at him longer. "I've never thought of us as ghosts. To be honest I don't really know what we are. Somewhere between living and dead. Our souls belong to the sea. But perhaps ghost is a good word for it."

"And what does all this mean for me? Why do you both want my necklace?" I shifted to my other leg to take the weight off my injured ankle.

"Katrina, I can't explain it all right now. But you're in danger as long as you have it." He started redirecting our steps back towards the dark forest behind the shore. "It's not safe to be out on the shoreline right now. Bellamy may come back, or worse. We'll use the forest for cover and make our way back."

I stopped.

"I just don't understand. Bellamy told me not to trust you. And the problem is I don't think I can trust either of you." My throat was scratchy from thirst, irritated further by the salty night air.

"Well, you never really can trust a pirate. But right now, you have no choice. I understand why this is confusing for you," he said hurriedly. "But we don't have a lot of time. I'll make sure you're safe. I'll take you home. But I can't protect you fully without the necklace. Bellamy was only using you to get it. I can't say what he might have done to you if you didn't give it to him. But I won't hurt you. Please believe me." His voice sounded desperate, but I wasn't ready to trust him that easily.

I'll make sure you're safe.

His words rolled around in my head. No one had ever told me that before. Though I wanted to deny it, it felt nice.

I caught him glancing down at my chest and neck. He must have been looking for the prized piece of jewelry.

"Wh—where is the necklace, Katrina?"

"I must have dropped it. I don't know." I lied, refusing to look at him.

"You're lying. You still have it."

I was getting flustered with his persistence.

"How do I know you're not using me for the same thing?" I demanded firmly.

"Katrina, please listen to me, I beg of you." He reached out to take my arm to stop me from walking. I braced against his grip.

I had had enough of these men putting their hands on me. His princely voice did nothing to charm me in my anger. Without fully thinking, I whirled around to face him and whipped my hand across his cheek with an unforgiving slap.

He stood, a shocked expression on his face.

"Are you always so difficult?" He asked, rubbing his jaw.

"I'm difficult?" I huffed. "You're the one who grabbed me."

"You're right." He spoke after a long pause. "I'm sorry. I suppose I deserved that."

"Yes. You did." I was surprised by my own confidence, but even more surprised by his apology. But it wasn't enough.

I continued without waiting for him, stepping over mossy roots as I slipped between the dense combination of towering Floridian oak and palm trees. I secretly cringed with each step. The forest floor wasn't very forgiving against my bare feet.

"You don't even know where you're going!" Milo called out behind me.

I stopped dead in my tracks. He was right about that. I wasn't sure which direction was home, and for all I knew the park was miles wide and closed at sundown. No one would be out there to find me as I wandered in the dark.

"Look," I bit my lip and let out a heavy sigh of aggravation as I slowly turned around. "You explain to me exactly what is going on, and then maybe, *maybe*, we'll talk about the necklace. Tell me who you are. The truth. What do you and Bellamy want with this necklace?"

"I suppose I have no other choice then. We'll follow the coast, but we need to use the trees for cover." He led the way, despite the impenetrable darkness before us. With the towering oaks surrounding us, cascades of greenery draping down from their gnarled branches, we pressed on. "There are many who are looking for you right now, Katrina."

"Why is anyone looking for me? I'm tired of this guessing game. Tell me."

"In time, I promise. Just a little further." His steps began to slow. He looked around him, surveying the tree trunks encircling us. "This way." He moved into a thick patch of branches, pushing away their leafy frills aside with his forearm. As I tried to follow him, my ankle began to pulse more painfully as the grainy terrain became more uneven and harder to trek. I grimaced quietly, but Milo noticed.

"You're hurt."

"A little, but it's fine. Let's keep going."

"No, you should rest it for a bit. Just for a moment."

I didn't argue with him as I eyed a spot underneath a tree that looked somewhat promising. I hobbled over to it, just a few steps away, and wearily let myself slide down the trunk. I was so exhausted. Taking the weight off my ankle provided instant relief. Milo sat down beside me, to my left, adjusting the sword at his back to make it easier for him to lean back against the tree. It was a wide oak, with plenty of room for the both of us to rest against.

I let out a forced laugh. I couldn't deny that no matter how impossible all of this seemed, it was real.

"What?" Milo glanced over at me, sounding a bit irritated.

"I don't know." I leaned my head back. "I'm just sitting here in the woods with a ghost pirate. Why don't you look like you did on the island? You had pirate clothes. You might as well have been Jack Sparrow there."

"I don't know who Jack Sparrow is, but that *was* what I happened to be wearing 300 years ago when the ship went down. Unfortunately, eternal damnation didn't come with a wardrobe selection." There was a touch of humor in his regal voice. I remembered how he had made me feel back on the island, and that same sense of warm security seemed to be returning here and now.

"Well, I see you've kept up with the times—sort of." I gestured, referring to his more modern, but clearly seafaring inspired look. The draping clothes and earthy colors certainly embodied his nautical past, but it could just as easily pass for an edgy fashion statement.

"We have to blend in somehow. After a while, we figured out that if we come onto the mainland, we must at least somewhat look the part. We've learned to make it work."

"Well, just keep your sword on that side," I joked in return.

"You'll be grateful for this sword if they find us." The way he spoke in that silvery accent mixed with the slight smirk forming dimples at the corners of his mouth made my heart flutter. For a moment I felt embarrassed about it. Thankfully, he didn't seem to take notice. If he did, he didn't let on.

"Okay, time to talk. Who are 'they'?"

Milo looked down, a small breeze lightly rustling his free-flowing hair across his forehead.

"The crew. The pirates," he said solemnly. "On the island. There was a picture you left behind."

"I know. I didn't leave it there on purpose." I could picture Bellamy holding my photo between his fingers back by the bay.

"Well on purpose or not, Bellamy's not the only one who saw it. With one look, the captain recognized the scale around your neck. He knows what it is. And he wants it. Bellamy volunteered to find you and bring it to him, but I think he has his own intentions with the scale."

"So, what?" I looked at him closely, urging him to continue. "You're going to take it from me instead?"

"Well, not exactly. I mean, not like Bellamy would, at least. I'm a little more patient."

"So, what does your captain want with it?"

"To break our curse. Bellamy told you about that, I'm assuming?"

"I think so. The mermaid's curse?"

"Aye." He stared straight ahead, unblinking. "Before she dragged herself back to the water, she said something about chaining our souls to the sea. *'Lest to the depths is returned the last of her.'* The captain's been trying to understand what she meant for ages. Most of us gave up long ago, but he won't stop looking for the answer. Personally, I believe it was just her way of mocking us, cursing us with an impossible condition we cannot meet because she was the last of her kind—and she made certain we would never find her again."

He breathed a weary sigh, then rested his head against the tree, looking at me out of the corner of his eye. "But if that really is a piece of the mermaid's magic left behind on the chain around your neck...Valdez thinks it could be the answer we've been looking for." There was silence between us for a minute as I digested his words. Then he spoke again. "I'd normally hate to agree with Valdez, but this time, I think he may be on to something. Maybe the scale could be enough to break the curse. Who knows? At this point, I'll try anything to end this hell."

"What exactly is this hell?" My eyes drilled into him with a desire to understand.

"Being frozen in time. Never aging, never dying, never feeling the simple pleasures of life though they are right before us each night. Reliving the same end over and over. Begging for death from these tormented tides until the night takes pity on us."

"Okay so let me get this straight." I put my fingers to my forehead, trying to decipher the rules of being a pirate ghost. "You and your ship come up at night?"

"Yes, with the evening tide." He used his hands to make rising and falling motions as he talked. "When the moon rises and calls up the tide, we rise with it. And then when morning comes, we return to our fate, like the first time it took us down in the storm she sent. Our ship, our bodies, our souls. It's a never-ending cycle."

"How is all this even possible?" I blinked, still making sense of it all in my head. "What's it like?"

"Imagine, if you can, your lungs burning as you drown without dying, as the water whips over you so quickly in different directions it feels as if it's pulling you apart. And there's no end to the torment. The sea seeks its revenge on our souls, because our flesh and bone can't survive it. That's why you saw Bellamy as a ghost when he stepped into the water. You saw his soul."

I pushed a stray lock of hair out of my eyes. "So, at night you get to be...normal?"

"Well, sort of. We were quite thrilled the first time we realized we could still set foot on land and walk among the living. But then we tried eating and drinking, and touching, and realized the sensation of it all eludes us.... well, except pain. That sensation stayed," he chuckled with a broken smile, as if he was wishing it was all just a sad joke. "Every day for 291 years we wait for the tide to pull us from that purgatory. But it's only a temporary, cruel tease."

What he was saying was too much to take in. If I hadn't seen the ghost ship with my own eyes, I would have refused to believe it. But I couldn't deny what I had seen. I looked at him, hungry to know more.

"So..." I swallowed, trying to wet my parched mouth as my words came out dry. "If the scale goes back into the ocean, it'll break the curse?"

Milo shrugged. His sage eyes drifted to me.

"I don't really know for sure. Every morning when the depths claim us again, the whirlpool returns to take the ship under, the same as the first one sent by Cordelia, the siren—or mermaid, as you call it. Valdez thinks we have to give up the scale to it. To return it to the depths, as she said."

"What if we try just putting it into the water? What if it just means it has to go back into the sea?" I stood up, ignoring the pain in my ankle, and began to head back to the shore.

"I suppose it's worth a try," Milo said, but he sounded unsure.

"Look, if it's this easy to end the curse, I'm happy to help. No one should have to go through what you do." I turned around, my mood lifting. This task, as strange as it may sound, was simple enough. I didn't want to let Milo or Bellamy suffer for eternity if I could stop it so easily.

"If this works," he said, following after me. "I'll die."

"I thought you said you're already dead."

"Yes, but I—" He couldn't seem to finish the sentence. "I supposed I'll just be gone for good."

"Do *you* want the curse broken?" I asked.

"Of course." He didn't hesitate. "I just hope there's some hope for me on the other side. I don't know how much mercy there is for a pirate."

"Well, I'll pray for you," I joked. I felt uncharacteristically bold with him, and I couldn't understand why. But I didn't mind it.

I knelt down when I reached the edge of the waves. Glancing over my shoulder to see if Milo was watching, I pulled the necklace from its hiding spot, careful not to let him see where I was keeping it. Here in the moonlight, the "scale" on the necklace shimmered with a pearly iridescence. Even if it wasn't magical, it certainly looked the part.

"Are you ready?" I asked.

Milo nodded.

I lowered the pendant down into the water, careful to keep my grip on it. I looked back at Milo, who was standing there with his eyes clenched shut, looking almost fearful of the uncertainty of what was about to happen to him. I braced myself in case something incredible happened. After all, I had never broken a curse before.

10

BATTEN DOWN THE HATCHES

I held the scale under the water for at least a minute or two, but nothing magical transpired. The lapping waves didn't even change their rhythm. Simply nothing.

"I didn't think it would work, but I was hopeful." He walked over to me and knelt beside me. I quickly yanked the necklace up out of the water and gripped it tightly. I felt a bit like Gollum from Lord of the Rings, from my peculiar need to be so protective of it.

"Easy there." Milo's low tone was gentle, but playful. "I told you I won't hurt you."

"I want to help you," I uttered, "I do. But I can't give up this necklace. Not yet anyway. I think I need it for something. For...for breaking a curse of my own, I guess you could say."

I shifted from my kneeling position to sitting crisscross in the sand, just out of reach of the rolling water. Milo joined me, facing me directly across.

"A curse of your own?"

"Let's just say, I think I'm supposed to keep it safe. Otherwise, I don't know what will happen. My mom, she's...she's not exactly well. And I think there may be something about this necklace that can help her."

And me. If these nightmares keep coming back.

"Hmm." he braced his chin on his closed hand, his eyes narrowing. "I see."

"So why don't you just kill me or something and take the scale? No offense, but aren't pirates like ruthless killers?" I couldn't resist asking.

"I'm *not* a killer," Milo's shoulders tightened, and he sat up rigidly, as if ready to defend himself from an attack.

"But if the mermaid cursed your crew for capturing her, that means you helped do it." My words came out with suspicion as I thought more about the story.

Milo became even more defensive. "I never wanted any part of it. I swear it. I'll admit I've done some regrettable things for Valdez. I wished I could have stopped him. But it was impossible to defy a captain like him."

"Sounds like maybe you were scared."

"You know nothing about me, Katrina." Suddenly, his words sounded like ice, much in contrast to the gentleness I was so used to hearing from him. "We all have regrets. Don't pretend you don't."

What he said pricked me as I thought of my own regrets. He wasn't wrong. How could I imply that he had been weak when I, too, had so often been driven by fear? The fear of feeling out of place had led me to do things I wouldn't normally do. The fear of being hurt again kept me cold towards my mom. And the fear of becoming just like her sometimes paralyzed me.

"Anyway, Valdez is a cruel man, and he won't care what happens to you if he finds you himself."

His words once again danced like poetry around my ears. Only a voice like his could make such threatening words sound like a lullaby.

"I think I saw Valdez." I remembered the wild-eyed man with the captain's hat from the ship that Halloween night. "He looked terrifying."

"He is." Milo cocked his head. "And he will get the necklace, no matter the cost."

"And what does Bellamy want with it?"

"I don't know for certain, but I don't think he plans to give it to Valdez."

"But you do?" I blinked. "To escape the ocean hell?"

"Ocean hell," Milo repeated under his breath. "Well...you're not wrong, but I've yet to hear it called that till now." A small laugh escaped his lips. "But yes, I plan to take it to him. I've hoped for an end to this pain for nearly half a millennium. I hate doing Valdez's bidding more than anyone, but if it means our souls can finally be at rest..." His voice trailed off without finishing the thought.

It all felt so absurd, so surreal. Here I was with a cursed immortal man who just told me he goes to hell each morning and my necklace could save him from it all. There was certainly guilt. But I didn't fully trust him or his story. Bellamy could have been telling the truth for all I knew. If the necklace was magic like he said, maybe it really could stop the nightmares. If I could figure that out first, I could help my mom. Maybe it could change her, save her. And then I could let the pirates have it if I must. But it would undoubtedly be a race against time.

"How is your ankle?" Milo's sudden change of subject jostled me.

"It feels a bit better," I said. "I'm sure I can go on."

"May I take a look?"

"It's not bleeding or anything," I mumbled.

He sat up and leaned over towards my left leg. As if he was about to pet a wild animal, he cautiously placed his hand over my ankle.

"It's okay. I won't bite," I said, noticing his wariness.

He shook his head, as if trying to snap himself out of his own thoughts.

"I'm sorry," he said, almost mesmerized, "it's just that I realized..." He swallowed as if choking down emotion. "...this is the first time in 291 years that I've touched someone like this. But I can't feel you." He kept his hand on my ankle, pressing against my skin gently.

"You're warm," I noted out loud.

"Were you expecting otherwise?"

"Well, you are dead, or whatever."

"Or whatever," he repeated. "Maybe I *will* take you to Valdez, on second thought."

I pursed my lips at him and rolled my eyes.

"Don't worry. I'm only joking." He looked back down at my ankle, still holding onto the base of my lower leg. The hand that had cradled my heel had crept up to the bottom of my calf. "Sort of," he added quietly with a smirk.

A tender spark rushed through me as his fingertips slid along my skin. He might not have been able to feel me, but I could feel him well enough. His touch made me feel at ease, and a part of me longed to reach forward and touch him back. I wanted to trust him, despite what Bellamy had said. However, I didn't want to be too quick to let him know that.

"It's definitely not broken, just a little swollen." He slid his hands off my leg and stood to his feet. "Can you continue?"

"I'll be fine, yes." I took his outstretched hand.

We continued back through the forest path along the shore, pushing palm leaves aside as we traversed off the main trail.

"If you don't even know where I live, where are you taking me?"

"I just want to get you back around to the other side, away from the shore. You can go from there once we get out of here. Believe me, I know where I'm going."

I responded only with an eye roll. But we continued on.

I lost track of time, so I couldn't tell if it had been 5 or 30 minutes. I used the flashlight on my phone to give us a bit of light, as the heavy oak canopies above us blotted out any remnants of moonlight. Milo was fascinated by all the things my phone could do, as he had never seen one this close before. I thought it was comical, the way he seemed to shy away from interacting with the modern world, but I also didn't understand how he and Bellamy could both be from the same crew and yet be so different. So I asked him.

"Okay, again, no offense, but how come you're so medieval, but Bellamy seems so—" I searched for the right word, "—adapted?" I thought back to how casually and confidently Bellamy spoke to me in the library. He certainly had me fooled that he was another student from ISA.

"Bellamy spends a lot of time on the mainland. Always looking for chaos or creating it. He's cunning, he studies. He'll be who he needs to be to get what he wants."

His disdain for Bellamy was clear, and I couldn't help but wonder how long their rivalry had been present. I didn't ask any more questions. However, the memory of Bellamy's warning came flooding back, accompanied by feelings of uncertainty about Milo.

Before long, we broke through to a clearing, stepping out from the brush into the edge of the park. The landscape was flatter, and I could see a familiar square of gravel dimly lit by the orange glow of a streetlamp in the distance. I recognized the parking lot as one near the entrance to Constantine Beach. There was not a soul around. Only a single truck parked, probably a late-night fisherman's, and a deserted motorcycle parked in the shadows off to the side. Now that we had escaped the dense canopy of trees, I could once again feel the breath of fresh ocean wind rush against my cheeks.

"You can get back from here?" He turned to me.

"I think so. But it's a long walk. I'll have to get across the bay."

"That's too far." He retorted.

"Well, what choice do I have? I could call an Uber." I suggested, walking on ahead of him through the parking lot.

"I don't know what that is," Milo said, "but I've got a better idea."

The sound of a rumbling engine firing up startled me. I whipped around to see Milo swinging a leg over the motorcycle in the lot, particularly a vintage Triumph Cafe racer.

"You can't just steal a motorcycle!" I shouted over the engine's roar as he drove closer.

"Who said I was stealing?" He chuckled. "When you've been around for as long as I have, you find ways to keep things interesting."

"So, it's—it's yours?"

"Well, yes. I found it a few years ago. I was fascinated. It didn't work at first, but I've had plenty of time to learn how to fix it."

"Great. So you're a motorcycle riding ghost pirate." I laughed, shaking my head in disbelief.

"See, I'm not so medieval after all," he chuckled, revving the engine.

"Of all the weird crap that's happened to me lately, this is probably the weirdest."

He rolled his eyes at me, playfully.

"Get on." He nodded towards the backseat, a few tresses of hair flicking across his eyebrows.

Still in disbelief, I stepped up to the bike. I had been on a motorcycle or two in my lifetime. On the rare occasion, when my dad would get one in to work on, he would sometimes let me accompany him on a short test ride when I was younger. But this was quite different. A little unsure, I stepped onto the footrest, placed my hands on Milo's shoulders to help steady myself, and swung a leg over. It was then that I didn't know what to do with my hands. I hesitated to wrap my arms around his waist, and I didn't anticipate how warm and secure holding onto him would make me feel. He didn't say anything and didn't wait for me to settle. With a flick of his wrist on the throttle, he urged the motorcycle onwards, and off we went.

The lights of the city blurred by, and the sea breeze combined with the wind from our speed sent my hair whipping wildly. I buried my face lower, closer to his back as the night air chilled me. It was only about halfway through the ride that I realized how tightly I was holding onto him. I found myself glad for the excuse to push my body so close to his.

I looked up just long enough to notice the moon, almost full, a larger than usual white glowing orb above us as we zoomed over the bridge. The roads were devoid of their usual traffic and everything but us seemed still. I still didn't even know what time it was.

Slowing the bike, he pulled it to a stop in front of the campus. I hopped off as he leaned the bike over on the kickstand. He stayed seated on the brown leather seat of the motorcycle and looked up at me. I couldn't manage to suppress the thought in my mind of how attractive he looked here under the moonlight astride the maroon Triumph with his wind-tousled hair. The urge to tangle my fingers in it was difficult to ignore, but I managed.

"Alright, you agreed that if I told you everything, you would give me the necklace." He held out his open palm.

Nearly stuttering, I pushed back. "Well—that's not exactly what I said. I said we would *talk* about the necklace."

"Ah, right, of course you did," he said sarcastically.

"That was the deal." I made my voice as firm as possible, tensing my brows together to shoot Milo a deathly stare.

"Fair enough. But you should know you're putting yourself in danger. If neither Bellamy nor I return with the scale, Valdez may very well come looking for it himself. You *cannot* be near the water at night. He can't know where to find you. Bellamy won't let on that he knows. He's got Valdez thinking he's on his side, but I don't know how long that will last."

"Sounds easy enough," I agreed.

"For you," he uttered. "I, on the other hand, will probably face a nice flogging waiting for me if they find out I helped you."

My face burned, feeling the impact of his indirect guilt trip.

"I want to help you, Milo." My words came out in nearly a whisper. I pulled the necklace out from its hiding place behind the top of my shirt, anxious to see what he would do once it was in sight. "And I will. But I have to try to save my mom, and until I've tried, I can't just let it go." I closed my palm around it. He hadn't even so much as flinched to try to take it. "I've got a lot of questions and too few answers. It's the only clue I have."

He reached up and rubbed the back of his neck with his hand, moving his dark honey locks aside, his jaw clenched with a slight sign of stress. He seemed to think before he spoke again.

"I half-expected it. And I understand. If it's real, it may just have whatever power you need. And maybe there's some kind of redemption waiting for me in the next life if I can end this curse with some honor. I will not take it from you by force." His eyes were fixated on mine now, and his words hit me like an ocean wave, settling into my core. He made it so easy to trust him, even with Bellamy's word of caution ringing in the back of my mind. We stared at each other for a moment, and I struggled to decipher the wave of emotions rushing over me.

Why was I so drawn to him? I wanted to be near him, to touch him. But I had to remind myself of one thing that could pose a problem.

He's a freaking ghost, Katrina.

"You're welcome." He broke the tension with his sudden sarcasm, lifting his tone.

"You are one strange pirate," I uttered, still looking at him.

"Well, maybe you should be glad of that." He grinned. "But my tendency to prefer *not* killing and marauding doesn't exactly make me very popular with the rest of the crew."

"I'm sorry." I became serious. "Will it really be so bad when you go back?"

"Maybe. They don't have to know I found you, though." He squinted one eye and bit his lip. "And it's nothing I haven't been through before. I always think of something to cover my arse." There was a pause. My expression gave away my concern. He brushed his shoulder, almost nervously. "Don't worry. They can't exactly kill me."

"Okay, look." A tired sigh escaped my lungs. I had resigned myself to giving up the scale if it meant breaking his curse—on one condition. "If you can help me figure out where this thing came from and how I'm supposed to use it to help my mom, then…" I couldn't find the words to finish the sentence.

"You don't have to make any promises, Katrina. I'm confident that once you learn the truth, whatever that may be, you'll do the right thing." His voice hummed over the low purr of the motorcycle.

Why did he have so much faith in me? I was not the best at making the right choices, especially not recently.

"Find out what you need to. Soon. I'll buy you some time by keeping the crew off your trail," Milo said. "Then call me."

I gave him a quizzical look.

"By that I mean leave me a message that only I would recognize underneath the pier when you're ready. On the second beam to the left. It's very important that you only go during the day. I'll find it at night when the tide comes in and find you."

"Well, what's something only you would recognize?" I asked.

"Hmm." he looked upwards, toward the sky, then back at me. "Do you remember our conversation about the stars back on the island?"

"Of course."

"Can you draw an 8-pointed star?"

I almost laughed. "I'm an art student! Yes, I can draw a star."

"Perfect." he tilted his chin. "Carve a star into the beam and I'll know it was you. Like this one." He rolled up his sleeve, revealing the same North Star tattoo that Bellamy wore.

I wondered if it was a mark of the crew. "Bellamy had the same tattoo," I noted. "What does it mean?"

"It's protection. A good luck charm, sort of. It was there as a beacon of hope when we faced treacherous waters. It always guided us to safety."

I nodded, touched by the sentiment.

"Okay." I took a breath in. "How do you know I'll do it?"

"I don't," he stated plainly. "I just hope you will. And if you don't, maybe I'll just have to kill you after all."

I thought he was joking, but I still watched him with untrusting eyes.

"That last part was a joke." He smirked. I smacked his arm playfully.

I wanted him to stay longer, to ask him more things, but he simply flipped up the kickstand before I could get out another word. "Be quick, because I can't guarantee your safety for long. Farewell for now, Katrina." And with that he disappeared into the night, leaving me standing in front of the East Wing campus dorms.

11

IN DEEP WATER

Turning the brass knob to our dorm, I shuffled memories of my conversation with Milo around in my head, still reeling from the impossibility of it all. But I couldn't deny the reality of it all after living it.

As I entered the darkened room, the subtle glow of the microwave clock caught my eye and I realized it was nearly 1 AM. I assumed McKenzie was asleep in her bed, so I was careful to tiptoe to the bathroom as quietly as I could, but it was difficult to be stealthy with my bruised ankle.

After showering in silence, I melted into the safety of my own bed, pulling the covers up around me. I remembered the blanket Milo had given me was still at the foot of my bed, so I reached forward to pull it over myself. I reluctantly admitted to myself that I found Milo attractive in more than one way, and now that he was gone, some part of me longed to be near him again. Our conversations echoed in my head as I let the memory of his strong but soothing voice lull me to sleep. I curled my fingers around his blanket and breathed in salty brine and amber.

However, a dark thought interrupted my fantasy as my hand brushed against the necklace I had returned to my neck. I would have to call my dad eventually to ask about this "scale" necklace. There was no other starting point I could think of. Dread swept over me and chased away my dreams of Milo.

I lay awake for what felt like forever, planning what I would say to Dad when I called tomorrow. Could he have possibly known what he had given me? Was it even he who had given it to me? Something told me it wasn't, but I didn't want to believe it.

Eventually, the questions faded as I dozed off into a heavy slumber, but it wasn't for long. To my misfortune, this was a night for bad dreams.

But this time it was a different type of nightmare. A new one. A shadow stood over me, and I couldn't move to escape it. It loomed over me as I slept, yet somehow, I could see it watching me.

My eyes flew open, but my body remained still. Lying on my back, I kept my eyes fixed up on the ceiling, trying to catch the breath that seemed to have left me while dreaming. The dim sliver of moonlight stretched across my small room from the slit in the blinds on the tiny window in my room. When a shadow crept across, I tensed. Nothing looked out of place, but I couldn't help but feel there was something there. My eyes fell on the window, and I wondered what could be outside.

I stood up gingerly, my ankle twinging when my feet hit the floor. I made my way to the window. It was only a few steps from my bed, but it felt like a half-mile walk. The heaviness of someone watching me was almost tangible. My breath was short, and I dared not blink. Mustering the courage, I ripped the blinds back to reveal the empty dorm balcony hallway, lit only by the moon. I checked the right and left but saw nothing. All was quiet.

"Is someone there?" I whispered hoarsely, trying not to wake McKenzie.

I whirled around, scanning the room, looking for any small sign of someone's presence.

With a jerk, I awoke, for what felt like the second time. It had been a dream, too. No matter how real it felt, it had just been a dream. But it left me with such an unsettling feeling crawling down my skin. Finally, I convinced myself to fall back asleep, and this time, I made it to morning.

The unfortunate part was that I had class that day. It was Wednesday. I had English Comp I at 8:30 AM. Was I really supposed to just continue on with the day like last night didn't happen? One thing was for sure. I needed to find out ASAP where dad had gotten this necklace. It couldn't wait. My eyes were barely open before making the call to my dad. No answer. It was early, but late by his standards. I knew by now he was probably already underneath an engine bay with his phone laying on the shop counter. So, I left a voicemail and also groggily typed out a text for good measure.

Hey Dad. I've been wondering about the note with the necklace. Where did you get it exactly? And what did that note mean?

I eagerly awaited his response as I beelined it to the kitchen to get a Keurig started. McKenzie was already in there, sipping on one herself.

"Hey girl!" She chimed. "Oh, you look rough. Didn't sleep well? Were you out with Bellamy?" Her concerned expression morphed into a mischievous one with barely a transition.

I let out a groan. "Sort of," I said, rubbing my head. "But nothing happened." *At least not what you think.*

"I need to hear all about it! Oh my God. You're limping!"

It was too early for this.

"I'm okay. It's just bruised. I...fell," I said wearily.

McKenzie flipped through her planner. "I have Chemistry at 9 and then French at 11:30. Wanna catch up between then?"

I nodded, though I actually didn't want to do any catching up. How was I supposed to make anything that happened sound even remotely normal? "That should work."

"Great! Yay!" McKenzie beamed, scampering to her side of the dorm to do whatever it was she did this early in the morning.

I looked at my phone with impatience. Still no response from Dad.

Mrs. Loftemberger droned on about the importance of the themes of heroism in the Odyssey, while I fought my own battle to stay awake. The tip of my pencil scratched back and forth as I found myself sketching tiny North Stars on my notebook paper. A vibration in my pocket alerted me to a text. I jumped to check the screen with lightning speed. I couldn't read the message fast enough.

Necklace? Note?

Yeah, the one you sent me for my birthday.

Trina, I didn't send you a necklace. I thought I told you. The gift I sent you was delayed.

I couldn't even manage to type a reply as the realization seeped into my core. Just as I feared. Who else than the same person who had decided to show back up in my life at the last minute? Mom. Mom *had* sent the necklace. The note about the nightmares and keeping the necklace safe was from *her*. The thought of having to ask her about it made my stomach turn. It was hard enough just talking to her without losing myself.

As I fought to accept that I would sooner or later have to call Mom about the necklace, I gathered my things as class dismissed. I was supposed to meet McKenzie at Sea Dogs Cafe to gossip about my date with Bellamy. But now I had a stop to make by Housing first. Shuffling as quickly as my sore ankle would allow, I sped to the student mailbox room and checked ours. Sure enough, there was a small package for me, obviously addressed in Dad's handwriting, marked as delivered two days after my birthday.

I tore open the little bubble envelope while I stood right there in the mail room. As I would have guessed, it was a gift card to an art store and a paint palette keychain. That was definitely the type of gift I would expect from my dad instead of a magical necklace. I touched the scale pendant around my neck. Now that I knew it was from Mom, I wanted to tear it off and stuff it in a drawer. But I couldn't be careless with it now in case it really did hold some kind of ancient mermaid magic.

I texted Dad a quick thank you and an apology for the mix-up, but I didn't offer him any further explanation. I didn't want him confronting Mom about it and upsetting her. I needed to ensure she stayed around long enough to get some answers. So, with a heavy dread washing over me, I forced myself to make the call as I walked along outside. With each ring, I felt sicker. I didn't want to talk to her yet, but I knew I had to. So, when she didn't answer, I couldn't distinguish my relief from my frustration, because even though I wasn't ready to confront her, I also wasn't looking forward to getting kidnapped by ghost pirates. I called once more. No answer.

Typical of her. Not being there when I need her.

Tucking the gifts from my dad into my backpack, I hobbled back out into the streets, trying to make it to Sea Dogs as quickly as I could manage without twisting my ankle again. I didn't know what else to do next. From the misty sky above fell a barely noticeable drizzle that left the cobblestone streets shiny with puddles that I was careful not to step in. My thoughts felt as muddled as the fog around me.

Once in the cafe, I ordered the usual for both of us while I waited for McKenzie. I had thought I was the one who would be late with my last-minute detour, but somehow, I'd still managed to get there first. It was only a matter of minutes before McKenzie walked in, her freshly curled orange tresses bouncing with each step. She hadn't even dropped her notebook on the table and book satchel on the floor before the words flew out of her mouth.

"So, what was he like?"

What was I supposed to tell her? She had believed me about the pirate ship, in her own way, but to tell her I just went on a date with a ghost...it was too wild, even for McKenzie.

"He was..." I tilted my gaze upward, looking to the light fixtures in the ambient little cafe for some help with my words, "...nice."

"Nice?" She slammed her hands down on the table in a playful way. "That's all I get?"

"Well, he sort of seemed like he had something to hide." That was technically true. "And I felt like he might just be using me to get what he wants." Also, true.

"Like, just to get in your pants?" McKenzie's eyes widened.

My sexual experiences were limited, to say the least, but I hadn't relayed that to McKenzie. I had a boyfriend in high school, briefly, but it never got that far. Nothing serious. Maybe that's why Bellamy felt so tantalizing in those moments he pulled me close. No one had ever caressed me that way. His seductive draw on me had felt like forbidden fruit. Either way, I couldn't tell her that he was just after my necklace. That would sound ludicrous.

"Yeah, like that's all he wanted, you know." I nodded, looking out the window at the horse carriage full of tourists clip-clopping by on the cobblestone, the sky gray and overcast above. "He just seemed like a bit of a player."

"Aw, I'm sorry, Katrina," McKenzie reached out to cover my hand with her own.

"It's okay," I started. "I still dreamed about him. I think." I immediately regretted adding that last part.

"Uh oh, falling for the bad boy." McKenzie's grin made me roll my eyes in denial. But in a way, she wasn't exactly wrong. Something *was* tempting about Bellamy.

"We'll see what happens." I told her. "But don't get your hopes up."

The barista called our names and McKenzie shot up to grab both of our lattes before I could even think to do it.

As she gracefully floated back down into her seat, still balancing both hot beverages in each hand, I decided to tell her about my mom. I half-hoped that talking about it would somehow prepare me for talking *to* her when I confronted her about the necklace.

"So, apparently my mom came back," I blurted out. McKenzie sipped her coffee, and her eyes grew the size of saucers when I spoke. I only nodded in confirmation. "I haven't said much to her. She tried to talk to me, but it's just so..." My words weakened. "Hard."

"Well surely, she understands how much she put you through. I don't think I would talk to her until she apologized."

I smiled at McKenzie's innocence. Her parents seemed so perfect. They took extravagant family vacations every winter and summer. I don't think she had ever fought with her mom, based solely on what she had shared with me.

"She apologized. She apologizes a lot, actually. The thing is her apologies don't exactly mean much."

"Well, what are you going to do?"

"I still don't know. But there's something I have to ask her, so I'd better figure it out."

"What do you have to ask her?" McKenzie didn't seem to recognize the boundaries of her prying. I didn't have the heart to deny her the information—at least part of it. "This necklace," I pointed to the pendant at my chest. "Turns out she's the one who gave it to me. And I want to know why she would do that after all this time away."

"Maybe she's trying to show you she's serious." She stirred her coffee as I sipped mine for the first time, just now realizing that I hadn't taken a drink yet.

"Maybe. It just seems unlike her. I don't get it." I looked down into my cup before speaking again. "Anyway, how are things with you?"

"Everything's great! Ty took me golfing the other day. He's great. So, all good there. I'm kinda worried about flunking Analytical Geometry, though. Ugh, why do we have to take math classes at an *art* school?" The way the words streamed out of her mouth without stopping prompted a little giggle out of me.

"What?" Her blue eyes shimmered. I couldn't think of a time when she didn't seem carefree, even when complaining about math. She switched gears with a blink as something came to memory. "Oh yeah!" Digging through her bag, she produced a double-folded piece of paper. Holding it up, her fingers folded over the top edge, she displayed it like a trophy. "Did you leave this on the table in the kitchen? It's got your name on it."

Taking the paper from her manicured fingers, I studied the eloquent penmanship in which my name was written. The paper was mine—*my* watercolor paper—but I hadn't created the drawing on the inside. The moment I fully unfolded the paper and laid my gaze on the image, I felt the blood drain from my face. It was a hand drawn sketch of a heart with two arrows, a casual sketch of Bellamy's signature tattoo.

I started to deny the drawing, but then I thought better of it, as I didn't want to scare McKenzie. So, I lied.

"Yeah," I muttered, blinking in surprise. "I must have dropped it."

I couldn't stop staring at the words scribbled below the image.

Milo's not the only one with a calling card. Here's mine for when you finally learn the truth. Be careful who you trust.

Bellamy. It hadn't been a dream after all last night. He *was* there.

Suddenly the weight of it all came collapsing onto me like the monstrous waves in my dreams. I couldn't turn a blind eye to this, not when an undead pirate had been prowling around in our dorm. He knew where I lived. What else could this haunted crew do? What if I really *was* in danger? The reality of it all hadn't gripped me until now. I couldn't risk endangering McKenzie in all this. If this was how things were to be, I had to piece together this necklace mystery sooner rather than later, which meant that no matter how much I didn't want it to be true, Mom was my only hope.

12

THREE SHEETS TO THE WIND

I was exhausted for the remainder of the day. Before class, I planned to talk to Mom. My fingers scrolled through my contacts to find her. I glanced across the empty corridor in my dorm hall as I pulled out my phone—perhaps making sure no one was around, or perhaps stalling, or maybe both. More than a year had passed since I last dialed that number.

Deep down, I didn't want her to answer just yet. I still didn't know what I would say to her, and I wasn't looking forward to figuring it out. Though the thought of any more ghost pirates leaving unwelcome notes still rubbed me the wrong way, the reality of actually holding a one-on-one conversation with Mom seemed scarier for the time being. But I still tried and was rewarded with old voicemail greetings and ignored text messages. I called and texted more throughout the day, every time I had a chance, but those went unanswered as well, not surprisingly.

Still, I texted Dad and asked him if Mom was around. I didn't want him to get suspicious or worry that something was wrong, so I tried not to make it sound urgent, though it very much was. When he responded with a call, I knew it couldn't be good.

"I really didn't want to tell you this yet, Trina." Dad's voice carried a familiar hopelessness that pierced right through me. He went on to explain and I listened.

She'd already relapsed. And she'd been gone most of the day, and stumbled home just a few hours earlier. Which was why every single text and call had gone unanswered.

Figures.

I wanted to summon Milo at once, to tell him to take the necklace and leave. It didn't feel worth it. Why was I risking my life for Mom when she couldn't even be strong for me for a few days? But I had to remember it wasn't just about her dreams. It was about mine, too. It sounded crazy, but I still wondered if the charm around my neck might be the only thing that could keep me from the same fate. If I could just make sense of it.

In the dorm that evening, I obsessively checked the locks on the door, trying to do it as discreetly as possible so McKenzie didn't get suspicious. Once I was satisfied with one last lock check, I closed myself up in my room. I was supposed to be working on an assignment. We were reading the Great Gatsby for both my art and literature classes, and consequently, we were tasked with using a motif from the book to create an illustrated piece.

But I had something else in mind, due to the circumstances. While Mom might have been of no help that day, I didn't intend to let that stop me. I decided to do some digging on Mom's side of the family. I remembered years ago, the first time we checked Mom into a rehab facility, I overheard her mentioning something about depression and hallucinations in the family, which was an unsettling bit of information I'd kept tucked away in the back of my mind. But maybe it could be useful now. Maybe I could find a diagnosis or disorder of some kind that was responsible for these nightmares

Sitting against my headboard, Milo's blanket draped across my lap, I opened my laptop and began an ancestry search for any records available under the only clue I had to go off—-Mom's maiden name: Gatlin. I didn't hesitate to sign up for a free trial under a renowned family tree database website, but I made a mental note to cancel it within a week so I wouldn't be charged later. I may have felt like an unstoppable sleuth on a time-sensitive mission, but I was still very aware of my true status as a broke college student.

The results turned up 26 different families with the same surname. I was only sure I was looking at the right family tree because I recognized the name of Lydia, my late grandmother. She died before I was born, so I had no recollection of her, but I knew her name. I dove in, eager to find something, but unfortunately, there were only marriage and death certificates available, and a few property records here and there, showing me Mom's ancestors always stayed close to home, either in Missouri or Arkansas. But the more I studied them, the more a pattern became more obvious. I noted the death dates on each name. One by one, I began making a list of their death years, going as far back as the records would allow.

Lydia Gatlin - 2003
Nelda Gatlin Harrows - 1971
Esther Graves - 1952
Alma Whitlock - 1922
Edith Barnes- 1900
Martha James Shores - 1874
Sarah Shores - 1840
Marina Samuels - 1819

Marina was as far back as I could trace. But it didn't matter. There was only one thing that was making my stomach turn, and it wasn't the names on the list, but the similarity I noticed in the dates. After calculating carefully, double-checking and triple-checking my math, I came to a chilling conclusion. Not one woman in the entire bloodline had lived beyond the age of 46. Mom was 45.

When I was finally able to still the churning in my gut and catch my breath, I could only think of one thing. The necklace. I dug the note back out of its place in the dresser that I still hadn't gotten around to organizing. Mom's note implied it had been in the family for a long time. Her family. So I was dying to know if each of these women had this necklace in their possession at some point. Which one found it first? And did any of them leave any clues for using it?

I had no idea how I was supposed to unravel any of it, but somehow, I knew I had to solve it, or I'd go crazy—if I wasn't already. And if I didn't do it quickly, I might just be in danger of having my dorm invaded by pirates.

My eyes grew heavier and heavier until they felt like anchors. Rubbing my eyelids to prod them open just a little bit longer, I checked my phone one more time. Even though I didn't want to see a reply from Mom, I knew I needed to, especially after the chilling realization I'd just uncovered. But I breathed a guilty sigh of relief when there wasn't one. With tiredness bogging down my thoughts, I surrendered to the call of sleep, tucking my necklace close to my chest, and glancing at the locked doorknob one last time before nestling down into the sheets. I'd talk to Mom somehow tomorrow. I swore it.

I don't know what exactly drew me to the ocean the next day after class when I finally worked up the nerve to call Mom. Days before, I wouldn't have dared to go there myself. But after my encounter with Bellamy on the shore, it didn't fill me with the same terror as before. I had packed myself into my Jeep and headed out to Half Moon Beach. It was a bit more of a drive than if I had just gone to Constantine Beach—but the promise of smaller crowds was enticing.

I wanted to feel untouchable when I called her. If she answered, I wanted the strength of the sea on my side. The ocean and I shared a love/hate relationship, just like with Mom, and looking at the sea felt like looking at her.

Stepping out onto the white sands of the beach, I drew a deep breath of salty sea air into my lungs. Beneath suppressed whispers, I tried to rehearse the speech that I'd been churning around in my head for when Mom picked up the phone. It wasn't exactly how I pictured my first day trip to the beach.

Mom, I need you to listen. I know you sent me the necklace for my birthday. Why haven't you said anything about it? And more importantly, where did it come from? How does it stop the dreams?

I'd been met with countless unanswered calls and texts to that three-letter name in my Contacts list through the years. Yet here I stood, daring like a fool to try once again. I twisted my lower lip under my teeth as I searched for the courage to continue. Then I pressed "call."

"You've reached Grace Delmar. Please leave a message."

I shouldn't have been so angry to hear the voicemail, but I couldn't help it. My first thought was to assume she was passed out after downing some hard liquor midday. Hanging up, I bit my lip again, harder. I trudged back to the car, almost embarrassed at myself for trying.

As I pulled the Jeep's door shut, my phone began to chime as "Mom" flashed across the screen. A pinch of panic rose in my chest. It felt like she was the one in control, and it wasn't fair. *She* was the one calling me, and I didn't like it. I had wanted her to answer *my* call, for once. But I needed her, so I had to give in.

I put on the speaker, sitting in my car, no one could hear.

"Hello? Katrina...did you call me...hello?"

I realized I hadn't spoken yet. Swallowing, I forced out a word.

"Mom." So far, the script wasn't going according to plan. Suddenly, I couldn't even recall a single word I had planned to say.

"Yes, I'm here. What is it, Trina?"

I didn't like hearing her use my nickname anymore. Dad seemed like the only one entitled to that. Not her. She shouldn't get to call me that.

"I—I have something to ask you."

"Okay.... Ugh. I have such a headache."

The inside of the vehicle felt like a cage, suffocating me with the trapped warmth of the sun. I climbed back out and began pacing in the sand.

"You sent me the necklace, didn't you?"

"Necklace? Oh, yeah. Yes, I did." She laughed, but it was stale and forced, sending a wave of uneasiness through me as I recognized she was far from sober. "I thought you should have it now. Maybe it'll help you. It's too late for me, I think. If either one of us should have it...it's you."

"Why? What did your note mean about it helping with the dreams?"

"Ohhh that..." She let out a lazy groan. "Well, I—I don't know exactly. It's a family legend. I never believed in it...but I'm starting to." She giggled strangely. "Your grandma did though...she tried. She believed it...but I think I waited too long."

"Grandma?" I repeated, clutching the phone. "Did Grandma have nightmares, too?"

"Well, yes." she hiccupped. "All the time. Just like us...I never told you? Wow...But that's why you need to keep it with you. That's why I brought it back. Mom always thought it could.... could...make us—make me—better. But I don't know, maybe it's just something we'll never understand, you know..."

I bit my lip as I registered her words, or what bits and pieces of them I could make out. She sounded as though she had just woken up.

"Katrina," she sniffed. "I'm sorry...Right now..."

"Are you drinking again?"

There was only silence.

"Mom, I know you're drinking. That was a rhetorical question." I just hoped she was mentally present enough to answer the questions I needed to ask.

"No," she breathed. "I mean, yes, I am drinking.... I was. But you don't understand. The dreams don't stop. It almost seems worse since I sent the necklace away to you...Worse than before...they've never been this bad. Even the alcohol isn't helping anymore...I should have tried sooner. Maybe I should've kept it...I couldn't do it. I couldn't figure it out. Maybe that damn necklace is just a lie and we're all just hopeless lunatics. But now it's your turn. I couldn't, but maybe you can. You...you're smart like your grandma was."

"Mom, don't blame yourself." It was the first hint of gentleness I detected in my voice since speaking with her. I remembered the death dates I had recorded earlier. "So we're all supposedly going crazy from nightmares. Then what happened to Grandma? What did she know?" I asked. Mom fumbled a bit and hesitated before answering. For a moment I wondered if she'd heard me. I repeated the question.

"Well, Mom...She...She really believed in that necklace. That it could...it can stop our nightmares. Somehow. Whatever that means...No one knows. But she died before figuring it out. She'd wear it to sleep. It helped sometimes, she said, but I thought it was just in her head. She thought she was close to figuring it all out...I just thought she was out of her mind. But maybe if I'd listened to her...before...Ugh, my head." Mom coughed, as if to try covering up the sounds of her sorrow.

I sighed. I knew what had happened to my grandma. Mom had found her hanging in her bedroom. And now, I was starting to realize why. It sounded like she'd lost it. Was this necklace really the answer to our curse or a death sentence?

"What are you saying, Mom?"

"I don't—" She paused before taking a shaky breath. "When I found her, it was more reason not to believe in all that necklace nonsense...I didn't want the thing near me. I got rid of it. But I don't know now. That didn't help. So I don't know anymore...Maybe it *can* do something. Because nothing else is working. You know I can't sleep...But lately, it's even now when I'm awake, I can't breathe." Her words came between sobs that only grew stronger the more she tried to speak. It was so increasingly difficult to follow her slurred disconnected sentences, especially with her trembling breaths added into the mix.

"It's okay, Mom. Try to stay calm." I allowed her a moment to collect herself as best she could before I asked my next question, her last sentence repeating in my head.

I can't breathe.

"Mom, what exactly *are* your nightmares? What—what do you see?" The words gushed out faster than a raging river. My heart was thumping through my chest.

"It's...it's always like.... like water. Like drowning. Always."

An icy grip squeezed my throbbing heart. I thought it would stop.

"Drowning?" I repeated.

"Yeah," she quivered. "I know it sounds.... sounds crazy, doesn't it? Like...why do you think...why do you think I never took you to the beach? I thought it was a warning...I didn't want to risk it." I stared in silence at the shoreline in front of me. She spoke again. "The rehab. The medications...it just numbed everything...but it's never strong enough. I don't know what to do...anymore. I just...I don't know how much more I can take."

Suddenly, in that one explanation, every drop of anger I'd ever felt for her turned into sympathy. I knew what those dreams were like. I just wished I hadn't missed that one detail all these years—that all this time we were both dreaming the same thing. This couldn't be a coincidence anymore.

"Try to get some rest, Mom. Please. We can fix this. We can fix this."

"I...No, I don't know. I'll try. I'm trying," she hiccuped through sniffs and sobs. "You're a good girl, you know. You're not too far gone yet. You're smart. You've got a chance...You need to be careful...Whatever you do. Oh, and happy late birthday."

I was losing her, I could tell.

"Mom, wait," I begged. "Please stay with Dad. Is Dad with you?" I could hear my own desperate breaths in the static of the phone. She didn't answer.

"Mom, just...just go lay down and stay home. Don't let yourself be alone. It's going to be okay." I forced myself to reassure her, needing to hear the words myself.

An uncomfortable silence followed, neither one of us knowing how to end the call. I finally spoke.

"Mom, I have to go now."

She hiccuped. "Be careful."

And she hung up.

I walked back to my car. Deep within me, I felt a heaviness that settled into my bones. As I pulled myself into the driver's seat, I suddenly longed for some warmth to come and take away the winter that had just overtaken me. Even the Florida heat wasn't enough for that. I fiddled with the pendant around my neck. The last thing I wanted was to push Mom over the edge, by asking her such intense questions, but I had no choice now. We both wanted me to figure out the necklace's secrets. This was the only way.

Even still, strangely, for the first in a long time, a small glow of hope for her felt within reach, like a lighthouse in the distance. I was starting to wonder if the necklace might just be the key to mending the broken pieces between us. Maybe ancient mermaid-pirate curses weren't the only kind of curse it could break. There now seemed to be something between us, a new connection that wasn't there before. Even a secret was better than nothing.

Back at my dorm, the thoughts wouldn't slow down. But I knew I wasn't any closer to unlocking the secrets of this necklace than this morning. If I kept thinking about it, I was going to lose myself. Despite the exhaustion in my soul, I felt a new spark of inspiration for my showcase piece. I indulged myself in the moment, just for a little while, to keep myself grounded.

Prepping some small cups of water and wiping my finger across the paper to be sure the last layer had dried properly, I sat down to work on it. The star had already begun to take form, but I needed to do so much more with the blending and layers to really make it "shine" on paper. With the ocean's surface filling the landscape at the bottom, I decided to add a tiny depiction of hope—a lone lighthouse out in the sea. I selected one of my finest-tipped brushes to create its towering figure in the distance. It might have easily been missed in the painting at first glance, but it was there, buried in plain sight, a hidden secret in the middle of a dark night at sea.

T hat night it rained. There were no bad dreams, no haunting feeling that someone else was there. The necklace stayed on me now even when I slept. Maybe Mom was right. The dreams had been less frequent since I'd worn it. At least it seemed that way. Or maybe it was just in my head. Because they weren't gone completely, so it was always a gamble to close my eyes.

As I lay there, resisting the powerful draw of sleep by twirling the scale between my fingers, I couldn't stop my thoughts from drifting to Milo. It was inexplicable, the way that I yearned to have him there so that I could tell him everything. I wanted to tell him about the unsettling findings I'd uncovered about my mom's lineage, and about how my earlier conversation with her haunted me. But that felt idiotic. What reason would he have to care?

As I listened to the rain pummeling the rooftops, I wondered where he was. What did a cursed pirate crew do in the middle of the night? I tapped my phone to check the time. 11:06. The tide would have long been up, releasing him from his prison for a while. I closed my eyes and imagined him on the phantom ship, drifting in the shadows, a figment to the rest of a world he couldn't explore. Was he thinking of me, too? Or was I only a solution to him? It would be unfair of me to expect otherwise. I hadn't even known him for that long.

13

HOIST THE COLORS

I t was Friday. It had now officially been a whole week since my encounter with the pirate ship on the island, and just a couple of days since I met the two pirates. Things were surprisingly quiet, but I couldn't help looking over my shoulder at every turn. I was heading back to my dorm after class, books in hand, thinking of too much at once. Milo. Bellamy. Mom. The necklace. Next week's exam. I barely heard the voice snap my name.

"Hey!" It was Russell, the groundskeeper, hobbling over in his worn khaki coveralls that contrasted against his deep umber skin.

I whipped around, thinking that perhaps I had stepped on some prized landscaping or something.

"I'm sorry. What's your name again, missy?"

"Katrina," I said, hoping I wasn't about to get in trouble.

Russell nodded.

"Do you have a minute?" he asked.

"Um, sure."

Nothing could have prepared me for what came next. Placing his hands on my shoulders, he looked me dead in the eyes.

"That boy you were with last week is not safe."

"You mean Bellamy?"

"I mean *either* of them." He drew in a breath and looked around. "They are not of this world."

"I know," I uttered, hesitating with my words. "I know that they're...dead."

"They're demons!" His voice raised and his eyes bulged. I almost backed away in shock from the fearful expression manifesting on his face.

I glanced down at my sneakers in the grass before speaking up. "What do you mean? How...how do you even know about this?"

As if expecting me to ask that, he pointed to the work van across the campus, parked in front of the central office building. "There's something you need to see." He began hurtling towards the vehicle, and I trailed close behind. It was anybody's guess what he was planning to show me. I certainly had no idea what to expect.

He swung the driver's side door open and leaned in, digging around underneath the seat for something he had clearly placed there with this intention. Then, turning to face me, he met my gaze, a glassy, almost tearful look between the creases of his eyes. He placed a newspaper in my hand.

"I don't understand," I confessed.

"Read it. Front-page." His voice wavered as he gestured towards the paper in my hands.

It was old. I could feel the layer of dust and mold settled into the pages, as I pressed my fingers against the underside of the yellowed paper. Swallowing, I glanced down and read the headline, dated July 19, 1988.

Local Mermaid Performer Drowns at Sea.

"Should this mean something to me?" I asked, naturally a bit unnerved at the mention of mermaids.

"Serena was my daughter. *They* did this," his tone hardened like stone. "She didn't drown by accident. She was murdered. They couldn't prove it. But I *know* what I saw."

I felt my pulse quickening, and I shifted uneasily.

"And what did you see?"

"She did the mermaid shows. And she liked to free dive. One day, she went to the pier, and they took her. It just so happened I was fishing off the pier that evening. I saw that boy—Bellamy—I saw him sneaking around the shore—and another fellow with him—the blonde one."

Milo, I presumed. I pressed him to continue with a pleading stare.

"I could tell they were up to no good. They ran under the pier. When I heard her voice—her screaming—I went running. But the pier is so long. By the time I got there, no one was there. They'd vanished, and so had she. There was a woman there lying unconscious. I carried her to a pay phone and called an ambulance."

I took a deep breath in through my nose. How painful this must have been for him to relive this incident right now as he described it to me.

"But then I immediately went out looking for Serena on my fishing boat. I knew that was her scream. I was out on the water all night. Near the island I found her, floating in the water, bloody. The bastards cut her open." He drew out an imaginary cut across his chest with his finger, a tangible ache in each motion. His lips trembled as he went on to finish the story. I stood there, speechless, hung on his every word.

"Then out of nowhere that cursed ship was right in front of me. And the captain—he was the devil himself—told me to go back to shore. Said he'd kill my wife and son, too if I ever came back. I shot at him, but the bullets went right through him, and he laughed. He couldn't be killed. And Bellamy and the other were right there on the ship with him. Of course, when I told the police about it, they never believed me. The ship had disappeared, along with the captain and everyone else on it. They thought I was crazy. My testimony didn't mean much to them. And her death was ruled a suicide. Closed, just like that."

Russell snapped his fingers as he uttered the last sentence. Then he paused for a long moment, as if holding his breath. I couldn't find words to fill the silence. He finally spoke again.

"My Serena." He ran his fingertips over the image of the smiling young girl in the print. "She was only eighteen."

Some combination of what he was saying and the wrenched expression on his face shook my nerves. The typically quiet, cheerful groundskeeper was now mere words away from a tearful breakdown as his lips quaked fighting back his own sorrow. Who could have possibly suspected that this old man who maintained ISA so faithfully was harboring such a dark burden all this time?

"Russell, I'm so sorry. I don't know what to say." I started to put a hand on his shoulder.

"Don't say anything," he snapped. "Just have the sense to stay away from them before the same thing happens to you."

There was another long bout of awkward silence as I glanced down at the ground once more.

"May I take a picture of this?" I finally uncovered the courage to look up and ask.

"You're not going to go sharing this with the world on one of those social media things, are you?" A little prickle rose in Russell's voice.

"No." I shook my head vigorously, as if the harder I shook it somehow demonstrated the truth of my words. "No, of course not."

"You don't believe me. You think I'm crazy, too."

"No, I...I believe you. Trust me, that's not the craziest thing I've heard lately." As I spoke, I could sense anger swelling up in my stomach and flooding my chest. If this was true, I would ensure Bellamy and Milo never saw me or my necklace again. If this was true, a part of me was convinced that they deserved their curse all along. They had lied to me, especially Milo. But he was clearly right about one thing when he said you can never really trust a pirate. "I want to have something to use against them, something they can't deny, if they come back for me." I closed my fingers around my necklace instinctively.

When Russell was silent, I began to turn away, but then I looked back when I had a sudden thought. "You wouldn't happen to know anything about this necklace, would you?" Russell examined the pendant at my neck for a moment.

"I'm sorry, no." He shook his head as though I had confounded him. "Am I supposed to know something about it?"

"No," I sighed, careful not to feed him any more information that might only make him more paranoid. "Just wondering if you've seen it before."

Or knew how to use its power to save a hallucinating alcoholic.

14

LOOSE CANNON

As I walked back to my dorm, I hung my head low, fragments of Russell's story still shifting around in my mind. Captain Valdez was truly a monster, by that account. It took everything in me not to bite my lip all the way through as I chewed it in frustration and pondered if Bellamy and Milo could truly have been just as monstrous.

The moment I walked through the door McKenzie's sparkly, high-pitched "Hello!" greeted me. She was brewing a Keurig with a big grin on her face. But I wasn't in the mood. I was so hyper-focused on digging into this nightmarish story that I didn't answer her. Instead, I stormed to my half of the dorm.

"Hey, everything okay?" McKenzie's question irked me. Everything around me irked me. I had never felt anger rising so fast. I'd been angry many times, like when my mom broke her countless promises to "get well," but being intentionally betrayed like this by someone new—two someones to be exact—opened an entirely new realm of fury in me that I was quickly losing control over.

"I'm fine." I growled.

"Are you sure?" She moved away from the coffee maker and practically danced toward me.

"Yes! I'm sure! Can you please take that for an answer?" The words snapped out like bitter frostbite, and I immediately wished I could reach out and pull them all back in. But the damage was done.

"Okay, sorry," she mumbled, turning her attention back to the coffee. In my four months of knowing her, I had never heard such dejection in her soft voice. Embarrassed and even angrier, I retreated into my room, closing the door behind me with a slow push. I stood there, released a heavy sigh full of countless emotions, and then my gaze caught on the stupid blanket wrinkled over my bed. Though I imagined tearing it to shreds, I could only manage to toss it into the floor for lack of strength.

As the evening hours droned on, I hauled myself out of my wallowing, and lazily reached up for my laptop from my nightstand. Pulling the little computer into my lap, I braced my back against the nightstand for support as I sat upright on the floor. My fingers couldn't type in the information into the internet search bar fast enough as I skimmed the photo I had taken of Russell's article.

Serena Alice Loveday 1988.

I began wading through what little information I could find. It appeared that there had been a few rumors surrounding her death, but nothing quite matched what Russell had told me. On a few true crime websites, there was something about how some people claimed she had run away with a lover that night, only to turn up dead with her chest cut open. Another source claimed she had been stressed with the show schedule, so she went to drown herself after one particularly hectic performance.

It wasn't long before I realized the mystery shrouding the case had meant law enforcement slammed it shut with a lock as fast as they could. After all, I imagine they had a hell of a time trying to find a ghost. But this only meant the internet wasn't going to give me any real leads. I'd have to look elsewhere.

The sound of the front door shutting ripped me from my concentration. McKenzie must have left. I suddenly remembered my awful treatment of her. I may not have been able to make any progress on the case of Serena's death, or my mom, but mending things with McKenzie was certainly a situation I could do something about.

I scrambled to my feet. Thankfully, I had been too upset to even take my shoes off when I came in earlier, so I was ready to go. Rushing to the front door, I swung it open and stuck my head out, glancing both directions across the outdoor hallway. By some stroke of luck, I caught a glimpse of that tangerine hair flouncing down the hall just at the top of the stairwell as McKenzie's head fully disappeared down the steps. My feet sped up through the corridor, and as I neared the stairs, I called out her name.

I nearly came to a sliding stop at the top of the stairwell as I caught my breath. She stood at the bottom of the first flight and turned her face up at me.

"Yeah?" There was a deadness in her tone that just didn't match her bright spirit.

"McKenzie, I am so sorry." I took a step down towards her. "I've just had a bad day, but that was no reason to be such a jerk to you earlier." I pleaded with my eyes, waiting for her response.

She stood there without saying anything for what felt like hours.

"Well, I really appreciate your apology." She trotted back up the steps, her signature smile returning to her face in less than a second. Linking arms with me, she crossed her brows and looked up at me through a mocking sad face. "But try not to do that again, please. I've never seen you so mean."

I was relieved that she was so readily willing to forgive.

"You got it." I smiled, realizing I probably looked near homeless with my tired eyes in contrast to her freshly made-up face. "Where are you going anyway?" I asked.

"Oh," she tucked a loose strand of hair behind her freckled ear. "Ty invited me over. He's just down on the 1st floor. Do you wanna come?"

"Do you think he'd want that?" I drew one corner of my mouth back, not so sure that Ty would be thrilled about me showing up with his girlfriend—or whatever she was to him. "It just seemed like I pissed him off at the Halloween party."

"Oh, I'm sure he's forgotten about that by now." McKenzie pulled me with her arm, still intercrossing with mine, and led me down the steps. "It's not just me. He invited a couple of other friends too."

I breathed in, not really wanting to go, but also thinking that being alone back in the dorm with a murder mystery tormenting me wasn't the best place to be either.

"Okay, fine, just for a little while," I agreed.

McKenzie turned the knob to Ty's dorm with the confidence of someone who lived there. She pushed the door open, and we were engulfed in a puff of fruity fog as someone vaped from the couch. The only light in the room came from two dim lamps on either side of the sofa. Including Ty, there were four people in the room—a couple seated practically in each other's laps, sharing one big lounge chair, and another guy next to Ty, each invested in their phone screens playing a round of a trivia game hosted on the TV screen.

"Hey hot stuff." Ty winked at McKenzie as she slowly shut the door behind her. "And hey—uh—what's your friend's name again?" His gaze jumped to me.

"You remember Katrina? From the boat party." McKenzie proudly leaped to remind him.

He squinted, trying to recognize my face.

"Oh yeah." He spoke with such minimal effort I could barely hear him over the whimsical music from the game. "The Ghost Girl."

I rolled my eyes, already wanting to turn on my heels and leave.

"Don't take it so seriously, geez." He flung himself back against the couch, sinking into the cushion. "C'mon you guys. Sit down and play. Beers in the fridge."

McKenzie waltzed to the little mini fridge in the corner and pulled out two glass bottles. She offered me one, and for some reason, I took it, though I immediately set it back down on the coffee table. Part of me did contemplate taking a few swigs, just to ease my mind of all the nonstop thoughts running through my head, but I persuaded myself not to when I thought back to my last conversation with Mom.

"Don't worry, no one's going to care if you don't," McKenzie assured me.

I nodded, appreciative that she had been more attentive to my discomfort than she had been last time.

I participated in a few rounds of a trivia game with the group, but after an hour, I felt it was time to leave. A feeling of being out of place crept up on me. I could tell everyone was a touch buzzed and no matter how much I fought it, the singe of exclusion was getting to me.

"I think I'm gonna head back up to our dorm," I murmured to McKenzie.

Her ivory hand patted me like a child on the back. "Sure thing. I'll be back up soon, too."

Standing to my feet, I waved a quick, awkward goodbye towards everyone and darted past the TV, ducking to keep from hindering anyone's view.

I had no sooner clicked the door bolt into place that I caught a glimpse of an arm reaching across my shoulder to rest on the edge of the doorway to the right. With a gasp, I whipped around to see Bellamy, propping himself up against the wall. If not for the flickering lights of the hallway, I wouldn't have been able to make out his face—but I knew that brooding shadow and dark jacket from anywhere.

"Leaving so soon? Without even just one drink? You could've at least grabbed one for me. We've been out of rum for 300 years."

I failed to suppress a scoff as he inched closer.

"I did not appreciate your little note the other night. How—how do you even know where my dorm is?"

"It wasn't hard to figure out, love." He flashed a handsome smile that I had to force myself to ignore. "You told me everything about yourself at dinner."

"Don't use your pet names on me," A wave of mortification came over me as I realized I *had* told him so much. The charming picture of deceit standing in front of me stirred my anger once again.

"Wow." He grinned, but his voice betrayed a sense of frustration. "It's truly fascinating how quickly Milo managed to turn you against me."

"He didn't turn me against you." I corrected, brushing a moth away from my face as it flitted about the hall lights. My heart was beating as fast as its wings fluttered. "You did that all on your own. If you want this necklace so bad, why didn't you just take it that night you broke into my room?" I dashed to the left of him in an attempt to walk past his brooding figure, but he put out his arm to stop me.

"I was protecting *you*. From any potential unwelcome visitors."

I bit my lip and restrained a lump in my throat by swallowing. Refusing to meet his gaze so he wouldn't see my blushing cheeks, I looked ahead, his strong arm still holding me in place.

"You like pet names so much? I have one for you." I turned my head to connect my stare with his. "Murderer."

He relaxed his arm, and I used the opportunity to shove it away back towards him, continuing onward.

Without looking back, I could feel his eyes on me as I marched toward the stairwell.

"What are you talking about?" He called after me.

"Serena Loveday," I projected over my shoulder, so he was sure to hear. "That should ring a bell."

When there was no response, I stopped at the steps with my back still turned, waiting for him to offer some sort of pathetic excuse or attempt an explanation.

Instead, I heard the click of a doorknob and McKenzie's delicate voice echo through the cold concrete hall.

"Katrina, who are you talking to?"

Turning to look back down the corridor, I saw nothing but shadows and an empty hallway, excluding McKenzie emerging from the dorm. Bellamy was gone.

"No one," I said, trying to think of something to cover myself. "Just...singing out loud to myself."

That sounded so lame and stupid, Katrina.

McKenzie walked with the grace of a ballerina to accompany me at the base of the stairwell.

"Well, I'm glad you are in a better mood," she beamed.

Hardly.

If only she knew the way my heart was pounding through my chest as I fought off a tsunami of emotions. Instead, she only saw me standing there in front of a flight of stairs, ready to take a step upward, without the faintest idea that moments earlier I had been hashing it out with a cold-blooded ghost pirate.

15

HIGH AND DRY

As we headed back upstairs together, I twisted my fingers around each other, shifting nervously as I decided whether or not to let McKenzie in on the case of Serena. Based on how many 'true crime' podcasts I had heard her listening to through the other side of the wall, I thought it entirely plausible that she might recognize it. Then, something she had said previously suddenly rang in the back of my mind. Something she had said the night I first told her about Bellamy.

I couldn't get the idea out of my head. There was no way I could wait, not when the solution could very well be the person right beside me. I prepared to ask her, thinking of a way to make it sound as least suspicious as possible.

McKenzie kicked off her shoes at the door with a princess-like yawn and then retreated to her side of the dorm. I hesitated to go into my room, planted there in the middle of the kitchenette. Loneliness came over me as I thought about what I was up against. If the story was true, and Milo and Bellamy really had helped kill Serena, was I really so confident that I could keep them from what they came for? I doubted I could. Deep down I had a feeling that the longer I kept this necklace from their psycho captain, the closer things got to becoming a game of survival. I turned around and shuffled to my roommate's door.

"McKenzie, didn't you say your cousin works at the PD?" The words leaped from my mouth before I could think it through any further. I was more desperate than I realized.

"I did! Why?" She beckoned for me to join her in her room. She was seated on a fluffy bean bag chair that nearly engulfed her, and I sunk to the floor next to her.

"This might sound weird, but I'm doing this project for extra credit." I was making it all up as I went, hoping the end result wouldn't sound too ridiculous.

"I have to find an alternative source about this old newspaper article and write about it." Scrolling through my photos, I stopped at the picture I had taken of the article and faced the screen of my phone at her. "But I'm really having a hard time finding anything else on it."

McKenzie's eyes scanned the page, straining to read the small print. I could tell when she got to the part about the body found in the ocean by the way her eyebrows lifted so high, they nearly tapped her hairline.

"Oh, man, this is that island legend I told you about. Creepy. I guess it really happened." She raised her eyebrows. "This is kind of a freaky project." She leaned back in her bean bag, wearing a disdainful scowl. I could sense her suspicion.

"I know, super weird assignment." Lying to her felt wrong, but I had no choice. There was simply no way to make the truth sound normal. McKenzie was silent.

Please believe this.

"Hmm." She pulled her lower lip up into her teeth. I grasped at the anticipation of what she could be thinking, waiting with my breath. She shot up from her seat. "Eh, what the hell. Let's ask him!"

"Really?" My eyes lit up with hopefulness.

"Yeah! I'll text him and get his email. Then you can see if he can help. But no promises. I don't actually know how all that stuff works." McKenzie sent the text right away and assured me she would let me know the next morning if her cousin had responded.

Stretching my tired arms behind my head, I wearily stood to head back to my side of the dorm. My feet almost crossed the threshold of her doorway when I thought how grateful I was for McKenzie. I turned around, leaning on the door frame.

"Hey." I smiled at her and made her look up from her phone. "Thanks for your help. You're an awesome friend."

"Pshh! You're too sweet." She flapped her hand at me playfully.

"I just thought you should know." I proceeded to flash one last smirk her way.

"Anything for you, boo." She closed her eyes and puckered her lips into a slight kissy face.

I walked out of her room with a step that was lighter, a little less burdened than when I had walked in. The next day couldn't come fast enough for me because I knew my mind wouldn't be at ease until I unraveled this mystery.

Before I crawled into bed, I considered removing my necklace and putting it somewhere safe. But where was truly safe? If Bellamy had already snuck into our dorm to leave his little note, he or Milo could just as easily come back for the necklace. Bellamy had already tried when I was awake, so I had no doubts he wouldn't give it a shot again. I didn't believe anything he had said about protecting me. And if they really *had* killed Serena, stealing a necklace would seem like child's play. But if I hid it somewhere in the room, I would make it all the easier for them to find it while I slept.

Always keep this with you...It's the only chance we've got.

I repeated the note's instructions in my head as I laid my hand over it, pressing it to my chest. I reclined back onto my pillow, my long hair fanned out around me, and I breathed in deeply, hopeful that tomorrow I might get some answers.

To keep my swirling thoughts at bay, I began softly humming a tune. It had seemingly come from nowhere, like some far away memory I couldn't quite recall. The melody taunted me with its familiarity. Where had I heard it before?

As my own strange lullaby coaxed me to sleep, I wished for a full night's rest, though I knew it was unlikely. But the next morning, I awoke with no recollection of any dreams, bad or good, and no figures lurking in the shadows. I was especially surprised to see that it was half past noon when I opened my eyes. It was rare to feel so rested.

I checked my phone to see that I had missed a text this morning from McKenzie, and it immediately snagged my attention.

A spark of excitement bubbled within my chest as I read the name of the contact info she had shared with me—Lt. Jared Burke. I wasted no time typing out an email on my phone, introducing myself and, asking for any information available on the closed case of Serena Loveday.

I checked my email obsessively for the next hour in between my routine of armoring my unruly hair against the Florida humidity with some leave-in conditioner and touching up my already dark lashes with some quick flicks of mascara. But no matter how many times I refreshed my email app, a reply never appeared in my inbox. I knew I was being absurdly impatient. It was Saturday, so I had to accept that it was unlikely McKenzie's cousin would be checking his email today.

I knew my time could be better spent figuring out the dark history behind my mom's heritage and the necklace. I certainly wasn't about to hand it over to those barbaric pirates when it was my only clue to changing my mom's potentially fatal destiny...and maybe my own.

I grabbed breakfast from the kitchenette, gulping down the sugary cereal so that I could begin another day's research. Nestled on a bench in the South Lawn, I traced everything, every date, and every name, making notes in my sketch pad like an obsessive conspiracy theorist. I practically had my maternal bloodline memorized by now. Marriage dates, baptisms, census records, medical records.

I hoarded every bit of information I could find, but none of it connected. My great-great-great-great-great grandmother Martha had been institutionalized in an asylum. Interesting, certainly. There was nothing on record telling why, though I had some obvious theories.

I did manage to find one grainy PDF of a letter copied from the late 1700s addressed to Marina, begging—or perhaps more like demanding—her not to marry some fisherman and move with him to the harbor in Massachusetts. The writer referred to Marina many times as "my daughter," so it seemed promising in tracing things back before her. But many parts of the letter were too faded to make out, and the author's name was obscured by some definite fading. The only thing I could make out was the first letter of the name—a large cursive "G." I saved a copy of it to my files, along with everything else I found, but it seemed to be yet another utterly useless piece of the puzzle. Nothing led to any information about the necklace, or what caused the nightmares in the first place.

Before I knew it, the sun was starting to set. I didn't know where I was safest, but I knew I shouldn't be alone at sundown if there was truly a bloodthirsty captain tracking me by night. Standing up to think, I heard a familiar voice not too far off, but enough to make me look around for the source.

I glanced in the direction of the crosswalk connected where I stood to the other side of the street, and to my surprise, I saw Ty goofing off and laughing with a small group of friends, including McKenzie. My first instinct was to look away and hope they didn't notice, but I remembered that my goal was to keep myself from being vulnerable. And they just might be the perfect solution for that. I purposefully strode across the crosswalk, positioning myself in a way where I was sure McKenzie would notice me. She did.

"Katrina!" She gasped. I thought I saw Ty roll his eyes, but I told myself I was probably just being paranoid. "I was gonna invite you to hang with us, but you were still asleep earlier. What are you up to?"

"I just came to do some…. Homework." I shrugged. "What're you guys doing?"

"Oh, just a little bit of everything really. We got lunch at this cool little place by the bay. Now we were just going to do a little bit of shopping." McKenzie turned to the group of people next to her, who were all obviously students. "This is Jade, Liam, and Caylin. You probably remember them from parties."

I didn't recognize them, but I nodded anyway. I was certainly too traumatized at the Halloween party to pay attention to who was there, plus everyone was in costume. And every other party was a blur of just trying to get through the night.

"I remember you! You're the watercolor girl." Caylin grinned, squinting, and brushing back a strand of light blond hair as she clung to Liam's arm. Now I remembered them. Caylin had been the one who had told me I would be completely fine if I had three mixed drinks in the span of an hour. I wasn't sure if I'd ever heard Liam speak, but he seemed pleasant.

The other girl, Jade, glared at me through hazel eyes of steel. Her sleek black hair hung to her shoulders. She smiled, but it was cold and unfocused. I couldn't help but notice the way she seemed to be fixated on Ty the rest of the time while McKenzie was talking.

"We're just about to hit up some shops in St. Augustine. Wanna come?" McKenzie asked, eyes brimming with enthusiasm.

"Actually, yeah. That'd be great." I meant it, but I knew how uncharacteristic of me I must have sounded to come across so eager.

"Really? Well, come on then. Good thing you wore sneakers. There's a lot of walking through the historic district. Right, babe?" She looked at Ty, who didn't appear too thrilled with the new addition of me to the group.

Piling into Jade's Range Rover, we crossed into Constantine's larger, sister city of St. Augustine for an afternoon of high-end shopping, though for me it was mostly a spectating event. Each time we entered a boutique, I'd mosey over to something that caught my eye, take a look at the price tag, and nearly gag. At some point, I just stopped checking the prices and accepted I wouldn't be buying anything.

I spent a lot of the time listening to the constant playful bickering between Ty and McKenzie, but keeping a close eye on Jade, who seemed to interject her own banter into their conversations, wanted or not. I wondered if McKenzie was oblivious to the shots she was shooting at Ty, or if she was merely ignoring them. Liam and Caylin kept to themselves, but sometimes Caylin would try making conversation with me whenever things got too quiet. I learned that her dad was a commercial lawyer, and her mom owned a posh salon in town. She was at ISA solely for the "experience," but her major was theatre. And Liam was there for game design. They were nice distractions.

"Who's hungry?" Caylin asked. I couldn't have been more grateful. My stomach had been growling for hours, having burned through my lunch of sugary cereal long ago.

"Let's head back to Constantine for dinner and drinks," Jade suggested. It was one of the few times she addressed the group as a whole.

"Sounds good to me," I added, and she simply scowled, but softened when Ty chimed in to agree as well. I only hoped they would pick something that wouldn't cost half my earnings of a painting sold in the antique shop around the corner.

As we headed back to the small strip in Constantine lined with quaint eateries and cafes, we passed the outdoor diner where Bellamy had first told me about the mermaid curse. I shuddered, feeling a sudden sense of apprehension as my gaze fixed on the exact table where we had sat. Something in the air shifted, and my thoughts grew heavy.

The group settled on a mid-range Greek bistro with outdoor seating beneath a trellis canopy of ivy and string lights, sans my input. I had been too preoccupied with my thoughts to offer my opinion. Waiting for our table, we leaned against a brick wall right by the outdoor tables as the live entertainer serenaded us with classic ballads on his guitar. My stomach growled ferociously as servers walked by carrying fresh bread. The smell of olive oil and feta made me salivate.

By now, we were all too tired and hungry to make much conversation, so the chatter that had been so prevalent on the way there was basically nonexistent now. As I debated with myself on whether to order the souvlaki or a salad, something about the downtown scene made my hunger pains dissipate.

Mingled within the crowds passing by our outdoor waiting section, a peculiar group caught my eye. A small throng of maybe 6 or 7 men, some middle aged, some closer to thirty walked about, prowling suspiciously as they eyed each person they passed. By the way their threatening presence darkened the air, as they slogged through the walkways in their worn ripped jeans and heavy boots.

I could tell they were trying not to make it obvious, but to me it was clear they weren't just strolling around for a night on the town. Something about the way they watched other pedestrians made my throat dry and my body cold. I hugged myself defensively as they inched closer to where we waited just outside the restaurant.

That's when I caught the quickest glimpse of dark gold hair that I recognized all too well. Amidst the three burly silhouettes of the men in the front of the group, I could just make out enough to reveal Milo standing amongst them, behaving in the same shady manner. He muttered something to them, and as if on command, they turned their attention away from my direction and towards something else entirely. As I watched, with eyes wide and palms sweating, Milo's gaze caught mine and his expression changed from scrutinizing to concerned. He pulled his brows together as if he was worried, while holding his eyes on me. With the men still locked into some type of heated discussion, Milo gestured a shooing motion with his hand towards me, while his mouth carefully formed the silent word "hide." My gaze fluttered to the ground beneath quivering lashes, still afraid of what I didn't know about him.

With my heart bouncing off the walls of my rib cage, I risked one last glance back up, recognizing a commonality amongst the men. The hoops in their ears and nautical ink on their arms indicated they were either a biker gang or an immortal pirate crew, and it wasn't hard to guess which one. I yanked down my ponytail to let my thick hair fall and shield my face and neck, while doing my best to use the shadows of my friends as a barrier. A grimy shudder slid over my skin. They were here, looking for me just like Milo said they would. And now Milo was warning me. But why? Surely if he could do something so terrible to Serena, he wouldn't be trying so hard to help me. Unless...was this what he wanted redemption from?

My chest tightened as I silently pleaded with fate for an available table so that we could escape their path. With nerves rattling and my jaw clenched, my gaze followed them from the corner of my eye through my curtain of hair. I was grateful for Ty's stout, athletic frame, as he made it easy enough to stay hidden behind his silhouette. But if they came closer, and if they noticed me, there was nowhere to go. I clutched my necklace and tried shifting my body inward towards the ivy-covered wall behind us.

I was mortified when Ty, who by now had caught onto the strange men lurking nearby, threw up his middle finger and shouted, "Can I help you with something, creeps?" Though to my surprise, it proved effective, and the men turned their gazes away.

Peering between a small open gap between Caylin and Liam, I noticed Milo talking to the men again. This time, he almost appeared to be arguing with them, and he was pointing back in the opposite direction. After a brief exchange of words between him and one of the older men, they all directed their attention back the way they had come. Another moment, and they changed their route, heading back that way. A trio of them separated from the group and walked down a neighboring corridor, still lurking with their predatory eyes.

I breathed a sigh of relief, and I felt the warmth of blood returning to my face. As the hostess came to seat us, I noticed my hunger had vanished, replaced by a sickly, weak feeling in my stomach. If Milo wanted to kill me, why did it just seem like he was trying to save me? Maybe Russell was wrong. He never did say he actually *saw* Milo taking Serena. Maybe Bellamy could have had something to do with Serena's death. He seemed like he had something to hide. But Milo? No. I didn't want to believe it.

The rest of the night was a blur. I picked at my food, forcing down a few bites, and participated in the conversations when I had to, but my mind was anywhere but there.

"Well, guys, it's been real but we've gotta get going," Jade suddenly laid her hands down flat on the table. "If you want a ride back to campus, speak now."

"What?" McKenzie objected. "It's not even that late!"

"No, but some of us actually have a job to go to in the morning. I can't afford to be exhausted tomorrow."

"You have a job?" Caylin raised her light brown eyebrows with a smirk. I was just as surprised as she was.

"Don't ask. My dad's making me do it for the 'experience.' You of all people should get that Caylin, considering you're literally only at ISA for the same reason."

Caylin's face turned a shade of hot pink beneath her pale foundation.

"So anyway, if you want a ride back to campus, it's now or never," Jade continued, standing up and picking up her purse without missing a beat.

"Ugh, fine," Caylin groaned.

"I'll ride back, too." Ty suddenly joined in.

McKenzie's jaw dropped dramatically, and her eyes darted to him in shock, as if he'd just spoken in a foreign language.

"Well, I'm not ready to go back yet, okay?" she scoffed. "So just count me out."

"Suit yourself," Jade said smugly, not even looking her way. "Katrina?"

Her voice saying my name felt like a splash of cold water to the face. I glanced at McKenzie, who I knew wasn't going to budge on her position.

"I'll stay with McKenzie," I said. Then I added, "I can't just leave her alone."

"Whatever. Your choice, ladies."

I couldn't help but look at Ty, then at the way Jade's eyes were navigating his features.

The friends all said their goodbyes and then departed back to the car, leaving McKenzie and I standing alone outside the restaurant.

"Well, now what?" I asked, turning to her.

"I don't know. Why don't we see what else there is to do? It's Saturday night. There *has* to be something interesting."

Oh, there's something interesting out there, all right.

I glanced around, making sure there were no pirates on our tail. They couldn't be far if they'd stayed in the city. We began to walk, following the preset paths through the lit streets. A horse carriage plodded by, its thunderous hooves clip-clopping on the cobblestone like some kind of romantic melody.

"Can I ask you something?" I blurted out to the redheaded friend at my side.

"Um, duh?" she teased with a chuckle. I laughed back, but then made sure I sounded serious.

"Don't you notice the way Jade is all over Ty? And he doesn't seem to mind?"

"Yeah," she sighed. "I do. But that's just how guys are. They don't notice when they're being idiots."

"Aren't you worried about him going off with Jade? I mean, he didn't even offer to stay with you. If I hadn't stayed, would he have left you all alone?"

"That's a good question actually." McKenzie tapped her chin with her manicured index finger. "You may have a point."

We turned a corner where the streets were less crowded, and the alleys were a bit darker.

"All I'm saying is...watch out. I'd hate for—"

I sucked in my words, unable to finish my sentence as I noticed movement in the shadows ahead.

"What?" McKenzie asked, looking in the same direction. She hadn't seen the burly man with the skull tattooed on his forehead turn our way. But I had. And my eyes were locked onto him as I answered McKenzie.

"Run."

16

DIRE STRAITS

We swiveled around before I could take my next breath and went sprinting back towards the town. The man didn't hesitate to follow, and I realized he wasn't alone upon glancing back over my shoulder. A couple of the other men from the crew with Milo seemingly appeared from nowhere and flanked his sides. But where was Milo?

The crowds were starting to die down this time of night, but there was still enough sidewalk congestion to create the perfect maze of bodies for us to push through, slowing our pursuers down in their tracks. With my pulse pounding in my ears like the rapid roll of war drums, I forced my stride as far and as fast as it could go. We darted through the streets, crossing to the other side while dodging honking taxis and scooters. The men trailed us with unbelievable speed.

"This way!" I thought fast, swerving into a narrow alleyway that had caught my notice at the last second, barely noticeable wedge between two buildings. The brick walls closed around us like a funnel as we ran further into the shadows. There was only one direction to go. Forward. The pirates were close, and I knew I'd have to do something unexpected if we were to lose them. They would know every inch of these streets. They'd had plenty of centuries to learn them.

There was a wall at the end of the alley, glazed with ivy coiling up and around its edges and over the top of it. We climbed over, tense, and clumsy in our fright. McKenzie didn't quite land on her feet, but I wasted no time yanking her back up by her arm.

"Who are they?" McKenzie panted, her voice shrill with panic as we scrambled.

"I—I don't know. Just some disgusting A-holes." I couldn't tell her the truth. "It doesn't really matter; we just have to get away from them." My ankle throbbed. It had almost healed, but so much running was agitating it. We approached the opposite end of town, horns blaring at us as we charged into another street. For a split second, I considered throwing my necklace to the filthy crew and not looking back, but I reminded myself that it could be my only clue to saving Mom. So, I protectively clutched the pendant at my neck and kept running.

My fear was a current, carrying me away swiftly before I could think. I didn't realize where my feet were carrying me until I caught glimpse of a familiar street name I recognized on the sign at the intersection ahead. Bay Side Relics, the antique shop where I sold my paintings on commission was right around the corner.

Without hesitation, we careened to the right, briefly shielding ourselves from sight as we disappeared behind the building at the corner. I glanced back, making sure our assailants weren't visible as I approached the only place familiar to me. Within seconds, I found myself pulling at the door of the antique shop, desperate to find a way in. McKenzie pounded on the door, peering through the glass at the dimly lit shop inside. It was closed, as I feared.

I knew the pirates must be gaining on us. Any second they would veer around the corner we'd just taken, and they'd have us trapped within reach. There was no way we could make up for the time we'd lost just trying to get inside the shop. "There!" I pointed, careful not to shout too loudly and draw attention. I rushed towards a parked old 70's Bronco. In one quick swift motion, I swung myself up into the open back seats. McKenzie followed, and we ducked down.

The moments waiting in hushed silence felt like an eternity. I could have sworn the sound of my thumping heart was going to give us away. I expected to hear footsteps soon, so when they came in the form of hustling boots on pavement, I wasn't surprised. But I *was* terrified. Then the steps slowed. I buried myself deeper into the floorboards, holding my breath.

The steps slowed, coming to a halt right outside the vehicle, so it sounded. I glanced at McKenzie, who was balled up with her face pressed against the bottom half of the backseat. She watched me with wide, glassy eyes, distress plainly painted on her tensed expression. We waited. And waited. The silence was torment. I tilted my ear up towards the open sky, straining to hear. Finally, someone spoke.

"She ain't here," a man grumbled, his abrasive voice like crumbling cinders.

"Aye. Are we even so sure it was her?" another one, equally as ineloquent replied.

"Had to be," the cinder voice snapped. "Now, let's keep goin' er we'll lose 'em for good. They can't be far."

Relief flooded over me to hear those words. I looked at McKenzie to see if she'd heard, but she didn't seem to have acknowledged it.

Good. Fewer questions.

Just then, a crisp bell jingled from a few yards away. I recognized that jingle as the bell on the door to the antique shop that announced every time someone entered or exited.

"Looking for something? If so, come back tomorrow." A smug voice leaped in, confrontational, and much younger than the others. "Shop's closed."

"We were just on our way. Don't pay us no mind." Cinders spoke in contrast to his words, like he was ready to pounce, but from the shift in his volume, I could tell he was walking away.

As heavy footsteps faded fast into the night, I slowly peeked my head up over the rim of the back door. I didn't see anyone. Ducking back down, I motioned for McKenzie with a thumbs up and gestured above us. We both slowly sat up to see a guy about our age standing in front of the antique store's doors, fidgeting with a full set of clanging keys in the lock.

He turned, walking towards the Bronco, muttering things under his breath the entire time, and looking down. It wasn't until he finally looked up to see the two frazzled girls sitting up in his backseats that he yelped in surprise.

"Get out of my car!" His deep brown eyes burned into us, particularly McKenzie.

My friend held up her hands and attempted to explain.

"We were just hiding! We're sorry, but those men were chasing us!"

I nodded as his gaze jumped back and forth from her to me.

"Really?" He raised an eyebrow.

"I swear it," McKenzie pleaded.

"Okay, well now that they're gone, get out of my car."

"Really?" McKenzie folded her arms. If she was still nervous, she hid it well. "You're not going to offer us a ride? We can't just walk around alone with those creeps on the loose."

"How do you know *I'm* not a creep?" he jeered.

"I don't. But one thing's for certain, you're not very nice. What's your name?"

"It's Noah." He flashed a smile with sarcasm, his white teeth contrasting in the moonlight against his dark skin. He blinked a few times before speaking again. "Look I'm sorry," he sighed. "It's just been a rough day at the shop."

"I'm Katrina. And sounds like we're the perfect trio. We've all had a bad night," I interjected. "McKenzie's right though. Any chance you could give us a ride to Isabel? I'm not so sure walking back is the safest choice right now. It's getting late."

"Yeah, fine," Noah grumbled, just before looking like he'd noticed his hands were empty. "Dang it! I forgot my laptop. Wait here—er actually, I guess you two can come with me. Don't need you attracting any more weirdos out here."

Without protest, we followed him back into the store. The lights were out, except for a few low-light lamps in the store-front window, casting a warm glow in the place. I glanced around casually at the antiques, old furniture, record players, and the variety of artwork placed around the building. My eyes caught on a dusty old portrait, the first in a stack of other frames, leaning against a wall. Immediately I remembered seeing it months ago when I'd brought in my own artwork to sell. But now, something about it held me captive, and I understood why the necklace had seemed so familiar to me when I first saw it. The woman in the portrait, with deep, soulless eyes staring back at me, was undeniably wearing my necklace around the collar of her Victorian-style dress. A chill blew through me like a snow flurry.

"Noah, where is this portrait from? Do you know who it's supposed to be?" I gestured to the painting as he walked up with his retrieved laptop in hand.

"Ahhh, I don't know. I think that whole corner came from a donation from some old asylum building somewhere in Kentucky. Just cleared out the crap and gave it to us. It's been here a while. Nobody wants that stuff."

"I do." I blurted out, compelled by the mention of the asylum. "I'll take it. Right now." McKenzie shot me a quizzical glance. "For one of my art classes," I added, to throw off any suspicion.

Noah groaned. "Look, I don't have time for this. I just want to go home."

"Here," I said, pulling out all the money in my wallet. "Take whatever you want for it."

"The owner hasn't even priced this stuff yet. I dunno..." His face grew flustered. "Look, just take it. We don't even have inventory on it. It won't be missed."

Without hesitating, I scooped up the portrait, thanking him over and over. My gratitude only seemed to annoy him further as he locked up the shop a second time and climbed up into the driver's seat of his Bronco. "Whatever. I'm glad. Just stop being so chatty. I've got a headache."

We rode along in the open backseats, and I stayed quiet, keeping my portrait still as it rattled against the floorboard. With a watchful eye, I did my best to keep my face hidden as I scanned the roads for any further pirate sightings. I was extremely surprised when Noah suddenly spoke to ask about the men who chased us. I let McKenzie do the talking to avoid any further grumpy remarks.

"Any idea what they wanted?" he asked.

"It's not hard to figure out." McKenzie wrinkled her nose. "A gang of men. Two college girls walking alone. Connect the dots."

"Well, we really should call the police," he uttered.

"Oh, look who cares so much now, hmm?" McKenzie teased.

"Those guys were hanging around the store, too. It was my night to lock up and I really don't want a robbery on my shift."

In my head, I couldn't help but find the notion almost comical, despite the seriousness of it all. They had no idea that even a hundred police reports wouldn't do any good against these men. It was useless.

If only you knew...

I was grateful to Noah for the ride back to campus, as my aching feet were throbbing, especially my ankle which up until then had recovered nicely.

As McKenzie and I started to separate to our individual bedrooms for the night, she flashed me a warm smile.

"I know tonight was insane, but before all that, it was nice to have you with us today. I never thought I'd see the day when you'd *ask* to hang out with my friends," she giggled.

"It was nice." I nodded.

Except for the part where we were chased by immortal pirates.

But even then, I was glad for the time I had spent with her. I returned her smile and hugged her. "I'm just glad we are both okay."

Once McKenzie was out of sight and back in her room, I tore the portrait from its frame, desperate to see what clues lay hidden behind it. I almost didn't notice the faded black ink written on the backside of the canvas until I looked a second time.

Martha James Shores - March 22, 1851

From my research, I knew the name. This was my 5th great-grandmother—either the artist or the model. Or perhaps both. Either way, one thing was certain. This necklace had been around for a long, long time.

Every following hour of that night was unsettling as I chased sleep. With every passing shadow, I flinched. I imagined noises. Outside my door, across my room, tapping at my window. For the first time, I felt more afraid of being awake than asleep. And that night I would have almost welcomed a guaranteed nightmare if it just meant I could close my eyes for only a moment. Was I destined to go crazy? Maybe I *should* have a drink. I hadn't tried that. No.

With all hope of sleep lost, I turned on my low-light lamp and crept over to my painting. The ocean beneath the painted starlight needed a nod to the darkness. Something to hint at an ominous presence lurking in the shadows. I smudged some black and charcoal grey into the corners of the indigo waters. A few dabs of purple and blue to create depth. While it dried, I pulled a piece of scratch paper before me and started on something, for me and me only. I traced the rough outline of a ship sinking with my pen, half under the water. On the bottom half, under the water, I dabbed on some orange, white, and pinks to create the reflection of a sunrise, and on the top half, I painted the night sky. Drowning in the depths by day. Rising with the tide by night. Darkness.

17

Make Up the Leeway

I opened my eyes to a bright room basked with morning sunlight. My cheek was pressed to the table, against something damp. I lifted my head, wet paint on my cheek, and looked down at the smeared painting of the ship that was now nothing more than an unrecognizable kaleidoscope of blue and orange. A part of me sank, and a part of me twisted like an out-of-control current. I saw myself in that distorted blob of colors clashing together. What was happening to me? I was just grateful I hadn't fallen asleep on my showcase piece.

Sunday was a day spent out on the South Lawn, finishing my reading in an attempt to chase away my all-consuming thoughts. I relished being outside when I could, because as soon as night came, I shut myself away till morning.

I wanted to call Mom again, to talk to her more about our "curse," but I didn't know what I could ask her that I hadn't already. Besides, she wouldn't be coherent anyway. I wondered if she was aware of our ancestors and their dismally shortened lifespans. And if I told her, would it just make things worse? What motivation would she have if she thought she was guaranteed not to live another year? I needed answers. I needed to do *something*. Until I figured that out, maybe I could at least focus on the other mystery plaguing my conscience. Serena.

That night, I googled Serena's name one more time, to no avail. I don't know why I had hoped for a different outcome, but just like last time, there was nothing of value available on her case. And I had heard nothing back from the lieutenant.

I tried researching mermaids, sirens, and magic, but that only led me to the usual myths and fairytales, none of which had any information on using the scale that I hadn't already thought of. I felt frozen in time, and I loathed it. Not knowing the next step, hindered by some mysterious piece of history that I may never be fully able to unravel.

For the next few days, I was gridlocked. Dad would text me each day with an update on Mom. And every day it was the same. Blacked out, stumbling, or finally sleeping. I waited, sent a follow-up email to the Lieutenant, and waited some more. And I spent each night trying to make sense of the dates and the names of my mom's ancestors after finishing the day's homework.

With each passing day, I felt something threatening was drawing close. My nightmares were still erratic, but when they came, they were stronger than ever. Singing that strange lullaby seemed to help sometimes, but even that was inconsistent, so I never knew for sure what to expect. Nothing terrified me more than the thought of sleeping, though my body constantly ached for it. I was afraid of what could enter both my mind and my room while I slept, so I lay awake each night, waiting for the worst.

Locked in the dorm each night, I kept myself busy with schoolwork and adding every small detail imaginable to my showcase piece. As each uneventful day passed, I almost convinced myself that none of it had ever happened. That the pirate ship, the mermaid curse, Bellamy, Milo, Valdez—that they had all been figments I had hallucinated. But the delicate chain around my neck constantly reminded me otherwise.

Beyond that, though it seemed absurd, I was convinced that someone was watching me in some way. Either that, or I was going off the deep end. Each afternoon when I'd walk back to the dorm from class, a regal white bird with dark wings, much larger than a seagull would glide down overhead alongside me and perch on the wall of the bay. It would stay there until nightfall, when it would finally take flight and fade away into the setting sun. But whether to keep tabs on me, or to protect me was unclear.

The next Wednesday morning, my alarm shook me from my sleep. I had an 8:30 class, and it was my third snooze, leaving me with a mere 15 minutes to get dressed and get out the door. Unbothered by this, I rolled over to snatch my phone and pulled it close as I tucked my nose beneath the covers. With groggy eyes, I checked my email, praying for something from the PD. I nearly squealed with triumph when I saw the Lieutenant's name appear in my inbox. Finally.

Hi Katrina,

Good thing you know McKenzie. These records are public information, but this probably would have taken a lot longer to get to you if you hadn't asked me directly. There are a lot of weird stories around this one, but hopefully this helps. Good luck with your project. -Lt. Burke

Attached to the email was a scanned PDF of the records. My trembling fingers couldn't tap the attachment fast enough to open the document. I knew I needed to get ready for class, but I didn't care. My eyes were glued to the report, skimming the information I already knew, searching desperately for something new. And there I saw it. The name and address of the only witness to the incident. The name of the only person who could tell me what I needed to know—the owner of Vista Laguna Marine Circus—Cynthia Gutierrez.

With the name and address fresh in my head, I quickly googled the street name. It was about a 25-minute drive from Isabel. The thought occurred to me that the address might not even be valid anymore given that this report was written more than thirty years ago. And Cynthia might not even still be alive. But it was the only chance I had to uncover some sliver of the truth.

The numbers at the top of my phone screen demanded my attention as the minutes counted forward. I was already running late. Five minutes until class. But my mind was racing, and I was powerless to slow it down. Though I was normally a stickler for attendance, today it didn't matter. I didn't care, because knowing the truth about the two mysterious pirates vying for my allegiance was of greater importance. All our destinies were at stake.

Deciding to forgo class, I dressed myself with jittery fingers and hurried motions. Slinging my backpack over my shoulder, I shuffled out the door, ignoring the faint pain in my ankle and praying this trip wouldn't be for nothing.

The drive only made my anticipation grow with each passing minute, and each stoplight strengthened my sense of urgency. Turning into the little subdivision, I held my breath, questioning my own mental stability. Was I really doing this? Talking to strangers wasn't my strong point, but I had forgotten that fact up until this point. Was my plan really to just walk up to some random person's door and ask them about a murder case from the eighties?

My clammy grip on the steering wheel tightened as my nerves whirled. The proper robotic GPS voice commanded me to turn right, and I obeyed. This was it. Lucille Street. Now I just needed number 405. Inching the Cherokee past the rows of townhouses, I kept my eyes glued to the mailboxes, all the while fighting a tingle of dread that made my stomach turn.

As luck would have it, a woman was standing outside on the porch of the little yellow townhouse at 405 Lucille Street. The sole spot on the driveway was taken, so I slowly nestled my vehicle along the curb. Closing my eyes and breathing in deep one last time before stepping out of the car, I did my best to make a friendly approach toward the woman watering the hanging plants.

She looked to be in her thirties and tired, her toffee-colored hair dangling in a loose bun. She flashed me an uncertain smile, as if to seem friendly, but it was more like a quick, awkward show of teeth. I could tell she was a bit wary of my approach, so I threw up my hand to gesture a wave.

"Hi, good morning!" I tried to sound as sweet as possible, wishing my voice was as charming as McKenzie's at that moment. "My name is Katrina. I'm looking for Mrs. Cynthia Gutierrez. She used to live here. Do you know her?"

"*I'm* Cynthia." The woman released her hold on the trigger of the water hose nozzle and the shower of water ceased. "How can I help you?" She didn't sound bothered, but she didn't sound nice either. I was a little shocked at her age. How could she have owned a business thirty years ago yet appear to be younger than my mom?

"Well," I braced myself for the lie. "I'm working on a research project for school, and I'd like to ask some questions about the Vista Laguna Marine Circus. You were the owner?"

The woman paused, looking at me as though I had just revealed some kind of secret I shouldn't know about. Lowering the hand holding the hose sprayer, her gaze became solid as she spoke.

"That would be my mother. We share the same name," she uttered, growing serious.

"Is—is she here?" I bit back the surge of discomfort that made me feel guilty for bothering these random strangers.

Cynthia sighed. "She's here, but..." her words trailed away. "She's not exactly in the best shape."

"I'm sorry." I looked down and cleared my throat, which was dry from my nerves. My usual self would have accepted that answer and left, but I couldn't let myself back down that easily, not for this. "Do you think she'd be able to just answer a question or two? It'll only take a minute." I tried my best to sound convincing.

"Her Alzheimer's has been getting worse lately. She isn't going to be able to answer anything."

My heart sank at the mention of the disease. If time had ravaged the one thing I needed from her—her memory—there was next to no hope of me ever finding out the truth of what happened that night.

As Cynthia stared me down coldly, I withered into myself and began to turn away, when a creak of the screen door on the front porch caught my attention. A small, feeble figure crept out, sticking her head out the door.

"What—what is...*Que está pasando?*" A frail elderly woman draped in a pink robe and holding a coffee cup pushed her way through the door onto the porch.

Cynthia flashed me a look of aggravation as she dropped the hose and stepped toward the old woman, taking the mug from her, and attempting to turn her back around.

"It's *nadie*, Ma. Go back inside." I recognized the Spanish word for "no one." Dad hadn't taught me much, but I had picked up enough from the Salsa radio stations he always kept playing in the garage.

The old woman resisted her daughter's redirection and locked her glassy eyes on me. She looked at me as if trying to recognize someone, squinting eyes that were already nearly pressed closed by sagging skin and wrinkles.

"Serena, is that you?" Those wrinkled eyes widened, and a spark of joy ignited on her face, though she stumbled through her words. "I haven't seen you...since Christmas."

"No, Mrs. Gutierrez, my name is Katrina Delmar." I corrected, stepping forward. "But I do know Serena. Or at least—I know about her." The old woman's look of excitement crinkled slowly into one of confusion. Cynthia, still glaring at me, wore a puzzled expression as well.

"Who is Serena?" She asked.

"Don't be silly, *hija*," Mrs. Gutierrez scolded. "You know Serena. Serena *La Reina*. She's.... she's..." The woman paused, taking a deep breath. "...our star performer."

She gestured to me with a trembling hand etched with creases. "Come here, *Reina*."

I walked with a hesitant step up the wooden steps to meet her on the porch. She took my hand, her speech suddenly a bit smoother.

"Oh *Reina*, you need to rehearse for the show tomorrow...The new fins...you saw the fins? Custom..."

"Mrs. Gutierrez," I pulled the humid Florida air into my lungs. "I'm not Serena. But can you tell me about her?"

"Oh, hmmm..." she uttered. "And when did you get here? Who...who are you?" I could tell by the way her eyes wiggled around that she was still terribly confused. It was then that I pulled my phone from its place in the back pocket of my shorts and pointed the newspaper picture of Serena at her.

"I'm Katrina." I reminded her.

"Oh. W—where's Serena?" she sat up, alert, as if looking for the girl.

"I'm sorry to tell you this, but Serena passed away a few years ago." Cynthia tilted her jaw at me with a threatening stare.

Mrs. Gutierrez's hands shook as she took the phone from me. She studied the image for what felt like hours as both Cynthia and I waited for her reaction. I silently prayed I didn't upset her.

The old woman turned around, still holding my phone.

"*Mamá?*" Cynthia put a hand on her mother's hunched shoulder.

We heard a trembling tune emanating from the old woman's lips. It began as a mumble, but then her voice grew until the words were clear. She sang each lyric perfectly, without one stumble or stutter.

Down by the shore
Meet me once more
By the light of the moon
Love me, then leave me
With the dawn rising
Haunt me forevermore

I clutched my necklace instinctively as the song ended. It felt oddly warm in my hand.

"What was that song, Ma?" Cynthia asked, bewildered at her mother's sudden clarity of speech.

"Serena used to sing it. All the time. In fact, she was singing it when—"

"When what?" I didn't mean to jump in, but her words held me captive, and I couldn't allow her to stop there.

She turned to look at me over her shoulder. "When she was taken."

M rs. Gutierrez had invited me in for a cup of Café Bustelo, much to Cynthia's disdain, but she couldn't argue with the feisty little fireball of an old woman. In my mind, she was everything I would have liked to have imagined the grandma I never got to meet would be.

"Now, you remind me so much of her..." Her voice trailed off as she patted my hand from her place across the table. I felt my lips curve into a smile as my gaze roamed the little kitchen. The old cherry red wood of the table contrasted the pastel yellow cabinets and the frilly white curtains in the best way. The smell of baby powder and coffee filled my nostrils.

"Serena sounds like she was loved by a lot of people," I said, blowing on the piping hot drink in my mug.

"Oh, she was!" Mrs. Gutierrez closed her eyes. "She was quite the star. She loved performing. She lit up when she put on those fins. She was more comfortable swimming than walking. We always joked that she was a real mermaid." Suddenly, she put a finger to her cheek. "I think I have some pictures, come to think of it!" She turned to Cynthia. "*Oye, hija.* Get the little photo album from the bookcase. The blue one."

Cynthia shook her head and stood up to do as she was asked. Returning with it, she set it down in front of her mother, who grinned with delight, the pink lipstick cracking across her creased lips. But then it faded as quickly as it had come.

"Why...what is this?"

"You asked for the picture book, Ma."

"I...is the coffee burning? Did you get...the groceries yesterday?"

Cynthia closed her eyes for a moment, sighing.

"Maybe you should go," she said to me once she opened her eyes.

"Don't be rude," Mrs. Gutierrez snapped. "Show me the pictures."

With a defeated groan, Cynthia thumbed through the photos in the booklet until her mother stopped her, making her pause when she saw a small section of pictures from her show.

"*Mira*," she said, pointing, "Oh, look at Serena. Orange...she loves orange. And the gold...braids in her hair..."

I leaned over the table, admiring the photograph. Even though it was a bit fuzzy from age, I could easily make out the image of a beaming girl waving at some spectators who watched her through a glass barrier. Her tail fin was sunset orange flecked with gold, and she wore a matching seashell and starfish bra the color of coral against her delicate brown skin. For a moment it was easy to forget her terrible fate.

"She seemed wonderful," I nodded. "Where was your show exactly?"

The old woman leaned back. "Well, you remember...a place downtown. By the bay, see?" Her finger guided my eyes to the image of a structure with big yellow circus font letters, a blue striped curtain hanging over the entrance. It could have been anywhere in downtown St. Augustine or Constantine, but I supposed that didn't matter.

"Sometimes, Serena would make a special appearance by the ocean near Constantine Beach. They all got such a kick out of it." The old woman thought for a long moment.

"They?" I asked.

"Tourists. Locals. Children...Admirers. They'd leave her notes...send...send her flowers. But there was one she admired back. He'd come to see her in the evenings, and she'd bring him backstage. Sometimes I'd catch them coming back late from a swim in the moonlight. *Un tipo muy* handsome, he was. Black hair, nice face. All that."

My ears perked up at the mention of this special admirer. "So, what happened to her, if you don't mind me asking?"

Suddenly the woman's warm tone became frigid.

"*Bueno*, you have the newspaper clipping right there. It says what happened."

I blinked back the hotness I felt in my face from a twinge of embarrassment.

"Yes, but do you really believe she drowned herself?" I forced out the question.

"I don't know...She drowned herself? Who? No...she wouldn't. Is she here?" she was curt in her response. She glanced around, calling her name. "Serena. *Reina*, where did you go, dear?"

I couldn't shake the feeling that this little old lady knew more. I believed she knew something. If I could just get it out of her. I needed to guide her to another spurt of clarity. And then I recalled Russell, how he said Valdez had threatened him if he told anyone. Maybe it was the same for Mrs. Gutierrez. Digging down deep, I drew some courage to help me press her for more.

"Can you talk about what really happened that night? This night?" I pointed to the newspaper clipping.

Cynthia shot up, nearly tipping her chair over. "Okay, that's enough."

But, to my surprise, Mrs. Gutierrez held out her hand and motioned for her daughter to sit back down.

"I couldn't...I can't prove what happened. No one believed me...No one... no one is going to believe me." Her drooping eyes began shining with wetness, and I could only guess she was trying to hold back tears.

"Serena's father would believe you. He knows she didn't kill herself. He knows the police covered it up because they couldn't piece it together." I paused, and I don't know what kind of bravery came over me to do so, but I gently placed my hand on top of hers from across the table. "And I think you know that, too."

The old woman burst into tears and began sobbing uncontrollably with her head down.

Cynthia cursed under her breath and then stood up again.

"I don't care, girl, you need to leave. Look what you are doing to her! You come in here asking her questions about all this weird stuff, bringing up a past she barely remembers—"

"Oh no, *hija*," Mrs. Gutierrez sniffed, trying to recompose herself. "I remember it well. Too well. But they think I'm *loca*. You think it, too." She paused, looking at her scowling daughter. "But now, maybe here is someone who will listen."

I looked at her, hanging onto her words. Desperation had never manifested so strongly in me before.

Mrs. Gutierrez settled herself in her chair and began to stare into a spot on the floor beside her.

"I was with her that evening," she began, unmoving. "It was right after our show...a Friday. She took her fins out to the pier for a swim on her own. She was learning to free dive in them. I went with her of course, for safety. That tail was so heavy. I really don't know how she swam so well in it..." She paused. "What did I tell you already? I...I'm sorry."

"You said it was Friday night with Serena."

"Oh, yes...I was waiting there on the shore. She had gone under a while ago. I was getting worried. It was too long for her to be under, I thought. But then she finally came up, smiling. I said it was getting late, and we should be going. As I walked back to the van, Serena wanted to stay behind for a minute and watch the waves. Then..."

Her voice trailed off and her eyes began to shine. I nodded to reassure her.

"A man...he attacked us. I have no idea where he came from. It's as if he came from the water itself. And he had a...a sword. A dagger. I remember...But I couldn't get a good look at his face because of his long beard. It was the strangest thing. I thought maybe he was a lost street performer or something, but he had a look of *el diablo* in his eyes. He...he wanted something...from Serena."

I was shaking my foot to keep my nerves from taking over. I suspected she was talking about Valdez. If it was anything like the fearsome look of the man I had seen on the ship, I knew exactly what she meant. She took a breath and then continued.

"I tried to stop him, but he knocked me unconscious. I woke up...for just a minute. I couldn't move, but I saw him taking Serena. And two young men came rushing out of nowhere to stop him."

Bellamy and Milo.

"One of them I knew—her lover. He kept shouting 'She's not what you think!' He...he begged the man to leave her. I didn't recognize the other, but he was about the same age. They tried to pull him from her...but I didn't see what happened after that before I blacked out again. Someone carried me to safety. I woke up in the hospital."

Russell.

Cynthia looked back and forth between me and her mother. By her expression, I could tell she thought we were both unstable. Mrs. Gutierrez wiped a teardrop that was threatening to roll down her wrinkled cheek. "And I couldn't prove any of it. The idea of a murder was thrown out. No evidence."

I searched for the words to respond. Her obvious heartbrokenness was reminiscent of how Russell had shattered right in front of me.

"I'm so sorry you had to experience that. And I'm sorry about Serena. She didn't deserve it." I squeezed her hand and she looked up to meet my gaze. "But there's someone else who needs to know the truth. Serena's father thinks her admirer helped kill her. It might help him find some closure to know that all this time he tried to save her."

Mrs. Gutierrez nodded and pulled the pictures of Serena from her photo album. "Take these pictures to him and tell him what I told you. Tell him who I was. If he still doesn't believe you, you can send him here and I'll tell him...I'll tell him myself."

"Thank you so much, *Señora*," I told her as I took the small collection of photographs from her. "I'm glad to have met you and your daughter. It means a lot to me that you took the time to talk to me."

Cynthia, arms crossed, still looked at me as though I was a nuisance, but I flashed her a genuine smile anyway.

"I hope you got what you needed for your project." She made a quotation mark symbol with her fingers around the word "project."

"I did," I tilted my chin at her. "This was exactly what I was hoping for. And I can't thank you enough."

"Thank you, Katrina," Mrs. Gutierrez interrupted, "because now I don't have to take what really happened to Serena Loveday to my grave."

A wave of relief flooded over me. I was elated at the thought that Russell might finally know what happened, and maybe he could put his hatred for Bellamy and Milo to rest.

As I sauntered down the porch steps, the old woman stuck her head out the front door one last time to wave goodbye. I was so grateful that she had been welcoming, and almost felt a bit sad to leave. When I turned to leave, she spoke out again.

"Who...Who are you, lovely? I don't believe we've met. I must've been up-stairs while you were visiting."

"I'm Katrina. Katrina Delmar. I'm—" I thought up something quickly. "I'm a friend of Serena's." I smiled.

"Oh...*Delmar*. 'Of the sea,' you know?"

"I suppose I'm in the right place, then." I grinned back at her.

"Oh, yes, I believe you are, *nena*. *Dios te bendiga*! And don't forget the groceries!" And with that she disappeared back into the house, closing the door shut. And as I backed away, I couldn't help but look at the little white house on the corner, with its screen door and hanging flower baskets, and think what a secret it was harboring all these years. So far there was one thing I was starting to understand about Constantine—nothing was ever as it seemed.

18

SAILING CLOSE TO THE WIND

I felt a sore spot in my heart as I drove back to campus, still putting together the things I had just heard. Bellamy was the admirer Mrs. Gutierrez spoke of, I suspected. And that meant that he had to watch Serena die after failing to save her. And I had been so awful to him the last time I saw him. I had accused him of murdering the woman he loved.

And Milo—I had assumed he was capable of something so horrific, when quite the opposite was true. He tried to save her. They both had. But why did they seem to hate each other now? And what could Bellamy want with a mermaid scale, if not breaking his own curse? My mind was a hurricane.

Mulling these things over, I knew I needed to see Milo and Bellamy. Not just to set things right, but to see if maybe there was a possibility of breaking their curse any other way. Perhaps Bellamy knew of a way to break it without giving up the scale. If they knew it was the only clue to saving my mom, surely, they'd understand. And maybe it could be their chance to mend whatever was broken between them. I could call on them both tonight and maybe we could all figure out what to do with the scale. So, I took a detour towards the pier.

Midday lunch hour presented a bit of a challenge to do anything discreetly on the beach. Even in November, there were always a few beach goers, usually bundled in a blanket reading a book, or just walking the coastline. But I disregarded their presence and a few wandering eyes as I marched along the pier entrance.

There were rocks below, creating a ledge from which the pier was supported, along with the fishing pier pay-to-enter toll building right behind it. I didn't need to get on the pier, only below it, so I swung a leg over the railing along the rocky ledge and carefully climbed down the rocks to the sand. The waves reached for the beams, coming up just enough to kiss the third one, but couldn't quite reach the second.

I headed to the left side of the beams. Milo had told me to carve the star into the second post. With what, though? I hadn't thought that far ahead in all my eagerness to summon the pirates. My car keys were going to suffice, until all at once I remembered the box cutter knife in my glove box. A little token from Dad that he always said I should have for a seatbelt emergency or whatever other emergencies dads worried about. I climbed back up the rocks and nearly ran back to the Cherokee, parked in the sand just before the beach entrance.

Grabbing the knife, I tucked it in my pocket as I made my way back down the ledge, the warm sun fighting off the nip of the November sea breeze against my skin. It was almost chilly when I stepped into the shade of the pier, and I snuggled my face down into my hoodie, though there wasn't much I could do about my bare legs in the shorts I was wearing. The underside of the pier was a floor of packed sand and foaming bubbles as the beams creaked and groaned under the weight of the boardwalk above. It made the hairs on my neck stand straight up to think this could very well be where Serena stood on the night of her death. I stood in front of the second beam, clicked the blade into place, and began to carve.

The blade grated against the red flakes of rust on the metal post, turning my fingertips orange. I tried my best to shape the star, all eight points, separate from the other various sharpie-written names and doodles on the metal, though there were fewer of those than I expected. I hoped Milo was serious about this, because in the moment I felt a bit foolish. Next, I remembered Bellamy. Where once his attempt at leaving me his "calling card" had angered me, I was grateful for it now. I just hoped he intended to look for it in the same spot.

With one last stroke of the blade, I took a small step back to admire my work. The outlines of a North Star and a double-arrow-struck heart stood out like yellow threads etched into the red barnacles and rust surrounding them. There was no way anyone who knew to look there could miss them. I smiled with a sense of accomplishment.

Walking back to the car, I thought about what Milo had told me about rising with the night tides. I could be there waiting for them, to make sure they each knew I had summoned them both. I tapped my fingers on my phone screen to do a quick search.

Scanning through the tide times listed on a fishing website, I quickly learned that tonight's tide would begin rising just after sunset. I'd be sure to be there, keeping watch. I knew Milo had told me it wasn't safe to be near the water, but considering my run-in with the crewmen back in town a few days earlier, I didn't think I was truly safe anywhere. Besides, he didn't even know where my dorm was, did he? I doubted Bellamy would share that information with him. Surely, with my head start, I would be able to see an approaching pirate ship before any danger could reach me. Though, that hadn't been the case for Serena...

*As long as I'm *on* the pier, not under it...Right?*

I weighed my options, well aware of the danger, and perhaps foolishly, decided to risk it. Besides, I couldn't just have two pirates bursting through the door of my dorm with McKenzie there.

D riving back to ISA, I thought about missing class this morning and wondered if I'd miss anything important. I checked my student email through my phone, and noticed the date, November 18th. The showcase gala was at the end of this week, and I felt a small panic roll over me. All this pirate ghost and family curse nonsense had kept me so busy I had lost track of the days. I desperately needed to work on my painting. It wasn't far from being complete, but I knew it still lacked something. There were a few details I needed to go back over as well now that everything had dried enough to be painted over. I was already missing class, I thought, so it would be wise to at least do something productive.

However, my first mission was to find Russell, to give him the pictures and tell him what really happened to his daughter. I only hoped he would believe me. I wandered around campus, looking in all the usual spots where I often saw him. He wasn't anywhere near the South Lawn that I could see, and I didn't notice his van in any of the parking lots. But I did finally notice a mop and bucket rolled next to the bathrooms in the student center, and that's where I waited.

It was only a matter of minutes before he emerged, lugging a wet floor sign in one hand and a full trash bag in the other. He walked with the same short step he always did, and his benevolent, friendly expression had returned. When I stopped him, the surprise on his face was evident.

I took a step toward him, unsure of how to start the conversation. Luckily, I didn't have to, as his eyes wandered down to my hands, and he immediately recognized the pictures of his daughter in my grasp. No words were exchanged, but I simply held out the photos to him. He took them in silence, still seemingly at loss for words.

"I...I talked to the owner of the show. She was with Serena that night. She was the woman you saved." I started, having to clear my dry throat just to get the words out. "The captain attacked her and took Serena. But Bellamy and Milo were only trying to stop him. Cynthia saw it all."

I waited for him to say something, but he only kept his gaze fixated on the photos now in his hands. He rubbed his thumb along the edges of the top picture. I waited for him to say something. I wondered if I should mention Bellamy and Serena's relationship, but then thought better of it. Something told me he already knew. There was nothing left for me to explain. He only had to decide whether to accept it.

The seconds felt like eternity, but Russell never looked up, and he never spoke. I watched him processing it with such reverence, and I realized there was nothing more to expect.

After moments that dragged on in uncomfortable silence, he looked up at me through eyes glistening with welling tears.

"Thank you," he muttered with a small nod. He turned away slowly to walk off, but stopped to look over his shoulder with three last words. "Please, be careful." The only option I had left was to walk away, too, hoping he had believed the truth.

Within the next few minutes, I was scurrying up the stucco-textured steps to my dorm with a newfound vibrance. All at once, I had hope that maybe things weren't all as foreboding as they seemed. Some strange weight had been lifted off me, and I could only hope that Russell now felt some sort of closure, too.

The dorm was quiet when I entered, and I guessed McKenzie was still in class. With the showcase painting on my mind, I prepared some water and set to work. I thought about the pier, and how it had come to mean something so significant. It was where I—shy Katrina Delmar—could beckon a personal visit from literal ghosts from the past. And that notion seemed unreal to me the more it lingered in my head. I started to question everything all over again. Was any of this even real? Maybe this was all just one very long dream and I just had yet to wake up. I didn't know, but I knew a strange excitement was welling up inside me, knowing I had connected the pieces for now.

I painted the pier. It was easy to incorporate, simply by using dark paint over what was already there, it was merely a silhouette. I considered adding a matching silhouette of a girl, waiting to see what the sea would bring in. But I decided to wait. I wasn't sure of that part yet.

When I finished painting the pier to my satisfaction, I left it to dry. I wondered what to do next to keep myself occupied until evening when I planned to head back to the pier. There was always studying to be done, but my mind was running too wild for that. Instead, I jumped up to grab something to satisfy my rumbling stomach. Cereal, protein bars, bananas, and ramen noodles were about the only things consistently stocked in our kitchenette. Both McKenzie and I were still getting the hang of dorm life and grocery shopping. So, I opted for a protein bar and a banana and then made myself comfortable back in my room.

It wasn't long before the tiredness began to settle in. My eyes became heavy, and a feeling of cozy cradling overtook me. Of course, I never slept well regularly, and I knew I would likely be up most of tonight if I planned to talk to Milo and Bellamy. So, I let the creeping sleep have me, there sprawled out on my stomach across the bed.

Wave after wave gushed down on me, as I fought to swim back up. The salt water burned not only my desperate lungs, but also my skin, as I was bleeding from open wounds, like lash marks along my arms. The water was heavy, like a damp towel covering every inch of me that I could not unravel. As I tried with all my strength to resist the merciless tossing of the ocean, a darkness engulfed my vision. The blue of the ocean around me became black, and an ominous presence loomed overhead. I looked up, my eyes on fire as if someone had rubbed pepper into them. Above my head drifted into view the underside of a wooden ship, shrouding the sea under its shadow wherever it moved.

A single text notification from McKenzie awoke me, making me grateful that I was a light sleeper. I noticed that somehow in my sleep, I had managed to become partially entangled in Milo's blanket, which had been folded at the foot of my bed when I closed my eyes. Trembling and soaked in sweat—or ocean water—I couldn't tell which, I clumsily gripped the phone to read her message. She simply said that she'd be out late, so I shouldn't worry if she didn't come home till the middle of the night.

Perfect.

Despite the frantic feelings I was still trying to suppress from my dream, I sighed with relief at the thought that McKenzie wouldn't be here when I left later. I wouldn't have to come up with an excuse to cover up where I was headed off to when I went to meet Bellamy and Milo. So, I wrote back to her that I would be out quite late as well.

She replied with a kissy face emoji, and I bit my lip, acknowledging the double life I was leading. I envied other students whose greatest worries this time of year might be passing midterms. But for me, I was saddled with hiding from ghost pirates, unraveling mermaid curses and family legends, while keeping it all behind the scenes. And I had no other choice.

I waited at the edge of the pier. It was closed this time of night, but it was no challenge to climb over the gate to the entrance and walk through to the other side. I moved with all the paranoia of someone trying to hide a body, and I couldn't stop checking over my shoulder to make sure no one was watching.

I silently cursed under my breath that I never carried hair ties with me. The ocean wind whipped my hair in all directions as it met the shore. I checked my phone for possibly the tenth time to see that only six minutes had passed. The sun was long gone now. In November, the sunsets came sooner, so I practically had the moonlit pier all to myself as I stared into the distance. I decided that I would paint the girl on the pier after all.

A strange wind blew in, caressing me like frostbite, reminding me of the one I had felt on the island when I saw the pirate ship rising for the first time. I pulled my denim jacket close as I braced against the ghost wind. As if it had blown some sense directly into my head, I started to think this was a bad idea. What was I planning to do? Tell Bellamy and Milo that I was sorry for falsely accusing them of a murder 30 years ago and then ask them to kiss and make up? Would they even come? That wouldn't change the fact that they needed my necklace. And I wasn't about to let that go until I knew how to stop Mom's nightmares. But maybe, just maybe, resolving one problem could lead to the solution to another.

Besides the strange wind, it was a calm night. The waves were docile, and the sky was clear, except for a few light wisps of clouds that dotted the canvas of stars behind them. I looked once more at the time. The ship surely would have risen by now. Would I be able to see it on the water? Did I want to?

After what felt like forever, I noticed a small dark figure along the ocean's foggy horizon. I ducked behind the railing of the pier, my breaths short and tense. It drew nearer, and the rhythmic sound of oars against water trickled to my ears. Suddenly the rowing stopped, and the boat bobbed in the water for a moment by the pier. A panic drew over me and I turned away, afraid that I had just made myself a sitting duck for this alleged pirate crew that was hunting me. The pier was empty, not another person in sight. Nervous and regretting my choice to come there, I quickly told my feet to move faster, and I began to do something in between a run and a walk back towards my parked car across the entrance to the beach.

I just reached the end of the pier, about to hoist myself back over the closed gate and make a break back to the parking lot, but a voice to my left snagged my attention and whisked my fears away.

"I told you not to come to the water at night. Especially not here." Milo called from below. I looked down, and there he was, glowing misty white like an angelic being standing up to his ankles in the water.

"I didn't think you'd come if I didn't." I crossed my arms.

"Why not? Haven't I kept every promise I've made you so far?" He stepped onto a rock that was barely peeking above the water. The glow instantly vanished, and he took his flesh form, his golden tan skin serving as a touch of warmth in this dark seaside scene.

I glanced down.

"Well...yes. Except for last week when some of your crewmates attacked me and my friend."

Milo's eyes darkened and he put a hand to his forehead. "You think I told them to do that? They split up to look for you. I tried to keep them away, but I can't have eyes everywhere. I wish you trusted me a bit more."

"Well, I *was* afraid to trust you. Because I thought you'd done something terrible."

"I've done plenty of terrible things." His jaw tensed. "I'm a pirate."

"I know. But you've been protecting me...I think. Why do that if you're so terrible?"

"I already told you. I've got to earn some redemption for my soul somehow. And right now, you're the only chance I've got." He paused, looking back out at the water. "But many of the crew are starting to doubt me. They're catching on. And that's exactly why you can't be here when the tide is coming in. They will find you. They're getting suspicious. They don't believe that I'm trying to help Bellamy find you, since Bellamy is obviously not helping to keep up the illusion that I'm on his side."

"Hold on. Let me just make sure I understand this. Both Bellamy and you have convinced the crew that you're looking for me? And you're both trying to keep them off the trail, but separately?" I could almost feel my eyes crossing as I tried to make sense of it.

Pirate logic.

"Yes, but I've no doubt Bellamy has taken no issue with filling the crew's heads with suspicions about me to make it easier for him to shift around unnoticed." His voice was weary.

I leaned over the railing of the pier to see him better. From head to toe, he was all swashbuckling pirate once again, his 18th century loose V-neck tunic billowing in the wind. Looking up at me, Milo put a hand on one of the beams below, still standing amongst the rocks as the tide waves beat against them. I couldn't deny the way I found his movements attractive.

I shuddered while he climbed up to the top of the rocks, then faced me from across the railing when he reached the sand. I gasped when I saw his face. A red gash stretched across the side of his cheekbone and his eyes were dull.

"What happened to you?" I asked, touching my hand to my own face.

He ignored my question. His voice softened with his next words, but he still breathed them out in disappointment. "You aren't supposed to wait for me here. I would've come to you."

"I'm sorry, I know." I looked away, chiding myself for blatantly disregarding his instructions. "I was just afraid you wouldn't. It's been so long. I needed to talk to you and Bellamy about something."

"Why would you call Bellamy?" He snapped.

"Because I thought both of you did something horrible, and I realized I was wrong. And I want to know why you two hate each other, because how can I help either of you if I don't know who to believe? I want to help you, but I can't give either of you the scale just yet. There has to be something we can do. Bellamy seems to know a lot about it. I thought maybe if we just spoke to him..." The words spilled out of my mouth without me even having to think about it.

"Well, look around. Do you see him?" Milo held out his hands across him as he gestured to the empty space around us. "It doesn't matter. Bellamy is the only one of us who doesn't want to break the curse, and he's not going to see it any other way."

"Just because he's the only one doesn't mean he's wrong. How am I supposed to know who's right and wrong?"

"Because there is no right or wrong amongst us. There's only regret or revenge. Bellamy only wants the latter."

"Revenge?" I squinted at him. "Against who?"

Milo looked out at the ocean. With only the starlight and faint moon above, I couldn't read his eyes.

I thought he was about to answer me, when suddenly his expression grew somber as he took in a hurried breath.

"Take my hand, quick." His tone carried an urgency that made my blood run cold. He reached forward and held out his hand. I couldn't help but glance out to the horizon to see what made him react in such a way. The silhouette of a ship in the mist was only visible to someone who was looking for it, and it seemed to almost levitate above the water.

Without another word, I understood. The crew was coming.

19

GET UNDERWAY

"Come on, quickly," Milo urged.

I took his hand, and he helped pull me forward as I climbed over the railing. He started to lead me in the direction opposite the parking lot.

"Wait!" I stopped him with my words. "I drove here, let's take my car."

He simply nodded, and we both booked it to the Cherokee in the parking lot behind the pier.

Milo jumped in the passenger side, and before his door even was shut, I peeled out of the lot.

"Where do I go?" I asked.

"Just get away from them. Go inland," he ordered. "They must have followed me. I don't know if they could see you from there, but they're going to be looking."

"How did they get here so fast?" I asked.

"The *Siren's Scorn* can go under any time and rise back up somewhere else. There aren't many limitations on a cursed ship."

"The what?" I raised an eyebrow.

"It's the name of the ship."

"Oh." I nodded. "I guess that makes sense."

I maneuvered the car out of the beach area, driving aimlessly along the coast highway, hoping to get far away.

"If you had just listened to me, this wouldn't be happening." Milo clenched his jaw and shook his head.

"I realize I made a mistake, okay?" I confessed. "But I really didn't think it would be such a big deal."

"Does this not seem like a big deal to you?" Milo whipped his head around to me and tilted his chin, directing my attention to the gash on his face.

"W-what did they do to you?" I shuddered the words out while still trying to focus on the road.

"The captain was so kind as to give me this nice reminder before I set out to search for you, since I lost you the first time. It was supposed to remind me to be more...vigilant."

There was a pause between us for a moment, with only the hum of the road filling the silence.

"Aren't you scared of what he'll do if you keep lying to him?" I asked.

"What can he do to me, exactly? Kill me?" He laughed dryly.

From the corner of my eye, I watched him hesitate before speaking again.

"I told you before. This isn't who I wanted to be. I never asked to be part of this crew. I helped them do terrible things in life, but I've spent the afterlife—or whatever this in-between life is—trying to keep them from doing any more."

"Is that why you tried to save Serena?" I asked, speaking before I thought.

If Milo had a heartbeat, he acted as though it stopped right then.

"How do you know about that?" His voice shook, reminding me of a child in trouble.

"I know her father. He works at my school. He told me to stay away from you and Bellamy."

Milo seemed to be thinking of what to say next. "We didn't kill her. Valdez did."

"I know. That's what I wanted to talk to you both about." I added. "But I'm sure Bellamy hates me now. I called him a murderer the last time I saw him. That was before I knew the truth. I didn't know."

"Bellamy doesn't need your apology." Milo spit the words out like venom.

"Clearly not since he didn't come." I turned onto a narrow road in a tightly knit neighborhood, still having no clue where I was going.

"When did you speak to him, anyway? Did you see him again after the night I took you home?"

"Yes," I replied. "He—he just showed up at my dorm hall."

"He's too brazen." The agitation was obvious in Milo's rising voice. "Did he hurt you?"

"N—no. Don't worry. I didn't give him the necklace. I was too busy accusing him of killing someone."

"I can see that," Milo said curtly, eyeing the jewelry around my neck.

Just then, the low thumping of a helicopter slowly began to grow louder until it was impossible to ignore. It worsened the more I drove, and the wiggle in my steering wheel made me realize it was no helicopter, but a flat tire.

I switched on my hazard lights and pulled to the curb. I didn't recognize this neighborhood, but I knew we couldn't have been too far from the school because it was only a few miles from the bridge crossing over the Matanzas Bay.

"Great." Flustered, I switched off the ignition and leapt out to view the punctured left front tire which was still deflating as I spoke. "You've got to be kidding me."

"Do you have another?" Milo asked.

"You mean a spare?"

He shrugged.

I closed my eyes and compressed my lips, remembering that I was supposed to buy a new spare a month ago, but never did because I needed the money more. My paintings at the antique store weren't doing so well and the money for the tire was my only option—a little secret I had managed to keep from my mechanic father.

"I'm certain the *Siren* has come to shore by now. They'll be looking for you already." Milo uttered.

I crossed my arms and surveyed our surroundings. Here in this little neighborhood, someone was bound to come out at some point if they heard us, and what would they see? A Jeep with a flat tire, being looked over by a frantic 19-year-old and a pirate.

"We have to get out of here, Milo. What if someone sees us?"

Milo turned his head, scanning the neighborhood with an intense focus.

"There." He took off running towards a driveway where a blue 90's Yamaha was leaning against the side of the garage. It wasn't hard to guess what he was thinking.

"You can't just take that!" I tried to be loud enough but was forced to whisper discreetly as I tagged along after him.

But it was too late. He was already astride the bike, hotwiring it with confidence.

"Do you have any better ideas?" He asked. "Right now, we have to go somewhere no one can find us. If they find me, they find you."

He flicked his head towards the back seat. I really couldn't argue with him. He was right and stealing a dirt bike seemed like the least of my problems at the time. So, I hopped on, and before I had barely connected my hands around his waist, he kickstarted the engine, and we were off.

20

A Pirate's Life

The bike zoomed through the streets, weaving in and out of traffic. As people honked at us, I couldn't help but wonder what we must have looked like, a smug pirate and a girl on a motorbike. I felt my face heat up when I caught myself thinking how strangely attractive I found the man in front of me in his rugged state. I used the tight turns and leaning around corners as an excuse to inch myself closer against him, though I would never have admitted to it.

Before I could think too hard about it, the bike veered off the road and into a dark thicket of trees overgrown with Florida moss. The moon above was blacked out from the overhead spread of treetops, with only the headlight of the bike to illuminate what was before us. I clung to Milo for security, with an actual real reason to do so this time, because everything felt so unstable as the bike accelerated over the forest floor, flinging out sand and leaves in our wake.

"Where are we going?" I shouted over the sound of the wind and the engine.

"Somewhere they won't think to look. At least not tonight." He spoke, keeping a solid gaze on the road ahead.

As we continued our off-road adventure, I couldn't help but realize he was taking me back towards the beach, but through some strange, wooded shortcut unknown to me.

I only noticed when we crossed a bridge back over across the river that looked like it hadn't been touched in decades.

"Back towards the beach? I thought you said to stay away from the water!"

"Just trust me!" He called out, glancing back at me out of the corner of his eye for half a second. "They're not on the water anymore. You need to get out of Constantine."

"You told me not to trust a pirate," I argued.

Trust him.

Did I really have another option?

After a few more minutes of peeling through the landscape, the canopy of trees gradually thinned out, and gave way to the light of the full moon. The forest floor turned into sand, and Milo loosened his grip on the throttle. We rode slowly through this shore I didn't recognize. It could have easily been 10 or 20 miles from where we started. I had no idea. But it didn't look like any other beach I'd seen since living in Florida.

There were rock formations along the edges. Not man-made like the ones back at the pier, but true, natural rocky ledges staggered along the coastline. Wild plants carpeted the sand around us, and bits of driftwood and seaweed littered the coast. It looked as though it hadn't been touched in years. Nestled amongst the rocks was a lighthouse from an untold number of years past, riddled with mold and sun faded paint on its outer stone walls. The top of it was partially destroyed, as if blown off by a hurricane, and the remains had crumbled, becoming part of the rocky foundation below.

"Where are we?" I asked over the sound of the waves battering the stones.

Where once the dark ocean before me would have made my blood run cold, now it seemed less threatening, here in this peaceful place.

"This old lighthouse has been here a while," Milo said. "I don't know its name." He switched the bike off, then gestured for me to remove myself from the back seat. I swung my leg around, touching my boots to the stony sand below. I was glad for my choice of skinny jeans and Chelsea boots, because the rocky terrain didn't look welcoming to sandaled feet, and the chill of the night sea air was even more unforgiving out here.

"And you think we'll be safe here?"

"I think they certainly can't get here in time if they're on land, not before low tide, anyway. And Valdez would have a hell of a time getting the *Siren* out here amongst the rocks."

"If you say so," I mumbled. "So, we're just going to wait here all night?"

"Well, the alternative is going back and risking them finding you. We can do that if you want," Milo's voice, though smooth as always, was riddled with sarcasm. He began to hike across the rocks and towards the lighthouse. "Fortunately for you, Bellamy has been trying to throw them off your trail, and they seem to believe him. Valdez has always had a soft spot for him."

"Why is Bellamy doing that for me?" I gingerly followed behind him across the rocks.

"He's not doing it for you. He's doing it for himself."

"Okay, new question. Why do you hate him so much?"

Milo jumped down from a large wide rock with the grace of a cat to a jagged stone below, then turned around to look at me.

"I don't hate him." he cocked his head. "He's just...well, we just...disagree."

"On what?"

He cursed audibly as he ran a hand through his honey locks. "Do you ever stop asking questions?"

"Well, what else should I do?" I put my hands on my hips to express my offense. "Last month, I was just an awkward art student trying not to get another hangover, and now I'm in the middle of nowhere with a 300-year-old pirate, hiding from other pirates. You expect me not to ask questions?"

He held out a hand to me, as I had yet to join him on the rock below. I was a bit intimidated by the drop, and though I was agitated with him in that moment, I accepted his assistance as I took a small jump down.

"I'm sorry," he said, adjusting the loose belt that held his vest to his waist. "It's just that Bellamy doesn't want to end our curse. He wants Valdez to keep suffering for what he did to Serena."

I shivered as a cool blast of salty sea air sprayed a mist from the water below around us. Milo put his back to me and lifted his chin towards the lighthouse, which was now only a few feet before him.

"Let's get out of this wind," he said.

I towed behind, admiring the majesty of the cracked stone and castle-like architecture of the old lighthouse.

"Do you have the lantern thing with you?" He asked as we entered the entrance to the tower. Standing in the doorless threshold, shoulder to shoulder with Milo, I looked up into an eerie void of blackness.

"You mean my cell phone?" My chuckle echoed on the stone walls. I pulled it out and utilized the tiny flashlight feature.

"Aye, that."

"It's creepy in here. Can we go to the top? I bet the view is amazing," I suggested, thinking of all the wondrous ideas that the top of the tower might inspire for my next painting.

"It is." Milo ducked underneath a support for the stairwell above our heads.

"You've been up there before?" I wondered how often he visited this place.

"Many times." He smirked at me as he pushed ahead of me. "You remember what I told you about the stars back on the island?"

I nodded.

"It's the best place to see them." An energy I hadn't hear before rushed to his voice as he spoke. In all this chaos, he genuinely seemed excited at the simple mention of stars.

As we followed the spiral staircase to the top, the darkness grew heavier, and I slowed my steps. The lack of lighting played tricks on my eyes, and I was fearful of missing one of the narrow stone steps and slipping. But I followed eagerly as I thought of the view.

Without any prompting from me, Milo suddenly picked up where he left off talking about Bellamy, almost like he was thinking out loud.

"I understand why Bellamy wants Valdez to suffer forever. Serena loved him." His satin voice echoed through the hollow tower, filling the damp darkness with warmth. "And he must have loved her, to be willing to live under this curse for eternity just to feel that he's avenging her." He shook his head. "But the rest of us shouldn't have to pay for the wrongdoings of Valdez forever. Not if there's a way out. Nothing could make me choose this hell over escaping it."

I was quiet. The air already felt thick with a distinct chill of wetness mixed with the cool of the lighthouse's cement walls, but the pain in Milo's voice made it seem even heavier.

"If you can believe it, before Serena was killed, Bellamy and I were friends. I told him not to spend so much time on the mainland." Milo continued. "But he was more desperate than we were, and he looked everywhere for an answer to our curse. He would also mingle with people throughout the ages, seeking a thrill I suppose, despite my warnings. And sure enough—it backfired when he met her."

The way Milo said "her" sent a tingle down my spine, the way he had managed to portray so much emotion—regret, wonder, and bitterness all in one single syllable.

"What about you? Did you ever love anyone?" I couldn't silence my curiosity and took the risk of asking the question. He was charming and undeniably, ruggedly gorgeous, to be frank. There *had* to have been a lover in his past life.

The darkness began to succumb to the haze of moonlight above, and I knew we were near the top. With one more step up to go, my foot managed to slip and I lost my balance. I reached for something to steady myself on the walls, but there was nothing but flat stone. Just as my heart dropped in my chest as I began to stumble backward down the steps, a steady hand caught me by the arm and pulled me up to the top of the stairway. Milo drew me to him as I steadied myself with my hands on his shoulders. His gaze drilled into mine, and I yearned to stay there in his embrace. He answered my question with a note of broken-heartedness as his eyes softened with sadness.

"No." And he let go.

He turned away from me and stepped towards the edge of the tower. "Nothing more than some short-lived flings with a few tavern wenches." He peppered his words with a weak chuckle, staring out into the ocean. "I never had the chance for love. Valdez forced me onto his crew when I was barely fifteen."

I carefully guided my feet to the edge next to him. The top of the lighthouse tower was in ruins, missing the roof so that only the platform meant for the light remained, with crumbling edges. And so, we stood under an open sky, the stars twinkling above in quantities that surpassed the night on the island.

"How old are you now?" I looked at him, but he kept his gaze on the horizon. "Er, I mean, how old were you when..."

"Twenty-one." He put both hands behind his head in some sort of a stretch, then turned to me.

"I'm sorry that you've had to be part of Valdez's crew so long." It was the weirdest form of sympathy I'd ever tried to offer, but it was genuine. "He sounds like a real ass."

A small, crooked smile lit up Milo's face, causing warmth to pool in my core. I thought of how he'd made me feel seconds before when he stopped my fall. The feeling of his arms around me was electricity, and I longed to feel it again. But it was his own words reverberating in my mind that made me think better of it.

Never trust a pirate.

I'll admit, I never thought I'd have to apply that warning to real life. I made an attempt to change the subject.

"You know, aren't pirates supposed to say things like 'arrrg' and 'shiver me Timbers?'"

Milo arched an eyebrow, looking down at me over his shoulder. "Ummm...no, sorry to disappoint you, but that is just about the most absurd thing I've ever heard." The way he laughed made my heart jump. "Arrrg?" He repeated.

I laughed with him. "Sorry," I covered the grin across my face with my hand. "You can blame the movies."

"Movies?"

I had an idea that I was sure would lighten the mood. "You know what? Let me show you." I moved myself to a section of the platform where the wall of the tower still remained, and sat down crisscross, leaning my back into the wall. Milo followed, but the expression on his face made him appear to be questioning my actions, seemingly more from curiosity than suspicion.

My fingers tap-danced over my phone screen as I navigated to a video website and began to search for iconic scenes from any pirate movie I could think of. Without further explanation, I pointed the screen at Milo, whose green eyes lit up at the amazement of the moving pictures, but then his wonder turned to confusion as he watched Johnny Depp's iconic scene as Captain Jack singing about his jar of dirt.

"This is what you all think pirates were like?" He turned to me and asked, almost as if he was insulted.

I couldn't help but snicker at his bewilderment. "I'm sorry." The snicker turned into a full laugh that I couldn't contain. "But your reaction is priceless."

I was relieved when instead of letting it upset him, he joined me in the laughter and nudged me gently with his elbow. "Well, I'm glad I could offer you some entertainment." He joked.

As our laughter filled the night air, I looked at him, straightening myself against the wall at my back. I was glad for the windbreak it provided.

"Okay, so then what was it like to be a *real* pirate?" I asked. "And did you really hunt mermaids?"

"Well, most pirates were just exploited sailors and naval officers that grew tired of being taken advantage of. I can't say I blamed them, but I never *chose* to be part of it."

"So then how did you end up on Valdez's ship?"

"Well," he drew his knees up to himself and used them as rests for his elbows, "We lived in Nassau. It was set to become a colony, but instead it became overrun with pirates. Taverns and brothels everywhere. Absolute lawlessness. A pirate's paradise, really.

"My father had no choice but to work with the pirates to survive, but I planned to move to Cape Cod to make my own luck once I could afford my own ship." He began to trace a crack in the stone floor with his thumb. "We were merchants, so I spent my whole life sailing. We made a good profit for our black-market deals with the pirates. Unfortunately, my father became mixed up with Valdez, and did a lot of his shipping for him to transport goods into ports that banned pirates. But one day, Valdez asked too much of my father." He looked straight ahead into the darkness of the sky and swallowed.

"What happened?" I urged him to go on.

Milo drew in a heavy breath before speaking again. His voice was beginning to sound dry. "Valdez wanted us to transport a pair of mermaids. He offered my father a lucrative penny for the job, but it was one line my father couldn't cross. He didn't want to be part of the mermaid trade. He refused, and Valdez threatened him, so I jumped in to defend my father. Valdez shot him in front of me, told me to learn from his mistake, and forced me aboard to join his crew. With my father's charts, and my knowledge of the trade routes, I was invaluable to Valdez. I've been the ship's Sailing Master ever since."

I studied his face as he spoke. It might have been a trick of the moonlight, but I thought I noticed a glimmer of a tear forming in the corner of his left eye. So many dreams had been ripped from him. My heart became heavy, and I wished I was better at finding the words to comfort others when they hurt. I knew I had to be crazy for the allure I felt towards him. But his story only pulled me in further.

"I'm so sorry," I whispered. "My mom didn't die, but she left me for a while. In more ways than one. And I know it hurts."

He reached up to scratch his jaw, but it seemed like he was using it as a guise to bite back emotion. "I'm sorry about your mother. I hope she realizes what a great daughter she's been missing out on."

I smiled sadly. "I know it sounds crazy, but I think there's some secret about this necklace that can make her better. It's been in our family for generations, I think. If I can figure out its power or what I'm supposed to do with it, maybe I can help her..."

"I can't fault you for trying. I'd do the same. My mother died when I was young." He uttered. "I wish there was something I could have done to give myself more time with her."

"I'm sorry life's been so harsh to you." I hadn't realized until that moment how close we were. Shoulder-to-shoulder, we leaned into each other, and I was so close that I could see the undersides of his brown eyelashes as his tired gaze drifted over me.

"Harsh? Maybe so. But it's a pirate's life for me," he uttered.

There was a long silence as we sat. The waves rolled like an ethereal song in the distance until I spoke again.

"Did you have to help Valdez capture mermaids?" I pressed, hoping he wouldn't end our conversation on his previous ominous words. Part of me didn't want to know the answer, but I knew I needed to.

"Yes," he blew out a puff of breath from his bottom lip that flipped a lock of hair upwards out of his eye. "Sirens—or mermaids—were thought to be legends. Until they weren't." He turned to me, and half his face became obscured in shadow. "Once it was discovered that their tails could be used for magic, there was almost no price too high for them. The elite. Kings, Royals, Officials. Everyone wanted a piece of the magic."

"Were they really magic, though?"

"I don't know. I mean, mermaids certainly had magic of their own, but if anyone besides them could figure out how to use it, I never did see. The crew would cut off their tails and ship them off to private buyers who believed in it all. But there must have been something real enough about it to keep it going. Some secret amongst the high society, I suppose." He shrugged. "A mermaid out of the water too long acquires legs. It was just the same when losing their tails. Their human form would take its place. So, they could have survived it…if it wasn't for their hearts."

"What about their hearts?"

Milo gave me a grim look. "There was a preposterous rumor that anyone who possessed a mermaid's heart could live forever. So, you can imagine how that legend sent the elites into a frenzy. There was no price too high for a mermaid's heart."

"Is that why Valdez killed Serena? He thought she was a real mermaid?"

Milo nodded. "He thought it was possible. He thought maybe she was the last one left, hiding, living out her days on land. And he doesn't take chances. It just became another one of his failed attempts to break the curse. He thought giving Serena up to the sea could do it. And he cut out her heart thinking he could cheat death while the rest of us met our end. He's all but a madman, now. Reason is lost on him. That's what the years of torment have done to him."

My expression twisted into a look of horror as I thought back to the report of Serena's chest cut open. Instinctively, I put my fingers to my chest, as if to make sure my own heart was still intact.

"I know." He continued, looking down. "Don't think I don't feel remorse for working for Valdez. He owned the monopoly on mermaids because he had Cordelia."

"That's the mermaid who cursed you, right?"

"Yes," he explained. "Valdez manipulated her into believing he loved her. He used her as a pawn to find other mermaids—until the sea had no more to give. That's when Valdez tried to capture her, and she turned on him, realizing her mistake. She cut off her own tail and destroyed it with its own magic. No one could stop her. She destroyed all evidence and records of Valdez's mermaid trade. And with new legs, she cursed us and disappeared into the sea."

I imagined it all playing out in my head. A scorned mermaid sending a storm to pull the souls of those who'd wronged her to the bottom of the sea. It seemed like a fitting reaction. Would it really be right for me to end Valdez's sentence after what he had done? Was it justice for all the mermaids he'd slaughtered? But Milo...there was no way he could be deserving of this eternity of punishment...

"I know you probably think poorly of me," Milo added, interrupting my thoughts. "But just know that I spent many sleepless nights knowing there were captured mermaids on board, treated as nothing more than cargo on their way to meet their end. I thought of every conceivable way to help them. But there was nothing I could do. Eventually I just had to harden myself to it...for survival. But now it weighs heavy on my soul. If I could go back in time, I would challenge Valdez myself, though it undoubtedly would have cost me my life." His eyes became sullen. "At least I would've died without being damned to this eternal fate." I saw his fist clench and his arm muscles tense.

I fought the urge to reach for his hand as I spoke again, but I wanted him to know the genuineness of my words.

"Milo." his name left my lips as a gentle murmur. "I promise that once I figure out what I'm supposed to do with this scale to save my family, I want to set you free. I will do everything I can to break your curse." I chewed on my own words, realizing that I had no idea how long that could take, or even if I *could* break either of our curses. I immediately regretted making such a promise, for fear I wouldn't be able to fulfill it.

"Thank you for your willingness to try," he said, "But you probably shouldn't make promises you can't keep."

"But I can promise I'll try."

"I suppose that's all I can ask of you. Perhaps before, I would've considered disappearing with that necklace by now. But maybe I can wait a little longer."

His eyes snaked down slowly and followed the curve of my neck. I felt his stare settle on my necklace, only for a second, and then it fell even lower, hovering across the rest of my body. I tried, without success, to suppress the wave of warmth that flooded into my cheeks.

"You could take it any time. You could snatch it right off my neck and disappear." My voice was a bit hoarse from the salty night air.

"Don't think I'm not tempted," he whispered, locking his eyes with mine, he reached forward and touched his fingers to the necklace. He held his touch there for only a few seconds, then slid his calloused fingertips over my skin. I tingled at his touch. He traced gently upwards of my neck until he reached my chin and tilted it up to him. I stared into his rugged handsome face, his wind-blown hair and beard scruff softening his strong features. His gaze held mine for a moment.

The tenseness in his forehead eased, and he cupped my cheek in his hand. I froze, but not from fear. I became still, waiting for him, longing for him, to continue, to come closer to me. My heartbeat thrummed in my head. As I sat there entranced by him, he suddenly looked as if he realized he had just remembered something important. He curled his fingers back into his palm and quickly withdrew his hand from my face.

"But I wouldn't." He cleared his throat, as if trying to casually brush off the tender moment that had just happened between us. "I know you have your own curses to break with it first."

Still trying to will my heartbeat to settle down, I dropped my gaze to the floor. Why did he care about what I wanted or needed? Was it really to redeem his soul from the terrible things he had done as a pirate? Or was there a reason beyond that? Because the way he had looked at me just then made me wonder if he yearned for more than just his soul's redemption.

21

TURNING TIDE

A s if the tender moment hadn't just happened between us, I stood to my feet. Leaning over the ravaged ledge of the lighthouse rim, I looked up at the stars. I knew that would be a safe topic to curb the lingering awkwardness.

"Okay, Star Man." I joked. "Are there any other important constellations I should know about?"

Milo joined me at the ledge, about an arm's length away. He began to tell me all about the patterns in the sky. He told me how the stars moved from east to west, and how every sailor worth his salt knew how to watch their movement carefully. I listened carefully as he described the tricks of celestial navigation. The enthusiasm in his already beautiful voice made me smile.

"What?" He stopped pointing at the corner of Ursa Minor and looked at me with bewilderment.

"Nothing." I shook my head, snickering. "It's just that you really light up when you talk about stars. No pun intended."

For once, I seemed to have been the one to have left *him* speechless. He blinked slowly in surprise as the edge of his gaping mouth lifted into a smirk.

"What can I say? It's in my blood. I'll always be a sailor, pirate or not." He threw his hands up in a resigned fashion. "I'm sure there's something you're passionate about as well."

I chewed my bottom lip for a second.

"Painting," I mumbled.

"Okay." He crossed his arms and looked up at me through a rogue strand of dark blonde hair. "Your turn. Tell me all about it."

"Well," I straightened my shoulders, "Watercolor is my favorite. It's kind of... chaotic and peaceful at the same time, if that makes sense. But it can be tricky, because if you make a mistake, it can bleed over into everything else pretty quickly. But I think that's part of the challenge. Trying to keep everything together. Trying to control something as fluid as water. And of course, there are ways to blot out some slip-ups, but you have to know what you're doing." I suddenly realized how much I was talking.

I almost sounded like McKenzie, rambling on about paint. I had never felt so open with anyone before, and I had certainly never spilled out so many facts about watercolors in one sitting. And yet through it all, Milo listened to me as intensely as if listening to directions to buried treasure. "You know, you actually gave me the idea for my art showcase piece."

Milo's eyebrows lifted.

"I did?"

"Yes, after you told me about the North Star on the island. I decided to paint it." I smiled with pride. "I've just got a few finishing touches left to add, but it's almost finished."

171

Suddenly I had a thought that seemed incredibly stupid, but something in that moment made me feel brave enough to say it out loud anyway. "The art showcase is kind of a big deal. I'm really excited about putting my painting in it. But it's part of a gala. I'll have to dress up and everything." I paused. "And...." I couldn't finish the thought.

Milo leaned an elbow along the rim of the ledge, his nodding eyes telling me to continue. Suddenly I couldn't look him in the face as I grasped the reality of what I was trying to ask. I turned around and walked away from the edge towards the center of the platform, where the light would have been if it remained.

"And?" I could feel his eyes on my back.

I turned around slightly, so that I was looking out at the ocean, but not directly at him.

"And...you could see the painting. I could show you if you come." I swallowed uncomfortably, regretting my words.

Milo took a few steps toward me, his leather boots silent on the stone floor.

"Are you implying that I could accompany you?"

I grimaced at my own embarrassment, "Well...only if you want. I mean, that is if I haven't broken your curse by then, or your captain doesn't kill me first." I tried to mask my humiliation with my sarcasm, but it didn't help. All of a sudden, being captured by a pirate crew sounded like the better fate.

"Katrina," Milo inched closer. "Don't think I don't want to. If our circumstances were different. If I wasn't—" He paused. "There are just too many reasons that's not a good idea."

I pressed my lips together nervously.

"Right, I don't know what I was thinking. Sorry."

"No need to apologize," his voice teased my ears like the sweet hum of a nightingale, "but you have to understand, we shouldn't get too close. It could be dangerous for you. And..." he hesitated, "I don't want to confuse you. This has to stay about breaking the curse. Nothing more."

Nothing more.

The phrase hit my heart like a hammer against an anvil. I took that as my answer as to what he wanted from me. Was I crazy to think there was even a remote possibility that a ghost pirate could be my gala date? I truly questioned my sanity for even entertaining the idea. I couldn't blame him for turning it down. Of course, there would be few things on anyone's mind more important than escaping eternal torment. But the way he had looked at me earlier had left me with such lingering confusion.

"Right. You are definitely right." I took the opportunity to change the direction of our conversation. "Anyway, when do you think it will be safe to head back?"

"I'll take you back right before dawn." Milo sat back down on the ground, leaning back on his hands, and tilting his gaze up towards the sky. "So, you might want to make yourself comfortable."

I groaned out a tired sigh.

"This is going to be a long night." I joined him on the floor but left at least a foot between us so as not to create any more confusing circumstances. Neither of us spoke a word, but together we lay there on the cold platform, staring up into the canopy of stars overhead as the sea crashed against our lighthouse.

I didn't even notice that I had fallen asleep. I didn't mean to, but I was so unaware of the time that my tired eyes had decided for me. My dreams hadn't been letting me sleep much lately, except on the nights when they seemed to stay away. My body constantly yearned for rest.

I thrashed violently trying to brace against the waves in my nightmares. My eyes flew open to see Milo kneeling over me, a frantic look on his face as he called out my name.

Catching my breath, I glanced at him, then felt the ground beneath my palms. My skin was frigid, but another nightmare had made my blood run hot.

"I'm so sorry," I said between desperate pants. "Bad dreams."

Trying to shake it off, I scrambled to my feet. "You don't have to say you're sorry," Milo uttered. "I used to have them, too."

"Really?"

"Aye." He nodded. "After Valdez killed my father, and after what I saw them do to the mermaids, I could hardly get a full night's rest." He looked down at his hand that was beginning to become wispy around the edges. "Luckily, now it doesn't matter because we never sleep."

I snorted at his dry humor, but then turned serious.

"You're disappearing." I noted, looking at his arm becoming hazy.

"Dawn will be here soon," he said. "The tide is lowering. We need to get you back."

We hurried down the steps of the lighthouse. Climbing back onto the bike, we zipped back to Constantine. The faint hues of morning hinted at their arrival over the flat Florida horizon, as Milo pushed the bike to its limit.

My mind raced about what I would do when I got back to the dorm. Could I really keep up this dangerous nightly routine for long? I knew I needed to do more to uncover the secrets of my mermaid scale, but I would have to do it soon. Milo couldn't protect me forever. And Mom's fate was likely sealed if I didn't.

He wheeled to a stop behind some bushes near the entrance to ISA. Lifting a finger to his lips, he motioned for me to stay put. I waited as he quietly snuck away and checked around the hedges. Once the coast was clear, he came back for me, and he looked as though the color had been drained from him. I knew it was moments before he'd have to return to the depths with the sunrise.

"I have to get back to the ship," Milo whispered.

"I know," I blinked. "Thank you for helping me tonight. Next time I promise I won't wait at the pier."

"Good." He nodded firmly. "But I'm going to be honest with you, Katrina. I'm not sure how much longer Bellamy and I can keep them from finding you. Especially working separately. Whatever you still need to do, try to do it as fast as you can. They *will* eventually find you."

"I know. I know." I sighed. "Just let me talk to my mom one more time. Maybe there's something I missed the first time. I'll call her tomorrow."

"Fair enough." He smirked, but his eyes held a sense of sadness. I knew he must be dreading the fast-approaching torment that awaited him.

He parted his lips as though he was going to say something more, but then pulled back and simply brushed the light brown scruff on his chin with his knuckles.

"If you can, tell Bellamy I'm sorry for what I said to him." I decided to ask the favor, though I wasn't sure if he would do it.

His brow stiffened and he tipped his chin, as if he was agreeing to do it, but there was obvious reluctance.

"See you tomorrow." Without further explanation, he sped off into the purple mist of morning.

Tomorrow?

My time left for uncovering the scale's power was running short.

22

STEM THE TIDE

I crept into the dorm, and silently closed my bedroom door behind me. The shadows outside were slowly turning to gold as the sun made its appearance. I felt a twinge of sadness as I imagined the ship returning to the clutches of the depths, knowing Milo was being taken down with it.

I also wondered what wrath the captain would unleash on him if Milo continued pretending not to know where I am. I couldn't wait any longer. I realized I was starting to care about Milo, more than I probably should have. And that meant if I could save him from such a fate, I owed it to him to do that.

The morning came and went in a blur. When McKenzie saw me in passing as we both prepared for the day ahead, she couldn't stop teasing me about being out all night. I didn't have the energy to counter it, and I let her think what she wanted. In her mind, I was out making the most of my college experience with a hot, new boyfriend. But things couldn't have been farther from the truth. I was so drained. I couldn't concentrate in class. Even if I had somehow managed to get in a full night of sleep, I doubted I could've focused any better.

How could I think about Comp I when I knew someone, I cared about was enduring unspeakable suffering? I counted the minutes as the day droned on, and before the start of my last class, I wrote out a quick text to Dad.

I need to talk to mom this afternoon. Can you make sure she is around? And as sober as possible?

It was a good half hour before he responded. I knew he was probably busy leaning over an engine bay or standing under a lift, but I couldn't suppress my anticipation. When my phone vibrated, I almost dropped it from trying to pick it up too fast.

I'll try, but I can't promise anything. I've been meaning to call. She's been acting strange lately.

Great. What did that mean? The death dates of my grandmother and great-grandmothers flashed across my mind. I had to figure out how this stupid heirloom around my neck was the key to stopping that, and my time was running out. I needed to talk to her more than ever.

I didn't even wait to get off campus and back to the dorm. After barreling out of class, still within the halls of the school, I pulled out my phone and tapped the icon of Mom's face on the screen. My hands were shaking. I hadn't even thought about what I was going to say, but I refused to end the call without some more clues. There had to be something, *anything*, more.

No answer. I left an urgent voicemail, begging her to call back. Frustrated, I shoved my phone back into my pocket, but then whipped it out one more time to send her a text.

Mom, call me ASAP.

I retreated towards the dorm, with each step hoping the phone would ring, only to be disappointed. All at once, I remembered my car that was still stuck out in the middle of a random neighborhood with a flat tire. Unaware that my roommate was already home, sitting with both fuzzy sock-covered feet propped up on the table doing homework, I burst through the door with a heavy sigh.

"Hey, hey, grumpy Juliet." She winked. "Surprised you're not out with Romeo. What's his name again? Miles?"

"Milo," I uttered. "But no, he's busy till tonight. He, uhhh, he works during the day." Satisfied with my plausible lie, I quickly changed the subject. "Do you think you could give me a ride to my car? I got a flat tire last night and we had to leave the car in the middle of some neighborhood."

McKenzie looked up from the notebook in her lap.

"Sure," she smirked. "And I'll call up Noah to see if he can help."

"Noah? From the antique store?" I wasn't expecting to hear his name again.

"Yeah, he's good with cars. I'm sure a flat tire is no problem for him."

I shook my head. "How...have you been talking to him?"

"Not since the night he gave us a ride home. But I did convince him to give me his number. And look how well that's paying off for us now."

I was secretly glad of something to distract me, but I didn't expect to be seeing our grumpy acquaintance again, at least not until I had to go back and restock some paintings in the store. The minutes were ticking until I saw Milo again and I had no idea what I was going to tell him. I was failing miserably at unlocking the necklace's secrets. Maybe if I could just talk to Bellamy. Maybe he knew something about the necklace's power.

I barely heard anything McKenzie said as she drove me to the neighborhood, because I couldn't calm the ocean of thoughts swirling in my head. I had a bit of a hard time recalling the directions, so it took a few tries to get there, but we eventually found our way. Noah was already there waiting when we arrived, sitting casually in his old Bronco.

"You guys must have really been loaded to not remember where you were going last night." McKenzie teased as we pulled up behind my outdated Cherokee. I shook my head.

"For the last time, it wasn't like that." I held my tongue and instead checked my phone again for what felt like the hundredth time. Still no notifications from Mom.

We hopped out of the convertible while Noah made his way to my Jeep to examine the damage. As we stood waiting, I couldn't help but glance over at the house from where Milo had taken the dirt bike. My gaze hovered over the empty spot where the bike had once rested, and I wondered if the owner had noticed it missing yet. I felt bad, but I also wished they could somehow know their unintentional donation had allowed me to outrun a psycho pirate captain and his crew.

After Noah so kindly patched my tire, it was nearing sunset. I expressed my gratitude and even offered to pay him something, but he refused. He was much friendlier than he seemed the night of the chase.

With nightfall looming, I wondered exactly what Milo had meant by "See you tomorrow," so naturally I was keeping an eye out for any unusual appearances. With the coming of night and the rising tide, he would be back before long. And I hoped he didn't expect me to have figured it all out since I last saw him. Back in my room, I played with the pendant on its chain, feeling the small ridges in the scale with my thumb. Milo would have to understand I needed more time. I hated to disappoint him, but something selfish in me was glad it would mean he was around just a little bit longer, even he was just using me for his afterlife redemption, or whatever he believed he was doing.

I sat down at my canvas, which was lowered and angled horizontally flat so that the water wouldn't run while I painted. I really needed to declare the North Star painting complete, as the gala was in less than 24 hours, but part of me ached to add one more little detail. Reassuring myself that it would dry in plenty of time, I touched my detailer brush to the black paint and carefully formed one last thing. I added the small silhouette of the girl on the pier. I started to add a second figure, but my mind stopped my hand in motion, scolding myself for encouraging the idea.

I couldn't have him, no matter how much my heart wanted to find a way. He would always be, quite literally, a ghost of my desires, close enough to touch but never enough to grasp. And soon even the ghost of him would be gone forever. There was no way around that.

So, I put my brush down and walked away, leaving the painting to dry for the last time before I would take it to the showcase venue in the morning.

Just then, the long-awaited sound of my ringtone jolted me from my solitude. Mom was calling. Finally.

I answered before the third note could even fully play.

"Mom," I gasped. "Thank God. I've been trying to talk to you all day. Why don't you ever answer?"

"Because I *can't*. Don't you see? It's so bad now, Trina."

She was frantic.

"What? Mom." I tried to still her, but her words unnerved me. "Mom, what's so bad?"

"It happened just like this to your grandma, too... I hoped I could be stronger. I thought..."

I could picture her face red from crying and her bloodshot eyes from drinking. She probably hadn't slept in days. That made two of us.

Just then, as I listened to her soft sobs, a strange shadow passed by my window. I quickly closed the curtains, holding the phone pressed to my ear with my shoulder. I heard a strange tap at the window as I turned my back to it.

"Hang on a second, Mom," I whispered as I whipped around to the window. Cautious, my hands shaking, I slowly pulled the curtain back to peek with one eye outside. There, drawn with some type of black coal on the brick arch of the balcony was an 8-pointed star. I looked around for Milo, but I saw no one. I feared it could be a trap. But Milo did say he would see me today.

I began pacing my room, holding the phone in front of my face, trying to decide what to do or say next.

"It's going to be okay, Mom." Suddenly I was ten years old again, calming my mom's nightmares by crawling into bed with her and letting her hug me. Just once, I wished we could speak to each other like a normal parent and child should. Instead of calming her hysteria, I wished I could be telling her about my semester. But even that was anything but normal.

As she cried quietly, I tiptoed to the kitchenette. Through the crack of McKenzie's nearly closed door, I could see that she was lying on her bed, wearing large headphones with her back to the door. Perfect.

I shuffled to the front door and pulled it open just enough to poke my head out. I saw nothing but the flicker of a hallway lamp. I stepped out, cautiously.

Suddenly, a touch on the shoulder from behind startled me. It was Milo. He put a finger to his lips and looked out into the shadows, making me feel as though anyone could be watching us. In silence, I pointed at the phone in my hand. He nodded in understanding, and then I gestured for him to hurry inside.

We quietly returned to my room, where I shut the door behind me. Milo leaned against the wall in the corner as I sat on my bed, holding the phone to my ear.

"Katrina, are you there?" Mom's voice startled me on the other end. She sounded like she had composed herself somewhat, but her voice still wavered.

"Yes, mom, I'm here. Sorry, there was just...I heard a noise outside. But it was just a stray dog."

Milo shot me an offended look. I mouthed the word "sorry" to him, shrugging.

"Mom," I whispered. "How did the necklace stop Grandma's dreams? You said it helped her sometimes, right? Until it didn't?"

"Did...did I say that?" She gasped. "I don't know how. She just wore it a lot, and they seemed to be.... less. Until one day they weren't. And she snapped when they all came back. They came back with a vengeance. I'm so afraid they'll get worse for you, too. Just like hers did. And just like mine. I know I wasn't around a lot, Katrina...but I thought about you...Maybe if I just believed it all and tried using the necklace sooner, maybe it would've worked."

"No, no, it's pointless to blame yourself. We have a whole line of generations who couldn't stop it. What did Grandma know? When she gave you the necklace...before you packed it away, did she tell you *anything* about what she knew?"

With desperation washing over me, I prayed in silence that she could remember something about this damned necklace.

"Hmmm...wait. Yes. She did. I remember. I think."

"What, what was it? What did she say?" The words leapt from my lips.

"Something about a box," she fumbled with the words in between. I couldn't make them out. "Yes, a box...no one has ever been able to get it open...She was trying to open it."

"What does that have to do with the necklace?" I pressed my lips together, confused.

"I don't know…. I just…she said something about a box when she gave me the necklace. Maybe a jewelry box or music box? I don't know. I didn't pay attention. I didn't care then."

"What box? Where?"

"I—I wouldn't even know. Maybe in the attic…I never tried to open it. It's locked." She yawned and sounded agitated all of a sudden when she spoke again. "Anyway, why are you asking? I'm so tired…"

She began humming softly. Before a moment, I recognized it as the lullaby I'd been singing to myself sometimes. And then I remembered it all at once. It was a tune she'd hum so long ago when I was a child, before things became got so bad. I began to hum with her.

Slowly, her voice faded, and it sounded as though she was breathing softly. But her panic had calmed.

"Mom. I'll be seeing you soon. Very soon. I'm coming home the day after tomorrow. Hang on…Please, stay near Dad and try not to think about the dreams. That's all they are. Dreams." I sighed, trying to reassure myself, "Everything will be okay. I promise…."

Milo raised an eyebrow at me. I remembered what he said to me back at the lighthouse about making promises I couldn't keep as I met his skeptical gaze. But I had to console her somehow.

"Goodnight, Katrina. I love you." Her suddenly clear words startled me.

The response became stuck on my lips. They didn't want to leave, but I forced them out despite their salty bitter taste. "I love you too, Mom." I breathed in. The words weighed heavy like lead on my shoulders. They carried so much hurt, so many negative memories, but I was starting to see her failures in a new light. It didn't excuse them, but it made sense. I, too, had wondered if alcohol could curb the dreams, but I had fought the urge to try it because of her. I meant it when I told her I loved her. It just felt so foreign. But it also felt as though I had finally leaped across a bridge I had been trying to find a way across for a long time. "Call me if you need me."

With that, the call was over, and I looked over at Milo, who stood with his arms crossed, watching me.

"Well, my mom doesn't really seem to know anything that can help us. And my grandma, my only hope, has seemingly taken all she knew to the grave with her because my mom just thought it was all some stupid fairytale." I shrugged, briefly touching the pendant at my neck.

Milo uncrossed his arms and took a step toward me.

"You mentioned something about a box when you were speaking to her?"

I looked up at him. "Yeah, she said there's some box that my grandma thought had some connection to the necklace...she didn't really make much sense. And anyway, it needs a key, so..."

As my shoulders hung low, Milo straightened himself, facing me as he spoke with strange enthusiasm in his voice.

"Do you remember how I told you Cordelia destroyed Valdez's records in her anger before throwing herself overboard?" I nodded as he continued. "Valdez kept those records in a box. A box that she had given to him as a gift years before. Maybe she didn't destroy it..." Milo stepped closer and then sat down beside me on the bed, eyes vibrant. "Maybe it could be the same one."

I massaged my temples in disbelief, trying to process it all. It was too far a stretch.

"It can't be, can it? Unless..." I blinked before stopping myself. "But even if it is the same box, she said there's no way to get it open. There is no key."

"Oh, there's a key." Milo rubbed his jaw with his thumb as he spoke, locking his eyes on me. "And I think I know where it is."

23

THROUGH THICK AND THIN

Whether from lack of sleep, information overload, pure disbelief, or a combination of all three, the room was spinning. How could my mom be in possession of Cordelia's box? How could my family be connected to a vengeful mermaid from centuries in the past? There was no way it could be the same box. It had to be a strange coincidence. But what if it wasn't? I had sought answers, and now that I was finally getting some, I wanted to deny them. They were frightening possibilities, and I wasn't sure if I was ready to learn the truth.

"Okay," I swallowed. "Then where is it?"

Milo straightened his shoulders as he held my gaze.

"Valdez keeps it somewhere in his quarters. I'm not exactly sure where, but I know it's in there."

I breathed in. "So, what does that mean? Can we get it?"

Milo pulled his lips together and let his eyes wander away from mine.

"Not we. *I'll* get it."

"That's dangerous."

"It is dangerous...for *you*. *I'm* not letting you go near the ship. It's never left unattended."

I scoffed with frustration.

"Exactly! Which is why you need someone to watch your back! You can't do it alone."

"No, I won't risk it. If you want the key, you'll have to agree to let me find it my way." He spoke with a somber expression that darkened the atmosphere of the already dimly lit room.

I was so focused on him that the soft tap at the door jolted me upright. I scrambled to my feet at the sound of McKenzie's voice on the other side of the door.

"Hey Katrina, do you have the notes from Mrs. Loftemberger's class?"

With wide eyes, I shot a panicked glance at Milo, then at the door.

"Um, no." I tripped over my own tongue. "I mean yes—er, maybe. Which ones exactly?"

I shooed Milo away, motioning for him to crouch behind the bed or hide in my closet or something. He didn't even have time to stand up before McKenzie decided to let herself in. As I watched the doorknob wiggle and turn, my heart dropped into my stomach as I realized I hadn't locked the door.

The instant she had pushed the door open, she stopped mid-step as her eyes lit up like electricity, looking at me first, then at the attractive guy seated on my bed. A light snicker escaped her lips, and she pretended to look down at the floor in feigned embarrassment. Mine however was completely real.

"Oh," she mumbled between giggles. "I didn't know you had company right now."

She turned her head to Milo, her thick red waves bouncing around her face.

"You must be Milo." she grinned.

Milo hesitated, then held up a hand in an awkward wave and tilt of his head.

"That's me," he greeted with a nervous lilt in his voice.

"Oh, gosh, I just love your accent. So hot," McKenzie fawned. "Katrina, I'm seriously a little jelly."

I shifted uncomfortably as my roommate lingered in the doorway. Forcing out a laugh, I went along with it.

"Oh yeah, I totally love it." I felt like I was going to throw up.

"Well, I'm so sorry I interrupted. Give me a heads-up next time, so I don't walk in on anything weird." McKenzie batted her eyelashes and flipped her hair over her shoulder with a laugh. "I'll leave you two lovebirds alone. And I'll make sure to wear my headphones...if you know what I mean." My chest was entangled in knots as wave over wave of awkwardness battered me.

She turned to go, then glanced over her shoulder. "Oh, and don't worry about the notes. You can just text them to me when you're not busy." She winked and then wiggled her eyebrows at me as she sauntered away, closing the door behind her.

I would almost rather McKenzie had discovered he was a pirate than what she was thinking. My cheeks were on fire from embarrassment. The fact that I truly *was* attracted to Milo made it all the worse. The second she was gone, I let out the breath I had been holding and immediately turned away from Milo, clasping both hands over my face in humiliation.

"Your friend is certainly lively," he said, standing up.

"Oh my gosh, I'm so sorry," I groaned. "McKenzie can be a little...unfiltered."

"Sorry?" He laughed, "No, don't be sorry. It was most entertaining. And I liked the compliments well enough." He paused, thinking with a smirk. "Do you really love my accent?"

"Well, I wouldn't say *love*," I said smugly. "Anyway, I'm just glad you weren't looking too historically accurate when she saw you." I shook my head, gesturing at his jeans and loose shirt. "I would've had a tough time explaining boots and a sword." I paused. "Where do you keep all those outfits anyway?"

"Who said anything about keeping them?" He nodded. "What's a pirate to do when he has to blend into the 21st century?"

"Are you saying you steal them?" I stuck my chin out disdainfully and put a hand on my hip.

"'Steal' is such an incriminating word." Milo shrugged. "But honestly, do you think that is the biggest of our worries right now?"

I rolled my eyes, "I guess you're right." I walked to my window, hugging myself as a chill came over me, remembering what we had been talking about before the interruption.

"So, anyway," I started, staring out at the empty corridor on the other side of the glass through the slits in the blinds, "You need my help to get the key."

"No, I don't, Katrina." He remained standing where he was. "Let me do this alone. For you."

I pivoted around to face him, my eyes stinging.

"Again, why? How does this help you?" My voice rose a bit.

Milo seemed taken aback at my abrasiveness. "Katrina, I've told you a thousand times—"

"You've told me you want to redeem yourself. Yeah, yeah. I get that. But this...this seems like more. And I won't let you do this for me. Not alone." I stepped toward him. He was handsome enough as he stood there with a confused expression taking over his face, but it didn't matter in that moment. All I wanted was to make him understand. "This is turning out to be something so much bigger than I realized. It's all starting to seem connected somehow, and I don't know if I'm relieved or terrified. Because of course I want to save my mom...but I want to save you too."

I drew in a big breath of air as Milo looked at me with pained eyes. His silence begged me to continue. "I feel selfish. To know I have the very thing that could end your suffering. I've always been so angry with my mom for hurting the ones she was supposed to care about. And now I'm doing the same thing. But I feel like I have no other choice. How can I save both of you?"

I clenched my eyes shut one last time to keep the frustration from becoming too visible, but one small tear snuck out and glistened there on my cheek. I quickly turned away so Milo wouldn't see. A torrent of emotions rained down on me as I reached up to the clasp on the necklace behind my neck. Then, tears blurring my vision, I tossed it to a corner of my room, where it hit the floor with a thud. "Just take this stupid thing! Ever since I've had it, everything has gone to hell."

Milo turned and walked over to the corner where the necklace lay and reached down to pick it up. Immediately regret rushed in. I had just given the scale to him. It was the only hope I had, and I had just thrown away. He was going to take it and leave.

But he turned around and stepped toward me, the amber glow of the room shifting as he crossed the light of the lamp. He reached forward, without a word. Then he covered my hand with his, dropped the chain into my palm, and curled my fingers back closed around the necklace.

"No. Put it back on." There was the slightest shake of his head as he spoke. "What's a few more days in the depths if it means you have a chance to unravel this and stop your family's curse?"

I was speechless. He just had the perfect opportunity to take the scale and run. I had practically given it to him. And he didn't.

"Katrina," his voice was warmth in the darkness. "I know what it feels like to lose a mother. And I won't stop you from saving yours."

"But...but what if I can't give it up? What if we have to destroy it or something? Like Bellamy wanted. Maybe...maybe that's the way to break the curse." I stuttered.

Milo gritted his teeth, as though the thought was unpleasant. "Do you really want to take that risk before you know for sure? Let's just get the box open first before we do anything rash." He stepped forward and took the necklace from my hand.

I didn't expect it when he reached both hands behind my head, sliding his hands underneath my hair and around my neck with the necklace in hand. He stood at least 6 inches taller than me, so I tilted my head back to look up at him and traced the details of his handsome face with my gaze. I noticed a small scar across his eyebrow, which I found endearing, as he slowly worked to connect the clasp with his fingers.

"This belongs here for now," he said softly, his eyes resting on mine.

I fought every instinct within me to keep from reaching forward and touching him. I was sure he had reconnected the necklace by now, yet his hands still lingered around my neck. He let his fingers skim the back of my neck before caressing my ear as he pulled both hands away.

Left bewildered and hypnotized by his tender touch, I yearned for his hands on my skin again. I loathed the way his eyes, his touch, and his voice stirred my emotions every time he was around. Yet it was one of the most painfully pleasurable experiences ever to weave its way into my heart. There were so many things I wished I had the power to change, but meeting Milo was not one of them. It made about as much sense as a screen door in a submarine—or in this case, a sinking pirate ship. Somehow, he made me feel invincible when I was with him, which was ironic since he was part of the very reason my life had seemingly been capsized from out of the blue.

I ran my gaze over him, still trying to make sense of his intentions as he slowly stepped back and brushed his nose with his thumb, dropping his gaze to the floor. It was difficult to be sure in the soft glow of the room, but I thought I saw his cheeks flush from that rugged sun-kissed gold to a bright red. Was he wrestling with an undeniable attraction as much as I was? Or was he just so starved of human touch for so long that he just kept getting caught up in the moment? He didn't leave me much time to get lost in my thoughts before composing himself and rerouting the conversation back to the key.

"I'll get to the key tomorrow night." He rolled his shoulders as he spoke, as if trying to loosen stiff muscles. "I practically had to beg Valdez to give me another chance before he comes to find you himself. I told him if he could just give me a little bit of time, I would trick you into giving me the necklace. But he's not a patient man."

"Does he know that Bellamy also knows where to find me?"

"Not exactly." Milo paced a bit across my fuzzy gray rug. "For once, Bellamy's scheming ways are proving quite useful. He'd rather die than let Valdez get his hands on the scale, and consequently—you." He shot a quick glance at me through that untamed lock of hair that swept across his face. "He's been doing a rather good job keeping the crew searching the coasts down south about 3 leagues out, so we do have that to our advantage. But it's only a matter of time before Valdez catches on. If it wasn't for the soft spot he has for Bellamy, I'm sure he never would've believed him this long, but he tends to put a lot of trust in his son."

My jaw dropped like an anchor as I repeated his words. "His son? Valdez is Bellamy's father?"

Milo looked at me with a strange smirk. It almost seemed inappropriate. "How did that escape you?"

"Well, you never mentioned it and he certainly didn't tell me!" I exclaimed just as a memory came flooding back to me. I remembered the weird exchange between Bellamy and Russell, when Bellamy had called him a 'friend of his dad's.'"

"Ugh!" I motioned with my open hands, as if gripping the air in aggravation. "He really does like keeping secrets."

Milo nodded. "I tried to tell you."

"Well, he still didn't deserve to be stabbed." I shoved Milo on the shoulder lightly as I passed him to walk over to my painting. I knew it wasn't the time to be thinking about it, but in the back of my head I was thinking ahead about what time I would need to take it to the showcase venue in the morning. But I still managed to keep our discussion going. "I mean after all, his own dad killed his girlfriend. That's pretty terrible."

"I never said it wasn't. I understand Bellamy's anger, but that doesn't mean I'll offer myself up to Davy Jones Locker for him. Not if I can find a way out."

I turned around to face Milo, leaning my backside against my painting table. "When you said you didn't know what Bellamy might do to me for the necklace, did you mean it? Do you think he really would hurt me?"

Milo made a face, tightening his lips like the words were stuck on his tongue. "I honestly don't know. In the moment I just wanted you to trust me. I was desperate." Milo joined me by the table. "But he's desperate, too. Desperate and broken. That can be a dangerous mix. I don't know what he'd do. But I'd rather not let him get near you too long to find out."

"Well," I looked down, "He has been here before. I've seen him in the night sometimes. And he hasn't hurt me."

Milo tensed and clenched his jaw. "He's been here? In your room?"

"Y-yes."

"Why didn't you tell me?"

"I'm telling you now."

"Well, I—I...He shouldn't be coming here. He's lucky they haven't followed him. I would never have come here if I didn't know the crew was miles away tonight. He's put you in danger. He doesn't think things through. And what if he hurt you? I'd—"

"But he didn't." I stopped him before he could finish.

He huffed as though trying to compose himself. His clenched jaw seemed locked into place. I looked back down at my painting, still taped to the surface of the table.

"Is that your painting for the art show?" Milo's change of topic surprised me, but it sounded like a distraction. I stretched out my hand and touched the paper as if to reassure myself one more time that it was completely dried.

"Yes. What do you think?"

Milo leaned over the table and studied the painting for a moment. That stupid snip of hair kept falling in front of his eye, and it made him look as ruggedly attractive as ever. I started to feel self-conscious as his gaze lingered on the artwork, and I wished he would answer my question before I ripped up the tape and yanked it away.

"I think it's..." he looked back up when he finally spoke, catching my gaze and making my heart palpitate, "...beautiful."

I ignored the burning sensation nagging in my chest and replied with a simple "Thanks." As Milo looked back down, he touched the North Star on the paper.

"I've never seen someone able to capture light in a painting so well. And I've seen my fair share of artistries and paintings when we used to ship fineries back and forth."

I smiled proudly.

"I'll take the compliment. Maybe I'll name it after you." I teased.

He chuckled, creating little dimples in his smile that made me melt. "That would be a terrible name."

"Because you're a terrible pirate."

He nudged me playfully. "Perhaps."

"I'm glad you're a terrible pirate." My lips parted into a smile. "Because it makes you a good guy. I never have thanked you for not just taking my necklace and ghosting me—er—-well maybe not so much on the ghosting part."

"Ghosting?"

"It just means disappearing without a trace."

"Oh. Well, if your necklace breaks the curse, I guess you can then consider yourself ghosted."

My smile vanished. Though he was clearly joking, the realization that he would truly be gone if the necklace worked struck me like a kick in the gut. I pushed the thought out of my mind with all the willpower I could summon. It wasn't like I was unaware that helping him would mean letting him finally die like he was meant to 300 years ago. But thinking about it too long stirred a bitterness in my soul as salty as seawater.

"Well," he said, shifting back over to my bed and plopping down. "If your art gala is tomorrow night, that might just work in our favor. I think I've got a plan to get this key."

I ambled over to the bed and sat down beside him, careful to leave a small space between us. I fought the urge to inch closer, instead using all my energy to listen intently to his plan and offer my input as needed. I didn't let him know that I had no intention of letting him go alone.

As we constructed the blueprint for stealing Valdez's key, I couldn't help but notice the way he would steal glances at me when he thought I wasn't looking. And I won't deny I was doing the same to him, secretly wishing we'd met under different circumstances.

Since September, I'd had a roundtrip flight home for Thanksgiving break booked, which would depart the morning after the showcase. That gave Milo no other option but to get the key the same night—tomorrow night. To lower his chances of getting caught, he told me he would wait till just before dawn to sneak on the ship. That way if anything went wrong, the crew wouldn't have long to do anything about it before they were sucked back under to the depths. And if he succeeded, he'd leave the key at the pier for me.

"And you're sure it's in Valdez' quarters?" By the time we had run through the plan more times than I could count, I was leaning against my headboard, hugging a pillow to my stomach with my knees tucked up close to me. Milo had made himself comfortable enough to sit crisscross at the foot of the mattress, facing me.

"It has to be. He always kept it close by, especially when we'd make our cargo exchanges. So, I can't imagine he would've gotten rid of it just because Cordelia took the box. If anything, I imagine he's made sure it's somewhere safe. So, it'll be a challenge to search the cabin quickly without leaving a trace."

"Which is exactly why you should let me help you. I could watch your back while you search. I leaned forward, hoping maybe he'd consider the suggestion.

"No," he said firmly. "If something happens to you, then everything I've done will be for nothing."

I rubbed my eyes and failed to suppress a yawn. "Do you even know where the ship will be? What if they take a detour?"

"It's been anchored in the same place for a while now..."

"Where is that exactly?"

Milo started to tell me, but then caught himself. "You'll have to do better than that if you think you can trick me into telling you where it will be. I won't put you in danger no matter what you say."

I shook my head, and then immediately yawned again.

"You seem tired." Milo placed his elbows on his knees, leaning forward.

"Well, I'm not exactly getting much sleep these days. You've practically made me nocturnal."

Milo adjusted his posture. "I'm sorry. I suppose I forget that you need sleep. I've practically forgotten what sleep feels like." He leaned over to pull on the boots he had kicked off into the floor an hour earlier.

I blinked the sleep from my eyes and sat up. "Are you leaving?"

Milo stopped, looking puzzled by my question.

"It's late." He pointed to the clock with a tip of his head. "You need to get some rest. It's quite a big day for you tomorrow."

As he stood up to leave, a strange fear welled within me. My chest tightened, and it was almost as if I could sense an oncoming nightmare while still awake.

"Wait," I croaked.

The young pirate took a step toward the door before hesitating at the sound of my voice. The way he looked back at me sent a warmth through me that closed around me like a hug.

"What happens if you don't go back to the ship?" I asked, now more alert than I had been in the past hour. "What happens if...if you stay?"

To my surprise, he turned completely away from the door and stood facing my direction. He shifted his jaw in a way that seemed like he was biting his cheek.

"We've all tried that before." He peered at me through a shaggy curtain of golden brown. "It doesn't end well. There's no escaping the sea when she comes to claim us."

I looked down and twisted the sheets between my fingers. Milo walked over without warning and stood over me, casting a looming shadow that made me shudder and blush at the same time.

"Are you asking me to stay?" The subtle hoarseness in his whisper created goosebumps along my skin.

"I just..." The words lodged within me were desperately trying to find their way out. "I don't know. I...I think I'm...scared. Of my dreams. It's stupid, I know. But I'm scared."

Until that moment, I somehow hadn't acknowledged the truth that I was genuinely afraid of going to sleep that night. Somehow, I knew with certainty a bad dream awaited me. Whether it would be the waves pulling me under or the sea tearing Milo from me once and for all, I was afraid of whatever came next.

Milo didn't say anything, but I knew he'd heard me. I looked up at him when he finally spoke.

"You have every right to be afraid." He nestled himself gently beside me and took my hand in his. "But I promised to protect you."

The fear had been replaced with every other emotion all at once. Calmness and chaos both battled for dominance in my heart as Milo's profound eyes rested on me. The welcoming warmth of affection and the bitter chill of apprehension simultaneously twisted in my chest in an unhinged cyclone, dueling for supremacy. Because I couldn't feel just one thing for Milo. He was dangerous, but I had never felt safer than when I was with him. He was dead, but I'd never felt more alive than when he touched me. He was temporary, and yet nothing else had ever felt so permanent.

"But what good is the promise of a pirate?" I asked, the edges of my lips forming a smirk.

"A pirate's word is everything when it involves his treasure," he whispered, leaning closer to me.

Treasure?

My skin tingled with warmth at his words, and I looked down shyly. As I sat analyzing his words, I noticed him looking at the blanket peeking out of my sheets. It was the blanket he gave me, and I knew he recognized it by his tender half-smile.

His gaze returned to mine, and with his opposite hand, he reached up and slid his fingertips across my cheek. I could no longer resist his touch and let myself draw forward into him until our bodies were no more than an inch apart. I reached up to take his hand that was now tenderly tracing my ear.

"Can you feel me?" I asked.

"Almost." he breathed. "And it's enough."

"Enough for what?"

"To make me want you."

Words eluded me. They didn't matter anymore. He had communicated enough to me with his touch alone. My heavy eyelids fluttered as I surrendered to his embrace. He pulled me to him, and I placed both my hands on his chest, feeling the solid, tight muscles beneath his shirt as he breathed. My hand wandered up his shoulders and along his neck, snaking its way up into his thick tresses of dark gold. I tangled my fingers in his hair before sliding my hand back down to rest on his shoulder. I parted my lips as he slowly traced the shape of my mouth with his thumb. With only millimeters between us, his warm breath danced across my skin, igniting a fire in my bones. Closing my eyes, I inhaled his familiar scent of amber, leather, and sea salt. His lips brushed the tip of my nose, and my heart hammered in my chest wildly as he lowered his mouth next to mine

.

Then, as quickly as the fire had been stoked within me, it was doused with the unexpected.

"No, we can't do this." Without warning, he swiftly pulled back right before our lips could make contact. "I'm sorry. I'm so sorry. Please forgive me."

I felt my face turning red and the warmth in me draining.

"I'm sorry?" I put both hands in my lap as if I'd touched something forbidden.

"Yes, I'm sorry." He quickly turned his face away. "I can't keep doing this to you."

"What? No." I shook my head, still a bit dazed and confused from what had just happened. "It's...it's okay."

"No, it's not okay, Katrina." The way he said my name made my still-rushing heart flutter. "I can't deny that I've begun to care for you. And for that reason, I can't hurt you."

I swayed back and forth there and shot him a confused glance. He had finally admitted he cared for me. And now I couldn't have him. Hot tears from exhaustion and disappointment threatened to break through, but I forced them back.

"Whatever is there between us, we have to ignore it, because if you break the curse, I'll be gone. Forever. And if you don't break the curse, I'm still just a ghost of the man I was. You will get hurt no matter how this ends. It just isn't meant to be."

Something sinister gripped my heart. I hadn't entirely thought of the consequences of falling for Milo, but he was right. It would be useless to give in to each other if he was only meant to disappear in the end. Whatever I felt for Milo, I had to be willing to resist, because it wouldn't be fair to either of us. With my heart sinking, I looked at him with a burning gaze. The one person I desired was right in front of me, yet somehow, he was farther than ever. No matter how painful, I'd have to find a way to quell the flame in my heart and lay to rest the insatiable yearning for this forbidden fruit.

"I get it," I muttered, "You're not wrong. But it's just so unfair."

I threw myself against the pile of pillows against my headboard, closing my eyes.

"In another life, I have no doubt you could have been mine, Katrina. But fate has decided against us." Milo crept forward across the bed to where I lied, pulling the blanket up over me and settling himself next to me with his elbow propping up his head. "But that doesn't mean I'll leave you tonight. I said I'd protect you, and that means even from nightmares."

The last thing I remembered was closing my eyes, resting against Milo as he gently twirled a lock of my hair between his fingers.

For the first time in days, my sleep was peaceful.

24

AS THE CROW FLIES

I woke up to the sound of rushing water, as if waves were washing into the room. Blinking quickly, I shot upright, looking around for the source of the sound unsuccessfully. Milo was still at my side, but he was already sitting up and watching me quietly.

"What is that?" I exclaimed with a quiver in my voice.

Milo's grim expression sent ice through my veins.

"Something's wrong." I clung to the sleeve of his shirt. "What's happening?"

"It's time for me to go back." He stared at me with pained eyes as his skin began to take on the frosty white translucence I had seen in Bellamy the night on the beach.

"No," I uttered weakly. "How can it be time already?" I glanced at the clock. It was dawn.

The room was still dark, and the soft haze of twilight lingered outside my window. Though I had known he couldn't escape his inevitable return to the sea, I hadn't expected it to happen like this. I don't know what I expected, but it was certainly not the despairing scene before me.

With shining eyes full of agony, Milo bid me one last goodbye as ghostly waves emerged from seemingly nowhere, wrapping around him like vines. They slowly covered him completely as the deafening sound of the ocean flooded my ears. Within seconds the waves had swirled back into themselves and crashed into an ethereal display of mist. When it all vanished, Milo was gone.

I sat in silence on my bed in disbelief. Reaching forward to touch the spot where he had been, trying to convince myself it had been real. Miraculously, there was no sign of even the slightest dampness despite the water that had just appeared to claim him. Not a trace that any of it had even happened remained. With my heart still battering against my chest, I put a hand over it. Instinctually, I reached up to check for the necklace. Knowing it was still there calmed me and made me feel that Milo was somehow still there.

But then I remembered the anguish I had seen in his eyes, and it forced me to acknowledge that he was doomed to another cycle of torment. I could only imagine the merciless sea dragging his soul down to the darkness. Sorrow drowned my heart as I thought of him and his fate. And I knew that I now had a reason more than ever to end this. I had to break the curse. I had to let him finally die to save him. But did that mean letting my mom take his place? I couldn't choose. This wasn't a choice I wanted to think about. There had to be a way. Maybe the box was the key.

It was impossible to return to sleep after that. It was almost morning anyway. I put my bare feet on the floor and slowly stood up. Walking over to my painting, I stared down at it in the darkness. The showcase was tonight, but did it even matter anymore? I hadn't even planned for what I would wear to the gala, and with the worries about my mom growing, everything with Milo, and the plot to get the key that same night, attending the showcase gala felt like the last thing I needed to be concerned about.

As the orange light of dawn started to roll in through my window, a chime alerted me on my phone. I huffed a half-hearted laugh as I read the text from Dad.

Happy Showcase Day! Good luck Trina... Can't wait to see you soon. Mom says hi, too.

I knew he was probably already up in his grease-stained coveralls with his tumbler of piping coffee in hand, heading out to the shop. At least one thing was still the same. I didn't have the heart to tell him I was considering backing out of the showcase, so I simply replied with a heart emoji.

I realized I'd probably need a coffee, too, if I was going to survive this day, so I wearily trudged into the kitchenette and brewed a cup. As I sat at the table with my head in my hands, staring down into the beige beverage in my mug, I couldn't stop thinking of both Milo and, to my surprise, Bellamy. I didn't know what I would do if I couldn't end their curse. I knew there was no chance I was going to walk away from any of this without some type of hurt, but it was more painful to think I might not be able to stop theirs.

I was so focused on my thoughts, I sat swirling creamer around into my coffee without ever even taking a drink. The sun had risen, filling the room with white light, and I hadn't even noticed.

McKenzie's dramatic yawn pulled me from my state of reflection.

"Hey." I let the word fall out of my mouth with minimal effort.

"Good morning, sunshine." She ruffled her orange mess of hair and yawned again. "Did your man stay the night?"

"Sort of," I uttered. "He left pretty early."

"Uh oh. Everything's okay I hope?" She pulled out a chair next to me at the table and took a seat.

"Yeah." I smiled weakly. "Everything's definitely okay."

We small-talked for a few moments more, but not about anything worth remembering. Finally, McKenzie looked down at her phone when her calendar app sang out a notification.

"Oh my gosh! I almost forgot. Today is the showcase, right?"

"Yeah." I took a breath. "But I think I'm gonna back out. I'm just not ready."

"What?" She nearly knocked the chair over trying to stand up. "Don't be a slacker like me. You've been working on that painting for too long not to put it in the showcase."

"I know, I know. But I've just got so much to think about. My mom's been weird lately, and I'm kind of worried about her. I have to leave in the morning for a flight back to Arkansas, which is probably for the best. I need to see her. Besides, I don't even have anything to wear."

"Oh, well I'm sorry about your mom, but not showing off your amazing work isn't going to fix her." McKenzie, now standing, pulled me up from my seat by linking my arm with hers. "And pshhhh! Don't worry about not having anything to wear. Do you know me at all?"

She practically dragged me to her room, and I stumbled trying to keep up with her.

"Stand here. We are pretty much the same size. Remember Halloween? That angel costume fit you like a glove."

I silently shuddered at the memory of the Halloween party. The event that marked the beginning of this wild saga I had been secretly living each night, and it was still as clear in my memory as when it happened.

"Okay," I agreed, curious to see what McKenzie was getting at. She was rummaging through her closet with the eyes of a hawk, whipping her analytic gaze over each piece of clothing as she slid them along the rack.

"I think I may have the perfect thing. I bought it for a debutante ball at the country club last year, but I ended up wearing something else. It just didn't quite feel right on me. I think you'll like it."

My eyes lit up at the gown my roommate pulled from her closet and held up before me. I was no fashionista, but I could certainly recognize a high-end dress when I saw one.

The sleek sterling evening gown glittered like the night stars as she flipped it back and forth in her hands. I was yearning to try it on, to my own surprise. I had never seen such a gorgeous thing.

"Let's see it!" She tossed the dress towards me like it was a T-shirt, hanger, and all.

I handled it as delicately as possible, admiring the extravagant diamond beading covering nearly every inch of fabric that dazzled in even the faintest light. I pulled the garment from the hanger and quickly stripped down to my underwear. McKenzie wandered over to help me pull the gown up over myself and zip up the back. Then she stepped back and grabbed my arms, positioning me in front of her full-length mirror.

My mouth hung open at the sight. The dress enhanced every gentle curve I possessed, hugging my figure all the way down to my thighs, where it then gently blossomed out into a cascade of glittering silver fabric that brushed the floor like a waterfall. It reminded me of the ocean in moonlight.

"You're a queen." McKenzie grinned.

I turned to her, speechless.

"Don't you dare say you're not going. No excuses now! Milo's not going to be able to keep his hands off you when he sees you in this."

"Oh." My excitement was suddenly dampened at the reminder that Milo wouldn't be there. "He's not coming."

"What?" McKenzie's aqua eyes flashed. "Douchebag alert. He stays the night and then can't even go to your art gala?"

"No, it's not that," I mumbled. "He just can't make it. It's a...family thing."

McKenzie raised an eyebrow, and I knew she wasn't buying it. Crossing her arms, she just said "I'm not going to tell you what to do, but watch out. You were worried about that Bellamy guy just wanting to get in your pants, but I think it might be Milo you need to be careful with. Just sayin'."

I knew McKenzie had no idea what was really going on, but I still felt a pang when she talked so negatively about Milo. And as if my mind wasn't already a swirling whirlpool of confusion already, she only added to it with her statements. She had made her way over to her dresser mirror and was carefully applying mascara as she spoke. "Whatever happened to Bellamy anyway?"

"That's a good question." I winced, twisting my arm to reach the zipper behind my own back. "I said something to him that I shouldn't have, and I haven't seen him since."

"Aw, that sucks," McKenzie made a little pout as she tucked her mascara wand back into her makeup bag.

"Yeah. Guys. What are you gonna do?"

Pirates. What are you gonna do?

"Well, you know I would totally be your date if I didn't have to head back home tonight. Surfside is almost a 5 hour drive."

"I know. Don't worry. I'm a big girl. I can handle it on my own." I brushed my hair aside and chuckled as I wiggled back into my jeans and T-shirt.

"Katrina, if you don't go, I'm going to hold it over you for the rest of our lives. And I want at least one picture as proof."

McKenzie was raking at the desire deep within me to go, and I could feel myself giving in for real. I truly did want to go, but it just felt so unimportant compared to everything else going on behind the scenes.

"Okay, okay! You've convinced me. But that means I need to leave yesterday to get the painting set up."

Hustling back to my room, I peeled the tape off the edges and carefully placed the paper into a leather case. I dashed out the door and down to the Cherokee, checking the tires out of paranoia. I could have walked there just as easily, but I had no time to lose. Gala submissions were supposed to be ready and on display by 10 AM. It was 9:40.

On the way to the venue, my stomach did flips, and the road seemed to rise and fall like waves. I felt guilty for being here when Mom was back home falling apart, and Milo was about to risk his skin for me. But McKenzie was right. What could I do about any of that right now?

I turned the wheel toward Valencia Grand Hall. This particular building of the school had once been a hotel for the elite in decades past, and it was now open to the public as a tourist attraction when it wasn't being used to host the school's extravagant events or being rented out for high-end weddings.

I didn't have many reasons to venture to this area of the campus often, so it was an entirely new world for me as I hurried across the gleaming cobblestone pathway, around the elaborate marble fountain and up the clean white steps into the ballroom. As I entered the building, still catching my breath, my eyes took in the sight of people scurrying to and fro, ensuring the finishing touches were in place as they prepared for the evening. I walked up to the rectangular table in the corner where a lady with a perm piled high on her head and thin lips sat with a pile of papers and a sign that read "Artist Check-In."

"Hi, I'm Katrina Delmar," I stepped up to the table, scanning the papers for my name.

"You just about missed your chance, hun." Though she looked a bit like she had just tasted something sour, her extreme southern drawl sweetened her face.

"I know. I'm sorry for being late."

"Well, you're only *almost* late. And that still counts," she shuffled some papers around as I scribble my signature on a line on the page. "Looks like you got spot #24."

"Where is that exactly?"

The lady pointed with her pen to the hallway next to her.

"Right through those double doors on the left. That's where the artwork displays and the silent auction will be."

I nodded and followed her directions. Painting in hand, I pushed through the lane wooden doors to find a wide-open room carpeted in scarlet and gold, with art displays lined up along the wall and a few placed throughout the rest of the room museum-style. It didn't take me long to find my empty spot, as most of the other displays were already filled. I pulled out my painting and placed it in the glass frame that sat on a pedestal near the end of the room.

My soul swelled with pride as I stepped back to admire the little painting that had started out so simply and yet had come to mean so much to me. I was glad that I had been able to show it to Milo the night before, but I silently wished that he could be there to see it underneath the shining display lights in this grand place. But I knew it'd be best to stop wishing for such impossible things to avoid disappointment. The goal here was to show off my artwork, nothing more. I reminded myself that this was why I came to Florida in the first place—to find new beginnings and start my art career, not fall in love with a pirate.

25

ROGUE WAVE

I returned to my dorm to get ready for the evening. McKenzie insisted on helping with my hair and makeup before she left for home, however I called dibs on the eyeshadow. My painting skills transferred over quite easily when it came to blending colors into my sun kissed olive skin.

With a careful hand, I worked the brush over my eyelids to create a natural shadow that enhanced my dark eyes, with just the faintest touch of shimmer to match the dress. I watched my reflection, hardly recognizing the elegant girl in the mirror. My hair cascaded down my back in a frenzy of loose coils pinned half-up by an ornate twist in the middle. And of course, the look wouldn't have been complete without the silvery mermaid scale hanging around my neck. Ironically, it looked almost as if it was made for the sparkling ensemble.

"Ugghhh, I am seriously considering just driving home tomorrow so I can go with you tonight." McKenzie squealed, doing an excited little sorority squat. "You look gorgeous."

I reassured her one last time that I would be fine attending alone. I didn't plan to stay long anyway. I would simply show up, stand in front of my painting for the start of the showcase long enough for the silent auction to get rolling, and then I'd leave to get myself mentally prepared for the heist on the pirate ship later.

"Thanks for being my fairy godmother." I smiled sweetly at McKenzie as we said our goodbyes. Hugging her, I truly hoped that the next time I saw her my world would be less complicated and I wouldn't have to feel like I was hiding half of myself from her.

"You know I've always got you, boo." She was teasing, but there was sincerity in her voice. She really was a wonderful friend, and right then I realized how profoundly grateful I was for her. No matter how things turned out, I felt encouraged knowing at least my sweet, bubbly roommate would still be part of the deal.

The last thing she did before walking out the door was whip out that vintage Polaroid camera, press her cheek against mine, and snap a picture of our grinning faces. She handed me the printout and all I could think about was Bellamy and how he had held the picture of me on our "date." I had so much to blame on that stupid little camera.

The minutes crept near to six-thirty. In the late autumn, night came early, so the golden glow of sunset was already fading to midnight blue when I arrived at the showcase. I slid out of the driver's seat, my dress slinking across the floorboards behind me. There was no way I intended to walk the four blocks from East Side to the Grand Hall in the heels strapped to my feet. I'd brought a change of clothes, because I didn't know how long I could survive in them.

Mostly juniors and seniors, the other artists were arriving in similar fashion in their exquisite gowns and pricey suits. Though I looked the part easily enough for tonight, I was not one of them. As I watched the Porsches and BMWs rolling in, I felt a twinge of embarrassment at my beat-up old Jeep with a patched-up tire. It was moments like this that reminded me just how life-altering one scholarship had been.

Scurrying past other guests, I made it my mission to simply get to my artwork quickly and take a picture for Dad. The fountain from earlier now served as the centerpiece of the entrance with gold lights strung above, hanging in drapes like curtains of fireflies. I lifted my dress to walk up the stairs, careful not to bump into any of the other gala attendees.

When I entered the ballroom, my jaw dropped at the glamour before me. I stopped with wide eyes as I shifted in my stiletto heels to keep from slipping on the polished floor. The area that had merely been a half-decorated venue this morning was now transformed into a fairytale setting. The shiny floor reflected the glistening lights of the massive chandelier overhead. Sophisticated archways lined the walls alternating between strong white columns of marble. A gentle melody of violins teased my ears over the chatter of the room. The hotel's history was manifested in this elegant display like nothing else I'd seen, and I could have believed for a moment that I had stepped back into the 19th century.

I weaved through the guests as delicately as possible, making my way to the silent auction room down the hall. When I got there, the bid sheet next to my piece already had a couple of offers, but I didn't even look at them. Thirty percent of the winning bid would go to the school, and the artist would pocket the rest. but I assumed my offers would be too low this early to really make a difference, so I didn't even bother looking. It was really the least of my worries.

As I stood by my work, sending a picture to Dad of the watercolor on canvas, people would stop and ask if I was the artist, or if I could explain the technique I used on the starlight across the water, or how long it had taken me to paint.

One stunningly beautiful woman who looked like a middle-aged millionaire stopped and lingered for a while, running her piercing eyes over the painting what seemed like a hundred times. Her thick hair was raven black, pinned up elegantly atop her head. She glittered with jewels and her silk blue dress rippled like liquid as she walked, reminding me of the sea. She finally spoke, introducing herself as the owner of a wealthy beach club and marina.

"I'd love to have such a piece in one of my resorts," she said, her delicate, lofty tone reminding me of the dramatic way 1940s movie stars used to speak.

"Thank you. I'm flattered. Of course, you can bid on it at the auction if you'd like." I smiled.

"Of course."

She studied the painting once more, and finally asked me where I had found the inspiration for such a piece. I hadn't prepared an answer, but I did my best to explain that I had met a friend who explained the stars to me in a way I couldn't forget, and I wanted to remember him through the painting.

If only it was truly that simple. If only I could somehow put into words the way the North Star in the painting represented the guiding light I longed for, and that one peaceful night where all my cares had drifted away under the stars with Milo. The lighthouse was a symbol of hope when everything seemed darkest, and the girl on the pier was the lonely figure watching it all, praying that star and lighthouse would be enough to keep her from going under as the night tide closed in around her.

The woman simply nodded and moved on, moving like liquid into the crowd. I felt myself blush with embarrassment. I probably sounded like a complete idiot trying to explain it to her. And it left a bad taste on my tongue. My conscious no longer felt at ease being there. My stomach turned and I wanted to escape, knowing there were much more important things to be dealing with right now. Being there, especially alone, just felt wrong.

I decided to leave the auction room to get one last glimpse of the ballroom before leaving for the night. All the glittering enchantment around me couldn't mask the troubles drowning me inside as I stood there alone. With one last glance at my painting, I made my way back to the ballroom.

Pushing through the throng of people, I headed for the door, but stopped still when I heard a familiar voice say my name from behind. A sensation of ice water trickled in my chest before I found the courage to look back. And that's when I fully turned around to see him standing there amongst the sparkling crowd—Bellamy.

26

TO THE BITTER END

He took a step toward me. Everything around me froze. I wondered if I had passed him earlier. But there was no way. How could I have missed him if that was so? He was devastatingly handsome in the dark suit he wore, holding the jacket over his shoulder in a casual fashion.

He held his ice blue eyes on me, walking towards me like a prowling panther. I fumbled for words. I never had the chance to apologize for accusing him of killing Serena, and I didn't know how deeply I had wounded him. Why on earth was he here?

I watched his gaze drop from mine to my neck. Quickly, I reached up to cover my necklace. Surely, he wouldn't try to take it in a place like this, not with all these people. As he approached me, I tilted my head upward to meet his eyes, the top of my head reaching just above his chin.

"Don't worry," his voice smoothed over me as he took the hand that covered my necklace in his. "I'm not here for that this time."

"Then what are you here for?" I asked.

"You."

I could barely hear his soft whisper over the melody of violins. He reached for my other hand with a gentle motion and guided me towards him.

"I'm a terrible dancer." I bit my lip, turning my head away. I couldn't look him in the eyes any longer. I was too bothered by what I had last said to him.

"And a terrible judge of character."

My gaze dropped to the floor.

"I'm sorry," I said "I had no idea. What happened to you was..."

"I can't really blame you for being suspicious. After all, only a fool trusts a pirate." He smirked with a wink.

Before I could gather a response, my footsteps were following his along the dance floor, slowly stepping in time with the music.

"You're not so bad," he chuckled, glancing down between us.

"I'm just following your lead."

"Good." His eyes darkened. "Where else would you follow me?"

I took a breath and felt a shiver across my bare shoulders as I felt him trying to get inside my head. "What are you saying?"

He leaned in and lowered his voice as we swayed in rhythm. "You seemed to have let Milo really corrupt that pretty head of yours. I can see he's got you eating from the palm of his hand. Sneaking onto the ship? He's going to get you killed. If it wasn't for me, I have no doubt they would've found you by now. I'm the one protecting you, not him."

"How do you know about that?" I snapped back, still keeping my voice low. "And why do you care what happens to me?"

"Because I may need you in more ways than one." He moved his hand from my back to the curve of my waist.

He was intoxicating. And it was maddeningly confusing. His scent of sweet rum and salty air filled my nostrils, and his touch made my muscles tense. Something about him always made me feel like a trapped mouse being taunted by a cat. But I couldn't bring myself to pull away.

"What does that mean? What do you want then?"

"I want you to realize that there are other options besides following Milo blindly. The scale *is* magic, and if you—if we—can figure out how to release that power, together we could become unstoppable. You can't let it anywhere near Valdez."

It was difficult to determine if he was serious, or if he was just grasping at straws to convince me not to break the curse.

"I'm not interested in world domination. But I want to stop the nightmares plaguing my mom and me. So, if you know how to use the scale, by all means, tell me. My family has been trying to figure it out for decades." I scowled. "Milo said he's never actually seen anyone figure out how to use mermaid magic except mermaids themselves."

"Exactly," Bellamy uttered.

"Exactly?" I repeated.

"Think about it, Katrina. Why would you have the scale? Why would this all be happening to you? Unless...What if..." he looked around the room as if to make sure no one could hear, then leaned in close enough that I could feel his breath on my ear, "...you're a siren?"

I tossed my head back and laughed at the absurdity of what I had just heard.

"I think I would have noticed by now if I was a mermaid. I've been alive nineteen years now and I haven't grown a tail so I think we can rule that one out."

I could hardly even believe the words coming out of my mouth. Trying to argue that I wasn't a mermaid was just one thing I never thought I'd have to say.

"But just imagine for a moment if you *were*. You could help your mom. And yourself. How could you turn away the chance to avenge who you are? Your own kind? After what my father did to them. Think about it. He exterminated them, one by one. And with that scale, you hold the last remnant of siren magic left. You can't just waste it by throwing it into the sea to let Valdez off the hook." Our dancing had slowed, but we still played the part, swaying and spinning across the dance floor.

"I'm not letting anyone off the hook," I shook my head. "Your father sounds truly awful. And he's been punished for it for 300 years now. Isn't that enough? He'll meet his justice in death. He *has* to die. Don't you think it's time? What he did to Serena...he'll never be able to do it again to anyone else if the curse is broken."

A shadow of sadness fell across Bellamy's eyes. I stopped our dance and held his gaze, losing myself in the ocean of his cerulean eyes. "Bellamy, you could finally be free from this heartache. If I can break the curse, you won't suffer anymore. You and your crew can finally rest."

"Will I?" His voice cracked. "I can't imagine what awaits a pirate after death, but it can't be anything good. Why do you think Milo wants to save you so much? You're just his second chance to make up for the barbaric lives we lived aboard the *Siren*. Every pirate knows his true place is in hell."

"You're already in hell. I can see it in your eyes. You're miserable, and you are willing to be miserable just to see your father suffer. Do you really want to be trapped this way forever?"

"I want Valdez to suffer forever. And this is the only way I can ensure that." Bellamy brushed my hair behind my ear with a gentle finger. We had resumed our dance, and the upbeat tune from the orchestra clashed with the grim topic we were discussing. "And you could be part of it. Just give me the scale. Together we could figure out its power."

As he spoke, I thought of Milo and how he had practically begged me to break the curse. And the crew was hunting me for the pendant around my neck. Why else would they want it if not to end their torment? But if Bellamy thought it could be used for more, what if Valdez did too? What if there *was* something more? What if he could use if for something terrible? But I had already promised Milo I would help him. I would not let him keep suffering. I cared for him too much to make him stay.

"No," I uttered. "Milo told me what it's like when the ship goes under. I won't be the reason he has to keep paying for something he didn't do."

Bellamy's grip on my hand tightened. He squeezed my fingers together.

"It's hard to believe just how easily you bend to him. Why? Do you think he really cares about you? He's not even here."

He was twisting a dagger into my heart with his words. I thought I had every reason to believe Milo after everything we'd been through, but Bellamy was planting second guesses.

"He told me you were once his friend," I said, wrinkling my eyebrows together. "Why can't you two just forget and forgive?"

"Because he seems to have won the heart of a siren, and he doesn't want to share." Bellamy slowly leaned into me, supporting my back with his strong grip as he dipped me backward in time with the music. He gently pressed his lips to my neck and kissed me right above my necklace. His voice crawled across my skin like a whisper in the dark. "But I'm a pirate, after all, so I intend to take it anyway."

"You're out of your mind."

Bellamy simply smiled with a gentle groan as he lifted me back up to him.

I was searching for words, but he had left me both breathless and speechless. He had a strange way of paralyzing me with his dark charm. But as I looked over his shoulder, I saw a face in the crowd that flooded me with light. Milo. I must've smiled without realizing it, and Bellamy made it clear that he noticed.

"I don't have to guess why you're smiling. I guess your Pirate Prince Charming showed up after all."

Milo made his way over, walking with an authority in his step I hadn't seen since the night he challenged Bellamy at sword point.

"Katrina." Milo was looking at me, but he tore his gaze away to send a threatening expression toward Bellamy.

"I thought you weren't coming," I said.

"I wasn't. But I can see it's a good thing I did." He looked down at Bellamy's hand on my waist and his eyes flashed. "Why are your hands on her?"

"Because she's dancing with me." Bellamy sneered. "Perhaps if you'd showed up for her, you could've had the honor."

An anger within Milo stirred plainly as the muscles in his neck and jaw tensed. "I'm trying not to hurt her."

"And yet you're putting her right in the path of danger, playing this little scavenger hunt aboard Valdez's ship. I can't imagine anything more dangerous." Bellamy was oddly calm as he spoke.

"She isn't going. I'm doing it for her. I'm helping her. What have you done for her, exactly?"

"I asked him to do it," I interjected.

Bellamy glanced down at me.

"I asked him," I repeated. "Because I want to find out the truth. You said it yourself, Bellamy. There has to be a connection between all this. Milo is doing it for me."

Bellamy looked at me like I'd just slapped him. He pulled his hands to his side and stepped back.

"I can see that I have nothing to offer here." He switched his gaze back and forth between Milo and me.

Without another word, as quickly as he had appeared, he stepped between the two of us and vanished into the crowd, but not before pecking me tenderly on the cheek. I noticed Milo watching him with a threatening gaze, and I thought if Bellamy were to return, he might kill him. It was hard to believe they were not always enemies. I hated to feel that I was only adding fuel to their rivalry.

Bellamy was mysterious. Like a dark, opulent wine that tempted me with the promise of drunken pleasure when he was in front of me. But Milo was milk and honey. Always. And I savored him every moment.

Milo watched Bellamy until he had completely disappeared. The flames of rage in his eyes kindled down to soft embers as he turned his gaze on me. He studied me up and down slowly, and my heart began to accelerate.

"You look stunning." his words were gentle as he drew near to me. "How about one more dance?"

I reached for his outstretched hand. He really did look like a prince—though a rugged one at that—with his loose open collar and his hair tied back loosely at the nape of his neck.

"I think I have one left in me," I teased with a curve of my lips.

We danced across the golden floor, waltzing, and swaying as sweet songs guided our movements, everything around us fading away. There was so much to worry about, but for now, I chose not to let any of it matter. Only the moment between us existed. as he spun me gently into his arms and then back out again. My dress was cut low in the back, so I could feel the warm brush of his fingers against my skin as he gently ran his hand along my waist. Our bodies were pressed against each other before the end of the song, and he held his fingers closed around mine as if he would never let go. Though no words were spoken, I had never heard him more clearly. I threw myself into his arms as he held me close against his chest.

"I can't feel your heartbeat," I sighed, breathing in his scent.

"That's because it stopped 300 years ago."

I looked up at him. I still didn't understand why he was here, though I was glad that he was.

"Why did you come tonight after every reason you gave not to?"

"I came to tell you something, Katrina." He pulled away and connected his gaze with mine. "I realized...well...is there anywhere we can go to talk, just the two of us?"

I nodded and he guided me away to the large doors of the entrance. We stepped outside to the little courtyard where the grand fountain awaited. Not many people were out here, as the dainty chill of a November Florida night was enough to discourage most people from leaving the ballroom. I however wasn't bothered. Arkansas was much colder this time of year.

The golden lights twinkled overhead like stars. The gentle trickle of the fountain prevailed over the muffled hum of the music from inside. It was just us now.

"Katrina," Milo started. I had never seen him look so uncertain as he fumbled trying to say whatever was next.

"Yes?" I leaned forward. "What is it?"

He took my hand in his.

"I came here to tell you that I've changed my mind."

"Changed your mind?"

"Yes," he looked to the sky and closed his eyes, breathing in before speaking again. "I don't want you to break the curse."

"What?" I choked.

"I know it's crazy. I know it doesn't make sense after everything I've told you. But I can't deny what I feel for you any longer." As he spoke, he closed the space between us. I remained captive to his emerald gaze. "Since the night I first met you on the island, I couldn't stop thinking about you. And when I found you again, I knew I had to protect you. I'll admit I did want the scale, but not at the cost of you. Yes, I wanted to end my curse as much as the rest of the crew, and that's what I tried to focus on. But then it became more and more difficult each time I saw you. And now..." He grasped my hand with both of his, holding it close to his chin. "Now I can't lose you. If our curse breaks, I'll die for good. And I can't let you go."

I stared up at him, my heart swelling in my chest and a burning in my bones. I had longed for Milo, and knowing he felt the same sent a song through my soul. I yearned to surrender to it, but I also knew we could never fully belong to each other in this life.

"And if I don't break it, you'll spend the rest of forever dying every day." My lips could barely utter the words, as I felt my throat closing with emotion.

"And you'd make each one worth it." He touched my chin tenderly and tilted my face up towards his. "Katrina, I'd die a thousand deaths over again if it meant I could be with you. You're the one I'd endure hell over and over again for. You are the one that I can't stop seeing when I look up at the night sky. You are the first thing that guides me when the tide rises. You are my North Star."

I could barely see him through the blur of tears I now fought back. What could I say? Standing here in this glittering gown of stars, listening to words I'd dreamed of hearing but knew weren't possible, gazing into the soul of this man who professed such beautiful things to me. It was a fairytale. But there could be no happy ending.

"Milo..." I couldn't speak and hold back my tears at the same time, so they rolled down my face as I spoke. "You have no idea how much I've wished you would say this to me. But I stopped wishing because I knew it would be cruel of me to want that." I caught my breath and swallowed. "I can't ask you to live this life of torment just so we can be together."

"You're not asking me." He dropped my hands and cupped my face between both of them. "I know what I'm saying. I know what I'm willing to give to have this."

"Milo, no...You can't ask me not to break the curse."

"You have no idea the depths to which I care for you." He breathed, drawing his face an inch from mine. His dusky pink lips tempted me, but I resisted, fighting to save us both the heartache.

"And I care for you, Milo. Which is why I have to save you. I can't let you suffer this curse forever. No matter how much it hurts, I have to let you die."

As the words left my mouth, I tasted my tears, and I had to squeeze my eyes shut to keep more from coming. I had never had to do something so difficult in my life.

"I don't care, Katrina," he whispered. "I'll suffer for you. I'll give up heaven just to touch you. I'll fight off Valdez and his crew each and every night to keep you safe. But I can't leave you."

I had argued all I could manage, but he called to my heart like the moon calls the tide. Never before had someone spoken such beautiful promises to me or held me like this. And when I had blinked back the water in my eyes for the last time, I opened my eyes to gaze into his handsome face.

I nuzzled the scruff of his beard with my nose, wrapping my arms around his neck. He tenderly pulled my waist against his.

"I can't do this to you." My voice trembled.

"I want you to," he whispered as he moved his mouth to my neck and began to plant gentle kisses along my skin, working his way upward. I moaned gently, both from the touch of his lips and the feeling of my heart breaking. But I couldn't hold back any longer. As his lips pulled away from my neck, he looked into my eyes, as if he was thinking of something else to say. But I didn't let him.

I pushed myself against him and pressed my lips onto his. Milk and honey. Our mouths danced together, breathing in one another under the stars. His tongue traced my lips and invited mine to taste him deeper.

His hand slid down along my waist, exploring each curve. Sparks ignited under my skin at his touch. I reached forward, raking my fingers through his hair as we strengthened our embrace. The tenderness of his mouth, the scent of him, the warmth of his breath, the strength and gentleness of his hands along my body. It took me to a place I'd never been. And it felt like I could stay there forever.

But a sharp pang of sorrow struck my heart, and I remembered we didn't have forever. We didn't even have tonight.

27

ALBATROSS

I don't know how long I kissed him. It could have been minutes. It could have been an hour. Time had disappeared in the passion. But when we finally pulled away, a part of me had been awakened, and I couldn't put it back to rest. I sensed more tears coming. It was such a cruel feeling to want him so much but to know he couldn't be mine.

But some stupid part of me toyed with the idea that maybe he could. If I didn't break his curse, what existence would that lead to? A life of meeting under the moon, hidden, waiting only for the dawn when he would be pulled back into the ocean.

No. That is not an option.

"Don't cry." Milo spoke soothingly as he wiped a tear from my cheek with his thumb.

"I just don't know what to do." I closed my eyes, regaining my composure. I didn't like to let others see me cry, but every part of me was unguarded with him. The reality was that I knew exactly what I had to do, and it hurt like hell.

"You don't have to figure it all out right now, Katrina," he whispered, circling the scale pendant at my neck with his tender fingers. "Let's just get the key like we planned and hope it'll help you understand what all this means."

I nodded, still holding him close.

"Come on." His voice contained the same excitement as when he was explaining constellations to me back on the island. "Let's enjoy the evening while we can."

I offered him a curious look.

"Unless you'd like to stay here longer." He smirked.

I looked back at the glowing building, then back at him.

"I'd bet whatever you have in mind is a lot more interesting than this place. And I brought a change of clothes. You didn't think I was planning to sneak on a pirate ship in these shoes, did you?" I winced at my aching feet.

"What?" Milo shot a second glance my way. "You're not sneaking aboard a pirate ship. Didn't you agree to let me do this alone?"

"Yes, but that doesn't mean I didn't hope you'd change your mind."

"Well, sorry to disappoint you and all your plotting, but I won't."

"If you insist," I said, my tone rising and falling as I mimicked his accent.

He didn't answer but nudged me playfully. With one last glance at the glow of lights and glamour behind me, I headed back to my car with Milo at my side.

As I opened the passenger door to collect the folded-up jeans, tank top, and knit jacket that forever seemed to be falling off my shoulders. I threw the stilettos in my floorboard and happily switched them out for sneakers.

"Wait here." Milo motioned for me to stay put as he disappeared between some cars.

In less than a minute, I heard the familiar growl of his Triumph motorcycle rounding the corner. "Climb aboard, pretty lass." His lip curled into a smile as he flipped some stray pieces of hair away from his face.

I shook my head, so he'd know how crazy I thought he was, but that didn't stop me from swinging my leg over the seat. I was grateful for the long slit in the dress that allowed me the mobility, and I had wrapped the jacket over my bare shoulders for the ride.

"Hold on." He called over his shoulder, giving the throttle a nudge.

Without hesitation, I wrapped my arms around him tightly. I held onto him as though he was the only other person in the world. We zoomed away, leaving the gala far behind.

The night air raked across my skin, and I breathed in the salt as we crossed over the bay. I leaned with him in the turns and clung to him when he went a little too fast. The streets were busy, so he whipped off the main road and we soon found ourselves on the shore. The water glistened like a black mirror beside us as the moon's light kissed the glass surface. The packed sand was an endless runway, and we could have easily been flying. We coasted along the shore, and I strained to see out over the infinite horizon, imagining glimpses of the ghost ship.

"I thought you said the shore is dangerous!" I called out over the wind, teasing.

"It's not if they can't catch us." The bike lurched forward, and the ocean roared to our left as the midnight waves rolled in.

This side of Milo was new and rejuvenated. Since I had kissed him, he had come alive in the most vibrant way. He was confident, eager, and just a little bit cocky, but I found it endearing. I wondered how long it had been since he'd truly enjoyed anything the world had left to offer.

I clutched the folded clothing tucked against my stomach, shuddering from the wind. After a few more minutes, I quickly recognized where we were heading. In the distance, I saw the eerie protrusion jutting out from the coast, reaching for the sky. The old lighthouse.

Milo parked as close as possible to the rocks and helped me off the bike. I nearly stumbled on my dress as I swung my leg over, but he steadied me. We laughed at nothing, hand in hand, making our way towards our lighthouse. I hadn't touched a drink at the gala, but I was euphoric. It was far better than being drunk. My gown glittered in the moonlight with each step.

"If I could only put you in the sky where you belong, starlight," he said through laughter.

"You are too cheesy," I teased. "But I do think it's time I changed out of this dress," I mumbled. "It's cold."

It wasn't *cold*. But the air had a way of clinging to my skin, and it was starting to nip at me through the thin dress.

"Agreed," Milo uttered, gesturing to his dark slacks and dress shirt. "I need to do the same. I'll have to look normal to the crew in case I'm spotted. It would be hard to explain why I'm dressed like this."

He walked over to the entrance of the lighthouse and squatted down, moving some cinder-block type bricks to the side to reveal his boots, neatly folded 18th century shirt and breeches.

"So that's where you keep it all." I smirked.

"It's worked well so far," he chuckled. He looked around, craning his head right and left.

"I'll...um...I'll change out here and you can use the entrance there."

My cheeks tickled with a sting of warmth.

"Aye, aye, Captain."

He winked and nodded, and we separated to our designated dressing spots.

As I fumbled in the dim tower entrance with the dress zipper, I sighed. I had managed to move it about an inch before realizing it was stuck. No matter how I contorted my arm behind me, I wasn't successful, and my shoulder grew tired of the awkward positions.

I figured Milo had to be somewhat clothed by now, so I took the chance and wandered outside to ask him to assist. As quietly as I could slink around the brick wall of the tower, I peeked around the corner. It would be a lie to say I didn't watch him in silence for a moment before speaking. He already had managed to get his pants and boots on, and he was picking up his shirt when I startled him.

"Do..." my tongue tripped over my words as I started to speak. "Could you help me for just a sec?"

He looked up, and didn't bother to pull the shirt on, instead tossing it over his shoulder like a towel. My eyes couldn't help but catch on his well-formed exposed frame. His powerful, muscular abdomen tensed in the most tempting way as he turned my direction, and I knew I was blushing.

"Help with what?"

"The zipper on my dress. It's stuck."

"Oh," he adjusted the belt on his breeches and ruffled his hair, smoothing it back from out of his eyes. "Aye, yes."

He stepped forward, still shirtless, and I couldn't stop watching him. His tan skin glistened in the moonlight across his muscular chest. His tattoos trailed from one side of his chest down his arm, all depicting various symbols. But my favorite was still the star.

I turned my back to him as he came near. I couldn't control the way my muscles clenched as he reached for the zipper. With one slow motion, he pulled the little zipper down and the dress relaxed its tight grip on my torso. I didn't turn around, but I could feel Milo still behind me. The shirt draped over his shoulder slipped off to the ground.

"Thanks." I let out the breath that was pent up in my chest.

"Of course."

He leaned forward and whispered the words into my ear. I wanted him to stay there. I turned my head and caught his lips with mine, but I stayed with my back to him, standing on my toes just to reach him. As he kissed me from behind, he reached forward and wrapped both strong arms around me. I leaned back against his chest. He was a wall around me, and I was invincible and powerless all at once.

We released the kiss and I remained in his hold, feeling each rise and fall of his bare chest against my uncovered back. I gasped at the sensation of his gentle lips leaving dainty puckers along my skin. He started at my shoulder and worked his way up my neck, until he was nibbling the skin of my cheek. I slowly spun around in his arms to return his affections, as the loose dress around me began to inch further and further down.

A blaze burned in my veins like a furnace as he continued to touch me, working his fingers along my bare skin. He traced the curve of my spine and down to my exposed lower back. The top of the dress fell away, only still barely hanging on by my hips.

Pressing his lips once more on mine, our breaths intertwined. I sighed as he wrapped his hand around my waist and slowly drifted upwards, tenderly brushing across my breast. I trembled like palm fronds in a hurricane. My heart raced, thumping louder than the crashing waves below us. The fire between us fought away the damp chill on my skin. I had never been this vulnerable with anyone before. Certainly nothing like my high school romance.

After a moment, he pushed me backwards gently against the lighthouse wall. Our hands took turns wandering each other like ships on uncharted waters. He teased my skin tenderly, his hot breath trailing down my neck as he gently pulled my skin between his lips. I ran my fingers through his hair, stroking back stray locks and lost myself in his hazel irises as he paused to look at me. I relished every desperate breath, every unbridled touch, every muscle flinch as he caressed me. But I silently reprimanded myself, remembering that he could never be mine. Not like this, knowing we would lose each other. And yet that's also what made me crave him in these fleeting moments all the more.

"Do you remember..." He paused to kiss my forehead. "Do you remember when I told you that the curse keeps me from feeling?" His words drifted out between slow, heavy breaths.

I nodded, my frenzied pulse still throbbing in my veins as I lingered in his gaze.

"With you, I *can* feel...I feel...something. But it's not in the way you think. I feel *you*...almost in my soul. And it means more than any touch on my flesh ever could."

I rested my head against his, breathing in his scent and the salty smell of the sea. I placed a hand on his chest and began tracing the bird tattoo underneath his collarbone.

"What does this one mean?" I asked, my voice quivering.

"The swallow," he said, looking down at me through his lashes. "It's the mark a sailor gets when he's traveled 5,000 miles at sea."

"And the anchor?" My eyes pointed to the design on his upper arm.

"That's a merchant's mark. Or a mark for those who have crossed the Atlantic. I've done both so I suppose I especially deserve this one."

"Do you have the heart and the arrows? Like Bellamy?"

Milo's expression became rigid. He tensed at the mention of Bellamy's name. "No," he uttered. "I don't have that one."

"What does it mean?"

"That one was personal for Bellamy." His voice sounded tired as he explained. I didn't offer a response, but I felt a small pinch of sadness in my heart for Bellamy. "You don't have to worry about him," Milo said. "I don't know why he always seems to be on your mind."

"There are so many things on my mind I wouldn't know where to begin to describe them. But you don't have to be jealous."

"How can I not? Any pirate worth his salt will steal another man's treasure without hesitation."

"Well good thing for you I am not a treasure to be stolen. I'll give my heart to who I want."

"Then I pray I am the one you choose, my star."

He smiled slightly, taking my face in his hands. I peered up at him, smirking back. But a dark thought intruded, and my smile slowly faded. The warmth within me suddenly turned to frost.

"Milo." His name trickled out of my lips. "What happens if something goes wrong tonight? What if the plan doesn't work? What will happen if they catch you? What if they take the key?"

"How many times must I ask you to trust me? It *will* work. You'll see. I know the ship inside and out. I've certainly spent enough time on it. Don't worry, I—"

"No!" I tossed out the word before he even had a chance to finish talking. "This is *my* quest. *My* problem. I don't want you to do it alone. At least let me come with you to keep watch. You've already suffered enough because of me."

"Suffered?" He lifted his eyebrows as though I'd said a word he'd never heard before. He looked away, towards the ocean, but kept his hands on me, sliding them both down my arms until he was holding my hands. "It is not suffering to know you."

Had things been under any other circumstances, his words would have sounded as sweet as nectar. But instead, the guilt they carried stung like salt in a fresh wound.

I once believed that there was never a reason to push away the ones you loved. But the only way to save the man in front of me was to do just that. I was willing to make whatever sacrifice it meant to keep him from eternal damnation. Did that mean I loved him?

I entwined my fingers with his and whispered as gently as I could manage.

"Stop making this harder."

It took every ounce of strength within me to let him go, to walk away from him. But I did. I slipped out of his embrace, unable to say more, and walked back to my pile of clothes in the lighthouse.

I changed, surprised that Milo hadn't followed me. Now much warmer in my jeans and jacket, I started for the top of the lighthouse. Climbing the stairs carefully, I paced my steps as fast as I could manage without slipping in the dark. I just needed to feel the open air from the top of the tower. I just needed to see it once more. I just needed to think.

Once at the top, I stared out at the endless sea before me, wondering where the *Siren* was sailing at this very moment. My heart turned in my chest. I didn't know what was going to be scarier. Going aboard the *Siren* or going home to Arkansas and opening the box. Of course, the latter depended on the success of the first. And then I'd have to do the hardest thing of all.

As I watched from the tower, alone with nothing but these thoughts, the sound of flapping startled me. A massive shadow passed overhead. My heart froze in my chest as a massive white bird with wings like black sails landed atop the crumbling lighthouse terrace. It peered at me, chilling me with the dead look in its glass eyes.

It was the same bird that had watched me every day by the bay back at Isabel.

"It's an albatross." Milo's voice made me jump. He emerged from the dark stairwell, his eyes on the bird. "Very rare to see one on these Atlantic shores. It was said that they carry the souls of dead sailors."

"That bird," I whispered. "It was always around. Every day that week I didn't see you."

"I suppose something was watching out for you on my behalf." He winked. I felt a shiver down my spine, but in a good way. "They were also thought to bring good luck."

"Then I guess it's a good thing he stopped by. We'll need all the luck we can get."

I hung my head before continuing. "How much longer?"

"A little more than two hours. I'll need to get you back home soon." Milo walked over to the albatross, which flew away as he leaned on the edge beside it. I joined him.

"Please," I began. "Please just let me keep watch from the shore. I'll stay hidden. Just don't make me wait back in the dorm while you're out here. I'm probably no safer there than if I'm with you."

He rubbed his forehead with an open palm, as though he was soothing a headache. "Fine," he muttered. "But only if you stay hidden. You *must* be careful and do exactly as I say."

"Aye, aye captain."

"You've got to stop saying that," he chuckled.

As I rested my head on his shoulder, one strange idea entered my mind from out of the blue.

"Have you ever had a cinnamon chai latte?"

Milo threw a confused glance my way.

"I—I don't believe so. I've never even heard of such a thing."

"Well, I think you should try one." I offered a half-smile. "If something goes wrong tonight, and it's the last time I ever see you, I can't let myself go on knowing I never introduced you to cinnamon chai."

Still perplexed, Milo laughed at my proposal. "I'm not convinced it can be better than rum."

"Oh, it is. Besides, you've shown me everything—constellations, giant sea birds, secret lighthouses. Now it's time for you to check out something from my world."

"I'd be delighted to try this—this cinnamon chai you love so much." He chuckled, but it wasn't a lighthearted sound. It was almost the kind of laugh you force to soften the blow before saying something unpleasant. "But I don't know if I could taste it. I'm afraid it would be a waste."

Again, I was yanked back down to this corrupted reality. Now *I* was the one making things harder. Cinnamon chai was yet another dark reminder of what I couldn't have—of what we could *never* have, because he was trapped in this cycle until permanent death freed him. And I had to remind myself once again to be brave for him.

Against my better judgment, we couldn't help but steal a few more kisses in the moonlight before heading back to the discreet outer shores of Constantine Beach, where the *Siren's Scorn* awaited us in the distance behind a cloud of dark fog.

28

CLOSE QUARTERS

T he black silhouette of the ship bobbed just offshore in the calm waters.
There was a single lantern on the deck casting a yellow glow on the
tattered sails, but otherwise, it was difficult to determine what the rest of the
ship looked like if you didn't know what it was. Even still, these outskirt coasts
were entirely quiet at 4 AM. No one would be out here looking for a pirate ship.
Except us.

Milo parked the bike in the shadows and told me to wait behind it. He quietly
walked across the sand to the five wooden dinghies parked ashore and checked
to make sure no one was watching or returning to them.

He motioned for me to come near once he determined it was safe.

"I guess this is where the saying 'the coast is clear' comes from?" I joked, though inwardly I was nauseous from the thought of being ferried across the water in such small boats.

Milo smirked and looked at the boats. His expression darkened.

I studied the size of the dinghies. They looked as though they could hold at least half a dozen men each. Valdez must've had a crew of close to 40 with him. And they were all ashore somewhere looking for me. I wondered how such a phenomenon had existed for so many years without anyone noticing. But then again, maybe some *did* notice. I guess that's where the ghost stories came from.

"You're sure no one is on the ship?" I stammered.

"No, I'm not sure." He hesitated. "I can only hope Bellamy was able to lead them all ashore." He leaned over to adjust his choice of rowboat. Now, find somewhere to hide. Back where you were was a good spot."

"Good choice, mate. Leave her in some capable hands." Bellamy's lofty voice startled us both. He appeared from the shadows, and it was the first time I'd ever seen him in his true pirate clothing—a dark coat covering most of it, save for his leather boots.

Milo cocked his head, stomping toward Bellamy. "You've been following us?"

"Quite the contrary. I just came to see the spectacle."

"Aren't you supposed to be leading the crew off my trail?" I threw in.

"Already done, love. You've got nothing to worry about." He paused as he looked at the moon. "At least not for now."

There was a long silence. Milo touched my arm, pulling me aside.

"Katrina, I'm not leaving him alone with you and the scale. I'm taking you back. I knew this was a bad idea."

"No!" I cried, freeing my arm from his grip. "There's not enough time. Sunrise is in an hour!"

"You heard the lass." Bellamy chimed in. "Time to go."

Milo looked around in an uncertain, hesitant way I hadn't seen on him before, and then refocused on me.

"I can't leave you here."

"Then take me with you. You don't have a choice. We're running out of time."

Milo stepped back, pressed his hands to his head and groaned.

"You heard the girl. Stop trying to control her. And here I thought you were a gentleman." Bellamy's voice was calm and collected, with a sly smile that seemed to further irritate Milo.

"Katrina, I—"

"Tell you what, old friend," Bellamy interrupted, opening his coat to pull out a pistol from the leather strap across his chest. I stepped back as he flipped it once in his hand. "I'll keep watch from here. Anything suspicious happens and I'll fire off a warning shot."

Milo glared at him with his neck muscles tensed. "I'm supposed to trust you?"

"What choice do you have, mate?" Bellamy grinned. "Besides, can you think of anyone more determined to keep that necklace from Valdez?"

"Fine." Milo stood squarely and spat through his teeth.

"Okay, that's enough," I said, annoyed with them both. "Now let's go."

With a shudder, I stepped into one of the boats. The wood was ancient. I gripped the edges of the boat with all my strength as Milo pushed the vessel out into the water and quickly leapt in. As the waves crested, they lifted the little boat up and down. I gasped as the dinghy rocked back and forth with each stroke of the oars. They glided through the water, making the only sound keeping silence at bay. The sea was a void on all sides of me, and I was at its mercy.

Once we reached the ship, I could see its rotting exterior much more clearly. It looked just as fearsome as it had the night, I saw it rising up from the ocean. Cannons lined either side, barnacles growing up the side of the hull. The Jolly Roger flag flapped proudly in the late-night breeze.

I didn't know much about pirate ships, but I had a feeling I was about to learn. As we neared the ship, Milo let the dinghy drift towards it, and leaned over the edge of the boat quickly to secure a tether to the ship.

"Ready?" He asked me once more with pleading eyes.

I took in a breath of air heavy with the scent of brine and fish. "Yes."

"I'll go first, just in case there is someone up there," he whispered.

I watched in fascination as he stood in the rocking boat with perfect balance and reached up to grab the rope ladder dangling from the ship's starboard edge. With the grace of an acrobat, he heaved himself upward and climbed.

Once at the top, he peeked over the deck, and then looked back down at me. Nodding, he began to climb back down. He held out his hand and helped me up. Standing in the swaying boat was enough to make my heart jump in my throat, but his steady hand supported me as I found my sea legs. He pulled me up towards the ladder, and I struggled to find my balance as I grabbed the thick, algae covered knots. My hands slipped as the rope bent whichever way it was pulled. Dangling from the ship's edge as the rickety ladder swung back and forth, it took everything in me not to scream.

Milo climbed back up quickly, and I found the willpower to follow up, taking each rung of rope at a time. When we reached the top of the backside of the ship, I surveyed the deck before us. The smell of salt, rotting wet wood, and iron overtook my nostrils. The masts towered over us, their sails gently billowing. It was still nearly impossible to believe it was all real. And yet, there I stood, sneaker soles flat against the deck of a 300-hundred-year-old pirate ship.

"Valdez's cabin is right there. In the quarter deck." Milo shifted his gaze to the left. There was a wooden door built into the smaller deck at the back of the ship. He held his hand out, telling me to stay put once more as he stepped toward the rickety steps leading to the door. He knocked once, then gently pushed it open to peer inside.

"All clear."

I stepped forward.

"Maybe you should keep a lookout, too," I told him. "Just in case."

"Agreed. I'm not relying on Bellamy's signal," he replied. "But make sure you leave everything exactly as it was. Valdez is organized enough, so he'll notice if his quarters look out of place." His whispers came out fast, almost nervously. "I'll be out here watching, guarding. If I see them coming before you're out, I'll tap on the door three times. You'll come out and we'll make a break for it back on the jolly boat."

I nodded, feeling sick to my stomach. But I had been the one who wanted to come, and I wasn't about to abandon my mission. I looked at Milo once more.

"If anything happens, be careful." I warned.

He opened his jacket to reveal a pistol strapped across his chest and gestured to the sword at his side. "Don't worry. I'll protect you. Remember?"

My feet were as heavy as lead. I willed them to carry me forward, passing through the threshold of Valdez's chambers with a chill in my bones.

The door was heavy and groaned when I opened it. The floorboards creaked and swayed beneath my feet, shuddering with the ocean's movement in a way I wasn't used to. A sense of suffocation crept upon me in the darkness, warded off only by the moonlight and the light of a lone candle on a writing desk in the corner.

A rolled-up hammock swung gently in the farthest corner of the room, with tattered linens that were obviously once of the highest quality. A large leather chest sat against the wall, rotting away beneath a blanket of algae and barnacles. Beside it was a small bookcase of maps and parchment, strangely in better condition. A deteriorating ornate table and broken chairs occupied the center of the rounded room, and there was sea sludge coating every corner of the walls, casting an eerie green glow about the room.

I let out an audible breath, reaching up to feel my necklace. It was still there, of course. But I felt as though a phantom could appear to snatch it away at any moment.

I approached the writing desk first. On it, there were maps—hundreds of years old, a compass, sextant, and a spyglass. But no key. I wondered what use Valdez could have for these things now. Maybe they now only served as reminders of a time long past. Maybe he was using them still all this time, searching for an end to his curse. It was impossible to know.

I carefully opened a drawer, as if it would shatter into pieces if I pulled too quickly. Blank parchment, some quill pens. But something different did manage to catch my eye.

It wasn't a key, but a scribbled note on some crumbling parchment. I was careful not to touch it. It looked ready to disintegrate. But I leaned close to decipher the words written.

With the moon you shall rise,
As the night calls the tide.

By day, bound to the depths
Forevermore this curse shall be kept
Lest to the depths is returned
What was taken; the last of her.

I recognized the last part. The mermaid's curse. Beside it there were stacks of papers, with notes and annotations, particularly about the last line "the last of her." From the looks of it, Valdez had been racking his brain about the meaning of this curse for decades, probably longer. He was desperate to find the answer, to shatter this unbreakable spell on him and his crew. Who knew how many innocent souls had been caught up in his quest to free himself? I thought of Serena. And now me. Who else throughout all those centuries had he dragged into this?

I pulled my thoughts away. There wasn't time for these dark reflections. I had to focus on finding the key. I searched the other drawers, keeping everything in place as best I could. But the key wasn't in any of them.

Next, I moved to the chest. I opened it, but found nothing but clothes, glass bottles, gunpowder, a few swords, and blunderbusses. I unfolded each piece of clothing, searching in the pockets for anything that might resemble an old key. But I had no luck with that either. I was beginning to worry. Milo was silent, and I assumed that was a good thing, but I couldn't help but feel unsettled by the creaks and groans of the old ship.

I searched the bed last, pulling the blankets away slowly to keep from wrinkling them. It didn't take long to realize it wasn't there either. I huffed and pulled my hair over my shoulders, thinking. As I surveyed the room before me, the eerie moonlight poured in through the foggy glass window, lighting up an area I hadn't noticed before. From this angle, beside the bed, I saw a thin drawer on the side of the desk that looked oddly out of place, as though it had been added in after the desk was built.

I tiptoed over to it, though I wasn't sure why I was trying to be so quiet if no one was aboard. It was just a precaution in my mind. I reached for the drawer, pulling it open as though I expected a snake to jump out.

When I looked, I saw a small stack of letters never sent. All addressed to Cordelia. My curiosity got the best of me, and I couldn't ignore the urge to read at least one.

My dearest Cordelia,

How cruel and ruthless of you to leave me suffering for so long. But of course, the same was often said about me. Perhaps we really were meant to be together, just like you wanted. I know there is no mercy for me, and I wear that proudly. I regret nothing that I've done. Only that I chose too cold and clever a siren for my own good. Still, I'm offering you a proposal. Release my son from this curse, at the least, and you can have my soul forever. Let Bellamy die once and for all, and I'll stop seeking to be free from your punishment.

Once yours,

Captain James Valdez

I nearly dropped the letter at the mention of Bellamy's name. Of course, I knew Valdez was his father, but there was something all too real about the words on the page that made me shudder.

And I was perplexed. Did Bellamy know that his father was willing to give up himself to end his pain? Or did Valdez merely write the letter in an attempt to trick Cordelia back to the ship as he had done once before? Or maybe he just hadn't known where to send it. The possibilities were endless, but I couldn't help but wonder if I had just glimpsed a small sliver of evidence of Valdez' humanity.

That letter was one of many, written, but never sent. But it was the only one not sealed with the captain's wax signet seal. The others were made out to a "Maria," but I didn't dare break their seals to read them.

I needed to hurry, but I was running out of ideas and there was nowhere in the room left to search. I glanced down once more at the letters. That's when I noticed one of them seemed just a bit thicker than the rest. Like there was something wrapped between the folded parchment. I didn't want to break the seal, but it was the only way. I pulled the wax from the paper, and the iron key slid out. I cradled it as though it was precious treasure, still in disbelief that it was even real. The seconds were ticking, but I opened the letter, thinking I could at least skim it before putting it all back.

Cordelia,

You may have sent me to hell, but remember they call me the devil himself. Don't forget how you turned on your own, leading the sirens right to me, one by one. You betrayed the sea, not me. The blood of your sisters is on your hands. And for that, you have a debt to pay as well. And what consoles me each morning when this ship sinks to those god-forsaken depths, is knowing that you'll still never possess what you wanted most—my love. For you see, my Maria took all the love I had with her to the grave. And I'll be damned before I'd resurrect it for another, least of all you.

With love,

Captain James Valdez

Of course, I had no way of knowing how much of the letter was true, but it made me suspect Cordelia could have very well been as formidable as Valdez. The more I read, the more they both seemed unhinged and lethal. It was no wonder such tragedies followed when the two of them collided. A sudden muffled bang outside made me jump. Like a distant gunshot.

Bellamy.

Whatever other secrets lied behind Valdez' past would have to wait for another time, because my time was up.

I tucked the key away into my smallest jean pocket, making sure it was snug. Then as quickly as my trembling fingers would allow, I moved everything back into place. I gave one last glance over the room to ensure nothing looked out of place and strode back to the door.

Milo had never knocked or responded to the gunshot, which I found odd, but I expected to see him waiting for me, ready to head back to shore. But when I opened the door, what I saw was far from my expectations.

Milo was waiting for me, but so were a dozen pirates. They encompassed the cabin door so there was nowhere to go. And there in the middle of them, grinning at me with a wild-eyed stare, like an animal ready to tear into its prey, was a giant of a man in a scarlet coat. He loomed over me, peering at me down the barrel of a blunderbuss. His voice was like steel on steel and made the hairs on the back of my neck leap up.

"Pleasure to finally meet you, lass." He tipped his hat at me, then addressed Milo. "And thank you for arranging the introduction, Master Harrington."

29

TROUBLED WATERS

A fraid to move, I stood, planted in place, glancing back and forth between Milo and the man. It was Valdez. His accent seeped out through his thick dark beard, as he continued. His powerful voice rattled my bones. In some strange way, he could have almost been handsome, but his formidable presence overshadowed even that.

"You beat Bellamy to it, Harrington. Maybe you knew what you were doing all along, but you know I don't like wasting time. Good thing you're already dead because I would've killed you days ago for this goose chase."

Milo stood at Valdez's side, watching the scene unfold as though he didn't even know me. I looked at him, hoping I was wrong to think he had betrayed me like this. He averted his gaze as soon as my eyes fell on his. He wouldn't look at me. My racing heart began to sink.

Tears of fear and anger burned behind my eyes. Valdez stepped forward, still aiming his pistol at me. I fought with all my strength to keep my terror from showing, but my panicked short breaths gave me away.

Valdez stared at my throat like he was hypnotized. I glanced down at my necklace, careful not to make any sudden movements, but trying to think of a way out of this.

"Aye, men." He pulled in a heavy breath through his nostrils as a faint grin cracked at the corner of his mouth. "That'd be the siren's scale without a doubt."

A crewman spoke up from the back, a dry, desperate cry, "Then what are we waiting for, Cap'n?" The men grumbled in accordance.

Valdez held up his hand with command.

"Patience, you bilge rats," he grunted. "I'm still trying to decide what to do with this young beauty aboard our vessel. It'd be a shame to simply take the scale and not enjoy the other pleasures so long denied us..." He licked his teeth while eyeing me in a way that made my skin recoil. I felt every muscle in my body tighten in defense. Trembling, I glanced once more at Milo, who remained expressionless. But I noticed his hand coiling into a tight fist at his side.

"She's all yours, Captain." Milo spoke to my surprise, nearly blurting out the words. "I've already had my fun with her." Whistles and obscenities erupted from the crowd of pirates looking on.

I blinked in disbelief at him. A burning bubbled in my chest, singing every inch of me with hurt and repulsion.

"You're disgusting," I hissed at him. He only looked away, up at the mast overhead, which only infuriated me further.

"You'll not be disrespecting my crewmen like that, lass." Valdez' tone was one of amusement. "Let's see you on your knees for that."

I wanted to spit in his face. But not as much as I wanted to slap Milo's again.

Milo pulled the cutlass from the holster at his side and pointed it at me, stepping close enough to reach me with his hand if he wanted.

"On your knees." His voice was stone. "Captain's orders." He put a hand on my shoulder and pushed me to the side a bit, adjusting me where he wanted. "Get down."

The way he said the words struck something within me. It wasn't threatening, but more urgent, like he was pleading with me to do as I was told. With a pistol and a sword both aimed at me, I couldn't argue. With the coldest glare I could manage, I lowered myself to my knees. Valdez put his pistol away and began to remove his coat, as Milo held me at sword point.

"You remind me of a certain woman I knew, rather powerful and cruel. Beautiful, too." He paused and gestured to the deck. "Do you know she gave me this ship? She could enchant any man to obey her, and she sent an entire naval crew overboard with just a song. Just for me. And she stood right where you are. Except, if I remember correctly, she stood fully unclothed, and hadn't an ounce of shame about it."

I had no idea what he was referring to, but I wondered if the woman he spoke of was Cordelia. He looked down at me from under thick, dark eyebrows as he drew closer, adjusting his belt.

"But you, lass, you're shivering like a dog in the rain. Like you've got something to be ashamed of. Like you've got something you don't want me to take."

I gripped the necklace with both hands and drew into myself. His boot rattled the wooden floor as he took a step toward me.

"I'll let you do the honors of setting the scene, Master Harrington. Think of it as a reward."

Milo used the tip of the sword to lift the edge of my shirt. I flinched and pulled away, but he grabbed my wrist with his free hand. I resisted, but he managed to hold me still, and he leaned in close to my neck for a half second. I barely managed to catch the whisper that grazed past my ear, but I heard him clearly.

"Trust me and hold on."

Then with one lightning-fast swipe of his sword, he whipped around to slice through a rope in the rigging that was tied taut to a hook in the deck. He pulled me to him with his free arm, and I threw my arms around his shoulders. He grabbed the rope as it snapped upward, and we were yanked off our feet and hoisted up with it. We zipped up to the crow's nest, and Milo tossed his sword to the deck below to free up his hand so he could grab onto the mast as we rose past it.

"Damn you, Harrington! You'll *wish* you could die after this. I'm going to spend my eternity making sure yours is hell." Valdez reached for his pistol and fired, but Milo and I had quickly climbed into the crow's nest for cover. Wood splintered around us as lead bullets pelted the floor beneath us, and the smell of gunpowder filled my nostrils.

I looked at Milo as we ducked for cover. I realized he had been playing a part to save me. I wanted to smack him and hug him both at the same time.

"That was vile," I told him. "But...I know why you did it."

He winked at me. "I told you I'd protect you. I didn't say how."

"What happened to 'knock three times?'"

"That's a little hard to do when you're ambushed. They had a boat on the other side waiting before I even heard Bellamy's warning shot."

More gunshots fired and pirates tossed out profanities from below, Valdez's booming voice the most audible.

"Now what?" I asked.

"It's almost sunrise. Now I just have to get you off this ship."

"What about you?"

"You know what happens to me."

"I mean...What happens tomorrow night? When you come back? What will Valdez do to you?"

Milo squeezed his eyes shut, as if trying to swallow something bitter. The pirates below were shouting threats, and two were beginning to climb the mast. More pistol shots rang out.

"Don't worry about me." He took my hand in both of his and pressed his lips to them. "But whatever happens, know that you need to stay away from the shore. When you come back from your trip, stay away from the sea. You can't come back to this ship. Ever. I'll find a way out. Somehow. And when I do, I'll come back to you. Every night. I promise."

"Weren't you the one who told me, 'Don't make promises you can't keep?'"
I asked.

He only looked at me in response, then pulled me to my feet and glimpsed over the edge into the water at one of the dinghies in the black water below.

"There's your ride," he muttered.

"What?"

He didn't explain.

As one of the pirates began to reach the underside of the crow's nest, swinging his cutlass, Milo pulled his pistol from the strap across his chest and fired. The man toppled to the deck below with a curse and a grunt. But there were more coming. And Valdez had his gun locked onto us.

Milo took the rope from before in his hand. It was still attached to its loop in the rigging in the masts. "Hold on." He plunged his lips forward into mine and I melted into him. It was exhilarating. Even with my life in immediate danger, I somehow felt safe, as we embraced, nestled amongst the sails under the moonlight. The sounds of swords and bullets faded away as the warmth of Milo's lips made mine tingle. A quiet whimper escaped my throat as he kissed me with relentless ferocity, holding me to him as if it would be the last time.

Without warning, he pulled his lips from mine and leaped from the crow's nest, clinging to me tightly. The rope was a pendulum, and we were the counterweight. As we soared past the deck, he fired a handful more shots into the crew below. I felt him push for as much momentum as he could muster while still holding me, and we swung just over the edge of the ship, where a small boat bobbed in the water below.

With the urgency of someone rushing to put out a fire, he brought his lips to my ear, leaving a message in my ear that rippled through my core. "I will *always* find my way back to you, Katrina. My North Star." He left me no time to respond.

With those final words, he released me over the dinghy and let the swinging rope carry him back to the deck, swords begin to clang. I pushed myself up from the floor of the boat, looking up to see Bellamy sitting across from me, oars in hand.

"Grab an oar, love. It's almost dawn," he ordered calmly.

I did my best to assist Bellamy in rowing back to shore as fast as possible. The faint light of sunrise began to show over the horizon, and the sound of the chaos on the ship had begun to drift away as we distanced ourselves from it. I could also hear the sound of the maelstrom forming as it began its ritual of taking the ship down into its depths. We were silent.

Something was different about Bellamy. I watch as he let the boat drift to the shore with only gentle nudges with the oar. His usual air of confidence was missing, and instead, he wore a broken expression I had not seen before.

"Bell—" He stopped me before I could even finish saying his name.

"Don't." He lowered his head and looked down at the water. "I saw the way you kissed him. Don't say something just because you pity me."

"I just wanted to say thank you," I partially lied. I wanted to tell him something else, but I just wasn't sure what.

"You already know I want to keep the scale from my father." He leaned on his knee with his elbow. "But..." he raked a hand through his hair "looks like Milo and I finally managed to agree on one thing."

"And what's that?"

"That you're very much worth protecting."

I offered him a weak smile, but it was all I could manage. Did he know Valdez had written about sacrificing himself to free him from the curse? I debated on telling him now, but it just didn't feel right. There was still no chance it could make up for what happened to Serena.

Before I could think of what to say next, Bellamy began to fade before my eyes. In the same way that the phantom waves had come for Milo before, the water rose around Bellamy to swallow him down. The little boat slowly vanished after him, becoming nothing out from under me, and I leapt out into the water that was just shallow enough to wade in. When I turned around, I saw the last glimpse of the ship in the distance as it was pulled beneath the surface. And then the beach was silent, normal, and the sun was coming up. As if none of it had ever been there at all.

30

DOWN IN THE DOLDRUMS

I zipped the key into my carry-on as I made my way through airport security. I dreaded this trip for various reasons. I was excited to see Dad, but I anticipated seeing mom for the first time in so long would be uncomfortable. Most of all, it would be impossible to think of anything but Milo and how he would be at the mercy of Valdez until I returned after Thanksgiving to break the curse.

But I had to stop whatever curse was plaguing my mom and me, first. It was all part of the plan, I reminded myself. If I really *could* save him, Milo would be free soon enough, no matter how much it would ache to let him go.

On my flight! Should be landing this afternoon.

I sent the text to Dad right before the plane departed, but I didn't wait for a reply before closing my eyes and leaning my head back. It was nearly a 4-hour flight, and I planned to catch up on some much-needed sleep after my eventful all-nighter. I held onto the necklace, praying it would work its mysterious magic and guard my dreams this time.

W hen I woke, the plane was landing. How was I supposed to just step off the plane onto Arkansas soil like everything was back to normal? Like my life hadn't drastically changed from one impossible encounter no more than a month ago. Hours ago, I was nearly murdered by pirates on a centuries-old ship. And yet, now I was just a college freshman returning home for Thanksgiving Break.

I had expected a text from Dad to come through after the plane was on the ground, but to my surprise a slew of text notifications and three mixed phone calls lit up my phone screen. Something was obviously wrong.

As I hustled out of the terminal and through the crowded airport, I hastily returned my dad's call. My eyes felt heavy and the space between my forehead throbbed with pain from sheer exhaustion. Adrenaline had fueled me all night, and my brief nap on the airplane did little to combat the crash I was feeling now. But I ignored it as best I could, fumbling to hold the phone to my ear while hauling my duffel bag and carryon. Dad picked up right away.

"Katrina? Did you land okay?"

"Yeah, I'm making my way to the pickup line now. Are you here?"

"I am, but your mom isn't. She's in bad shape. That's why I called so many times."

"W—what do you mean she's in bad shape?" I repeated.

"I mean this morning she was...crying...screaming...hysterical. I ran to her, but she was absolutely out of it. I couldn't shake her from it. It's worse than usual. Something's wrong."

"Oh no..." I pressed the phone to my ear, my fingers curling around it. "Where is she now?"

"The hospital," he sighed. "I couldn't wake her up. She was screaming like she was in a dream or hallucinating, but I don't think she was ever awake. She's been unconscious since then."

"Oh my gosh," I groaned. "Okay, well I'm coming down the pickup line. I'm—wait—I see you!" I waved in his direction as I rushed into the lane where Dad's '99 Dodge Ram pickup awaited me.

The familiar brisk November air brushed against my skin, but I hardly noticed as I hoisted myself into the passenger seat and flung myself into Dad's open arms.

"I missed you," I uttered into his shoulder. He smelled faintly like oil and engine grease, and it was the most reassuring smell in the world in that moment.

"I missed you so much, Trina. Your mom has been wearing me down." He drew a deep sigh. "I tried so hard to shield you from it. You shouldn't have had to be worrying about all this."

"It's okay, Dad," I said. "I didn't want you to worry. I'm hoping there's a way we can get Mom out of this now that I'm here, before..." I gently pulled away from his hold and sat back in my seat. "...before it's too late."

"Hope is the best thing we have, Trina. Whatever happens, don't stop hoping."

I nodded quietly and offered him a weak smile as he drove forward. I assumed our destination was the hospital, twisting my fingers together as Dad maneuvered out of the airport traffic.

Breathe.

"I can't help but feel this is somehow my fault." I pressed my forehead to the glass window.

"*Hija*, no," Dad reached over and put a strong hand on my shoulder. "We've been through this. It's *never* been your fault. "

"I know," I breathed. "But maybe if I'd just never left. Maybe if I stayed here instead of moving to Florida, I could have stopped her from doing this...if I'd just been here."

I failed to understand why Mom's relapse felt so heavy on my shoulders. It certainly wasn't the first time. And it wasn't my fault I couldn't figure out the necklace's secrets. Clearly, no one else had been able to either. And yet, ever since she had told me about her drowning dreams, I had sensed a new connection to her that antagonized me.

When we first arrived at the hospital, I stared upwards at the entrance. It had been a long time since I'd been here. The last time I was here, Mom had broken her wrist and hit her head stumbling up our porch and falling after a typical night of drowning away her demons. She had made it home just after dinner. Dad had rushed to take her there, and I rushed home from my high school homecoming game to stay with her that night. The memories were anything but good, and they were flooding back now, perching in the back of my mind like a threatening shadow.

As we approached the front desk, I began to wonder what I would feel when I saw her for the first time, conscious or not. She had been away for over a year, and though I had heard her voice many times over the past few weeks, I hadn't actually *seen* her in what felt like ages. Would my anger towards her return? Or would I feel pity for her like so many times before until I had decided to harden myself to it?

A few turns down the hallway and we were there at the entrance to the room. I held my breath as Dad opened the door. Mom's eyes were closed, and her shoulder length hair was pulled back in a ponytail to one side. A menacing thought snaked its way into my head as I watched her. Had she done this on purpose?

No. There's no way. She wasn't that bad off yet...was she?

I stood over my mother as she breathed like she was sleeping. Was she at peace, I wondered? Or could the nightmares find her here, too? I wanted to hug her and hate her all at the same time. Attempting to dam up the tide of emotions within me, I bit my lip as tears fought their way to the surface.

"Grace," Dad uttered. But Mom didn't respond. There was only the quiet of our breaths and the beeping of the monitor connected to her. I feared I didn't have much time left to figure out how to save her.

We stayed with her as the day turned into evening, taking turns staying at her side. Dad refused to go home, but he offered to take me to the house to get some rest for the night. I ached for sleep, like always, but little did he know I planned to spend my time alone in the house searching every corner of the attic for that box. I thought about telling him about the box and the death dates, but how could I possibly explain what I knew? There was nothing he could do to stop it anyway, and he'd think I was going just as crazy as Mom if I told him. That's what *I* would have thought if I hadn't seen it all with my own eyes. But if he only knew how the clock was ticking...

On the ride home, I stared at the road ahead, focusing on the yellow lines on the pavement sweeping up underneath the truck headlights as we passed over them. Gray soft clouds billowed overhead, creating a horizon of shadows and gloom. The leaves had mostly all fallen now, but a few remaining gold and crimson stragglers still clung to branches for dear life.

"So, what happens, now?" I turned to Dad. "What if Mom doesn't get over this one?"

"Don't say that, *hija*." I clung to the steadiness in his voice. "Don't give up hope. Not yet."

I swallowed, still pestered by the feeling that it was somehow my duty to do something about this. Hoping wasn't enough. For so long I *did* hope. I hoped Mom would change for so many years. I hoped we could be a family. And when that didn't work, I hoped I could forget about it all and start over on my own. When I finally thought I had left the past far behind, it caught right back up to me like it never left. But it was becoming clear to me, in more ways than one, that the past was never dead, just buried beneath the surface for a little while. I had let go of hope a long time ago. Now I was scrambling to get back like a kid chasing a runaway balloon before it floated away for good.

As I pondered all this, Dad took a turn along the same road I used to drive to school. For a moment, I was back in 11th grade, a socially awkward nobody just trying to make it to graduation and find a fresh start, applying for art scholarships around the country. How I had so desperately wanted to escape from this small town that had caged me for so long. It was cozy. It was safe. But that was the problem. Cages were safe, too.

And now nothing felt safe, and oddly enough, something primal in me longed for the security of my boring home in Ozark, AR. But what I wanted didn't matter. There was nowhere I could go to outrun the struggles I faced any longer. They would always be there. In Arkansas. In Florida. Literally at the bottom of the sea, even. And it was time to stop looking for a way out. I couldn't run any farther. Instead, I was ready to swim against this tide head on.

31

BURIED TREASURE

The Diesel engine of Dad's truck growled steadily as we rolled into the driveway of the little one-story ranch-style house. I had never known a different home beyond those walls until moving to my dorm this year. Once he turned the engine off, nothing but the sound of crickets remained as the silent night sky looked down upon us. I wasn't wearing a jacket, and I shivered as the cold air hit my bare arms from the truck to the entrance. Stepping through the front door wrapped me in a cloak of familiarity.

The decor looked identical to the day I left, with the bright green fake plants contrasting sharply with the out-of-date wood paneling on the walls. Baby pictures of me and some old wedding photos of my parents hung throughout the house. I stepped into my old room, so many of my artwork still pinned to the wall, right where I left them. My mismatched socks still strewn across the floor. The wall behind my headboard featured my own attempt at Van Gogh's 'Starry Night,' stretching from floor to ceiling. I hand-painted that wall when I was in middle school. Turns out I had liked sleeping beneath the stars for longer than I realized.

I flipped on the room light and tossed my bag across my bed. I tried to stifle a yawn but failed. My body was weary, and my mind was murky. My dad stood, eyeing me in the doorway.

"I'm going back to the hospital once you're settled in." He gestured to the bag on my mattress. "Please don't think I don't want to spend time with you, Trina..."

"Trust me, Dad. I know." I reassured. "I'll be there tomorrow. I'll call you when I'm ready for you to pick me up." I whirled back and around and began pulling my things from the bag. I scattered my clothes out across the bed, not bothering to keep them folded. After I received no response from Dad, I glanced over my shoulder. "Go. Don't feel bad, Dad. You need to be with her."

"I don't want you to think I'm not happy to see you."

"Dad, of course I know you are." I stood to face him, holding my elbow with my opposite hand. "But right now, you are the one Mom needs. You've always been there for her, and I'm the one who gave up on her. If she wakes up, you are the one she'll be looking for. I'm still not sure I'm ready."

The last part was partially true. I wasn't ready, but for more reasons than just that. I left out the part about needing time to dig around the house for a box I wasn't even sure existed.

Once Dad was gone, I took a breath, fighting another yawn, and made my way to the luggage I had carried in last night. Producing the key from my carryon, I cradled it in my hands. It was the first time I had the chance to study the ancient thing. I analyzed the exterior, darkened and roughened from corrosion and salt as I turned it over in my palm. The iron was carefully crafted with intricate swirls molded into the handle.

After everything I'd gone through to get it, I prayed it would all be worth it. I needed answers. Answers that could hopefully become solutions. And I needed this key to unlock them all. But I was afraid to find out. What if it couldn't even open the box? What if none of it was connected like it seemed? What if there really was nothing special about the necklace? What if I couldn't save Milo? What if I would spend the rest of my life knowing his soul was damned to the seas forever? What if none of this had anything to do with my mother or me and she really was just a hallucinating alcoholic beyond saving? What if this destiny was unavoidable for both of us?

The cyclone of voices in my head spiraled without relenting. The questions. The fears. This little key in my hand was summoning them all. Determined not to waste any more time, I started for the attic, where I had only visited once before as a child.

I tugged on the cord, watching the steps expand out before me in welcome. With no one else in the house, an eerie feeling befell me as I crawled into the dark attic space alone. I quickly diverted my attention and retreated to the kitchen looking for one of Dad's many emergency flashlights. It didn't take long to find one, and I was back at the base of the steps within seconds, clutching the light in my hands.

The stale air from the attic wasted no time ambushing my lungs. It was musty and oddly stuffy, and I was more than thankful it wasn't summer. There in the corner, I saw the pile of toys I had carried up with Mom eleven years ago. Among other things, old chairs, small grimy car parts, and random house decor that looked like it belonged in an old lady's living room claimed nearly all the space in the cramped attic. Where was I supposed to begin? The daunting heap of disorganized junk before me made my chest tight. It could take forever to find the box. I didn't even know what it looked like.

"Where would it be?" I said to myself. I searched in frustration, pulling boxes down from everywhere and moving every object I physically could. But nothing. There was no sign of this legendary box.

I plopped down and sat resigned in the floor, a stirring in my chest building like a wave. And then the ocean I was holding back finally came crashing over me. The broken wail that escaped from me echoed off the hollow walls of the attic. My teardrops dotted the dusty floor as I fell forward, my sobs fast and heaving. I hugged myself tightly, trying to catch my breath, rocking back and forth. I couldn't do it. I couldn't save us. And I was so, so tired.

The horn honking outside woke me up. My eyes burned as I opened them to realize I had fallen asleep there in the attic. I scrambled to my feet and quickly rushed downstairs to the bathroom, to brush my teeth and shower. I made sure to close the attic behind me.

"Trina, I'm here!" I heard Dad call through the hallway.

I peeked my head out from the bathroom door. "Sorry, Dad, I slept in. Must not have heard my alarm."

Dad didn't mind waiting on me to finish getting ready, and I tried my best to act more rested than I felt.

Back at the hospital, I turned over every bit of the attic in my head that I could remember. What had I missed? I planned to try looking again tonight, but I was losing confidence that this box was ever truly in Mom's possession.

When dusk came, I curled up in a spot by the small window in Mom's room. I studied the horizon, noticing the way the pale oranges and gray hues clashed together like waves in the sky as the sun crept downward. The wisps of color were woven across the sky like silk threads, making me yearn to have a paintbrush in my hand. But the closest thing I could get was the sketchbook stuffed in my duffel bag. Watching the moon take the sun's place, I allowed my heart to guide my hand as it began to trace an outline of a face. From the strokes of my pencil came tousled hair, a strong jawline, and smoldering, fierce eyes staring back at me from the page. As I shaped the velvet lips, I silently called on the memory of the nectarine taste that still lingered on mine.

The smell of marinara sauce and garlic tore my focus from the sketch. Dad entered the room, carrying a pizza box and placed it on the small table, casting his gaze my way.

"Who's that?" I noticed him eyeing my sketchbook.

"Oh...um." I quickly put the book down flat to obscure his view, feeling my face flush. "It's no one."

"Well, I don't believe that for a minute," he laughed. "I've never seen you draw a person like that. Usually, it's butterflies or flowers or clouds."

He was only sort of right. Sometimes I sketched and painted people, but portraits certainly weren't typically my thing. Especially portraits of attractive men.

"Trina, you don't have to tell me, but don't think your old Pops can't figure it out. I've been in love for a long time." He grinned, showing his wide set teeth beneath his mustache as he flicked his gaze to my mom. "And I know you well enough to know *you* don't just fall for anyone."

With a flutter of my eyelashes, I tried to keep from looking at him, but he came closer. "He must be something special if he could capture your attention."

My lips were dry, and I held my mouth open as I croaked out a reply. "He's definitely...different...from other guys."

"And what's his name? Op! But you don't have to tell me. I'm fine with *secretos*." He laughed, and a hint of his accent snuck out within the words of his last sentence.

"Nah, it's no secret," I surrendered with a weak giggle that came out more like a huff. "His name is Milo."

"Well tell Milo if he causes any problems, I may be a fourteen-hour drive away, but I know how to get there in three if I need to."

I shook my head and playfully rolled my eyes. "Don't worry," I said. "He's great." My half-smile faded, and I pressed my lips together. "But he's not from the area, and he may have to leave soon. For good."

"That's too bad, *hija*. If he knew what was good for him, he'd stay."

Something stabbed in my chest as my dad spoke. I knew Milo would stay for me. No matter the pain it brought him. And that's why I couldn't let him. But I let Dad go on talking.

"Just know something, Katrina." I perked up, listening. It wasn't often he called me by my full name. "Sometimes doing the right thing for the ones we love hurts. Sometimes it hurts us. Sometimes it hurts them. Many times, both. But we still must do it. And we have to be strong. *Fuerte.*"

I knew Dad couldn't possibly have known about my secrets back in Constantine, but his words struck right through to my core like a javelin.

With a complete shift of mood, Dad reached for the pizza box.

"Now I don't know about you, but I'm starving. Pepperoni and pineapple. Still your favorite, I hope?"

I nodded. "Of course."

Dad put an arm around me and lightly kissed the side of my forehead, probably noting the dullness in my voice. "Don't worry, *hija*. Everything is going to be alright in the end. I promise."

His words reminded me of McKenzie in that instance. With their constant reassurance and willingness to listen, I realized that both of them were the reasons I had gotten this far. And I was more grateful for them than they would ever know. I only hoped that someday I could be the one to say the right thing to someone the way they had done for me so many times.

After we ate, Mom stirred in her bed, groaning a bit. Dad had nodded off in a chair, snoring gently. I reached for my mother's hand, but I didn't know why. Some part of me was glad that I couldn't tell if she could hear me or not, because I didn't know what I would say to her if she was awake.

As I watched her, her eyes began to flutter, but quickly shut again. She took in a gasp for air, and tried to lean forward, opening her eyes again, in a panic, as if suffocating.

Dad jolted awake and quickly took in the scene before him as I quickly released Mom's hand.

"I'll get the nurse." Dad whipped out the door, calling for help.

My eyes stayed locked on her, my nerves leaping back and forth. She suddenly grabbed my wrist with both of her hands, clinging to me with a white-knuckle grip.

"Don't let me drown. Please. Please. The water's getting too high. Please..." She squealed the words out between choked breaths, but I heard them clearly.

As Dad burst back into the room with two nurses trailing close behind, her eyes closed again, and she fell back against her pillow. Though she looked calm,

I knew waves were raging inward. The nightmares were undoubtedly here. And they were pulling her under.

I *had* to find that box.

O nce Dad dropped me off at home again, I didn't waste a second. Without time on my side, I got to work again in the attic, with no regard for the mess I made as I searched in desperation, pulling out objects and sliding boxes across the floor. I strained to pick up an old rocking chair that had some antique-looking objects behind it. It looked like a spot where a wooden box might fit in perfectly. But rummaging through them, I soon realized it was only an accumulation of collectibles from my grandmother.

I pushed Grandma's things back where I found them. It was then that I noticed a cardboard box labeled "Lydia"—my grandmother's name—at the base of a stack of boxes in the far dark corner behind the others. The box was the size you'd expect to contain a few books or something similar. I had been looking for the box among in Mom's things. It wasn't until then that it occurred to me that maybe the box was packed away with my grandma's.

I started on the stack of boxes, opening each one and peeking inside, but found nothing that resembled a music box or jewelry box. I wasn't even sure what it looked like.

The nagging sensation of my time ticking away whispered constant discouragement into my ear. I should be with my mom, it said. I knew it wasn't wrong. But if I was with her, then I couldn't be here helping her by unraveling the mystery of this curse on our family. Either way I chose, I felt that I was failing someone I cared about, and my heart was heavy for it.

I took one more peek into the last box with my grandma's name. There, at the bottom, underneath a faded and moth-eaten handkerchief, I spotted the corner of something wooden. My heart stood still as I uncovered it to reveal a wooden rectangle roughly the size of a loaf of bread.

With frigid fingers, I lifted the box out, my eyes caught on the intricate designs across the lock that perfectly matched those on the key. It was clearly of the same craftsmanship. As I studied them more closely, it occurred to me that the same pattern of delicate metal swirls and curves also matched the very design holding the mermaid scale in its place on the silver pendant of my necklace. A shudder trickled down my spine as I connected the three and could no longer doubt the connection between it all. Whatever I had to do with Cordelia and Valdez, I was about to find out.

32

X Marks the Spot

The lock groaned as it clicked into place for the first time in centuries with a careful turn of the iron key. I was almost afraid the lid would crumble off its hinges as I lifted it with gentle hands. I pointed my flashlight beneath the dark wooden lid to illuminate a stack of yellowed and ravaged papers, neatly arranged and held together by a string that was ready to disintegrate upon the slightest touch.

As carefully as I could manage, I pulled the papers out, trying to untie the stiff, dried string, but it snapped immediately. The papers seemed to be a mix of letters and merchant records, specifically showing where the *Siren's Scorn* had made port and how many "units" were processed and sold. Eerily enough, many of them bore the signature of Daven Harrington, who I supposed was Milo's father selling on behalf of Valdez. But that was far from the majority of papers. The rest were detailed ink hand drawings of specific areas in the sea, with significance placed on certain spots over others. Some showed the Caribbean, some the Atlantic, even the Baltic as well as a few others.

As if on cue, the bottom from underneath the box gave way to a rotting secret compartment, obviously added in some DIY fashion. And as I poked the extra compartment, I noticed, tucked within the box's carved out frame, a journal obviously well-used. It looked like it could have been at least a hundred years old, with its worn leather binding and chipped, yellowed pages. More than anything I longed to delve into its pages of secrets, but of course it might require more time than I could afford there in the attic. I did, however, mentally note that I intended to take it with me later back to the hospital to read.

I shuffled through the sales records and business notes, but a single letter was the document of most intrigue. The handwriting was immaculate and elegant, and my eyes swept over it, pulled in by each word.

My dearest love, Captain of my heart,

What you have asked of me is no small task. I bear the burden of turning over my sisters in exchange for your love. But if the fleeting moments we have spent together are any indication of how it will be to love you forever, I consider it a worthy exchange. I trust you will leave Maria and the boy, as discussed. I shall be the only one who holds your heart, my love. And with this single piece of me, I give you my promise, that as long as you are mine, I shall continue to share my power with you so that you may conquer, and when you someday rule the seas, I will be your queen. With this, you are bound to me.

Forever yours,

Cordelia

I reread the last 2 sentences over again. The piece of her. It was the scale. It had to be. *The last of her.*

As if to confirm my suspicions, when I lifted the journal nestled underneath the letters, there was a spot carved out, with the remnant of a dark velvet surface that had long been worn away. The hollow spot was carved as if for a charm on a chain—a necklace.

With trembling breaths, I slowly reached behind my head to take the necklace off and placed it in the mold. It fit perfectly, down to each individual imperfect edge of the scale.

So now I knew. Valdez was right. It *was* a mermaid scale. Cordelia's scale. And it was no wonder he wanted it. All this meant that it really *could* set the crew free from their torment. But I had to figure out how to use its power to save Mom first. And there were still questions left to answer. Personal ones.

That's when I ran my finger along the crinkled edges of the old journal. It was so brittle from age; I'd have to take extreme care not to damage it.

Just as I began to open the book, Dad texted that he was on his way to pick me up. The hospital was about 15 minutes out. Fifteen immensely valuable minutes. So, I made myself comfortable on the floor, adjusted my flashlight onto the pages, and began to read.

33

MAYDAY

The first page was an entry by my great grandmother Nelda, who seemed to be a young teenager at the time of writing. It was dated December 25th, 1943.

Dear Diary,

Firstly, I want to give you a name. A name of your own. Some-thing more personal than simply 'Diary.' During these times of war, everyone walks around with a frown. But I hope for better days. I know they are coming. So, I think I will name you Hope. As my first entry, you should know it is Christmas and you were given to me as a gift from Father. I hope to write in you every day. But if I can't, please forgive me. There isn't much to do here in Missouri, so I might not always have anything exciting to tell you.

Mama said Father wanted me to have you so I would stop talking about traveling the world so much. They say it's dangerous, and I can do all the traveling I want by reading and writing about it instead. Maybe that's somewhat true, but I still plan to see the snowy mountains and the oceans someday.

Well, it's time for Christmas dinner. Mama's calling. I hope she made sweet rolls. Until tomorrow.

Love,

Nelda

I skimmed the next two pages. There wasn't much of anything except for her writings about the snow and New Year's Day, when everyone hoped this year would bring the end of World War II. From the looks of it, she had managed to keep up with her goal of writing every day, but only for about a month. After

January, it dwindled to sporadic dates with missing days in between, and entries grew less frequent, but more detailed. She spoke a lot about wanting to travel, but never mentioned where, specifically. At least not until one entry that caught my eye from the summer of 1944.

June 7th, 1944

Dear Hope,

I have been begging Mama to take us to the beach this summer. I ask every year, and she always says no. She never has a good reason either, it's just that Grandmama Alma used to make her fret with her stories all the time when she was growing up. Mama also says folks can't be traveling like that right now during the war. I guess that part makes sense. But someday, I'm going to beg until she can't stand it. She will have to take us eventually. When this war is over. It can't be much longer now. But until then I'll keep imagining. I just want to feel the sand under my feet and look for seashells and feed seagulls and—

The text from my dad whisked me back to reality. It was already morning. Had I really been up here all night?

He was here. I placed my thumb on the page to save my place and stuck an old receipt between the pages. Before leaving, I snapped a quick picture of the box with my phone, inside and outside. I wanted to show Milo when I saw him again. I had thought about taking it back to Florida with me, but I decided I didn't need another thing Valdez might want to hunt me down for.

I quickly scurried to place everything as I found it, carefully keeping the journal close to my body. With a jumpiness that wasn't typical of me, I climbed back down the attic stairs and managed to shut the entrance just as Dad opened the front door.

"Morning, Trina." He smiled, but there was exhaustion in his eyes. The poor man worried himself so much. Without a doubt, his heart truly belonged to my mom, no matter the pain she caused him.

"Hey, Dad," I stepped toward him for a hug. "How's Mom?"

He looked down and pinched his forehead with his thumb and middle finger. "The same. No change."

"Yet." I put my hand on his shoulder and pulled my lips into a small but sweet smile. It felt weird to be the one offering encouragement for once, but I knew he needed it more than ever. The truth was, I did, too. I still had no useful information whatsoever on what had caused my generational curse or how the scale was supposed to stop it.

The ride back to the hospital was borderline awkward. The usual connection with Dad just wasn't there. I could tell he was trying to act as if things were normal, but something was missing, and the issue at hand just hung in the air like a dark fog. I thought of something to say to break up the silence.

"So, how is Thanksgiving supposed to work this year?"

I asked, acknowledging that it was only two days away. Typically, the holiday included only us three sitting at the walnut-stained table in the dining room with a turkey and some mashed potatoes, since neither set of my grandparents was around. Last year was a bit different. It was just me and Dad, and a slew of unanswered calls to Mom. This year wasn't looking much better, though that was obviously the least of our worries.

"I don't know, *hija*. I haven't even thought about it to be honest," Dad loosened his grip on the steering wheel and adjusted his shoulders, as if trying to force himself to relax.

"Well," I rubbed my knuckles together, "I could try to make something. If Mom's still at the hospital on Thanksgiving, we can just all eat there." I was no chef, but I could manage to follow some recipe blog instructions as much as anybody. And I could whip up some mean instant mashed potatoes.

"We'll see." Dad nodded. "What's important is that we're together again."

"Dad," I drew in a breath. "If Mom gets better now, but goes right back to drinking, what are you going to do?" I didn't have the heart to fully express what was in my head. Did he plan to live this way forever? In a constant state of worry for his wife who would forever be just one more drink away from her own demise? "I love Mom, but I want you to be happy. Her vice has you just as chained down as it does her."

My father started to respond, but then pulled his words back in. I watched his mustache quiver a bit as he gathered his thoughts.

"There's something I've been meaning to tell you. I should have told you when you first got here." He blinked, keeping his eyes on the road. "But I was scared. And I didn't want to make you scared, too."

I urged him to go on with a lift of my eyebrows.

"I think your mom was..."

"What? She was what?"

"I think she did this to herself. I think she was trying to take her life."

My jaw dropped, and I stuttered my reply.

"You—you think she did this on purpose?"

"I—I found a bottle of pills next to her along with all the empty bottles. It was enough to knock out a horse. The doctors said it's a miracle she's still alive."

I was speechless. I tried to drag up words from within, but the well in me was dry. I felt my face burning and I blinked to hold in the tears that begged to gush out. That was what I had been afraid of.

"So, then what do we do?" I asked, my voice cracking.

"I really don't know, Katrina." It was unusual to hear him say my full name, and it meant things weren't good. "We'll try to get her help. Better help. It's just one step at a time. Like it always has been."

I responded with a few weak nods of my head, knowing it was all futile, and knowing the curse was beginning to claim Mom just like it had all her ancestors.

We pulled into the hospital parking garage. Neither of us said anything else on the way up to Mom's room. I stayed with Mom, and Dad went to run some errands. I took the opportunity to crack open the journal once more, picking up where I left off. I could hardly look at Mom without crumbling, so I kept my head buried in the pages.

June 11th, 1944

Dear Hope,

I don't think Mama is going to change her mind. Yesterday Father was furious when he found out I've been pestering Mama so much. He said he'd switch me if I brought it up again. So I made sure to keep out of sight for a while. But today I asked Mama if she'd ever been to the beach before, and she said of course not. I guess I didn't think about it, but Grandmama didn't have a car when Mama was growing up. She couldn't have gone to the beach even if she wanted to. But between you and me, I think deep down she'd like to see it someday, too. She just won't admit it.

Lovingly yours,

Nelda

The more I read, the more I learned that Grandmama Alma had made quite the lasting impression in the family, though I couldn't tell if she was still alive then or not. Her daughter, Esther, seemed completely willing to follow in her footsteps, and as a result, to my knowledge, poor stubborn Nelda never got her beach trip that year. She seemed to leave it alone after that, and from what I could tell, relinquished the idea altogether. But after reading through the next bunch of entries full of trips to the park, dance lessons, starting the 9th grade, and one about lying to Father about practicing her cross stitching, I came across one entry in particular that stoked my interest beyond the others.

August 2nd, 1944

Dear Hope,

I had the most frightening dream last night. I was drowning, in the ocean of all places! I couldn't breathe. I could almost taste the salt water. It felt so real. Mama came to my room when she heard me screaming. She woke me up and told me it was just a bad dream. But I couldn't go back to sleep. I was so afraid of having that dream again. If that's what drowning feels like, maybe it's not worth ever going near the water. Mama told me this was a warning. She said she'd had it before, too. I think maybe she's right. Maybe it's a good thing we live so far from the beach. I don't think anything could be scarier than drowning.

Nelda

By the time I finished reading that entry, I was holding my breath as though letting it go would cause an explosion. The *same* dream. Centuries old.

Dad entered the room, and I put the journal away. I didn't want him asking questions, so I did my best to keep it out of sight whenever he was around. But I spent the rest of the evening aching to open it back up and explore the rest.

That night, I went back home again, and though I intended to read the rest of Nelda's journal, I also had something else in mind.

34

SINK OR SWIM

I opened my laptop, navigating to all the files I'd saved weeks back at Isabel with the death dates, the list of names, and the strange letter signed by "G." I thought that maybe there could be some clues in Nelda's journal as to who this "G" was. This "G" was as far back as I could trace. Maybe that's where the plagues of dreams and insanity began, too. I printed all the documents one by one and locked myself in my room.

I sat on my bed with papers scattered all around. There were still a few remaining pages of the journal that I hadn't gotten around to reading. My bloodshot eyes scanned the pages, faster and faster, searching and pleading with the faded ink on the paper to show me something new. Wading through entries about more dreams of drowning, the handsome new boy in class, and being on the cusp of the end of the war, I read with urgency. The beat of my heart sped up with each word as I drew closer and closer to the last page. The final entry tore my soul in two.

June 5th, 1945

Hope,

I should change your name. There's nothing hopeful about any-thing anymore. I can't even see through my tears to write this. Yesterday Mama made herself die. She's been so sad for a while, but I never thought she'd do this. Father says she didn't do it to herself, but I know she did. I'm the one who found her——

I encountered difficulty deciphering the smudged words through obvious tear stains blotted all over the page—

—so how do I go on without her? Father doesn't listen to me like she does. He never understands. And I know I'd be switched for saying this, but sometimes I believe this family is cursed. Or maybe we made God angry for something and he's punishing us. I don't know, but I don't want it to happen to me. But I swear I'll go down fighting.

Bye Mama. I'll never take off your necklace, so I can always be near you.

I love you to the depths of the sea.

Nelda

My heart nearly stopped, and I had to take a moment to regather myself before reading it again. After three rereads, my body quivered, knowing full well something dark was at work, and by the looks of it, had been at work for a long time. One line rang over and over in my head like eerie church bells. Though I'd already believed it myself, seeing it written sent chills through me.

"I believe this family is cursed."

I rolled the words around in my head, soaking in them, pulled in by one specific word that I couldn't seem to escape these past few weeks —cursed.

From the looks of it, not a single one of my ancestors had any clue or even mention of how to use the necklace. Did they even know what it was? Where did it even come from in the first place? Was I, too, destined to die at my own stupid hand after only living half a lifetime suffering from progressively worsening hallucinations? I rolled over, fully defeated. It was 3 AM. I wished Milo was there next to me like he had been the night we planned the key heist. I failed to keep the tears from falling, even as I clamped my eyes shut. I was powerless to keep myself from losing everything—my mom, Milo, and eventually, even myself. Our fates were sealed, and just like everyone before me, there was nothing I could do about it.

When I woke, dawn was just peeking through. Like the sky, my mind was clearer now. I could think. I took a deep breath.

Surrounded by loose papers, my notebook, and the journal still open to the last page, I sat up slowly. The letter I had printed signed "G" rested directly in my lap. Rubbing the sleep from my eyes, I strained to read it one last time, with renewed interest and an ability to think a bit more clearly. It was dated 1796, which was the oldest record I had been able to find aside from the birth date of Marina Samuels, who the letter was addressed to.

It was as I scrutinized the page that I noticed a grainy texture around the signature that I hadn't before. It was extremely pixelated and barely there, but there was something more to the name than what I had been able to see at first glance.

With renewed intrigue, I returned to the PDF file of the letter on my laptop and zoomed in on the signature. There was certainly something more, so I enlarged the signature area and reprinted it. Once printed, the marks were even more obvious on the paper than it had been on the computer screen. I looked closely, realizing I couldn't make out the entire name with my naked eye, and decided to use one of my micro-brushes to flesh out the shadows left of the signature. As I had done so many times before, I dipped the brush in some water, as if I was about to add some finite details to a watercolor painting.

As each small curve of the letters came into focus, I felt an icy chill slithering through my veins. I realized the "G" was not a "G" after all, but rather a "C," connected to a...a lowercase "o." A space, followed by "d". There were two missing letters that were completely faded, so I had to fill them in with my best guess. But I followed the faint pattern of the last few letters, fighting to keep my trembling fingers steady with concentration. My locked gaze followed the name slowly taking shape underneath the tip of my brush. As I traced the singular last vowel, my stomach flipped, and my chest constricted. I forgot how to breathe. The room was swaying as though I was back on the ship, being tossed with water's motion. I couldn't look away from the final product, the signature I had written.

Co..d..lia.

It wasn't hard to guess the two missing letters in the middle. I filled them in with the obvious, then stared in disbelief at the name on the page: *Cordelia*.

35

ABANDON SHIP

I t was a good thing I was sitting on my bed, because if I had been standing, I would have stumbled backward from the shock. Every excuse I could think of rushed to my head to convince me that I was wrong. That the name could have been anything else. Maybe I had just traced it wrong. Perhaps I was seeing things that weren't there.

But something in my soul knew that on the contrary, it only made perfect sense. For whatever reason, somehow, some way, the curse on Valdez and his crew and the curse on my family was one in the same. I still didn't quite get why or how. I only understood that everything had started with one vindictive mermaid, who may very well have been my 7th great-grandmother.

But there was one thing I was absolutely certain of: I had reason to break Valdez's curse more than ever now. It was my curse, too. It was the only way to save everyone I cared about. If I didn't, they would all continue to meet the same fate that had cycled through them for centuries.

And if Mom was going to survive, I couldn't waste any more time. Thanksgiving be damned. It already was anyway. I had to return to Constantine. I had to keep my head and break the curse, no matter how much it would break my heart to let Milo go forever. I had to set his tormented soul free. And I had to save Mom from herself and the dreams.

Only one problem stood in my way. I didn't have a way back to Constantine. My plane ticket wasn't for a flight until Friday, but I didn't think it could wait another two days. My Jeep was back in Florida.

I frantically checked the airline websites for the next available flights to Florida. There were plenty, but this close to Thanksgiving and on such short notice, they were all at least $400. I just didn't have it.

But I remembered something. Mom's car was parked outside. I could drive it back. It would be 14 hours of pure mental agony, but it would either be spent here doing nothing or on the road on a mission to save the people dear to me.

But how would I explain any of this to Dad? It would make me look heartless, to suddenly up and leave right before Thanksgiving with Mom in the hospital. But what choice did I have? Hurting Dad was the only way. I may never be able to explain it, but for now, I had to make him believe I still hadn't forgiven her.

I didn't think I could do it face to face. I didn't have time anyway. Tossing on a pair of jeans, boots and layering my top half with a light jacket, I went straight for the bowl by the door where Mom's keys sat untouched. I picked them up, flipping them in my hand as I walked outside, locking the door behind me. With a deep breath of crisp autumn air, I threw myself into the seat of her gray sedan.

I started to call Dad, but I was afraid he would talk me out of it. I knew he would be coming to pick me up later, and I would tell him before then, so my departure didn't surprise him. But I at least had to get out of Ozark first. I needed to be far enough away that I couldn't turn back. For once, I had to be brave, and let the consequences lie.

The steering wheel between my palms became slippery with sweat, and my heart pounded like a war drum in my ears. I felt faint. I hadn't eaten, but if I had I would have thrown it up. Over the next fifteen minutes, I kept trying to find the courage to call Dad. Every time I would reach for the phone, I'd panic and chicken out.

Five more minutes.

But then five minutes became thirty-five. I was already on the interstate heading south. I could imagine my dad's broken expression. It was going to darken his world. When he texted me to ask if I was awake yet, I knew it was time. I called.

"Dad." I started, trying to control the shakiness of my voice. "I'm awake. But don't come to pick me up today. I have to leave for a little while. I took Mom's car."

"What do you mean, Trina?" A subtle panic rose in his voice. "Where are you going?"

"There's something I have to do back in Constantine."

"You're going back to Florida? Now?"

"Yes..." I swallowed the lump in my throat. "Yes, because I can't keep looking at Mom the way she is right now. She made this choice, and I'm tired of always being the one who gets hurt." My chest ached as I forced out the lies.

"I—I thought you were okay. You were just talking about making Thanksgiving dinner."

"Yeah, well that was because I was trying to make you happy. But I'm tired of having to hide how I feel. I just need to get away for a while. I'll be back, don't worry."

"Trina, this is serious. Your mom isn't getting better. There was a lot of damage and—"

"I don't care, Dad." I fought to keep from crying. My words came out like venom. "There. I said it. It's always about Mom. It's always been about Mom in this family. I'm over it."

It was unusual for my dad to be left speechless, but he wasn't saying anything. I knew I had just destroyed him. If I tried to speak another word, tears were going to flow like a flash flood. So, I hung up.

I allowed myself the consolation of crying, careful not to let my tears blur my vision too much as I drove along the freeway. The sky was overcast, darkening my spirit even further. It was a long road, and I wasn't entirely sure what awaited me at the end of it.

I reached Constantine a few hours after nightfall. Fighting my tiredness from the long drive, I parked at the pier, hoping it wasn't too late to find Milo one last time. I had to tell him everything. About the box, the journal, and Cordelia. Maybe he'd already known. But he wanted to allow me the chance to discover it for myself, and I was grateful for that. If it wasn't for him, I wouldn't have known what I was saving my mom from. I wouldn't have even known my mom needed saving. If for nothing else, I owed him heavily for that. I would set him free, even if he thought he didn't want it anymore. I would end his curse and let him rest. But I at least wanted the chance to tell him goodbye.

I stood alone on the pier, wrapping my arms around myself to keep warm. The sea air was bitterly cold, and the waves below were choppy, as if a storm was brewing out at sea. By some instinct I had developed, I checked that my necklace was still around my neck every few moments. If I hadn't tried it already, I would have tossed it into the ocean below, but I remembered what Milo had said. It had to be returned to the depths, whatever that meant. Clearly just putting it in the water wasn't the answer, as we had discovered the night he fought off Bellamy.

The tide was high, and the choppy waters too dangerous to attempt climbing down below to carve my star into the pier posts. I didn't know how I was supposed to let Milo know I was here. But I needed to give him the necklace. I needed to beg him to let me break the curse. I needed him to want to die again. I needed to save him, though my heart was breaking at the thought.

As if by some strange magic, a hauntingly familiar melody began to sing in my head. I followed it, singing aloud the words into the mist of the dark sea. Into the wind, as the waves swelled, and the stars disappeared, I sang this strange song to the tune of my mother's lullaby. Serena's song.

Down by the shore
Meet me once more
By the light of the moon
Love me, then leave me
With the dawn rising
Haunt me forevermore

As the last chilling note escaped my lips, the mist over the water seemed to thicken, and the outline of an albatross came into view. within the fog before disappearing. The necklace around my neck began to shimmer with a soft iridescent glow. I felt a warmth, a small pulse of power, radiating from it against my skin. But it faded as quickly as it started. Had the song awakened it?

I breathed a sigh of relief as I felt footsteps behind me on the wooden pier. I closed my eyes as the steps drew nearer, and warm breath touched the back of my neck. Soft lips grazed against my ear as strong arms reached forward around me, pulling my trembling frame into an embrace. Leaning my head back to rest against his chest, I breathed in him in, expecting to inhale the warm scent of amber, but instead a familiar dark spice infiltrated my nostrils.

"I never thought I'd hear that song again. You almost sounded just like her, you know." Bellamy spoke delicately, and I could feel each movement of his lips along the tip of my ear.

With a startled gasp, I pulled away from his hold. He stood smirking at me with his smoldering blue eyes.

"I had no idea you could sing so beautifully," he added in a voice like rich velvet, "but I guess it only makes sense, siren."

"Stop calling me that," I pleaded. "What are you doing here? W—where is Milo?"

"Tsk, tsk, Katrina," Bellamy shook his head, taking a few steps towards me. "I really thought you'd be happier to see me after all we've been through. Don't forget I helped you escape."

He was right. I was glad to see him. But my gladness was overshadowed by the fear I felt for Milo and my mom.

"I'm sorry." I put a hand to my head. "I'm just worried about him. Has Valdez done anything to him?"

"Don't worry." Bellamy said coolly, "He can't kill him, remember?"

"Exactly, so I can't imagine what kind of torture he might have in mind as an alternative."

"Well, I'll tell you where he is, and how to find him, if you tell me why you're here."

"Really?" I blinked tears back down and pressed my lips together. I couldn't cry, not now. "You're going to blackmail me? Why didn't Valdez punish you for helping me, too?"

"He doesn't know it was me who got you back to shore. Besides, he tends to turn a blind eye to his son."

"So I've heard." I crossed my arms.

"It's too bad I'm not so willing to return the favor for him. Guess I didn't quite inherit his gracious mercifulness." Bellamy sneered with sarcasm.

The wind began to pick up, and my hair blew fiercely behind me in all directions as I raised my voice to talk over it.

"I know that you want him to pay for what he did. I get it. But this curse must end! You have to let go."

"Ah, as I expected." Bellamy's eyes darkened. "So that's what you're here for. You've finally decided you're going to try to break the curse."

"Well...yes. I am." I hesitated. "The curse is connected to my mother's bloodline. She's going to die if I can't end this."

"W—what do you mean?" Bellamy's expression became a genuine picture of concern.

"I mean..." I took a breath. "I found out that Cordelia might have been my 7th great-grandmother."

"And you thought I was crazy," Bellamy stepped forward, closing the space between us, and lifted my chin with his hand. "You see? You *are* a siren."

"No." I squeezed my eyes shut. "It doesn't mean that. Maybe Cordelia was a mermaid but that doesn't make me one." I spat the words out as if they were sand in my mouth. "Anyway, now I told you why I'm here. Now tell me where Milo is."

"He's aboard the ship, love."

"Take me to him."

"I don't think so," Bellamy leaned back on the railing of the pier. "Do you have any idea what will happen to you if you go aboard that ship again? If Valdez knows you're descended from Cordelia..." his voice trailed off, lost to the sound of crashing waves. He stared out into the water, looking past me, but then his blue eyes moved to capture mine.

"I'm going to ask you once more. You're practically making me beg." Bellamy straightened, leaving his position along the railing. He stepped towards me once more and took both my hands in his. "Let me destroy the scale. Go back home so you're safe. Let Valdez get what justice is due him. Let him spend his eternity hopeless, just as he's left me."

I failed to hold back the weakness in my voice, as I battled the raging tears within me. "No!" I shouted, burning my gaze into his. "Can't you see? If I don't break this curse, my mom will die! I will die! Cordelia didn't just curse your crew. She cursed her own daughters with dreams that made them go insane. It hasn't failed a generation." I pulled in a breath of sea air and steadied myself before speaking again. "And if I don't break the curse, Milo goes on suffering forever. Hopeless. He doesn't deserve that. And neither do you, Bellamy."

For the first time since I'd known him, I thought I saw some sort of emotion welling up in Bellamy. His eyes became glassy, and he clenched his jaw tightly. For just a moment, his witty, arrogant persona was gone, no longer there to act as his armor. As he searched for words, he pulled me closer, until we were mere inches apart.

"Please, let me save you," I whispered.

"I wish I could." He let go of my hand and traced my cheekbone gently with his fingers. My chest fluttered, in a strange way. I became rigid and unsure, as was the usual with Bellamy. My body leaned into him slightly, but my mind and heart were divided.

As I studied his handsome face in the shadows, fighting myself to keep from being pulled in by his charm, I lowered my guard, which caused me not to notice what he had done until it was too late

He backed away, looking at me through a pained but unwavering gaze, with the silver chain wrapped around each of his fingers and the pendant tucked tightly into his closed palm.

"No!" I screamed, grasping at my bare neck.

Then, with no warning, I found myself knocked to the ground with the weight of an enormous net. It was soaked through, making it even heavier than it already was. I strained to peek through the dripping seaweed stuck in the holes in the net, and I saw that Bellamy was trapped beneath a net, too.

A group of men—pirates—emerged from the darkness. They ignored Bellamy's insults and attempts to fight them from within the ropes. I groaned, pleaded, and did everything I could to work my way out from the tangles of the net, but it was too heavy, and they were too quick. They tripped my feet out from underneath me with one swift tug of the net. My body slammed against the wet pier floor with an impact that was sure to leave a bruise. I made more attempts to scream as Bellamy and I were dragged as though we were lifeless piles of fish. But no one heard my screams there on the empty pier.

When they finally removed the nets, after dragging us over the edge of the pier, I took a good look around. We were aboard the *Siren's Scorn*. The crew held us both at gunpoint with their pistols and swords. My eyes frantically scanned the deck to see a bloodied figure tied to the mast, his head hanging so low that his matted hair obscured his face. But I knew right away whose hair it was. He looked up at me weakly, through a face smeared with dried blood. Milo.

36

KNOCK SEVEN BELLS

"**M**ilo!" My scream tore through the air as I lunged forward, resisting the crew member who held me in place by my arm.

"Don't worry, lass. He's still alive, of course." Valdez stepped out from the throng of pirates looking on, his men parting the way for him to stand in their midst. "One good thing about this damned curse—it allows me to treat traitors accordingly. Over and over again. Your dear Harrington here has chosen mutiny. So many nights he spent leading my men off your trail. Wasting all our time. Making a fool of us all." Valdez drew his sword from his hip and slashed at Milo's thigh. The blade went deep, sending blood spatters across the deck as it swept through cloth and skin.

"No, stop!" I pleaded. I thought I had run out of tears by now, but I was wrong. My vision blurred as I watched a weary Milo groan in agony. I imagined he would've fallen over by now, but the thick rope across his chest held him standing in place.

Valdez only laughed, a menacing rumble in his throat, and took a step towards Bellamy and me.

"But to be honest, I should be thanking Mr. Harrington for wasting all this time. If he hadn't, we would never have learned about that shocking secret of yours, Katrina." With the bloodied tip of his sword, he moved a stray hair from my face as he came close enough that I could feel his breath on my skin.

"Cordelia's great-granddaughter. Mmm. That explains why you look so much like her. How charming to know she made such a lovely legacy for herself on land while she damned me to these pits of hell."

"As you deserve." Bellamy spat on the deck. His back was pressed against mine, and up until now he had been silent.

"Boy!" Valdez tore himself away from me and swiftly crept to Bellamy, his black boots trekking deftly over the wooden planks of the deck. "I've put up with your insolence long enough. I ought to have you chained up with Harrington over there. This wench has had you wrapped around her finger all this time. Just as is her nature."

The pirates scattered along the deck nodded and voiced their approval in unison.

Valdez turned back to me, his cold eyes narrowing as they searched my chest and neck.

"Where's the scale, whore? Will we have to take the pleasure of stripping you down and searching you for it?"

"Don't you dare touch her!" Milo shouted from the mast as he wrestled against his bindings.

Valdez twisted his lips into a grin. "Or will I have to gut your beloved in front of you to make you talk?" The tears streamed down my face faster than I could blink them away.

"No, no! Don't hurt him anymore, please!" My voice cracked as I cried out the words in anguish. "I came here to break the curse. You can have the scale. I came here to give it to you, but Bellamy took it. He took the scale from me just before you kidnapped us." My whole being shook as I watched Valdez stew over my words. He looked at Bellamy.

"Is that true?" He asked. "Hand it over, boy."

"I—I dropped it," Bellamy stuttered. "It must be back on the pier." I couldn't tell if he was telling the truth or not, but I felt my heart drop at the thought of him having lost the necklace.

"He's lying," Milo uttered. "Are you really so blinded by your love for him that you can't see that your own son despises you? He's lying."

"Shut him up," Valdez ordered one of the crewmen. A man standing near Milo hit him across the face with the blunt end of a pistol. I winced at the sound. Valdez watched both me and Bellamy with snake-like eyes, reminding me of a vulture as he circled us. "Men, throw these two in the brig for now and go back to search the pier."

A man grabbed me, and another took Bellamy, pointing swords into our backs as they forced us across the ship and towards the opening to a galley beneath the deck. Bellamy went before me, disappearing below deck. As I passed Milo, he looked up at me. I fought against the man pushing me forwards, begging for just a moment to speak to him. As if he found some inkling of compassion within himself, he let me stop long enough to meet Milo's gaze. My heart shattered in a way I'd never felt before.

"I'm sorry, Milo," I croaked through my whispers.

"Don't worry about me. I've always been meant to die, one way or another." He squirmed against the ropes cutting into his chest as he fought to catch his breath. "But not you. Just get the necklace from Bellamy, give it to Valdez, and get off the ship. Save yourself. I can't live with myself if anything happens to you. I'd kill myself a thousand times until it finally works."

"Oh, she won't be getting off the ship, Harrington. If she's descended from a siren, I'll be keeping that heart of hers for myself while you and the rest of this pathetic crew sink to the bottom of the sea for good. You know I don't take chances." Valdez appeared from behind us, and spoke lowly to Milo, as though he wanted to keep the rest of the crew from hearing. But I heard it, and I shuddered as my blood turned to ice.

"What?" Milo's voice splintered as his passionate cries turned to threats. "No, Valdez! You won't touch her! If you hurt her...I swear on my father's grave—"

I couldn't hear anymore as the door to the galley was closed behind me. The pirate behind me led me down to a dark cell, ravaged and rusted with barnacles clinging to the bars. He shoved me forward into the cell with Bellamy, who stood at the far end, in a corner obscured by shadows, with his back to the wall.

The pirate locked the cell door, and then retreated up to the deck. I quickly whipped around and grabbed the bars, shaking them in an attempt to break free. When that didn't work, I began desperately checking every edge and corner for anything I could use to break out. But there was nothing in the cell with us except a rusted bucket likely used for waste.

I noticed Bellamy wasn't moving or speaking. He seemed entranced as he stood staring into the wall. I felt the ship lurching forward.

"Bellamy, please help me," I begged. "I just heard your father say he's going to—"

Bellamy spun around to face me, his eyes flashing with anger even in the darkness. "He's not my father! I refuse to accept that monster as my father!"

He stomped towards me, and I stepped back, afraid of what he might do. He pinned my back against the cell bars, his chest heaving as he growled. "He's taken everything I ever cared about from me. And now he's doing it all over again." His voice became eerily calm as he stared into the deepest part of me.

I trembled as I spoke, afraid of what he might do next. It was all I could think of to do to try to keep him from having another outburst.

"I—I found a letter from Valdez to Cordelia, Bellamy. He wanted to save you."

Bellamy didn't say anything, but only leaned in closer so that his eyes were inches from mine. Then, he straightened his shoulders and began to chuckle with a laugh that chilled my bones. He pointed to his tattoo of the bleeding heart pierced by two arrows.

"Do you know what this tattoo means?"

I shook my head.

"The first arrow to my heart was when Serena was killed. The second...Well that one's from my father. And he's dead to me."

"I know Valdez is terrible, but I think in his own way, he loves you. In the letter, he was begging her to come back just to free you from the curse." My voice cracked as it quivered.

"You mean the letter never sent? You think that man cares about me? That was just a way to trick Cordelia into coming back. But even *she* wasn't so stupid," he sneered. "If he cared about me, do you think he would want to tear your heart out for himself just so he can go on living while his only son pays for his sins?"

He was right. It was a selfish thing to do, and it certainly negated the care Valdez seemed to exhibit for Bellamy in his letter. I was a fool to think otherwise. My thoughts swirled in my head out of control. I didn't know what to say or do next, and I grasped for some sense of hope, but I couldn't find it. I thought of Milo outside, and my mom back in the hospital. I was failing them, and it was tearing me apart.

Bellamy still had me pressed to the bars between his arms. He was still breathing hard, as if containing some raging beast within. He was hardly the charismatic charmer I'd met in the library so many nights ago. Now he was a broken, confused, and out of control shell of himself.

And I hoped he still had the necklace. It was my only hope.

"I know you're hurt and angry." I finally spoke. I was about to ask him for the necklace one last time, but I worried that if I suggested it now, it would send him over the edge. I couldn't afford to risk it. If he had the scale, it had to be somewhere on his person. But it could've been anywhere. The only option I had left was to manipulate it out of him, though it pained me to stoop so low. I reached for him.

"This doesn't have to be the end, Bellamy," I whispered, as seductively as possible. "You were right. There is no way out of this. Unless we figure out how to use the scale's magic." I slid my hand around his waist, underneath his loose-fitting shirt, feeling his skin and discreetly searching for anything that felt like the necklace. "Maybe we can figure out how, together." I leaned forward and spoke softly into his ear. My fingers trailed up his chest, and then along his neck until I was touching his face.

The way he looked back at me as I touched him almost brought more tears to my eyes. I never thought you could see someone's spirit breaking, but I watched his do exactly that, as he realized I was now the one offering affection. He looked into my eyes, but stared through them, as though they were someone else's. With short huffs of breath, he leaned into me as he gripped the cell bars in his unrelenting hold.

Then his eyes softened in a strange sort of way. I thought he would kiss me, but he didn't. With quaking breaths, I withdrew my hand from his face and sent it trailing down with the other, exploring his body for any sign of the necklace. I forced myself to remain as calm and unwavering as I slid my hands down farther than I had hoped to go, caressing the skin beneath his trousers, praying for the feeling of a small chain or pendant to graze my shaking fingers.

"Serena." Bellamy breathed, closing his eyes, and pressing his lips to my neck. I nearly jumped back from the sudden mention of the name, but I held my ground. When Bellamy's eyes opened, they were soulless blue voids, as deep and endless as the sea.

I hadn't even noticed that someone had entered the room until I heard the lock clicking behind me. The door to the brig swung open, causing me to stumble backward as I had been leaning against it. Bellamy snapped from his trance and grabbed my wrist with a ruthless grip. Without warning, he twisted around and sucker punched the crewman who'd opened the door, then snatched the man's sword from its holster.

"You think I don't know what you're trying to do, Katrina?" Bellamy bared his teeth at me. "Seems you've learned a few too many tricks from us filthy pirates. Or maybe you're just finally realizing what a siren can do."

He pulled me to him, his arm across my body and the other holding the sword at my neck. I resisted, but he only pushed the blade against my skin, further, and I knew he was serious.

He forced me up the steps to the brig, keeping the sword pointed at my throat the entire time. I could see that the ship had sailed far from any point of land now. We were back in open water. And I could see Valdez waiting for us at the top of the deck.

"Well, well," he spoke with a voice like thunder, standing at Milo's side, surrounded by his crew. "We didn't find the scale, boy. Where is it? It's nearly sunrise, so speak up."

"I'm never giving it to you." Bellamy choked out the words. "I'm never giving *her* to you either."

"Bellamy, let go of her! What are you doing?" Milo's voice pierced through the sound of the rioting waves below. The ocean breeze blew my hair against my face, plastering loose strands to my tear-soaked cheeks.

Bellamy turned his gaze to Milo. "If I had to watch the girl I love die, it's only fair that you should, too. If I don't kill her, Valdez will. And I won't let him win again."

I couldn't have imagined Bellamy would do this. I never dreamed he'd let his pain take him this far.

"Don't do this," I whispered, quietly enough that the rest of the crew couldn't hear me.

"I have to." He spat out his words through gritted teeth. I could feel the blade shaking against my skin as his hand trembled.

He blinked through his own tears and swallowed, and I thought, for just a second, he was going to change his mind. And he did. He tightened his grip and lowered the edge of the sword to my chest, right over my pounding heart.

"Go on, boy." Valdez's midnight voice hummed as he smiled, seemingly entertained with the whole scene. "Go on. Cut her heart out. Take it for yourself. At least I'll die seeing you finally become the pirate I always hoped you'd be."

Bellamy hesitated, pulling my head back as if to give himself more clearance to my chest. I thought I would faint if he weren't forcibly holding me up. I was dizzy, and my vision blurry from crying. I could only trust what I could hear. I heard Milo screaming, pleading in a voice of agony, begging Bellamy to stop. I heard Valdez laughing. I heard Bellamy's breaths coming fast as he kept me frozen in this horrific moment of anticipation.

"Go on, Bellamy." Valdez urged once more. "Take the heart. Maybe you can even use it to bring back that lass of yours."

I felt a shift in Bellamy as his father's cruel words took hold. as his face turned pale.

"Bellamy..." I choked. "Don't be like Valdez. This isn't you. Serena wouldn't want this." He loosened his grip and eased the blade against my chest, but kept it aimed towards my heart. I turned my head to look into his face. "You have the scale, Bellamy. The ship is about to go under with all of us on it. It's going to go to the depths either way. It's too late to stop it."

"I can destroy it. Or...what if...what if I *can* bring her back?" he said shakily, as if trying to convince himself, his empty eyes red with strain.

I shook my head softly. "No. No...you can't." In a moment of courage, I took his hand holding the sword and lowered it. He offered no resistance. I leaned forward, whispering as quietly as I could.

"But you can finally be with her," I uttered, and immediately pressed my lips against his. I could taste the salt from both our tears as we stood locked in our dark kiss of surrender. The sword fell out from his grasp, clattering on the wooden floor below. He slid his hand into mine and closed his fingers. When he let go, I realized he had tucked the necklace into my closed palm.

Valdez roared in anger and sent forth a flurry of curses as Bellamy pushed me to the side, raised his sword with a cry of anger, and cut Milo's ropes free.

37

THE DEVIL AND THE DEEP BLUE SEA

I ran to Milo, nearly collapsing at his side. Bellamy stood over us facing his father.

"I'm so sorry," I cried, pushing the hair back from his battered face. "Look at you...I wanted to tell you goodbye. This isn't how I wanted it."

He grasped my face between both hands. "All that matters is you're safe." He smiled that crooked smile through a bloodied lip and bruised cheek. "I'm the one who should be sorry. I promised to protect you. Whatever happens, you have to get off the ship when it goes down. The sun will be up soon."

The ocean was howling below. It had been growing louder since Bellamy held me at sword point. The air had shifted, in the same way it had on the island weeks before. Water spun slowly drawing the ship in as it rocked beneath the raging water. The maelstrom was forming.

I pressed my forehead to Milo's, breathing in his scent mixed with blood and brine.

"Katrina." he sighed my name as though it brought him relief just to say it. "I love you, Katrina." My heart stood still as his voice soothed my soul.

"I...I—" I searched for words, but they wouldn't come, and when they finally did, they were cut short by the captain approaching from behind.

"Give me the scale!" He ordered, standing over me.

I started to hand over the necklace to Valdez, but some strange burst of bravery within me told me to withhold it. *I* would be the one to break the curse, to ensure he didn't somehow cheat his way out of it.

"I don't trust you!" I shot back.

He reached for me, but Milo used a dagger he had hidden in his boot to deflect his reach. Trembling, I made a break to the edge of the ship. Leaping up onto the hull, I grabbed the netting fastened to the sails for balance. I thought I was going to be sick, but I held my ground, looking at Milo to give myself the strength to go through with my plan.

The wind whipped my face, and the salty sea mist stung my eyes. Lightning ripped across the sky in bright flashes, allowing me just a momentary glance at the swirling obsidian water below, beginning to funnel into a black abyss.

I heard a grunt that made me look back. Valdez and the crew stood facing Milo and Bellamy, and me. Somehow Milo had managed to swipe his pistol, and Bellamy had picked his sword back up. They stood with their backs to me, yards away, barely managing to hold off the approaching crew and captain. Someone fired at me, but missed.

"Don't shoot her, fools! I still need the heart out of her...alive."

I looked at the necklace one last time, smoothing my thumb over the scale pendant as its iridescent colors caught the lighting. With one last glance back, I tossed the necklace into the water below, making sure the motion was visible to Valdez and his crew.

Everyone on deck stopped dead in their tracks, including Milo and Bellamy. I gripped the netting as the ship fought to sling me overboard. The shouts and grumbles of the crew ceased. The clamor of swords and daggers came to a halt. There was only the sound of the wind and the waves. I didn't know what we were waiting for, but I wasn't sure anyone was getting what they hoped for. The necklace disappeared into the dark waters, and the maelstrom continued spinning, picking up speed as the ship began to creak and groan with the force of being pulled in.

After a moment of silence, the crew began to mutter among themselves. Valdez grunted in frustration and demanded the crew grab Bellamy and Milo. Milo fired into the fray, and Bellamy swung his sword, but the few crew members who took the force of their blows merely stumbled backward and others took their place. Three crew members grabbed Milo and Bellamy each, keeping them from moving. Valdez stepped forward, picking up Milo's dropped dagger. He looked at me, then at Milo, before ramming the blade between Milo's ribs. I screamed through new tears.

"Stop hurting him! What more do you want from me? I tried to break the curse! It didn't work!"

Valdez didn't speak, but instead twisted the dagger in his hand. Milo cried out in groans of torment, making my blood run cold. Bright crimson trickled from Milo's mouth as he caught his breath.

"Come down here." Valdez coaxed. "Save him. Your heart in exchange for him. If you don't, *this* is his eternity. He'll never see relief. Sundown to sunrise and everything in between."

"Katrina, no. Don't you dare..." Milo could barely spit out the words as he choked on the blood.

I looked at him and the puddle of scarlet forming below him. I didn't need to come down there for Valdez to rip my heart out. He was already doing it.

"It appears you're caught between the devil and the deep blue sea, lass." Valdez mocked. "There's no way off this ship."

My mind raced. I didn't know where to look for the answer. I had tried everything I knew to try. And Valdez was right. It was much too late to get off the ship. There was no way around the fact that tonight I would have to die somehow. I replayed my options. I could either let Valdez cut out my heart, I could hold them off long enough to go down with the ship, or...

A familiar phrase echoed in my head, but I wasn't sure.

"Bellamy!" I cried. "Do you remember the words to Cordelia's curse?"

"Of course," he called through his restraints.

"Recite it to me!"

The crew looked at one another in confusion, and Bellamy did, too.

"Just do it!" I screamed in desperation.

"Okay...um... With the moon you shall rise, As the night calls the tide. By day, bound to the depths. Forevermore this curse shall be kept. Lest to the depths is returned what was taken... the last of her."

I repeated the last part in a voice only I could hear.

"Lest to the depths is returned what was taken; the last of her."

The last of her. The last of her.

Then I realized. I knew what it meant. The curse wouldn't break from just returning the literal last piece of Cordelia to the ocean. It meant a remnant of her, a mermaid—the last mermaid—had to be returned to the ocean. And the dreams. The dreams were to keep us all from ever coming here. Cordelia never wanted the curse broken. Her hatred for Valdez ran *that* deep. So she cursed her own, too. To keep us from the sea. And *I* was the last of her. The chilling revelation seeped into my core like the icy rain soaking my skin.

The storm was strong now, and rain began pelting down like bullets. The ship leaned and tilted as the waves rose and the ghostly cyclone began to suck it inward. Gripping the net, squinting through the rain, I turned to Milo and Bellamy one last time. The crew was now watching me with as much anticipation as they were. They all just wanted to finally die, and I couldn't blame them.

I fixed my eyes on Milo. The rain had washed away his river of blood. He watched me with fearful eyes as the men forced him upright on his knees. I hoped I could save him from this fate. I hoped this worked.

I took one long, deep breath, forcing my fear back down into my chest. I leaned out over the edge of the ship as the water reached for me. Then, with my body rigid and my hammering heart clenched, I let my fingers slip one by one from the rigging and leapt down into the black, churning water.

38

DEAD IN THE WATER

The last thing I heard were shouts from both Milo and Bellamy growing distant from above. I don't remember the drop from the ship to the water below, but I vividly remember the ocean swallowing me whole.

The turbulent waters ripped into my flesh like daggers on impact. The cresting waves rolled over me, forcing me down with all their fury. As I fought to find the surface, the distance between my body and the skyline only grew as the maelstrom's current dragged me down.

I kept hoping I would wake up in my bed, in a frantic cold sweat, and Milo would be beside me to calm me. But that kind of relief never came. Instead, my lungs burned from the inside out as I pleaded for air, flailing helplessly in the pitch blackness of the water.

This was a mistake.

I prayed to whoever was listening that my sacrifice had been the answer. I clung tightly to the hope that somehow my mother would now be free from the nightmares, and that the souls of the crew above me could be put to rest once and for all.

I fought the voice in my head telling me otherwise until my last conscious breath. In the cold grip of death, I grasped in desperation at my senses as they faded one by one. With one muted scream, the pain of it all escaped me in the form of bubbles. Then the dark water rushed in, replacing my cry, and pulled me to the depths.

There was no way for me to know how long I was at the bottom of the ocean. I don't even know if what I saw or felt was real. But at some point, I opened my eyes to what I thought was the afterlife. I was floating, suspended underwater in a calm sea. Bright cerulean glistened around me in shimmering curtains, clear enough that the white sunlight broke through it, stretching to the ocean floor. With heightened senses, I could see as clearly as though I was on land. I could make out each grain of sand beneath me, and even the detailed stripes and speckles on the fish that swam past. Every swish and sway of the water reached my ears perfectly. The salt water on my skin felt as natural as air. And somehow...somehow, I could breathe. Only...I wasn't breathing. I didn't have to, somehow. It was beautiful and terrifying all at once.

I tried moving. I tried swimming up to the surface, but my legs wouldn't move no matter how much I willed them. Within moments, the heavenly scene around me began to fade. But it was me. I was the one fading. My eyes grew heavy, but I fought to hold them open long enough to spin around and take in the rest of my surroundings.

And in the distance, I caught one glimpse that reminded me it was all real. One glimpse that gave me the peace of knowing my plan had worked, and it wasn't all for nothing. Meters from me, nestled in its final resting place, was the *Siren's Scorn*, in all her lifeless, tattered glory.

Finally.

I had saved him. Both of them. And Mom, I hoped.

My head fell forward as I closed my eyes, succumbing once more. Through the ghostly wisps of my long hair floating freely around me, I thought I caught a glance of something strange below me where my feet should've been. I strained to see before I blacked out again. Something silver glittered in place of my legs. Something inhumanly beautiful. Something...

When I came to, I was face down in the sand. The tide washed over me, back and forth, just reaching my waist. Wet hair draped across my neck and face. My clothes were soaked through and clung annoyingly to me with every movement as I retched and coughed up seawater. Every inch of my body ached, as though I'd been hit by a truck.

I grimaced, struggling to muster the little strength I had left to get up on my feet. By the way each joint screamed at me under the pressure of any weight, I thought my bones were broken. Worst of all, I had no idea where I was. The beach didn't look familiar, and I didn't have my phone with me to call anyone.

Disoriented and sore, I finally found my footing. The sun was just coming up, slowly banishing the clear purple sky in favor of orange and pink ribbons across the ocean's horizon. I studied the area, looking for something I recognized. Something to get me home.

I tilted my head back, looking heavenward, when I noticed a bright star still shining. I smiled a broken smile. I knew that star. And I followed it, walking in the direction it faced along the coast.

As I trudged along the empty coast, the drying sand and salt made me itch. The brisk morning air kept me shivering. My bruised body sang out in pain with each step. But what bothered me more than any of that was the way the open ocean at my side mocked me.

It looked just the same as every day before, lazy waves lapping the shore. The tide would rise and fall just as it always had. As if nothing had changed. When, in fact, it hid so many dark secrets beneath. Secrets that I could never tell. Secrets it had harbored for centuries, and yet just like that, in one instant, it had swallowed them whole.

The lonely walk felt like an eternity. By the time I reached familiar shores, dawn had come and gone. I must have been going for at least an hour before I recognized the pier in the distance. Seeing it brought back a flood of memories I was trying to forget.

In just one month my life had been changed forever. In one night, I had broken ancient curses, both magical and generational. And I had managed to do it without getting my heart cut out by pirates. So why did it feel like it had been ripped out anyway?

If I cried any more, I thought I might shrivel up from dehydration. But it turned out I had one tear left. A tear for Milo. For the love I'd lost, but for the love I'd given by setting him free from his curse. A tear for Bellamy, and the pain he spent so long trying to escape. A tear for Serena, who had not deserved her fate. And a tear for Mom and all those in my bloodline who'd suffered from the vengeance of Cordelia.

I let the tear escape my eye with one last look at the sea before painstakingly crawling into the driver's seat of Mom's car. Reaching for my phone, I saw 9 missed calls from Dad, 3 texts, and one voicemail.

"Trina, your mom...She's waking up! She doesn't remember anything, but she's going to be okay."

His message reassured me once more that I had done the right thing. However, when I thought of the last thing I'd said to Dad, it felt like a kick in the gut. I was too drained to think about how I would reconcile that, but I knew I'd figure it out later. For now, I sent him the only text my brain could formulate, just so he would know I was safe.

Happy Thanksgiving, Dad. I'm coming back home.

39

Shipshape

I drove home the day after Thanksgiving. I was so wiped out, I would have much preferred to fly, but Mom would need her car back.

Mom was released from the hospital the same day, and she said she'd had the best sleep of her life overnight. Though she didn't specify why, I knew exactly what she meant. There were no inklings of nightmares to greet me in my sleep either. It was the most liberating rest I'd ever experienced, and my only regret was knowing my grandmother and all those before her would never get to experience i
t.

As we sat around the table with our Friday night late takeout Thanksgiving dinner, it finally felt like we were a whole family again. I heard Mom's laugh for the first time since I was a kid. And Dad's smile couldn't have been bigger. I was quiet. Still adjusting. But I allowed myself to be content. I owed myself at least that.

After dinner, I excused myself to my room. As I was unrolling the package I had brought back with me, Mom appeared in the doorway. I tucked the package away so she wouldn't see.

"Katrina." her voice, strangely light and free, drifted across the room.

"Yeah, Mom?" I asked, still a little hesitant, but trying my best not to let on.

"I just remembered. Did you ever find the box you were looking for?"

I shook off a shudder at the mention. "I did," I said calmly. "It had everything I was hoping to find."

"You were able to get it open?" She seemed shocked.

"Well..." I looked away, still crafting my full explanation, and wishing I hadn't said so much. "Yes. But trust me, it wasn't easy." That certainly wasn't a lie.

"Wow." She sat down at the foot of my bed. "You know, I remember my mom trying so hard to get it open when I was a kid, but she never could. She always wondered what was inside."

"It was practically just a jewelry box for the necklace, with some old letters and stuff." I was going to leave it at that, but something nagged at me to tell her more. It was only fair for her to know of our heritage just as I did. I knew she'd never be able to connect the part about the mermaids and pirates. I wondered if she even remembered everything she'd told me during her drunken phone conversations. Maybe telling her that every other woman in our bloodline was prone to the same mental torment she'd suffered might make her feel a little less guilty for something so out of her control. "Did you know about the secret compartment with my great grandmother's diary in it?"

"Really? I had no idea. I've never really messed with it much. It's one of those heirloom things I just kept it safe and didn't ask questions. Like the necklace. But maybe I should have believed in those stupid family legends and things wouldn't have gotten so bad. Who knows."

"Well, you should read it sometime." With a discreet glance, I noticed the key lying on my bedside dresser. I had no intention of taking it with me. "I think you'll realize you and grandma aren't the only ones who struggled. It was never your fault."

"We've all known it ran in the family. Every daughter. There's even a rumor one of them was put into an asylum because she really thought that necklace was magical. So, it became a bit of a family ghost story. Who knows if any of that was true. But it's always been passed down. But I didn't want any part of it. I thought it was all just stupid superstition. But I finally got desperate enough.... last year...and that's when I left. I went to get the necklace back. It was in storage with your grandfather's family in Missouri. I felt stupid, but I had to try *something*. It sounds ridiculous, but I actually believed it all for a minute there. I'm sorry I sent it to you. I can't believe I actually fell for all that."

My mom smiled at me, in a weirdly warm way that made me happy and nervous all at the same time. I wasn't used to talking to her sober, and it was still an awkward endeavor. But I was glad for it. Suddenly her eyes narrowed.

"Where is the necklace anyway?" she asked.

"I left it back in Constantine," I said simply. That wasn't a lie either. I just left out the part about it being at the bottom of the ocean.

"Well that just proves all along this whole nightmare thing had nothing to do with that necklace. We clearly didn't need it and things turned out okay. You're not having nightmares anymore, are you?"

I considered telling her about how the song I had sung on the pier seemed to have unlocked some part of the necklace's power, but I decided not to mention it. Mom was clearly set on being a skeptic. It didn't matter much anyway, now.

"No. I'm not." I chuckled at the irony, but Mom spoke with a sudden seriousness that caught me off guard.

"I'm proud of you, Katrina. And I know I can't make up for all those times I wasn't there for you. But I've already found a program to help me stay clean—for good. And I think it will be easy this time. Really, I do. Because I haven't even craved a drink once since we left the hospital. It's like...it's like I woke up completely new. Like a weight's been lifted." She breathed in like she was smelling sweet spring air. "I promise you won't have to worry about me when you go back to Florida. Don't let anything—especially me—keep you from the dream you started pursuing there."

I thought it was a strange coincidence for her to say that. After everything Constantine had brought me, I wasn't sure if I should go back. I was considering finishing the semester and then trying to transfer somewhere else. I didn't know if I could handle the painful haunting memories.

"Thanks, Mom," I said, finding the boldness within me to offer her a hug. Her eyes lit up, and she welcomed it with open arms. We stood together in my room, hugging each other tightly, without the smell of alcohol or feeling of resentment coming between us. I had lost all hope for a hug like that a long time ago, so I quietly cherished it all the more.

When Mom left my room, I continued unrolling the package I had brought home. It was 'Bad Dreams,' the infamous scholarship-winning watercolor that had started it all. Taking a firm hold of the rag paper canvas, I held it up in front of me, and looked it over one last time before tearing it in two, top to bottom.

I waited until Sunday afternoon to leave for Florida. Both my parents accompanied me to the airport and graciously paid for my extra plane ticket, since I had forfeited the original. It was an unreal experience, being able to say goodbye to both of them at the same time, with no lingering hang-ups present.

As the plane lifted, I watched the clouds from the window. I wondered what awaited me back in Constantine. I promised Mom I would at least finish the semester, but beyond that, I didn't know. I didn't believe my wounded heart could ever forget. In all honesty, I didn't want to forget.

After checking my single carry-on through security, I rushed to the pickup area, where McKenzie waited for me in her car, stalled in the blinding sun, top down, and music blaring. The sticky air of Florida greeted me as I hopped into the driver's seat, careful not to strain my still-recovering body.

"Thanks for offering the ride." I smiled.

"You know I got you! Good break?"

"Yeah, it was..." I squinted in the sunlight. "...eventful. My family's back together and my mom's not spiraling anymore, so I'd say things are good."

McKenzie leaned over and hugged me, while cars behind her honked.

"Chill out! One sec!" She cried over her shoulder, shooting them a prickly stare. Fighting with something buried under the unused jacket in her floorboard, she grinned at me as she produced that annoying vintage Polaroid.

"They can wait. We have to get our first airport pickup picture. For documentation purposes of course."

I knew my face was redder than a chili pepper with embarrassment from the drivers behind us cussing her out. But she couldn't be bothered. I leaned into the frame just to appease her as quickly as possible, and with one push of the button, she snapped her prized photo.

She shoved the camera and freshly printed photograph into my lap and sped off, jolting me backward. Despite her unnerving driving, I smirked to myself. At least one thing was still the same.

On the drive back to Isabel, McKenzie entertained me with stories about her extravagant Thanksgiving hosted at her aunt's racehorse farm in Ocala, where everyone gathered, including Lt. Burke.

"And the best part of all," she squealed. "I broke up with Ty."

That was one twist I hadn't seen coming.

"Really?" I shot her a confused look. "Would Noah have anything to do with that?"

"No, no, not at all! Noah had nothing to do with it. I dunno, Ty just didn't seem to appreciate me, ya know?" She flipped back her tangerine hair, despite the wind blowing it right back all over the place. "Besides," she added, "he's the type to come crawling back once he realizes what he missed. And that'll be fun."

I shook my head at the humor of McKenzie's seemingly unshakeable confidence. But I was glad for her. I'd never exactly been Team Ty.

When McKenzie asked about Milo, the world came to a halt. The few words I tried to manage became trapped in my throat.

"I...he..." I shifted my gaze towards the road on my side. "He left." That wasn't what I meant to say, but it was the only thing that came out.

"Ohhhh," McKenzie groaned. "Girl, I'm sorry! Are you okay?"

I nodded, brushing off the suffocating feeling in my chest. "Yeah, totally." I lied. "It stings a little, sure. But I'll be fine."

McKenzie picked up on my cues and eased away from the conversation just as we pulled into the parking lot of ISA. It was as though a dark cloud had been lifted over the town of Constantine, but instead now hovered over me solely. As we walked to the dorm, my eyes caught every strange shadow in every corner and corridor, trying to convince me that it might just be Bellamy or Milo. But I knew that was impossible, so I fought the intrusive thoughts away and focused on nothing but the floor in front of me. To distract myself further, I pulled out my phone and opened to my student email app.

As McKenzie fiddled with her jingling ring of keys, looking for the one to our door, an unopened email appeared in my inbox. The urgent title and flagged message caught my attention. I was worried I'd gotten in trouble for never picking up my showcase painting after the gala. Other matters had obviously been a bit more pressing at the time, so I had forgotten about it entirely.

IMPORTANT - Showcase Silent Auction

Dear Katrina,

We are following up with you regarding your showcase piece, which was sold at the silent auction. Half of the winning bid was donated to the school, but the buyer insisted the other half go directly to you. It was a generous offer. One that you'll need to come pick up in person. Please come by the bursar's office ASAP with your student ID to collect the payment.

As I read the email again for clarification, I couldn't refrain from the chirp of excitement that broke free from me.

"What is it?" McKenzie whipped around, equally excited without even knowing the reason.

"My painting sold! Apparently for a lot. Tomorrow I have to pick up the check." I grinned, hoping it would be enough to afford a new set of tires for the Cherokee. I smiled, grateful for something to lift the lingering ache in my soul, even temporarily.

We wound down the evening with a simple celebration dinner of homemade tacos which we threw together with various ingredients. When I settled into my bed that night, my foot brushed the blanket Milo had given me. How strange it seemed, that after all I had experienced, that silly blanket had remained untouched through it all. Pulling the wrinkled fabric close to me, I inhaled the scent of him that remained. As had become my habit, I reached up to my throat to feel the necklace. But the emptiness I felt in its place sent a wave of grief crashing into me, as I remembered it wasn't the only thing that was lost to me forever. I thought of sitting with him on the island, and I wished more than anything in that moment that I could go back there and watch the stars with him.

The morning brought with it the refreshing promise of a new day. I braced against my emotions as I fought to push the past behind me, eager just to keep my head above water for the day. I got out of bed earlier than usual so that I could visit the bursar's office before class.

Still admiring the unchanged beauty of the campus, I made my way to the building. Walking to the front desk, I explained the email and presented my ID.

"Just one moment." The lady excused herself as she turned around and disappeared into a back room behind a door. When she returned, she placed a check in my hand with a mumble. "Must have been some painting."

I unfolded the check the moment I stepped out the door. With eyes wide, I stood in shock as I read the amount written behind the dollar sign.

"Twenty *thousand* dollars?" I shrieked to myself.

Who in their right mind would give such an outrageous amount of money for my mediocre watercolor? I had expected maybe a couple hundred, if I was lucky, but this was beyond my comprehension. Confused, I checked the unreadable signature, then looked at the company name printed in the top corner. Tesoro Del Mar Club and Marina.

The name wasn't at all familiar, but it did make me think back to the mesmerizing wealthy lady who I'd spoken to that night at the gala. She mentioned her club and resort, so perhaps this was her doing. I couldn't be sure, but either way, it didn't matter to me. All I knew for certain was that I was set for my time here in Constantine. If I stayed, anyway.

Beaming with irrepressible enthusiasm, I tucked the check away safely to cash later, still in disbelief. My steps sprung with more energy, even though my body still felt a bit like a walking punching bag.

I had just entered the Maribel White Building, when the sound of a rolling cart around the corner made me slow down. No sooner had the bright yellow mop bucket and trash cart come into view did I see Russell behind it, turning in the hallway.

"Russell!" I waved slightly at him.

"Hello, missy." He stopped his cart. "How was your Thanksgiving?"

"It was probably the most exciting one yet." I chuckled. Leaning forward, my voice lowered to a whisper. "I broke the curse."

"I told you to stay away," he shook his head. "But I'd be lying if I said I wasn't glad you didn't listen. You helped me put my daughter to rest. Thank you."

"You're welcome," I uttered, suddenly sad again.

"It's time to put it all behind us." He put a hand on my shoulder. "And I'm gonna start by selling my fishing boat. It's sat unused since that night. And well, I just don't think I want it around to hang onto anymore." There was a twinkle of sadness in his brown eyes. "You don't know anyone who's looking to buy a boat, do you?"

"No, sorry I don–" I caught myself mid-sentence as an unfathomably wild idea entered my head. "Actually, how much do you want for it?" I asked, surprising even myself.

"Are you saying you want to buy my old fishing boat?" He raised an eyebrow.

"I'm saying there's a place I need to get to, and the only way I can get there is by boat. So name your price."

40

UNDER FULL SAIL

I knew it was crazy of me to buy Russell's boat. But he gave me a great deal, showed me the ropes for steering and piloting the boat, and even hauled it to the marina for me. I once feared the ocean, but now that I had conquered it, I saw it as my only ticket to chasing a distant memory in the only way I knew how.

It was a sunny afternoon two days later, and warmer than it had been in quite some time. I stepped onto the boat. *My* boat.

With my nerves tossing about like the waves, I steadied myself with a deep breath. I couldn't believe I was doing this. The same girl who once could hardly bear to even look at the ocean was now about to single-handedly sail it. Though some fear due to inexperience was indeed present, I refused to listen to it, drowning it out with thoughts of my destination.

Looking out into the horizon, I set my sights on the invisible island in the distance. I couldn't see it, but I knew it was out there. Confirming once more that my navigation app was working, I put myself at the helm and set forth on my maiden voyage. I hummed quietly to steady my nerves, the engine spewing water behind me as my boat coasted across the blue landscape.

What was a 30-minute trip only felt like moments, and when I saw the little sand bar coming into view, my heart leapt. Though I knew it couldn't bring Milo back, something about the island made me feel he was near. I slowed the boat and maneuvered as best I could to get near the tiny shore before dropping anchor.

I wasn't used to this daring, courageous version of me, and I still couldn't believe I was doing this. However, I had done things much more dangerous and terrifying, like diving into a storming whirlpool at sea, so this seemed easy compared to that. Kicking off my shoes, I waded across the sand bar, careful not to drop the backpack I carried. I had brought some scratch rag paper and paint, just in case the inspiration struck.

Once on the island, my eyes found the few pieces of trash and bottles littered across the sand from the Halloween party. Even the charred remnants from the bonfire had survived untouched. As I relived the memory of walking past the drunken crowd, I followed my footsteps to the edge of the island where I once encountered a pirate who changed everything. Standing in the same spot where I had sat that fateful night, I dropped my backpack. It hit the sand with a thud, and I followed suit. My legs buckled beneath me as I folded onto my knees. With the afternoon sun beating down on my shoulders, I sat in the quiet, wishing for just one more moment with him. I kept my gaze locked on the edge of the water, as if somehow his ship might rise up again and bring him back to me.

I loved him. I had never said it out loud, but it was impossible to deny. It drove me crazy that I didn't get the chance to tell him. But he had told me. And as I sulked there, dreaming of him, I could almost hear his voice whispering my name.

"Katrina."

No, wait. I *could* hear his voice.

"Katrina."

I whipped around at the unmistakable sound of my name. And there he stood, only feet from me.

"Milo?" My heart accelerated with both joy and bewilderment. Was I going crazy? Or was he real? My chest tightened, and a tide of emotion rose fast within me. If I was going crazy, so be it.

"I told you I'd find my way back to you." He took a step toward me.

I leapt to my feet and rushed into his arms, ignoring the soreness that no longer mattered.

He embraced me with a passion that ignited me, lifting me off the ground as I clasped both arms around him. With a kiss that stopped time, we breathed into each other, toppling to the ground. There in the sand, we entangled, clinging to each other as though either one of us might disappear again at any moment. Milo pressed his mouth to mine, and I drank in the sweet savor of his lips that I never thought I'd taste again. The heat of his touches on my skin made the sun seem like winter. Every part of me craved every part of him. We pried ourselves apart long enough for me to ask the obvious question.

"How?" I gasped through joyful tears, laying my head on his chest to listen to his heart. "You have a heartbeat! You're not hurt anymore. You're...you're alive! How?"

He placed a strong arm around me, stroking my hair protectively as he spoke.

"Well," he breathed, "I'm not entirely sure, but my guess is that the legend must be true."

"What legend?" I rolled over, lying close against his side.

"That any man who possesses a siren's heart can cheat death."

I shot him a quizzical look as he smiled at me with a strange confidence. But the longer the thought sat with me, the more it made sense. I had given him my heart completely. There was no denying that. But did that really mean...?

No, not now.

I refused to entertain any troubling thoughts right then.

"You promised me you wouldn't wait at the pier again." Milo nudged me gently.

"You know I have a habit of making promises I can't keep," I said, nuzzling my face into his shoulder. "So have you been here this whole time?"

He nodded, then kissed me sweetly before answering. "Yes. I woke up here to the first morning I'd seen in centuries. I was beginning to worry I'd have to start swimming to find you." He kissed me again, playfulness in his tone. "The worst part is I'm starving."

I threw my head back in laughter.

"Well for your first real meal in 300 years, what would you like?"

"Aside from rum, you mean?" I rolled my eyes and smacked his leg lightheartedly. "Alright, alright. Sorry. But I'm still willing to try the cinnamon chattays you mentioned."

"You mean cinnamon chai lattes," I corrected through uncontrollable giggles.

"Yes, those."

"We'll be sure to get some after you've had some real food. I've got a few ideas. Burgers, tacos, pizza, spaghetti. Take your pick."

"Uhhh..." he scratched the back of his head. "You pick for me."

"Pizza it is." I grinned.

As the sun faded behind the skyline, we climbed into the boat, ready to leave our island behind. Of course, I let Milo take the helm and steer us back. On the way, I told him all about my mom's miraculous turn-around and about how my painting had sold for an absurd amount of money that had enabled me to buy the boat.

"She's certainly no galleon," Milo laughed patting the steering wheel. "But she needs a name, you know."

"You're right," I said. "I've been thinking of one."

"Oh? What is it?"

"*La Esperanza*. It means hope." I smiled, joining him at the helm.

"I think that's perfect." He grinned, looking ahead. "Now, let's get you home. Under full sail."

"Aye aye, Cap'n." I saluted and pecked him on the cheek as the boat sprung forward across the blood-orange water.

After we docked at the marina, Milo showed me how to tie a hitch knot and secured the boat before leaving. We walked hand-in-hand towards Constantine, admiring the view of the old city by the bay. We strolled unhurriedly, laughing as I explained more of my favorite foods to him. I soaked in the sweet moments, liberated by the feeling that there was no longer a limit to the time we had together. We had tonight, tomorrow, and every day ahead, with no curses or tides to separate us.

"So, you're really alive now." I smiled. "What are you going to do with your second chance at life?"

"I don't know for sure." He paused. "But wherever it takes me, I hope it's with you."

"You can bet on it."

I leaned forward to kiss him once more, then pulled away, losing myself in his vibrant eyes of hazel green.

"*Te amo*," I whispered. "That means—"

He put a finger to my lips and interrupted me. "I know what that one means."

With a kiss to seal it, we continued into town, on a new hunt for the best pizza available.

Minutes later, we were carrying our large pepperoni and pineapple pizza back to the South Lawn, where I intended to make the most of this unseasonably warm evening and sprawl out beneath an oak in the grass.

"I think a picnic on the beach would be a little overrated, don't you think?" I teased, tearing a warm, steaming slice from the pie.

"I have to say I'd agree," he chuckled, biting into his slice. I laughed as his eyes grew wide with wonder as he experienced the taste. "This...this is delicious."

"I knew you'd love it."

"In my defense, I think anything would be delicious right now."

As we sat laughing and eating, one high pitched excited voice sang through the air like a bell.

"Ohhh my Gooooddd! Could you two be any more adorable?"

McKenzie came speed-walking over, some enveloped in hand. She stood over us and looked down at Milo.

"But...I thought you left."

"So did I...I thought I had to," he replied. "But turns out I just couldn't stay away from her." His gaze shifted to me, and I blushed at that mischievous crooked smile.

"Ugh, so romantic and sweet it makes me sick!" McKenzie squealed. "I wish I had my camera. Oh well, just stick around a little longer lover boy, and I'll snap a pic next time."

I shook my head with a smirk as Milo looked at me with an expression of confusion.

"I think he's planning to stick around for a while," I said.

McKenzie turned to me.

"And you, *boo*, you've got to get better about checking our mailbox. This was in there for you. You're welcome." She bent over to hand me an elegant little envelope, addressed to me with only my name handwritten in cursive on the front.

I thanked her, setting the letter down.

"Anyways," she chimed. "I gotta go. Bye lovebirds!" and with that, she trotted off to go do whatever she was on her way to do.

"You'll get used to the energy," I reassured Milo through a grin. "But anyway, let's see what's in this envelope. Maybe it's another check." I joked.

I carefully tore back the envelope paper. The texture was quality, smooth and thick. It seemed too luxurious to just rip open like any old letter. I slid the letter out to read. There was a note, on equally fine paper with two simple handwritten lines.

Dearest Katrina,

It was a privilege to purchase such a piece from such a gifted aspiring artist. I'll be expecting more from you.

But it wasn't the flattering lines that made my breath catch in my chest. It was the eerie signature right below it, unarguably clear. My thoughts flashed back once more to the lady from the gala with the piercing blue eyes.

"Milo," I whispered, holding the letter in front of him. "Look at the signature."

He squinted at the note, then looked at me in surprise as we read the name aloud in unison.

"*Cordelia.*"

Acknowledgments

Thank you to my mother, who always encouraged my strange and wild imagination, and read fairytales to me each night.

Thank you to my father, who taught me how to tell a good story and not be afraid to tell it.

Thank you to my grandpa, who reignited my love of writing with one simple gift.

Thank you to my husband, Cody, who encouraged me and listened to me endlessly talk in circles as I constructed and deconstructed this story like a madwoman. And for watching the stars with me.

Thank you to my best friends, Briley and Caylin, for helping me make decisions when I got indecisive.

Thank you to all my supporters, ARC readers, and critique partners for believing in me and reminding me that all our stories are worth telling.

Thank you to the city of St. Augustine, FL for inspiring this story.

And thank you to Captain Jack Sparrow, for obvious reasons.

FOLLOW THE AUTHOR

Thank you so much for reading. To keep up with my current works and be the first to hear about new releases and special reader opportunities, follow me on social media @authorvalelane or sign up for my newsletter at authorvalelane.c om